JASON ANSPACH   **NICK COLE**

THE HUNDRED

SAVAGE WARS   **BOOK 3**

GALAXY'S EDGE

Galaxy's Edge: THE HUNDRED
Copyright © 2020
Galaxy's Edge, LLC
All rights reserved.

This is a work of fiction. Any similarity to real persons, living or dead, is coincidental and not intended by the author.

No part of this publication may be reproduced, stored in a retrieval system, or transmitted in any form or by any means electronic, mechanical, photocopying, recording, or otherwise without the prior written permission of the publisher and copyright owner.

All rights reserved. Version 1.0

Edited by David Gatewood
Published by Galaxy's Edge Press

Cover Art: Tommaso Renieri
Cover Design: Ryan Bubion
Formatting: Kevin G. Summers

Website: InTheLegion.com
Facebook: facebook.com/atgalaxysedge
Newsletter (get a free short story): InTheLegion.com

PROLOGUE

"How fortunate it was for the world that when these great trials came upon it there was a generation that terror could not conquer and brutal violence could not enslave."

—Winston Churchill

The old leej came rolling off the civilian passenger star freighter, just in from the core worlds and venting her hyperdrive across the landing apron of New Vega City's brand new star port. His good leg worked with his bad leg and the effect of his lumbering walk was like an old sailing ship rolling from side to side across some storm-tossed sea. Scars, old ones, wicked and white, painted the sides of his face and neck. There were others all along his short, squat, time-shrunken body, but they were hidden by his simple traveling clothes. His fashion was thirty years behind the rest of the passengers—simple clothes for a hardworking man. Something for weather rather than to be noticed.

The old leej took an awkward step and winced from old wounds acquired long ago. When he was young. When he was among the first to call himself a legionnaire.

Burns, thought the PR handler watching "this one" make his way from the star freighter. She'd been calling him "this one" since she was assigned the veteran's case in the days leading up to the fiftieth anniversary of Hundred Day on New Vega, which was soon to be renamed Libertarion. A special honor afforded the new home of the House of Liberty, the galaxy's first and only representative government of all the known human and alien worlds, standing in direct opposition to the Savage nations still menacing their stellar borders.

Those whitish scars—those burns along his neck—were probably from the Second Battle of New Vega. It must have been awful. She'd read the history briefs about what happened that day. It was all part of her orientation.

The PR handler addressed the old veteran by his name and rank. Like some little ancient mole coming out at the end of winter, he blinked up at her, bleary-eyed from the long star flight and the quiet darkness most starship captains kept their vessels in during the jumps between distant worlds.

"That's me," he answered simply. A mumble. A grunt. But not an apology. Just a matter of fact.

They, the PR staff, had been warned that these old leejes were men of few words. They had seen much and had done much more than most free citizens would ever know, but the psych briefings that accompanied their handling packets indicated that to ask them about what they'd seen and done back in those desperate days when it looked like the Savages were going to make a clean sweep of the galaxy... well, to ask them about those days was not a thing to be embarked on lightly. Better yet, not to be embarked on at all.

"Don't hurt them by dredging up old and painful memories," had been the admonition from Event Management. The PR handler felt there was something infinitely kind in that sentiment. These men had lived out their lives with the burden of all that "much" they'd once seen. All that "much" they'd once done. There was no need for them to relive their horrors—and horrors they had been, if even half the stories were to be believed.

Of course, the admonition was driven more by practicality than by sentiment. Neither the planning committees nor the sponsors wanted any "psychiatric incidents." It was important to have the ancient legionnaire veterans in as happy a frame of mind as possible so everyone could honor what they'd done that day long ago. So everyone could celebrate.

Unless, of course, the legionnaire under her supervision *wanted* to talk. In that case it was considered best to just listen until you could gracefully steer the conversation toward more pleasant aspects of the massive celebration weekend on New Vega, and really across all of the known Republic worlds.

A young and beautiful girl exited the ship via the boarding ramp and came up quick and breathless with excitement. She took the scarred old man's arm, a startling contrast of age and youthful beauty. She was golden-haired, and her skin, especially her face, shone like a brilliant sun on some perfect day that should have been the shape of every day. Bright blue eyes flashed in the warmth of the morning, and the PR handler swore this girl could have been a model working for a high-fashion boutique agency had she chosen to. Instead she was dressed in last year's easy fashion.

3

The PR handler guessed she was probably some outer-world hick beauty undiscovered. The prize of the planet and the local community. The beautiful girl of the farming collective she and the old legionnaire came from, according to the brief. Which, when you thought about it, was probably quite good for marketing optics. Farm girl and hero grandpa. Citizen stock of the New Galactic Republic that was all that stood between the mass of its planets and people and the still-present Savage threat out there.

The Savage Wars were a long way from over. Longer than anyone knew. But the darkness was distant at this moment, not as clear and present as it was on the day they were gathered to celebrate.

"Poppa needs help walking," the beauty told the handler. "He doesn't like to admit it." She patted her grandfather's arm. "Here, Poppa. Hold on to me now." The girl's manner was exuberant and friendly.

Also good for optics, thought the handler. Her supervisors would definitely want some interview snippets from this one. The handler would remind the camera people to get a closeup of her during the unveiling ceremony. That would look absolutely great.

The old legionnaire stared up at the PR handler assigned to him. He seemed embarrassed that he needed help to move around. Fussed about it like it was a thing he needed to apologize for. Showing up to such a hallowed place in a state like his. Not ready for battle. Just an elderly man who had gotten old and never meant to. He blinked at the sun, and it was then that the PR handler could see he had only one remaining eye. The other was a prosthetic. Not even a cybernetic implant.

Seen much. Done much. Lived with all that... "much."

"This is my granddaughter, Sylvi," mumbled the old veteran. "Aaannnd..." he warned everyone, suddenly angry, a trembling finger pointed at all who listened, "I can take care of myself. If I fall down, then I fall down. I done falled before. I'll fall again! And I'll get up again until... until... well one day when I just can't."

Both women, PR handler and granddaughter, looked sheepish at this unexpected and brief winter storm. In the moments that followed, as passengers and crew hustled about to get the big starship turned around for departure, they just stood there, hoping this would pass.

"It's gettin' up that's the important part," the old leej added with a prickly harrumph at the both of them. And at unseen ghosts.

And then he looked around at the skies of New Vega. "Looks different," he mumbled.

"Are you okay, Poppa?" asked the granddaughter. "You're sweating."

He looked up at his granddaughter and gave her a hard look, his mouth working as if to say something. As if to confess some great sin. Then... "I'm fine. It's just... hot."

In that pause there was something else he wanted to say. Something neither of them would understand because they hadn't been there. Something that felt to him like an argument against the galaxy. A scream. A shout. A cry that everything gone had to be put back.

But he said none of that. Instead he muttered that it was just hot, but that he'd "get used to it."

The three of them began to walk toward the sled transports waiting curbside at the New Vega Interstellar Star Port. A fantastic city that had once been the site of two terrible battles back at the beginning of the wars.

"All the cameras will be on you and your friends, Poppa," soothed his granddaughter as they made the long walk across the wide modern concrete apron. "And it wouldn't do for you to be all bloody and banged-up when the ceremonies start if you happened to fall down."

The old legionnaire scoffed.

"I'm serious, Poppa. Gram wouldn't like that. Okay? She'd want you to look your best for today... so just let me help while we're here. The *whole time*, Poppa. Okay? That's our deal."

The old man scowled and looked around as though still trying to find something that wasn't there. Looking for buildings and markers that should have been there. Faces that had been there once too, long ago, on that worst of worst days.

He'd been bloody and banged-up then. They all had. He felt his cane and remembered what it felt like to hold a blood-slick N-1 and try to load it and not think about...

"Wish she was here," he mumbled as he was mothered by his granddaughter into the transport with some difficulty. He was missing a leg. And the prosthetic wasn't working too well lately. Still, he suffered the indignity of needing assistance and bore the scores of tourists coming in close to the operation of helping him get into the luxury sled, sticking their comm devices over the heads of the PR handler and the luxury limo driver who were busy helping to get him in and installed in the back seat. Trying to get a photo of one of the actual Hundred.

The heroes of that day.

The Hundred.

Sket, he hated getting old. Hated *being* old. Hated all... just all of this fuss. He just wanted to see someone he knew and then go home. Anyone from those days.

Someone he'd once known. Even if it was just a ghost he could meet in the night.

That was the only thing that had brought him all the way back to this place. He wanted to see even one of them, one last time. Because there wasn't much time left. Wasn't much of them left, either.

It was clear to the crowd and passersby that the center of the fuss was an old legionnaire here for the big celebration.

Hundred Day.

To them, to the sudden impromptu curbside crowd, all of them—the Legion buffs and historical fanatics who knew something of those early desperate days—he was a celebrity. *The* celebrity. He was living history. A piece of the glorious past. A hero from that lost golden age when they, the Hundred, were all Achilles, fighting the Savage monsters to save the galaxy firefight to firefight, battle to battle, world to world. He'd seen the dragon, as some called battle. He'd seen it and walked away to live and never talk about it again.

"He's gotta be one of the first!" someone shouted as their devices flashed even though it was broad daylight, snapping images as fast as they could. Recording it all to post and collect.

Some others who only saw the crowd thought it might be one of the stars here to film the new movies about the battle. Maybe even *the* star, actor Beau Clifton.

"Y'know only thirty-seven survived that day!" someone bellowed near at hand, erupting as though the man they were talking about hadn't known any of the sixty-three that didn't make it.

"That's not technically accurate," said someone else. But by the time the explanation was given, the old legionnaire was finally in the quiet limo, door closed, the silence of plush surrounding him. He felt embarrassed to the point of death.

He wanted to say something as the vehicle pulled away and the PR handler and his granddaughter made small talk about the weather and the upcoming festivities.

Hundred Day.

What was expected and what would happen next.

He wanted to say that if...

"No one cares..." he muttered to himself finally when the words he wanted wouldn't come.

"What, Poppa?" asked his granddaughter, breaking away from the scheduled talk with the handler.

But he just made a face and turned away, glad his old buddies and sergeants, and the general—of course the general—couldn't see what he'd become.

Wounded.

Broken.

Just plain old... and useless.

"I wish you were here," he whispered to the window as they made their way into the fantastic downtown of New Vega fifty years after the battle to liberate it from Savage control. But that wish wasn't for the buddies, the sergeants, or even the general.

That was for her.

"I wish you were here," he told her ghost.

No one heard, and for a moment he tried to talk to his wife as he'd done ever since she'd died. Tried to tell her about that day and all the emotions he was afraid of digging up again.

She was the only one who'd ever heard the real story of what had happened to him, and so many, that day, long ago. The only one who'd heard *his* story. She would hold his hand. Listen.

And now she was gone.

Two years now.

He wanted to see one of the boys, yes. But the only thing he looked forward to, *really* looked forward to... was just catching up along the trail with her. That was how they'd always talked about death. Not as something final. Just one of them getting out ahead in front of the other. They'd meet up soon enough.

They'd promised each other that. And he'd promised again as her hand grew cold and the doctors told him she was gone and they needed to take care of her now.

"Does he have his uniform?" asked the PR handler in the limo.

His granddaughter nodded proudly. Like someone accepting praise for some fantastically impossible triumph no one else had ever been able to accomplish. Climbing some mountain no one had ever climbed. She had done the impossible.

"It's packed and dress-ready," she assured the handler. "I even looked up all the current Legion regulations to make sure I got all his awards and decorations just right."

The PR handler would never know what a battle of the wills that had been. How much she'd fought a game of cat-and-mouse to get the dress uniform found and ready. Even just being allowed to pack it for their trip... that alone had been a fight. There had been battles and rages and long silences. But she had held the line. He would go in his dress uniform whether he liked it or not.

She'd never been off-world from the place where she'd been raised. Where Poppa had ended up after his service in the Legion was done. The place she called home.

Getting that dress uniform ready was the proudest moment of her brief life so far. Learning about the awards on the nets, the decorations and the stories behind each one he'd reluctantly and almost embarrassed to the point of death confessed to, had made her so proud of him and every legionnaire. She wanted to meet them all. Even the new ones.

She was proud of him.

Of the Legion.

And this was her chance to see them all. The ones he'd talked about, and the legionnaires who had come along since. The next generation.

The Legion's Honor Guard, formed from General Rechs's Dogs, would be here. And that just could not be missed.

The old leej stared out the window and tried to see... them. The men he'd served with. And even those who had died here. Like they might still be waiting near the intersections and streets where'd they fallen on that long-ago hot day. Still young. Still brave. As though nothing had changed.

But instead he saw sidewalks filled with beautiful people and young mothers pulling children off to school. Sparkling new taxi sleds and sleek buses hurtling toward important places.

Life was all around him. Not like that long-ago day. Life now. Death then.

"Settle down, Poppa," he heard his granddaughter saying to him. It would be a long three days and a lot was expected of him according to the schedule. "You need to pace yourself."

He felt his granddaughter's hand on his. She was watching him as he watched the city that had become New Vega after the ruins of that world and that war. Fantastic towers flung themselves skyward. Immense triangular buildings glimmered and shined. Advertising thirty stories high gyrated and thundered. Teased and promised a better life. Fantastic starships landed at private platforms high up along the faces of impossible buildings.

He looked back at her. She was a good girl. Beautiful and kind. *Like you*, he thought to his wife. Like the one he wished was here with him. She would have been proud of the girl their grandchild had become. Very proud indeed.

"It's beautiful here," his granddaughter said. She paused thoughtfully and added, "Thank you, Poppa."

The old man looked down, embarrassed again. His eyes kept watering and he couldn't damn well help it. He'd never been good at compliments or kindnesses, and so he swiped angrily at his face. Ashamed.

"Well," he began, his voice a rusty gurgle. He cleared his throat roughly and started over. "Well... I just thought you should see the galaxy a little. Get off Bakker's Run and see some things before... well, before you settle down or whatever it is you and that boy got planned to do."

She shook her head. Kindly. Mothering him. And then pointed her finger out the window at the fantastic civilization rising up all around them as the limo made its way to the hotel they'd been offered for the duration of their stay.

"No, Poppa. That's not why I'm saying thank you. I'm saying it before anyone else can. For what you and your friends did here that day... I just wanted to tell you that first, Poppa. Thank you, Poppa. Thank you for saving us all. That's why we're here. Not to see the galaxy."

Open-mouthed, he turned to stare out the window, seeing no more all the death, destruction, ruin, the ghosts, the living and the lost he'd been looking for out there. Instead he saw the wonderful, fantastic aesthetics that embodied New Vega now. The speeding taxis and tired commuters. The mothers dragging their children off to schools. The world the Legion had rescued from the Savages on that day the first Speaker of the House of Liberty had called *"The worst of all days. When only a few held the line between light and darkness. Between civilization... and an all-consuming madness. Between life and death. Freedom and tyranny."*

The old veteran now saw the return on the price that had been paid that day. The legionnaire saw a living world where there had once been only death.

That was what General Rechs had promised them they, and the dead, had invested in that day. A chance for humanity to try their hand in the galaxy and not disappear under the cruel weight of the Savages.

"Thank you, Poppa," his granddaughter whispered to him once more, squeezing his hand.

"... although many of the misconceptions populated by current media culture have the facts of that day... all wrong."

A memorial was being dedicated to the Hundred, and the speaker for this portion of the dedication—some fine and distinguished academic—was droning on about what "really happened" that day. As though he'd been there. As though he'd seen the bloody dead, and the Savages coming at the Legion in waves down there in the tunnels beneath what had once been called Hilltop.

"No thanks, of course, to that popular holofilm of a few years back," lectured the speaker. "Despite the narrative choices of the filmmakers, General Tyrus Rechs was not the only survivor of the battle. Nor is it true, as many conspiracy theorists would have you believe, that he was killed on that day. No. Here are the facts. One hundred legionnaires made it off the *Chang* at LZ Victory. Of those one hundred, thirty-seven survived eighteen hours of battle against a Savage force estimated to be at just under twenty thousand. Every one of those survivors was injured.

"Of course, I would be remiss in not reminding you that the Hundred, the first combat force of the Legion as we know it today, were not the only ones involved in operations that day. We must not forget the 295th Combat Engineers out of Britannia, who lost their home world nine months earlier during the opening moments of the Savage invasion into the core frontier. They were stationed in exile on Subica and joined the battle going in with the Hundred. That unit ceased to exist that day, taking over ninety-five percent casualties, the majority of which occurred at Kill Zone Alpha below Hilltop.

"Nor should we forget the efforts of the 17th Combat Support Medical Group, also a Britannian unit, along with her ships *HMS Nightingale* and *HMS Sparrow Hawk*. Disobeying orders from the United Worlds, they began medical evacuations in conjunction with the first Republic Fleet, which was at that time a ragtag collection of under-maintained and ill-outfitted warships assembled around the rogue carrier *Defiant*. These ships and their crews entered the battlespace in direct engagement with no less than three Savage hulks at the beginning of the battle."

The academic waited for a respectable applause to die down.

"And of course there was the Ninth Intercept Wing and the legendary Bloody Baron who would die just six months later in combat on Callayae, going into the skies that day against overwhelming odds, making strafing runs against the Legion's primary targets even before the Hundred were on the ground and fighting.

"And that fateful appearance of the legendary warship *Old Reliable*. I urge you to spend the day at the museum of that storied ship if you'll be here through this weekend's festivities. Its career began that day, when her captain entered the pages of history, joining the greatest commanders of all time."

He paused, scanning the crowd as though they were students in a lecture hall.

"But it is the Hundred for whom we are gathered here today, and it is to them we must pay the greatest tribute. It is to them we owe the galaxy. It is to them we owe our very freedom. If not for their actions that day at places history will remember as Kill Zone Alpha, the Highway of Death, and of course, Junction Eight—all sites of some of the most intense fighting the Savage Wars would ever see—then simply put: *we would not be here today*. The line between civilization and total darkness was that thin."

The speaker paused once more, and his voice took on a note of somber respect.

"We have the extreme honor of being in the presence of some of those great men, who stand with us here today. Please recognize—"

The crowd began to clap, then to roar, getting to their feet as all eyes went to the last surviving veterans of the Second Battle of New Vega.

It had been agreed that the five legionnaires able to attend the festivities—the sixth living survivor was in hospice and dying on Spilursa—that they would not stand when recognized. Three of them bore injuries that made it almost impossible for them to stand without pain. So they would sit while the Legion's anthem was played and the crowd rained down on them their gratefulness, honor, joy, and adulation.

But the legionnaires did not do that. Did not do as they were told.

First... one stood. Wavering at first, but then solid once he got his feet planted.

Then the next, until all were standing but the fourth in line, confined to a repulsor-chair. He nodded approvingly at his brothers.

Then those at either side of him, both of them little old men, bent and wrinkled, helped the leej in the chair to his feet, evoking a still stronger reaction from the crowd.

They stood there, not smiling, but firm. Like the men they had once been. Still legionnaires.

Overhead, Delta V Banshee interceptors tore across the sky.

"*PRE*-zent... arms!" bellowed the senior-most ranking of them, barely heard over the roar of the cheering crowd going nuts, drowning out all commentary on the entertainment and news networks.

Then the legionnaires rendered a salute.

They were men.

They were legionnaires.

And once, long ago, on that *worst of all days*, they had been the few who'd held the line between the light... and total darkness. Between civilization... and savagery.

They, these, they had been the Hundred. And these were all that remained of their number save a dying man gasping out his last in hospice.

Tears began to fall from the old veteran's face. Rolling down along his weathered scars and burns. He could hear his grandchild right behind him. Clapping harder than anyone. And shouting, "Thank you, Poppa. Thank you."

And in the sound of her, the sound of his granddaughter... was the sound of the one he loved and missed most. The sound of his wife. She was there.

He hated himself for the tears. But he held the salute with the rest of them. Held it until the highest ranking gave the command to "orr-derr harms," and to return to attention.

He hated himself for getting old. For surviving. For living when he should have died with them all. Soon... very soon... it would time be time to catch up along the trail. Catch up to his old friends and comrades who'd never left here in his mind. Leejes every one.

And to her also.

Soon. Very soon.

He would be catching up along the trail.

"Old soldiers never die; they just fade away."

—General Douglas MacArthur

THE SECOND BATTLE OF NEW VEGA

01

75th Legion, Strike Force Dagger
On Approach to LZ Intruder

Legionnaire and newly promoted lieutenant Aeson Ford had flown some old and beat-to-hell ships in his time exploring the frontiers of the galaxy before he joined the Legion. Turian starhoppers, Kohlo-Pehlo Slingshots, and countless cheap ships designed to get the crew from one point in the galaxy to the next—with no guarantee of ever making a return trip. One-shot coffins, the spacers called them. These had been some of the earliest models to make the first daring, and very dangerous, jumps into hyperspace and out to the limits of human expansion.

Ford had flown a lot of them; wrecks that could still get some lift after his crew worked out old problems and ancient system failures. They handled like pigs, little more than scrap heaps outfitted with frightening amounts of thrust. They didn't fly through atmosphere so much as crashed safely over a long period of time.

But all of them, each and every one, had felt much safer than the Savage light explorer he and his twenty-man team of Legion commandos found themselves currently in. Strike Force Dagger. They would be the first on the ground in the bid to retake New Vega and rescue the survivors imprisoned beneath the ruins of Hilltop.

But they weren't on the ground yet. For now they were falling—plummeting, really—through New Vega's outer atmo like a runaway comet going down for the last time. Their ship had been hacked and taken from the deck of the mini-hulk the Legion had secured during the final phase of training. The vessel had an alarmingly thin skin and used actual jet engines for atmospheric flight. Old-school jet engines. Two on either wing. Three of the four had barely spooled up to life and thrust. The fourth was set to windmill. Their unceasing scream filled the blacked-out interior of the ship where men sat, faces like shadows from the nether between stars. In the dark and rattle of the inner hull only the whites of the men's eyes seemed to offer any shine. The only life within the barely moving statues.

The noise of reentry was everything, defeating the best efforts of the men to make small conversation beyond shouting out a few words to the legionnaire next to you and hoping he understood you over the banshee scream of the atmospheric propulsion system. A few times amid the wash of noise, someone would try to scream out some motivation or tell a joke above it all. There was no time to slow down, to hit the brakes, as it were. They, all of them in the strike force, had to beat the Savages on New Vega to the punch and hit their objective before the main element arrived in the skies overhead. Provided they didn't get shot down on the way in.

"Hey," shouted Sergeant Kimm, and though Ford heard him, he had no idea who he was speaking to specifically.

Ford met the sergeant's eyes, and Kimbo continued. Evidently the new sergeant was talking to his new lieutenant.

"You sure we're gonna be able to just fly over the city without taking some kind of incoming?"

Ford shrugged and then nodded to Donal Makaffie. Their attached. As in attached to Strike Force Dagger. Not a legionnaire, but on mission all the same for his supposed technical expertise. Apparently it would be invaluable at some point. The scrawny little man in the wire-rimmed smart glasses had become obsessed with the Savages and their technology. His greatest desire being to "see what it's all about, man."

Even now there was a data scrawl running along his lenses. They were about to jump into the hostile pre-dawn dark sky and the little man was studying data. Half, if not all, of everyone here was thinking about death. Their death. Makaffie wasn't braver than the rest, he just... didn't pay attention to the same things. Lieutenant Ford thought he looked sketchier than a Chitterrat rat-monkey on Shubao leaves.

"He says so," Ford shouted back to the sergeant, tilting his head toward the twitchy adviser they'd been saddled with by none other than Tyrus Rechs himself.

General Rechs.

The words didn't seem to provide much comfort to the NCO in the dark next to him.

A patch of turbulence caused the hijacked Savage ship to jump violently, forcing arms and legs out to steady themselves as the ship crashed through atmosphere. It passed quickly, but the experience was jarring. Thankfully, this time no one threw up.

"We'll be fine, Sergeant," Ford shouted, figuring that it didn't matter if he was right or not. "Our job is just to kill them first. Keep it simple and think about just doing that."

Kimbo looked off into space, thinking.

"Yeah. I can do that, LT. It's gettin' *to* that moment when we get to start killing that's got me worried."

"Not your job," shouted Ford. "Guy up front is flying the approach. That's his job—gettin' us there. Our job is killing the Savages first. *Kill them first*. Got it?"

Kimbo nodded. "I gotta remember that. Thanks, Fast."

Ford nodded. And then as an afterthought, he added, "Make a memory trick out of it. That way you'll remember it and focus when it starts going down."

"A what?" asked Kimbo.

"An acronym. Make it an acronym."

Again the ship bounced hard and didn't stop. Something banged loudly aft, and to all the legionnaires strapped in and ready to go, it sounded like the old ship was coming apart.

Sergeant Kimm looked suddenly ghostly, his skin drained of color.

"KTF," shouted Lieutenant Ford over the noise. "Kill them first. Got it, Kimbo?"

Kimbo jerked back from the vision he'd no doubt just had of the Savage ship suddenly cartwheeling into a hundred thousand pieces over New Vega as it came apart structurally.

He nodded.

"Yeah. KTF, sir. Got it. Thanks."

General Rechs had apportioned twenty legionnaires for this operation. A crucial piece of a tenuous battle plan. Twenty legionnaires out of one hundred effectives. The numbers made figuring the percentages easy.

One hundred was less than a quarter of those who had set out to capture the honor of calling themselves the first legionnaires. Those who failed were put to work in efforts to support the mission, but they weren't Legion. They weren't the men General Rechs trusted to win the fight. Eventually there would be more—already others were training with Sergeant Major Andres back on Hardrock—but they weren't here now. There were only the hundred. And they would finish their mission or they would die on that rock. Every leej on this decrepit Savage exploration ship was prepared for that. Understood that in the big scheme of things, this was something worth dying for. But knowing that and being at peace with it were two completely different things in the dark before dawn riding a rocketing relic hundreds of years past its operational limit.

Filling out the boilerplate Last Will and Testaments that Admiral Sulla and Captain Milker issued had been a very sobering moment for those who'd earned the right to be legionnaires. No matter who you were. No matter how hard-as-nails you came off. That moment had put it all in perspective.

There was a very good chance you would die doing this.

Maybe it was Admiral Sulla's presentation on how to distribute your worldly possessions and leave your final thoughts that truly brought home the seriousness of it all. The meaning. The implications. The finality.

"If you've got someone in your life you need to forgive," said the admiral, a fellow legionnaire and Rechs's right-hand man, "or make it right with, then I'd suggest you do it now, Legionnaires. Make it easy on them that have to survive. Life's tough enough without having to go on with something that could have been made right if only you hadn't died. So clean it up now, because there might not be another chance."

Ford was at peace with what he'd written and to whom he'd written it. Wouldn't have signed up for the Legion if it were any other way. But the rest of the leejes in the dark...

he couldn't read their minds. Maybe they were at peace with dying, maybe they weren't. But he could see that failure was gnawing away at them, causing their faces to rest in a permanent scowl of worry. Because if they failed, if Strike Force Dagger failed, well, then the options were quite limited for the rest of the galaxy. The mission to retake New Vega would be scrubbed indefinitely, the rest of the Legion coming in on the *Chang* waved off from the LZ.

Or, said some quiet little voice inside Lieutenant Ford's head, *or Tyrus Rechs would push forward anyway and hope that the rest of his legionnaires would somehow get it done where Dagger had failed. And maybe that would be the end of the Legion right there.*

Because, according to rapidly updating intel from Admiral Sulla's scout frigates, the Savage air-defense artillery would shoot the *Chang* full of holes on the approach to LZ Victory.

The door separating the cockpit from the rest of the ship swung open on a whiny shriek that somehow pierced the wail of the jet engines. The co-pilot, hanging onto the handle, leaned out into the aft of the shaking cabin to shout, "Three minutes!"

Ford nodded at the UW Navy pilot and made a point of lifting his arm so the man could see him mark the time on his smartwatch. That was good enough. The co-pilot closed up the hatch, returning to the cockpit.

Ford looked to his legionnaires, who'd all seen the co-pilot come out and knew what that meant. He held up three fingers and could hear the confirmation run from his position to the back of the ship.

Three minutes to jump altitude.

Legionnaires all along the inner shadowy hull began final weapon and gear checks. Making sure everything was as it should be because it was about to be needed. Just as it had been when they dropped out of the *Chang*'s hangar hours ago in the approach to New Vega timed with phony jump signatures being emitted by the United Worlds scout frigate *Reece*. The plan was to make it look like the Savage vessel had jumped in right before the main body of the admiral's ragtag fleet.

On the flight deck an intel specialist was broadcasting Savage distress codes, requesting assistance. Ford could hear the target-lock sensors screaming bloody murder up there. No doubt the Savages were lasing them with targeting sensors and developing engagement and firing solutions to shoot them down out of the night sky.

It could all go very bad in the next...

Two minutes. Ford held up a 'V' and stood, the rest of the legionnaires dutifully following suit. No one was joking now.

There were no red lights going green. No comm traffic, not even the new L-comms created from salvaged Savage tech—more of the spoils of their raid on that minihulk. The chance, however slight, that the Savages of New Vega might pick up on any of these were too great a risk. Even a percent of a percent was too much. They weren't even allowed to wear their new buckets on the way down for fear that they might activate and announce, electronically, that there was a new player in the game.

Makaffie had assured the mission planners that the ship would fly in unhindered on the former city of New Vega. Long enough to deliver the commandos at least, even if the massive Savage air-defense installation chose to engage. And in the event that the ruse was discovered too soon, the ship would be transmitting a universal "all clear" code the Savages had adopted when they got it in their twisted little brains that the time had come for their various tribes to work together. According to the twitchy little advisor in the middle of the stick. That code, too, had been discovered aboard the mini-hulk, though none of the monstrosities still alive on that tomb of horrors had had the mental wherewithal to use it. Their ship had been receiving mindless communications from the other tribes, but it wasn't transmitting. Apparently the monsters on the mini-hulk thought their self-hybridization, their own Savage experiment, was Paradise found, and neither knew nor cared what was going on outside of their own little twisted sandbox.

The Savage tribes preferred the hells of their own making.

But none of that mattered now. What mattered was that there would be a window over New Vega for the Strike Force to insert. The UW crew flying the hijacked Savage ship would make that happen. Even now the jet engines were spooling up to their most urgent whine. Modified rocket boosters grafted onto the hull were dumping mass and propelling the ship forward into the battlespace as fast as possible. Racing to get ahead of whatever bizarre decision tree the Savages were currently climbing down to reach a firing command and shoot them down.

G-forces pushed the legionnaires around.

Now the acceleration dampeners, batteries really, burned all their charge just to get the ship to slow down enough that the legionnaires could exit safely.

Lieutenant Ford didn't need to hold up an index finger to indicate one minute to jump. The opening of the rear cargo bay at the back of the ship told everyone what was coming next. The not-so-long fall into the night before dawn. Wind suddenly whipped through the thin-framed

Savage craft, instantly making the legionnaires long for the warmth they'd settled into while sitting in armor. It was a taste of what they could expect throughout the chill New Vega night they would soon operate in.

"Thirty seconds!" shouted Sergeant Kimbo. Then: "KTF, legionnaires! Kill them first!"

All the glittering that had come to represent New Vega at night was gone beneath them, replaced with a rolling darkness that gave no indication of how close they were to the city itself. Did the Savages see well enough in the dark to not need the array of streetlights and brightly lit signs? Did they expect something and order a blackout? Or had the pilots misjudged the entry trajectory and flown them to the wrong part of the planet, sending them to jump hundreds of kilometers away?

Jumping was the only way they'd find out for sure.

Ford's watch vibrated gently beneath his gloves. He slapped the man in front on the shoulder and shouted close to his ear, "Go!" That man, LS-11, "Junior" to the rest of the strike force and every other member of the Legion, raced for the rear ramp. "Junior" because his older brother had been a legionnaire too. Killed when they took the Savage ship during the last phase of training.

Every legionnaire followed, hand on the shoulder of the man in front, running without hesitation toward the open doors at the back of the craft. Makaffie, too, took his place in line. There was no jumpmaster to wave the next man on and out. No such man could be spared for such a task in this desperately understaffed invasion. The pilots would be all that remained on the Savage ship. The Legion commandos knew their jobs inside and out. They'd trained incessantly. One by one in a stream of ones, they slipped out and away and into the night sky.

No one hesitated.

Lieutenant Ford felt the jet engines wash over his armor and fling him away as gravity greedily embraced him and pulled him down from the racing Savage craft. The fall lasted all of fifteen seconds before his jump system, sensing the proper altitude, deployed the dedicated chute pack slung over his armor. The lieutenant felt the jerk of the triangular chute as it ripped open and blossomed to slow his fall. He checked his N-1, knowing that it was the one piece of equipment he absolutely needed upon landing. Finding it still secured to him inside its case, he grabbed his chute's handles, not wanting to activate the auto-guidance system for fear that the Savages would somehow be able to detect it.

That was perhaps what was most unsettling to Ford as he drifted down to a world that seemed so still and asleep that you'd never imagine what monsters walked its surface waiting to be met. What, exactly, were the limits of what the Savages could do? How did you fight an enemy beyond your understanding?

The old man, Tyrus Rechs, The General, had given an answer before the Legion commandos departed on their mission:

"You find out what scares them, and then you make it come true."

Twenty legionnaires floated down at the witching hour. Determined to become that which even demons tremble at.

02

Ninth Intercept Squadron, "Sand Lions"
Aboard *Defiant*

He was tall and brooding. Tall for a fighter pilot. Brooding for a human. All around him air crew raced to get the ships ready, working fast to load the last of the AGM-105s. The pilots had slogged through briefing after briefing. Briefings ad nauseam, and finals. It was on now. They knew what was required of them to prep the battlespace for the arrival of the *Chang*.

This was the liberation of a Savage-captured world. But for the Sand Lions of New Britannia, this was something else, too. Revenge. Britannia was all but gone. The Ninth had survived only because they had been deployed on another world, Subica, when the Savages had come and stormed their home world.

Now the brooding pilot stood holding a letter in the darkness between the warship's missile stores and the pilot's briefing lounge aboard the rogue UW carrier *Defiant*.

A letter written on paper. Heavy bond stationery. Folded just like the sweet remembrances that ladies in castles from bygone ages might give to knights sworn to die defending their honor. Written by hand, in ink. Like some gentle art from a lost and elder age when fine things had been valued. A time this present darkness never imagined.

He read it once more. A cigarette dangling from his mouth devil-may-care. Glowing in the darkness, illuminating those brooding features and coal-dark eyes that would soon become legendary in the time that remained him.

And the ages after.

My Dearest Stone-Face,

I do not understand. And no. No. I never will. But that doesn't mean I don't love, and yes, there I said it, love you. But this is not our war. Not anymore. We lost. Britannia is dead. I watched New Londoneaux go up in a mushroom cloud. I saw it with my own eyes and I know this seems silly given, well... everything... but I shall miss Savoy Gardens and the Old Pipe and Baron Pub where you first took me that day it rained.

Do you remember?

And maybe we, just we happy few survivors (did you ever study Shakespeare? Or was it always just the piano?) of the old British Empire, should just sit this one out this time. Maybe that's been coming for a long time. Time's up. Retirement. Sod off you silly lot of Western Civ monks. You couldn't save Earth way back when and now you've lost the galaxy to the savage hordes. Once again, and once more.

Maybe.

Our time's up, Stony. As a member of the Royal gaggle, and a very minor one at that as you always liked reminding me, you could have come with us. We'll be safe where we're going.

I'm not saying we could start over. No. Not that at all. But maybe, what I tried to tell you on the platform when you kept flicking your silver lighter case, the one your father gave you for graduating Air Academy, and waiting for the damned bullet to arrive, maybe we could have tried... "retirement."

We could have tried it out, Stony. Like a dress or something you could return if you didn't like it so much. Someday when we'd managed to live and get old in a galaxy of death, we could decide if we'd made the right choice.

Imagine it...

The two of us on some island on that hidden world we're all heading toward. Ex-pats. The Royal Gaggle. Me with my poems and plays and garden. You with your piano. Always the piano. We could have been that batty old couple, someday (I'm in no hurry to get old; I rather like being slinky and twenty-seven in ways I never thought when I was slinky at twenty-six) that batty old couple who wanders the beach and collects shells. Taking tea at four and pretending to whomever happened by that afternoon that the Britannia we once all knew, loathed, and loved, was still alive. Somewhere.

We could have retired, Stony. I need you to know that was an option. An option you're passing on.

And I could have loved you forever, Stony. I promise you that. And you should know it. I do not want you to ever think that I thought you were tragic and noble and dashing in your flight kit going off to die on some forsaken world against the cursed Savages. I do not want you to ever think that I thought you were brave in the face of death or how extremely proud of you I am.

I wanted you to be like all these boys with military ranks and hereditary ranks all about me who are all talking very seriously about the war and all things war.

I wanted you to be like them.

Here.

And not there, actually doing all things war. I prefer the murmur of what must be done over the doing of it.

That's what I wanted.

Retirement, Stony. Sweet, blissful, endless days on the golden sunshine isle I'm sure we would have found... retirement. I fear that with your imminent demise, for in fact you are dead to me already, that I will have to allow one of these serious war boys to be my husband. And so, I close. You are not a hero. Neither dashing nor romantic. I am not proud of you.

I only wish that you were here. Instead of doing your damned duty. As every man must. Damn Nelson, whoever he was. Damn him to the hell where all old generals go.

Love (didn't you know that you idiot),
Gwen

Another pilot ran by in the shadows of the carrier's lower decks, noting the brooder reading in the dark by the light of his cigarette and those coal-dark eyes that seemed alive in the inky half-light.

"Oy, Baron. Ya daft or something? They just called Ready Five. We're due to launch. C'mon already."

The brooding pilot waved the man away, murmuring an upper-class-accented "Thanks, Cuckoo. Be along in a moment."

Now he could hear the APUs charging up the main ion drives of the interceptors. Crew chiefs were taxiing the birds into position on the flight line.

He stared at the paper in his hand once more. Watching the smoke of the cigarette between his fingers drift across the words. Her words.

All the things she hadn't said were there just the same.

He folded the letter just as it had been folded. Just as it had been sent. Crushed out his smoke, and dashed off to his ship.

03

75th Legion, Strike Force Dagger
LZ Intruder

Wild Man didn't like the out-of-control vulnerability of freefall. He found the violent deceleration afforded him by the deployed jump system to be even worse.

He counted himself as someone with a strong stomach, but the jumps made him feel queasy all the same. Not that he ever really thought he'd lose his lunch, just that he was heading in that direction. The quivering, sloshing feeling created a hyperawareness of the contents of his stomach. Churning and roiling like steady surf pounding sand. It didn't do wonders for his sense of control.

That's when she came back. Began to whisper...

Kill for me, babe.

"Gonna," grunted the Wild Man as night whipped his face and made his eyes water. As he fell and then floated toward the pitch-black dark below and the mission that was about to begin.

She'd stayed.

Through the additional jump training the old man wanted for this mission and the strike force put together to carry it out. Strike Force Dagger.

She was a changed woman now.

Maybe her time away had been good for her, thought the Wild Man. Maybe when she'd seen what he'd done on the mini-hulk... maybe she'd finally surrendered herself to him and let him just do his thing. Which was kill Savages. Kill them all. Decided that maybe he could lead the way after all. Maybe she'd seen how much he really loved her in all the killing he'd done. All the killing he was going to do.

"Gonna make 'em pay today," he promised the wind and the dark. And her.

Maybe…

She'd been back before now. Encouraging him during that training. Only he was too focused to realize it.

Oh baby, she'd crooned like some siren beneath dark waters, *think of all the Savages you're gonna kill after this.*

Hadn't she practically whispered in his ear during the after-action reviews where he'd performed beyond expectation? And couldn't he have sworn he'd felt her biting his ear one time?

Lieutenant Ford told him that as big as he was, as good as a shooter as he was, and as strong as his voice could be, he'd probably be able to get a few Savages to surrender out of plain old fear alone.

"Don't want 'em to surrender," Wild Man had mumbled where the lieutenant couldn't hear. "Wanna kill 'em all."

And now it was all about to happen. He'd hit the ground and then the payback could get underway once more in full. With interest. If he'd been a thorn in the Savages' side before, now he'd be a flaming sword. One that bit and twisted deeper with every gentle squeeze of the trigger on the big rifle he'd brought to play.

The wind beat at him and his gear. The darkness below was growing wider and wider as he fell.

The fancy new comms systems weren't to be used under any circumstances. That had been made clear repeatedly in the pre-raid briefings. Which made linking up with the rest of Strike Force Dagger first priority on landing.

But if you see a few, babe... you're gonna do 'em, right?
You bet he would.

He looked about, searching for the faint silhouettes of those who'd jumped with him from the speeding hijacked Savage scout ship, renamed *Tombstone*, that was tearing off into the sky, engines gleaming like forsaken comets. No one seemed to be above him, though perhaps they were blocked by his chute. Below, he could see two others from Dagger floating down toward the dark landscape further beneath.

The planet was like a hungry black hole. An ever-growing mossy shadow spreading unevenly beneath Wild Man's feet in every direction. Leejes seemed to fade and blend into the shadows as they fell nearer, like apparitions coming to tell him something and then receding back into the nether world all around. He watched the chute of one of the men flutter.

The Wild Man went over his parachute landing fall procedures. Reminding himself to look at the horizon and let his body react to the impact instead of trying to anticipate it.

In a gut-churning instant of manufactured doubt and fear, Wild Man checked his chute, afraid it had somehow failed and he was in freefall as the ground tried to get his attention and grab him. Smash him. Take him.

But the chute was good. He... was good. He floated down, watching those below him gracefully, easily make landfall, their chutes deflating as they hurriedly prepared for the fight.

The ground walloped him and he collapsed into it with little thought. It actually felt good. Felt like he was back in control again. He didn't lie there for even a second. He was up and going through the procedures that had been drilled into him to become routine. Disconnecting, gathering, folding, tucking, stowing. Weapon next.

He had the big rifle out of its clamshell and heard himself mumbling like a praying monk that it had survived the fall. Captain Milker and then little Makaffie had wanted him to use a new optimized version of the N-1 meant for snipers, but it was the general himself who'd allowed the Wild Man to go with his own weapon system. A surprising breach of the uniformity General Rechs insisted on within his Legion. The general had even eschewed his own notorious armor in order to wear the same kit that the rest of legionnaires were going in with. Uniformity. All as one.

But this was a no-fail mission. And maybe that was why the general had let the Wild Man bring the rifle he'd spent the last few years of his life killing Savages with.

"You take what you need to get this done," General Rechs had said, pointing at Wild Man. "Because if you can't get it done a lot of people are going to die, and that's on you forever."

Wild Man had learned to hate Tyrus Rechs during training. And the Wild Man had done fine qualifying on the modified N-1. But it wasn't his baby. So when the general spoke to him, he picked up his big rifle. His special rifle.

Tyrus Rechs was looking at him hard.

"With this..." he rumbled to his general, "with this, I won't miss."

Rechs nodded once and was off to sort out some other vital decision. Off to handle ten thousand other things that would lead to the next few hours on New Vega and the bloodbath at Victory.

The rest of the Legion needed Strike Force Dagger to knock out Objective Guard Dog and take LZ Victory. If Dagger failed, everyone would probably get killed on the

Chang in the skies over New Vega. So no matter what it took, even if "what it took" was for everyone in Dagger to get killed, or even if there was just one man left to finish the mission, they had to knock out Guard Dog so that *Chang* could put down on Victory.

I love you, the Wild Man told her in the darkness as the shapes of legionnaires began to rally up in the quiet field just before dawn.

Prove it, she whispered in the hiss of the trees all around as a cold wind began to come up.

Get some.

04

Dagger formed up into two patrol columns taking either side of a trail that had been identified by scout drones dropped during the recon passes leading up to the day of the assault. Dawn was still two hours off.

Lieutenant Ford sent two leejes forward on point, one from each element. Alpha and Bravo Dagger respectively. Kimbo was the sergeant in charge of Alpha, and a leej named Ian House, LS-89, who everyone just called Whistler, took Bravo.

In column and underway toward the objective a few kilometers to the west, Ford reviewed the plan General Rechs and Admiral Sulla had developed for knocking out the immense air-defense artillery platform. The one-shot scout drones had identified the target a week ago while Sulla was still assembling the ragtag fleet to take the legionnaires to their rendezvous with destiny. Intel also indicated that the Savages who'd taken New Vega had destroyed much of what the original colonists had built in the years since the last battle here, and had constructed several megalithic structures in and around the ruins.

"How will we even know the bunkers are still down beneath Hilltop?" some junior naval weapons officer had asked during one of the planning briefs. That had been where the civilians were stored the last time Tyrus Rechs had been on planet.

No one had had anything to say about that, because it was an unknown. There were a lot of unknowns.

Admiral Sulla had moved his pointer toward the base of the referenced area on the digitally projected maps they were studying. "The Savages are excavating here. It appears they're also building a sort of massive reflection pool, enhancing their view of the city they're building all along Hilltop. That's here."

The aerial image zoomed and expanded, telemetric data scrolling along the side.

"That pool will be LZ Victory. It's the size of *Defiant* and we don't expect it to be finished and filled prior to our arrival. Once *Chang* lands there, it will become the base of operations for the invasion. Look here..."

The pointer danced around the bottom of Hilltop. Caressing mound-shaped areas of reinforced duracrete.

"That's what remains of the old tunnel system built by New Vega colonists. A recon image from six months ago had it still exposed due to damage from the Titan strike during the Battle of New Vega. As you can see, they've patched and sealed it. That strongly suggests they're keeping the tunnel system and most likely maintaining their supply of civilians for their... purposes. It stands to reason that any survivors are still in there."

"Like food in a fridge..." someone muttered bitterly in the darkness of the briefing.

Admiral Sulla agreed with the frankness of the sentiment. "Yes. That's their nature. As best our xeno-psych specialists have been able to determine, the predominant form of Savage currently occupying New Vega seems to come from a group that shed their physical states in favor of an uploaded cybernetic existence of some sort. Intel from the last battle confirms that a lot of the resistance we were facing was little more than brains operating mechanized cyborg units roughly equivalent to human form. Not all of them. But the majority.

"We call this Savage tribe the Calorie Hoarders. Our scientists theorize that they shed their bodies in order to keep their brains alive due to some stellar catastrophe aboard their colony ship, something that disabled or destroyed their farming systems. Reducing their caloric needs down to just enough to keep their brains alive was actually a rather brilliant solution. Consequently, we think they'll still have that fear of lack. That calories will remain a major concern for them. And that being the case, the Savages are most likely keeping our people in a suspended state for a rainy day."

That horror of that statement was not small, and it had bothered Ford when the admiral said it. It still bothered him now on the march to the objective.

Ford had ordered Kimbo and Whistler to keep the men from putting on their ballistic helmets with the new L-comm system connection. Makaffie had told them that while the Savages couldn't hack the state-of-the-art quantum encryption the L-comm ran, the L-comm would still emit detectable electronic and quantum signatures, and the Savages' massive air-defense gun, with its powerful target acquisition radar, could definitely acquire those disturbances in the quantum spectrum. Especially this near to the objective. At a minimum, the Savages would know that something was up.

So it was helmets off until the objective was under actual attack. Until then it was hand signals learned during the patrol phase of legionnaire school.

Whistler signaled for a halt. As one, every leej in both columns sank to one knee and scanned their respective sectors out and away from the two columns, watching the field and forest dark. Ford, hunched and carrying his N-1, hustled forward to link up with both section sergeants. By default, LS-09, the L-comm operator whose mission it was to stay near Ford at all times, followed. Each platoon within the Legion had a designated L-comm operator who carried the bulky system that allowed all the legionnaires to communicate through their fancy new ballistic helmets.

"Buckets," everyone was calling them.

Ford checked his watch as they rallied. An hour until *Chang* arrived. They were running low on time.

"OBJ's over the hill," said Whistler's point man, LS-13. Everyone called him Bad Luck and he didn't seem to care much. "Have eyes on target. No OPFOR. It's wide open. Passive detection on the 'nocs indicates no lasers, but there are sensors. We won't get close without getting noticed, sir."

There was no need to pull out a battle board and sketch out what needed to happen next. They'd trained for this. They knew what would happen next.

Ford turned to his sergeants and whispered the execution orders. "Alpha will stack and clear just like we planned. Once the lower level is clear, Bravo will move to the identified generators and plant the explosives. Kimbo, you're with Overwatch on the road. We do not detonate until I get a signal from *Chang* that she's in atmo and on final to Victory. Then we detonate and move to rally. Got it?"

"Roger," both sergeants acknowledged.

The air-defense installation was a strange structure. Stacked discs rising up four stories before expanding out into a multi-domed platform from which the gun housing erupted. They had no idea what kind of gun it was, or what kind of munitions it fired. Though these Savages had used gas-fired projectile weapons in their previous encounters, strange coiled generators indicated the defense system might be a powerful energy weapon of some sort. Regardless, it certainly seemed big enough to seriously hurt if not outright destroy a capital ship that tried to approach New Vega City unauthorized.

Which was why Admiral Sulla and General Rechs had decided the weapon needed to be disabled prior to the invasion. There was no backup if the *Chang* was lost—it was the only ship going in while the *Defiant* and her fleet maintained orbital superiority above New Vega.

Unfortunately, there was no way to be sure that Dagger's explosives would be sufficient to outright destroy the weapon. And that was unacceptable. Failure was unacceptable. So the plan instead was to trigger a timed detonation that they felt certain would, at a minimum, knock the generators offline just prior to *Chang's* arrival, allowing a window for landing. If they brought the whole facility down in the process... well, so much the better. But *Chang* had to land. That was non-negotiable.

"Why ain't it guarded?" asked Donal Makaffie as Alpha readied themselves for the three hundred meters they'd need to cross to reach the main door. Bravo had already crawled up to the top of the wood line and had their weapons ready to engage. Alpha would make the mad dash to stack and breach across open ground.

It wasn't optimal. But there was no other way.

"Don't know," answered Ford. "Doesn't matter. Maybe the Savages aren't expecting an attack. Or maybe they think this thing can take care of itself."

"Yeah..." said Makaffie, rubbing his stubbly chin and peering up at the lieutenant through specs that constantly scrolled data. "That last part's the bit that's got me worried."

Two minutes later Alpha was hauling butt as fast as eight men could, sprinting to reach the glimmering steel door that was the entrance to the facility. They had made it halfway across the field when the entire fortress lit up. Massive lights sparkled to life, throwing powerfully blinding white beams of light across the field. A strange, almost alien doomsday klaxon began to bellow.

"Keep moving!" shouted Ford over his shoulder as he ran to cover the last one hundred meters as fast as he could. And fast he was, outpacing his men by a considerable margin.

A moment later small turrets erupted from the structure and began to spit out blurs of untargeted munitions in every direction. Star shells popped from canisters along the building's face and lobbed themselves up into the skies as green targeting lasers lanced away from sensors near the turrets and tried to acquire the eight legionnaires sprinting for the main door.

Two legionnaires went down immediately, cut to shreds by heavy automatic fire. Ford dove, and the surviving five did the same. At the same time Bravo opened up with the N-1s from the tree line, causing several Savage turrets to explode, cooking off their own munitions packs as they went up. Within a minute acrid smoke was drifting over the battlefield and the guns had all but gone silent across much of the structure. But far from all of it. The remaining Savage turrets sought to acquire the legionnaires of Alpha as they belly-crawled, inching closer to their objective. Lieutenant Ford sent a stream of concentrated fire that disabled a turret, then leapt to his feet in the midst of the melee.

"Get up and *move*!" he screamed.

He led the final charge.

Arriving ahead of the others and reminding them why they'd given him his nickname—Fast—he slammed his back into the door and shouted for them to move faster still. Hurriedly, he made a count. Six had made it, but Junior was hit, his hand shattered and bleeding, his face bone-white as he stacked near the door with the rest of the men.

"Hey," Ford began, and then took in an entire conversation just from looking in Junior's eyes. He had been about to tell Junior to hold the entrance while he and the other five went ahead try to clear the unknown corridors ahead. But Junior had lost a brother back in the Savage mini-hulk. He wasn't sitting anything out. His eyes told Ford he was all in.

"You sure?" Ford asked the wounded man, holding up his N-1.

"Passed right through," Junior said, holding up his own N-1 with his good hand. "I'm good, Lieutenant Fast." Then he lowered the N-1 onto his forearm as a brace, indicating how he'd engage once they went in. "I'm good."

Ford nodded. "Buckets up."

For the first time ever, the legionnaires became what they would look like for the rest of their history. The helmets came off their hips where they'd been strapped and were on their heads. L-comm was tapped, and the Legion was ready to take lives.

"Let's blow it," Ford called, stepping aside so Ringo, LS-19, could slap two thermatex discs on the door.

The leejes stood at either side of the entrance as the turrets fired and the sirens wailed.

"Ready..." said Ford over the ether of the new L-comm.

Junior gave a double-click over the comm. As did Shadow and Chalky, Dagger's medic.

Ford nodded at Ringo, who tapped the ignition fob he'd tac-taped to his left gauntlet. Five seconds until the device did its trick.

"Breaching..." Ringo whispered over the comm.

Seconds later the explosives sent their charge into two hinging mechanisms and then sent a powerful repulsor charge that sheared the door inward.

"Go! Go! Go!" shouted Ford.

Ringo and Shadow swept in, N-1s covering left and right, while Ford drove the tip of the spear forward. Chalky followed, sweeping left to right to support any initial fire.

"Contact!" Shadow shouted, acquiring the first Savage on their left coming into the entrance area at a dead run with some kind of heavy-caliber automatic weapon that wasn't even brought to bear. The leej double-tapped the Savage with two blasts from the powerful N-1, sending two streaking bolts of hissing blue at the bad guy. He followed the target down onto the floor, then fired again, once into the Savage marine's head, while breathlessly shouting, "More from the left!"

Chalky gave a cool, "On it!"

Ford and Ringo watched right and center but could only see smoke and debris ahead.

"Switching to NV!" shouted Ford.

"Pack out," said Chalky, who'd been pouring fire into his section of the room.

"Up!" shouted Shadow. He moved swiftly forward, shooting down three more Savages who came to play.

Ford couldn't see anything over the night-vision filter inside their new buckets. The bright blaster bolts were burning out the field of vision every time someone fired.

He tapped the filter switch over the ear and brought it back just in time to see a Savage marine fire into the room from a passageway dead ahead. But Ford had maintained his weapon exactly where he'd been taught to. That, coupled with his lightning-fast reflexes, had him shooting the Savage marine several times in the passing of a second. He simply shifted the N-1's reticular barrel over a bit and engaged the target.

But not without taking return fire. Rounds from the Savage rifle tore through the smoke and dust, streaking over Ford's head.

"Door to the center!" Ford called out, letting his team know where he was going to be occupied.

"Contact right!" screamed Ringo. "Junior, get up here!"

Savage automatic gunfire replied to Ringo's shouts, causing him to dance back and take cover, sending what return fire he could with his N-1 to keep any Savages with a mind to charge backed up.

Ringo peered around the corner into the right-hand passageway and ducked back before the Savages could get shots on target. "Some kinda internal bunker down that way!"

"Poppin' a fragger!" shouted Junior, before dumping an entire charge pack in the bunker's direction while shouting "Covering!" A second later, N-1 tucked under his arm, Junior pulled a grenade and yelled, "Frag out!"

There was a dull explosion and the barometric pressure changed for a second. Then a wave of heat came at them, pushing smoke past the legionnaires and out the door.

"Up!" shouted Junior, who'd swapped a pack during the interval and was now advancing into the ruined bunker to the right of the entrance area, shooting probably-dead-but-still-twitching Savages.

"Clear!" Ringo shouted a few seconds later. "Dead Savs all around."

"Clear," shouted the rest.

"Let's see if we can find a speedlift," offered Ford wryly over the L-comm. "Bravo, clear to move in on completion of your objective."

05

Ninth Intercept Squadron, "Sand Lions"
Aboard *Defiant*

The *Defiant* was shaking badly when she dropped out of jump just above New Vega. Not a few wondered how much more she could take. The hull groaned horribly before the ship settled in under its powerful ionic drive engines once again. It had been nearly a year since any kind of official shipyard maintenance had been done. That was how much time had passed since Admiral Sulla and his crew had gone rogue from the United Worlds Navy in order to serve Tyrus Rechs's new Legion.

All around Brett Shilton, the pilot known by the call sign "Baron," the carrier deck crew and chiefs hurried to destabilize the restraining locks that had held the first flights of the Sand Lions in the *launch*, *ready*, and *hold short* positions.

Over the dull hum of the comm, Flight Ops indicated Baron and Lion Two were authorized to go to engines ready.

Baron pulled his flight glove tight and took hold of the throttle along the right side of his thigh. He gave a thumbs-up through the canopy to Two and said, "Going Dark, Cuckoo."

"Copy," replied Cuckoo as both pilots darkened their canopies and waited for launch clearance. Already the powerful twin-engine interceptors were humming away beneath them. Down the length of the carrier deck the force-field barrier was shifting to egress while still maintaining enough presence to maintain atmo inside the hangar.

"*Chang* away and entering atmo over New Vega. Sand Lions, you are cleared to launch. Good hunting."

Baron checked both wings, waggled both rudders, and powered up to full while still maintaining the wheel locks. The interceptor tried to surge forward under the restraints.

The fighters of the Sand Lions hadn't been designed for use aboard a United Worlds carrier. Many of the launch and recovery systems were ad hoc. In particular, the Britannian fighters did not mesh with the repulsor catapult, so they had to launch off the deck under their own power. Which, given the current speed of the *Defiant*, would be like throwing a handful of grass out the window of a speeder.

"Go," murmured Baron calmly.

He saluted the deck chief, who threw her signal batons forward indicating a launch.

Wheel locks released and the fighter jumped forward to race down the too-short deck and then tumbled away from the massive carrier, grabbed by New Vega's atmosphere and basically in freefall, tumbling in uncontrolled as the powerful ion thrusters of the larger capital ship washed over them.

"Insertion in ten, Cuckoo," noted the Baron softly.

"If ya can call it that, be my guest," replied Lion Two. "But it feels like we're just falling, gov. Don't it?"

06

Strike Force Dagger

With the breach completed, Bravo element moved in to take the lead and sweep up the targets marked to disable the gun. But not before Lieutenant Ford told the medic to organize the wounded and the dead. Already there were two KIA. LS-45 and LS-10. Fritz Ausman and Chris Campbell. They were laid out side by side next to the entrance, and their gear and charge packs were redistributed.

Dagger's combat medic was an exiled Britannian man named Ellis Dobbins, LS-12. They called him Chalky because of one brutal day of training back when they were all going through the unarmed combat phase in a particularly dusty sand pit Rechs had found for them. Chalky had gone through an advanced medical training taught by a team of doctors from the 17th Combat Medical Support. Now he was dealing with Junior's shot-through hand.

Junior wasn't having it. "Doc, I'm fine."

"Are you?"

Chalky wrapped the wound in Gel-Set and pulled one of the undamaged armored gloves off one of the dead for use as a bandage. "This hand won't work," he informed his patient. "But it will at least be protected until you can receive further treatment."

"That's it?" Junior asked. "I can catch up with the guys?"

Chalky gave a tight smile. He knew that Junior should be out of the fight—and in normal circumstances, in a normal war, he would be. But there was nowhere for the wounded to go until *Chang* arrived. And that wouldn't happen unless Strike Force Dagger accomplished its mission. The medic's priorities, he knew, were to do what was needed to get men back into the fight. Even above saving lives. That was their level of desperation. That was what it would take to defeat the Savages.

Makaffie was poking at the dead Savages in the breach area using a pencil he'd produced from his pocket. "These aren't the Calorie Hoarders," he said, craning his neck to look at the waiting Lieutenant Ford.

Ford nodded. That much was clear. These were the Color-Codeds, one of the other Savage tribes that intel had confirmed was operating on New Vega during the last battle here. The Color-Codeds operated in functional groupings of reds, blues, greens, and yellows.

All around them were dead reds.

"Reds is s'posed to be warrior-types like you guys," Makaffie mused.

"Guess they weren't warrior *enough*," quipped Shadow from behind Ford. "Reds ain't Legion."

Three minutes later, Bravo element, with Sergeant Whistler in the lead, walked into a Savage ambush. Ford was bringing up the rear of Bravo, letting them work like the team they'd learned to work as during all the clearing exercises everyone had been forced to go through until they were blind with corners, angles, and engagement zones. Whistler had just called out "At the top. We're going in," when the shooting started. Loud, hard bursts of slug-thrower fire and the almost instantaneous whine and pulse of the N-1s in reply.

"Man down!" someone called out over the L-comm. "LS-36 is hit bad!"

Truth was, he was already dead. But they'd find that out later, after Chalky made it all official.

"Sir, Alpha is asking if they should reinforce." It was Shadow, standing next to Ford, looking like he wanted to be up at the front of Bravo and in the fight.

"Negative. Keep them pulling duty at the entrance and have them ready to support Overwatch if needed."

"Roger."

Ford did a tally of available men. Already Alpha had taken casualties, and now Bravo element was down to seven. He wished he had more, but he'd get the job done with what he had. No fail.

The firefight carried on with white-hot intensity before dying down almost as suddenly as it had begun. Ford listened to Bravo's comms, and was relieved to hear that LS-36 was its only casualty.

What LS-36 had died trying to take was a control room that looked out over the wide platform that was the bottom of the upper mount for the ADA gun assembly. The powerful generators were one level up. Then fire control, and finally the immense gun itself reaching way out into the sky.

"What was the resistance?" Ford asked Bravo's squad leader.

"Three bad guys," called out Whistler over the L-comm in reply. "More reds."

Ford checked his watch. Twenty-eight minutes until *Chang* arrived. "I'm on my way up, Sergeant," he said, taking steps two at a time.

The site of the ambush was some kind of power management station, but the screens and indicators were all offline, dark as night. The Savages had shut down power to the room.

But not to the facility. The massive gears and gleaming pistons all along the lower platform level were coming to life. The Savages knew something was about to happen now. They were readying their weapon.

"We're bleeding time, sir," said Whistler, coming to stand in front of his lieutenant. "Point has identified the stairwell outside the room over there as the only way up. But it's a safe bet that we'll walk into another ambush or get some explosives tossed down at us."

Ford tapped his chin controls for the L-comm. "Sergeant Kimm, we're preparing to set charges. Engage any Savage elements, but don't let your Overwatch team get cut off from the main group. Over."

Then he bent and unslung the det-cord he'd brought. "Sergeant House, I want your team to come up the sides out there along the platform. Two teams. Breach from both sides. Use the climbing rigs to get up around any Savage ambushes. Take control and plant your explosives. We're running out of time, and since this is a no-fail, I'm going to wrap the spine of the platform with det. Maybe we crack the motivator control and the gun can't swivel to acquire."

"Affirm," replied Whistler with little wasted time and gave his easily divided element their orders. The team led by Whistler would assault the north side of the platform. The other the south.

Lieutenant Ford was already wrapping the central core that the control room surrounded. It would take time. Time to clear out the wounded and time to set the charges and, hopefully, time to get clear before they went off.

This was going to be tight.

07

Wild Man spotted the incoming Savage mechs. Two. Coming down the main logging road that led back to the once-fabulous highway that circled most of New Vega. Main Highway One. Both machines had thrown out targeting lasers and searchlights making them look even more monstrous as they came pounding through the forest night. But their hydraulic legs were near silent. These were most likely some kind of scout variant.

He pointed them out to Sergeant Kimm, who immediately went to L-comm. "Overwatch to Dagger Actual."

Ford was on his third circuit around the central core and running out of det-cord. "Go for Dagger Actual."

"Got two Savage mechs inbound."

There was a brief silence, but not for a lack of words. The L-comm operator was positioned next to Ford as he should be, but was indicating trouble maintaining signal.

"Sorry Lieutenant," Shadow said, "but it looks like the Savages are tryin' to hack the L-comm. I can keep in front of it by scrambling as we go so they can't get a lock."

Ford nodded. "Say again, Overwatch."

"Two Savage mechs inbound. Say again: Two Savage mechs inbound."

Ford repeated his command, not wanting to cause any further latency delays. "Engage. Engage. Engage."

"Roger," said Sergeant Kimm.

There were two other leejes operating as part of the sniper overwatch with Wild Man and Kimbo. Both riflemen carried Achilles man-portable anti-armor "Javelins." Basically, a long spear inside a slender kinetic boost launcher. The launch system could dump a round up to eight hundred miles an hour and interfaced with special sensors attached to the carrying legionnaire's HUD that could be used for targeting. The powerful round was classified as armor-piercing and carried a secondary canister of gel-ignite that turned oxygen into living fire. It burned intensely hot but didn't last long. The designers of the Achilles Javelin system had hoped that providing an infantryman with a way to disable an armored, enclosed space with fire by melting controls and components would be a force multiplier on the ground.

Following behind the Savage mechs were close to twenty of the Savage marines they'd expected to encounter on New Vega. The Calorie Hoarders. Armored cyborgs. Life and machine integrated. To what level beyond brain stem... who knew?

Wild Man updated the situation report and got a terse "no change" in reply from Lieutenant Ford.

And why would there be? The clock was running out. They were now down to nineteen minutes before the rest of the Legion hit the main LZ at Victory.

Heart Attack and Jokes, the other two leejes on Overwatch, divvied up the two mechs. Wild Man would take the marines on foot and try to get them to halt their advance.

"Firing! Firing! Firing!"

A moment later one of the Achilles Javelins lit up in the dark, its engines boosting and sending the round shifting this way and that in the forest dark to acquire its target, weaving and dancing as it streaked ahead. Then with a sudden final push it shot straight into the lead mech and came out the back of the command cupola trailing fire and smoke, raining down debris on the scattering Savage marines.

Fired seconds behind the first, the other Javelin boosted hard and sheared off the right leg assembly of another mech, crashing the metal beast down into the forest shadows. It exploded, sending flames spreading into the nearby woods.

"Perfect," thought Wild Man as he selected his first Savage and pulled the trigger on the big rifle. Selection and pull had been almost instantaneous.

His satisfaction was momentary. He'd hit the Savage in the lower torso.

I know! he shouted at himself.

"In a hurry," he mumbled to her.

He blew the next Savage's head clean off. The massive rounds he fired were like small tank shells. He'd had to make them himself, and had spent what little free time there had been aboard the *Chang* hard at his passion of creating the perfect load. Even the general had come to watch him, as had just about everyone else at one point or another. Impressed with the dying human art of reloading.

He selected another Savage and killed that one too.

The lead mech was still moving forward, though it was unclear if this was because its pilot was still in control. It might have been carrying on some final death ritual, like the chicken with no head. But then Wild Man spotted the pilot inside the cupola, still alive, despite the flames crawling across the cockpit. The Achilles Javelin round had ignited as it left the vehicle after penetration. Wild Man shifted on the fly, led, and fired, blowing the pilot's body across the far side of the canopy in spray and matter.

Its controls unattended, the mech crashed into a big pine and stopped dead, burning fuel dripping down its legs. As if to punctuate the moment, the first mech to go down suddenly exploded yet again as its internal munitions racks cooked off.

Savage marines advanced cautiously forward, now forming up into a wedge as their armor burned in the forest.

"I see you," whispered the Wild Man.

He selected their leader and felt his finger caress the trigger of the big rifle once more, and not for the last time.

08

Bravo's attack on the generator level of the big air-defense guns was proceeding. Alpha was now split between pulling security at the facility entrance, moving casualties to the CCP, and assisting Ford with setting explosives in the control room and throughout the structure as Makaffie pointed out where the charges would do the most structural damage. But time was running out.

"Sergeant Kimm," said Ford over the L-comm. "Pull Overwatch back to the rally point. I want everyone clear and ready to move once we blow this gun."

"Roger."

Ford made his way to the stairwell, leaving Makaffie working on a terminal he'd somehow managed to power up. The lieutenant's L-comm operator followed, but Ford waved him back.

"Stay here for now, Shadow. And make sure Makaffie leaves with the rest of Alpha once you're done on this level."

The L-comm operator nodded and affixed himself to Makaffie, becoming the enigmatic little man's new personal shadow.

Ford moved his way up the next level, blaster pistol in hand because he was faster with it than the N-1. The fighting up top where Whistler had made his climb sounded as though it had drawn away any ambush the Savages might have had waiting for them along the stairs. But Ford wouldn't know until he finished the climb.

He passed an abandoned barricade the Savages had set up for their ambush—a stockpile of heavy equipment and cabinets. It had a clear view down the stairwell and excellent cover. This would have slowed them down. Would have cost a lot of lives. Maybe Sergeant House's entire element. Climbing the exterior of the structure, though time-consuming, had proven to be the right call.

Pushing on up the stairs, Ford reached the generator level Bravo had stormed. Chalky, who had moved with Bravo, was already working on two men with severe gunshot wounds. Another leej had already bled out.

Sergeant Whistler's voice came over the L-comm. It was clear that he'd been hit. His breathing was rapid and shallow. "They want this one real bad, LT!" he shouted. His team was assaulting the northern generator array, attempting to clear the defending Savages off so they could plant the charges. The other half of Bravo had already reported back success at the southern array.

"I'm linking up with you," Ford replied. "Pull your men back. Charges set on the southern side should do the job."

"Negative, Fast," said Whistler. "Crossfire is bad up here. Four-Nine and Seven-One are on their... way back. They can help Chalky handle ... the... wounded. I'll get it done at the generator." He coughed. "No fail, right?"

The sound of the firefight up there was reaching cataclysmic proportions.

In just that moment LS-49 and LS-71 returned. Both had been hit but were making their way on their own.

Chalky put them right to work.

"You two help him!" ordered the medic, gesturing to the most badly wounded at the CCP. Chalky then bent and hauled the other onto his boots.

"You got him?" Ford asked.

Chalky nodded. "He can still move his legs. We'll get down."

"Go," Ford ordered.

He looked ahead to where the fighting was taking place, squeezing the grip of his pistol. He did not like this. Did not like where this was going at all.

He checked his watch. Six minutes.

He opened L-comm. "Drop the charges and get out of there, LS-89." That was Whistler's official identifier.

No response.

Then...

"We got this, sir," came the broken and distorted reply. "No fail."

Ford hesitated one more agonizing minute. This was the hard part of being an officer. He had to leave his men to do their jobs, knowing the cost, and he had to keep himself where Dagger needed him. Which was back down the facility, preparing to clear out before the charges went.

He scooped up the dead legionnaire still at the makeshift CCP and began to fireman-carry him back down.

The level above Ford's head shook with the sound of detonating explosives. Fraggers. But belonging to which side? Had he just heard the end of Whistler and his team? Or were those more Savage dead?

It mattered to Ford and yet it didn't matter. Because no amount of lives lost made a difference when compared with the mission. Because everyone, the entire invasion, and therefore the united worlds of the galaxy, depended on what needed to damn well happen in the next few minutes.

09

**Rogue United Worlds Corvette *Chang*
Over New Vega**

"We're getting lased with target acquisition!" shouted the sensor operator on the flight deck of the sturdy flat corvette.

"Still not within range of their main gun engagement window," replied the countermeasures officer. "We can still break off, Captain. Your call. Three minutes to Do Not Exceed line."

The ship bounced and rattled as Captain Cami Dutton flew the approach to LZ Victory.

"Negative. All stations maintain watch," she ordered. "We'll go for it unless we're told to abort."

Admiral Sulla himself had wanted to take the *Chang* in. Just as he'd taken her out, pulling the last of Rechs's commando team off the buildings of New Vega in the last moments of the first battle. But the captains of the fleet that would support the Legion's assault on New Vega had insisted Sulla take overall command. If it was, as rumored, looking like they might actually face Savage lighthuggers in direct ship-to-ship engagement, they wanted the best combat leader with the most experience against Savage vessels directing fleet ops from their flagship, the *Defiant*.

That was inarguably Admiral Sulla.

Even Rechs had agreed, once it had been decided that Sulla would not be fighting as a legionnaire during the battle.

Though others had more overall experience, Captain Dutton had flown the *Chang* and had led her crew during the months when Admiral Sulla had been alongside General Rechs training the legionnaires. So she was the admiral's choice. She'd earned it. She would fly the approach to LZ Victory, get the Legion on the ground, and support their mission afterward.

When Admiral Sulla first told her she would have that mission, her reply had been, "Thank you, sir."

"For what?" asked Sulla in the quiet of the main SSM tube ejector where he'd found her supervising repairs. "You're going in with every likelihood of getting killed over the objective. And if you make it, you're going to sit there like a duck in the middle of one of the biggest firefights humankind has ever known. I wouldn't be thanking me for anything just yet, Captain."

She wiped the grease from her nose and stood straight, her chest out, eyes forward.

"For the honor of taking the Legion in, sir. Thank you for that."

Sulla hadn't known what to say. *Funny that*, he told himself later when he was in his cabin. Thinking about all the young men and women he and Rechs, and Reina, had known and watched die young for such ephemeral things as "honor."

Funny that.

"Drone strike inbound!" called the sensor officer on the *Chang*.

"Weapons free!" ordered Captain Dutton, her gloved hand gripping *Chang*'s powerful engine controls. She stabilized the angle of attack to give the PDCs a better chance to engage. A moment later a swarm of drones spat up out of the Savage city to meet the diving corvette, coming out of the dawn that was rising over New Vega like an angry explosion in the east.

"Captain?" asked the sensor officer over bridge comms. "What if the air-defense gun isn't down? We're still getting pinged, which means it's still active. That gun needs to be knocked out or we won't make the LZ."

"It'll be down," Dutton snapped. "The Legion put their best on it. They will not fail."

The PDCs erupted to life deliver their long *BRRRRRRRRRRT* blasts as they filled the sky with 20mm ball munitions to knock out the incoming drones.

"EMP projectors engaging!" shouted the countermeasures officer.

Everything was chaos on the narrow flight deck of the heavy assault corvette. Belowdecks the legionnaires were ready. As were the other non-Legion combat units that would be joining in today. The 295th Combat Engineers and the 17th Medical in support.

Drones slammed into the deflectors and exploded. Dutton took her hand off the throttles and adjusted her flight helmet, which appeared almost too large sitting atop her slim frame.

She straightened her comm. "Maintain course. All stations two minutes to DNE No Fail."

Do Not Exceed Line. No Fail.

Three drones smashed into the cockpit window and exploded away like pulped bats. And though the glass held, it was enough for the crew to duck and cover.

"That was close!" shouted the weapons officer.

Dutton scanned the cockpit window for signs of stress. Sensors would warn of impending breach, but sensors tended to get damaged. Best to check yourself. In the window's reflection she saw Tyrus Rechs riding in the jump seat behind her. Studying his battle board as though nothing else were happening.

Pending death was all around the captain. And yet she didn't feel fear—at least she wasn't overwhelmed by it. The only emotion that threatened to take her over, even with death this close, was an insurmountable sense of pride and honor.

"Damage to the portside thrust stabilizers!" barked damage control.

Bells whooped. Sirens blared. Cami Dutton did her job and flew the approach to all their destinies despite the litany of shrieking alarms.

Yes. It was still an honor.

10

Strike Force Dagger

Lieutenant Ford was dragging LS-87, who'd passed out on the way down. They were withdrawing from the blast zone of the Savage air-defense gun facility when the no-fail clock, calculated by the watch on his wrist, fell under one minute.

He was still moving across the wet grass as the sun began to erupt through the trees ahead. Off in the distance, near the logging road where the mechs approached, a fire in the woods sent drifting gray smoke through the canopy.

The three legionnaires still on overwatch were struggling toward the rally point. Move. Fire. Move. He could hear Wild Man's rifle banging out in slow tympani. Each shot a kill. That was for sure.

"LS-89..." Ford called over L-comm.

It was still a firefight up there on the power generator level of the Savage air-defense installation.

Off in the woods he heard the tell-tale *BOOM* of the Wild Man's big rifle again. Another one. And how many more?

"LS-89!" shouted Ford, a gnawing frustration and helplessness growing with each stretch of silence from his L-comm. "Whistler. Come in. That's an order."

Lieutenant Aeson Ford hated this. Hated it with all his soul. Because this moment, this situation, was the opposite of all he'd ever been. Free. Responsible for himself. No one else's life in his hand. No fate of the galaxy...

He pulled the detonator control off his belt.

"*Any* Bravo team element still engaged! Over!"

Thirty seconds.

The air around the ADA began to crackle to life with bright necrotic purple energy. The big weapons platform seemed to be inhaling everything nearby, like a great metal giant taking its first breath after a long sleep. Even the grass and the trees seem to be inhaled by the gun's power and intake systems.

Thing's getting ready to fire, thought Ford as he dragged the unconscious wounded legionnaire as far away from the facility as he could.

"Whistler," he tried again.

No answer.

Fifteen seconds.

No fail.

He tried once last time.

Five seconds.

Chang was due overhead and probably within engagement range. That was why the gun was powering up.

No freedom. He hated it.

Ford squeezed the detonator arms on the clacker, slaved to the charges and the det-cord.

The installation's central spine exploded, sending hot fragments and plating in every direction across the red dawn. Ford dove onto the man he'd been dragging, seeking to cover his wounds from further harm. Then the generators went up, sending up huge electrical snaps and even greater explosions. The barrel of the main gun, which had been swiveling away to engage its distant target, began to topple, slowly but surely, emitting a mighty groan of rending metal as it fell toward the ground below.

No fail, thought Ford as he lay there waiting to be crushed by some flying-falling piece of debris against which there was no defense.

They hadn't failed.

And now the attack on New Vega could begin in full. Still no fail. But with the first phase completed.

Strike Force Dagger had taken six KIAs and five wounded.

Ford did the math that had been drilled into them during patrol phase. Headcount. Wounded. KIA. Blue sky on charge packs. He got to his feet and watched the facility burn and explode. He hated this.

No fail.

11

Hundred Day Celebration Official Historical Program

p. 86 – THE BLOODY BARON

History has made quite a legend of the Bloody Baron. His shadow is so long, his record so impressive, that few realize just how young he was, or in how brief a time his exploits were achieved. During the Second Battle for New Vega he was just twenty-seven years old. Six months later he would be dead in a farmer's fallow field at Callayae, his body lying amid the wreckage of his famous Dauntless Nine. But in those six months the ace fighter pilot Brett Shilton, who would become known as the Bloody Baron for the rest of galactic history, would rack up three hundred and eighty-four air-to-air kills against Savage forces, including two capital ships and one Savage hulk.

An extraordinary aerial combat record that has never been, and likely never will be, surpassed.

Another interesting fact: He was, indeed, an actual baron. But only just. He was the fifth son of the Baron of Al-Hastings on Britannia, and his call sign "Baron" was initially a bit of a running joke in his squadron, because it seemed a certainty he would never actually become a baron, being that he was fifth in line. But when his parents and four brothers were killed during the Savage conquest of Britannia, his entire family wiped out at once along with the rest of that unfortunate world, by fatal default, the fifth son, a roguishly handsome pilot who no one much expected anything of, became the actual Baron of Al-Hastings. The galaxy would never have heard of the Bloody Baron—indeed, the Republic would likely not have survived to hear of him—had not he and his squadron, the Ninth Sand Lions of the Royal Britannian Forces, been deployed to the colony world of Subica at the time of the Savage attack on Britannia. Fate turns on such moments of chance.

Yet fate is but a catalyst. It is through men's actions that history is made. Chance may have made the young pilot a baron, but it was his deeds at the Second Battle of New Vega that earned him the name the galaxy would come to know him by...

The Bloody Baron.

Ninth Intercept Squadron, "Sand Lions"
Inbound on New Vega City

"Targets selected, Lions. Weapons free to engage. Cuckoo, stay with me. I'm going for the drone canisters at mark one-nine-five."

They called him Baron. Captain Brett Shilton, but call sign Baron. The rest of the squadron, ten Dauntless multi-role interceptors still camoed in desert sand and dust white, spread away from his lead interceptor. Still bearing the markings of a stellar nation that no longer existed, the Sand Lions were determined to have their revenge this day. But already the squadron of fighters was feeling the burden of attrition. Twelve craft were meant to fly, but two had been dead-lined for spares in the months since the fall of Britannia. And the United Worlds carrier *Defiant* did not carry spare parts for a Dauntless interceptor. Available munitions had likewise had to be modified to function in Britannian ordnance delivery systems.

Such was the desperation of those times.

The Dauntless, a multi-role interceptor, fired quad pulse guns off both wings. The ship carried two UW AGM-105s—bunker blasters. Only half their usual ordnance load of what the crew chiefs on the flight lines called "gravediggers." Nevertheless, the Sand Lions flung themselves off the carrier *Defiant* and into the New Vegan atmosphere to clear the air space of enemy fire and watch for hostile interceptors over New Vega City.

Weapons hot and inbound against selected targets around the area designated LZ Victory, dropping rapidly through the atmosphere to pick up the deck over the ocean just to the southeast, the sleek, bulldog-nosed fighters broke up into attack teams. Baron was lead and flight lieutenant "Cuckoo" Davies hurtled just aft of his port wing. Target solutions for the AGM-105s were appearing across the canopy's HUD, then fritzing out due to poor maintenance through no fault of the under-supplied crew chiefs.

Lack of supplies and spares conspired to make a bad day worse.

Baron, cool, calm, and dark-eyed, gave the canopy one swift strike of his flight glove. The readouts stabilized.

"That's better, baby," he murmured demurely.

Lieutenant Davies noted approach to target and incoming fire from the west. Everybody else might be scared to death, practically shouting their tallyhos just to burn off the fear and anxiety, but the Baron flew the attack like it was just another day at the drop range.

"Cool as a cuke!" is what their old squadron leader used to say of his most noble pilot. However much of that was meant as praise rather than as a remonstration of the flight leader born with a silver spoon was anyone's guess. And would have to remain so, because that squadron leader was now dead. As were so many of the Britannians the Sand Lions once knew.

At nine hundred meters and doing Mach 1, Baron's and Cuckoo's interceptors released ordnance over a drone pod cluster that scout intel had identified the week before. The AGMs smashed into the spreading farm of drone pods after streaking away from the fighters' outboard wings.

A-A fire, the Savage version of PDCs, was woefully inadequate. It merely chased both twin-tailed interceptors up and away, raking the ruined New Vega skyscraper Baron used for cover and disengaging from Lion Two altogether.

"Regroup over the expressway south of the city, Cuckoo," instructed the Baron over flight comms. "We'll go for the mech farms on the south side and then switch to targets of opportunity."

"Roger that, One. Coming in on your six now. Gorreee, look at the *Chang*, Baron. She's covered in tangos! Think maybe some of them UW F-1s might need to scramble to defend?"

Those fighters were held in reserve in case of a Savage naval attack.

Baron ignored the question. "Stay on target. We'll assist after we hit the mechs."

The Baron dialed in the target on his HUD and selected arm for the remaining AGM. The sky was turning to morning-glory red, and indeed the UW corvette was getting swarmed by enemy interceptors as she came in.

Nevertheless, reflected the brooding pilot as he pulled a hard-gee turn, taking in the morning, *It's a good day to be alive.*

They all were.

He flipped the weapon safety on his stick and pulled the trigger with one finger, his every motion fluid and natural despite the chaos around him.

Below, a fellow Sand Lion caught incoming fire and spiraled into a ruined building, her Dauntless's outboard engine and wing shot to pieces.

Huggins, thought the Baron. *Bad bit to go like that.*

No ejection had been noted.

"Sparrow away," he murmured, then flared the engines to pick up a new intercept to relieve the troop transport with the incoming legionnaires.

12

Rogue UW Corvette *Chang*

As *Chang* made her final turn to burn off reentry speed and then head for the LZ, she got jumped by a new type of fighter. One the Savages hadn't put up in any of the other battles UW forces had fought against their now mortal enemies. One that certainly wasn't on-planet the last time around.

Six craft, shaped like retro-future-age rocket ships with giant fin tails along three sides and no discernible canopy other than a sleek mirrored bubble forward, came in as *Chang* completed her turn. Neither agile nor light, these new fighters were the heavy turn-and-burn type. They raked *Chang*'s upper hull with heavy-caliber machine-gun fire.

"Damage reported…" called out *Chang*'s damage control officer. "Aft reactor. We're holed in cooling. Chief Summers says he's on it!"

Captain Dutton swore under her breath. *Chang* had two reactors, and while one wasn't a major loss—they could take it offline or even dump core and still get by—she didn't like that her ship had taken so much damage this early in the fight.

Still, damage control wasn't her biggest problem right now. *Chang*'s powerful targeting computers were getting ready to give fire control a solution for the single SSM the corvette was carrying. The rest of those unholy terrors, precious few there were, had been transferred to *Defiant*.

Chang's mission to deliver the Legion and act as a base of operations on the ground for the duration of the operation dictated minimal need for the powerful capital ship-based weapon that was the SSM torpedo. Captain Dutton intended to make the most of the one she had.

"Torpedo locked and loaded!" shouted the weapons officer midway down the flight deck.

Above the bridge crew, *Chang's* canopy was suddenly overshadowed by one of the streaking Savage fighters that Naval Intel was now tagging as Phantoms. A tremendous dull roar of incoming fire erupted over the chatter, electronic and verbal, on the bridge. The Phantom's target was further aft, and, judging by the damage control klaxons, it had found its mark.

"Breach on deck seven. Water tanks hit and bleeding!" someone reported.

That's for later, Dutton reminded herself. *Concentrate on controls.*

Her job as captain and pilot of the assault corvette was to fly the approach, fire the SSM, and then put the *Chang* down on a dime after pulling a high-energy reversal. And while every captain had pulled this trick in sim a couple of times, Dutton wasn't aware of many who'd ever done the theoretical tactic live under fire. Herself included.

"Cleared to fire, Captain," intoned the weapons officer over the flight deck comm. His voice was as dry and smoke-stained as the fingertips that incessantly held his cigarettes. He was an older officer who'd joined the crew after *Chang's* previous was killed in a chance engagement with a Savage lighthugger two months prior.

"Roger," acknowledged Dutton, maintaining acceleration and flight profile. The HUD painted the SSM's target ahead. "Count thirty on release and stand by for full reversal. Firing!"

Dutton reached forward to the weapons panel and tapped the torpedo release clearance. Two seconds later the powerful weapon shrieked away faster than once thought possible. Usually these things were deployed in the vastness of deep space. In atmo, they gave a sonic shriek and moved like an angry hornet on fire dumping Mach 6.

"Flight level a thousand meters and approaching, Captain," noted the navigator.

Captain Dutton stared at the fantastic new city the Savages had built, lit up by the rising sun. The ruins the Savages hadn't yet gotten around to cannibalizing remained in the shadows of the otherworldly Savage building project. There were gleaming, twisting towers whose sides shifted and climbed in the golden blue of morning, and Savage work crews and bots manned cranes erecting new towers that seemed to hang from beneath the ones that came before them. Massive arches, also still under construction, promised to someday cover the entire city in a single spider-webbed dome. Welding lights and safety strobes could be seen ahead as *Chang* approached the city. Flak and minor ADA fire reached up to pound the deflectors. And yet the Savage construction crews continued unabated, unfazed.

To the west, a column of smoke rose up where Strike Force Dagger had knocked out the titanic air-defense gun that would have made short work of the *Chang*.

"At least we got that going for us," muttered Dutton as she turned away from the smoking ADA platform to watch the SSM drive itself straight into the base of the old Hilltop District. That was the place where New Vega's early colonists had built their first settlement. Where the local government had constructed a series of deep underground emergency bunkers. Where the Savages now kept those colonists' descendants—stored away as food for monsters from the dark.

Chang's first officer was approaching twenty on the count to full reversal. Dutton shifted in her seat, ignoring the massive explosion just beyond the dirt field the Savages had been planning to use for their reflection pool monument. The SSM had hopefully done its job and opened a gaping hole into the lower levels of the bunker system. It would be impossible to know until the dust settled.

Ten seconds.

Five.

The first officer's count hit zero, and Captain Dutton cut all forward thrust while bringing in the starboard reversers to max at the same time. Repulsor power went to full to maintain lift. Repulsors six and seven, the ones she was the most worried about, blew out.

"Casualties on deck nine. Repulsor six is on fire!"

"Stand by, all hands," ordered the first officer.

Chang swung about hard to come out on a reverse heading to the one she'd been speeding along less than two seconds earlier.

Inevitably, unsecured gear shifted. People got hurt. Mechanical fractures were revealed as erupting faults. More damage-control klaxons picked up the litany of woe. One of the Savage Phantoms, and then another, desperately streaked away to avoid plowing into the suddenly dead-stopped assault frigate now looking to set down.

"Full port reversers now!" ordered Dutton, busy checking her cams to get *Chang* right onto the LZ. She would land as close as possible to the gaping wound in the side of Hilltop their SSM had hopefully just left.

Two Savage Phantoms streaked in and raked the upper hull and the bridge with bright fire. Canopy glass shattered a second after the forward shield array indicated a breach. Before the crew had so much as an opportunity to cry out in alarm. Huge rounds slammed into the glass and cracked it. Someone lay dying on the aft flight deck. Someone else, the radar officer, perhaps, was screaming bloody murder.

Dutton blocked it all out and tried to get the *Chang* down. The closer she got to the SSM's impact, the less open ground the legionnaires who were about to take the battle to the enemy would have to cross exposed and under fire.

Less than three hundred meters to go, she told herself as she watched two more Phantoms turn and streak in toward her completely defenseless ship.

She wondered why *Chang*'s PDCs weren't picking these up. Wondered if all the Sand Lions were dead, unable to help. But she knew more people were about to get killed. There was no wondering about that.

And she could do nothing about it but try to get the ship down as fast as possible.

13

Ninth Intercept Squadron, "Sand Lions"

"I'm on the lead. Pick up his wing when we break them up, Cuckoo," said Baron over the comm as the two Dauntless interceptors closed in on two Savage fighters. Phantoms, according to an updated status on their HUDs.

Coolly, the Baron flicked the safety off the trigger that activated all four of the pulse blasters his ship carried. He promptly smoked the lead Phantom with little to no effort. Remarkable given the high rate of speed over the battlefield with little room to maneuver ahead. His hits raked the long slender gleaming metallic hull of the lead Phantom, tearing into panels and exploding components. The enemy interceptor, which had been on a course to engage the assault frigate *Chang*, came apart and rocketed straight into the ground, leaving a long smoking trail of debris and ignited fuel.

Rather terrific, thought the normally stoic Baron.

The Phantom's Savage wingman broke off and streaked away.

"On him!" shouted Davies, breathlessly exuberant.

Moving at close to eight hundred kilometers per hour several hundred meters off the ground does have a tendency to make one lose one's breath, thought the Baron, who rarely got excited about much.

Tac ops off the *Defiant* reported a deep scan from its combat radar. "Sand Lion One, we have multiple bogies in your AO. Re-tasking the rest of your group to assist."

Baron was already aware of at least four other bandits in the area besides the one "Cuckoo" Davies was chasing down.

"Roger that," replied the Baron as he pulled a hard-gee turn. He guided the Dauntless in a climb to avoid painting the side of one of the alien-like Savage structures rising over the ruined city. A moment later he backed off thrust and looked "up" toward the distant horizon behind his ship to select his next victim.

Victim, not target.

He had no respect for a Savage.

Something the unit's psych officer indicated was unhealthy in combat. "Respect your enemy, or you'll be prone to make a mistake and underestimate your next combat encounter."

The Baron had said nothing in reply, merely smoking through the rest of the interview murmuring droll asides and "agreeing" to see things as he was supposed to if he were to maintain flight status.

But inside, secretly, his hate for Savages left no room for respect. And that UW naval doctor—the psych officer—what did *he* know of what it meant to be noble born?

It was a funny thing, the hatred. The disrespect. That was something he'd never agreed about with his father and brothers during countless arguments in the feasting hall over cigar and cognac.

Everyone is worthy of respect, said the defiant fifth son.

Not so, said they. *Never so.*

Only later would Baron find out just how right they were. Not that it would have made a spit of difference in his decision-making. All paths led him here, to this very moment, in this very cockpit.

He just liked fighting.

And his greatest weapon for the victim, as he picked up the flying Phantom, was his utter contempt for them. Those who had decided to play God and shed the great gift of being human were worthy of nothing more than disdain.

And he, the Bloody Baron, would show them the difference between his respect and his disdain. It was his noble obligation.

Weapons tracking, safety disengaged, rolling out upside down above and fantastically beneath the sky-climbing arches of the Savage picture of heaven on New Vega, he opened up with a leading burst that smoked the forward section of the Savage Phantom. She rolled away from his gunsights and went to full burn. It was fast, but its turn was slow, and he stayed right there in its shadow, never minding that his sensors indicated a lock-on by some new targeting system.

He heard the sound of their guns and felt his Dauntless shudder from a series of impacts. Onboard damage control sensors shrieked, and he slapped at them across the panel.

"Oh, shut up!"

He was busy killing now.

Another burst and his latest victim exploded midair. Pieces of the strange new ship streaked out and away to rain down on the new Savage dream of a better tomorrow.

Another burst of fire on his five or seven o'clock, definitely not six, and his ship took more hits.

Say what you want about the ol' Dauntless, he thought as he shut down a fire in the starboard intake and rolled, diving for the deck of the rooftops below, *but these Britannian fighters can take a pounding.*

And they were agile. He easily lost his sluggish pursuer and picked up another Phantom going for the *Chang*, guns blazing. The assault corvette was lowering her four massive landing gears and preparing to set down in the wide dirt scar before the giant hill full of strange Savage towers.

This victim was smart. *No firing willy-nilly*, thought the Baron. He was lining himself up for some kind of critical kill. Slowing his speed. Saving his gunfire for a select and particular target that might deal a lethal blow to the transport that was bringing in these new legionnaire boys to have a crack at the Savages.

"Should have fired, you poor slob," whispered the Baron as he raced in at the closing Phantom and sent pulse fire into its flaming engines. The Savage ship began to smoke badly, rolling away from its target as it lost what little altitude remained to it before smashing into the ruins of some pre-Savage New Vega building.

"Splash one!" shouted Cuckoo over the comm. "Got mine, Baron. Picking you up now. How'd you do?"

Three, thought the Baron. But all he said in reply was, "Well done, Cuckoo," before turning his attention to the damage the Savages had managed against him.

The inductor fire on the starboard thruster was now out of control. The Baron reached over and blew the fire retardant on that engine, effectively killing it for the rest of the combat.

"Oy, you're hit bad," said Davies as he fell in on Baron's starboard wing, just aft. They climbed for altitude. "Break off?"

"Negative. Two at two mark seven... mark six setting up on the frigate. Follow me."

"Tallyho," murmured Davies, pulling hard on his flight stick.

Baron managed to climb into a loop even with one bad engine and then set up to dive straight down onto the two approaching Phantoms.

Neither the climb nor the hostiles would be good for a ship running on only half power. The climb required energy, as did the breakaway from the dive. And loss of the final remaining engine in either of those scenarios meant certain, and sudden, death.

As for the hostiles, well, that was obvious.

"Careful, Lion One," warned an obviously concerned Davies. "Remember what Ross always says: Your bird might forgive you, but physics won't."

The Baron smiled. He would have his way without concern for a flamed-out engine trailing black smoke and fire retardant all over the sky.

He engaged from the top of the dive and would continue to do so until the last second. Anything to get the Phantoms off the *Chang*. Anything to distract them. The galaxy and all its treasures to get them to break away from their intended attack against the fat, stupid, and slow corvette sitting there like a vulnerable sylph chick waiting to be gobbled up.

Pulse fire raked the city and ruin below as the Baron slipped his Dauntless into a sight picture that would allow him to score some hits. Never mind that he was more falling than flying.

His first shot to hit tore off a fin stabilizer on the outboard Phantom. The Savage ship pulled up and away, breaking off and clearing the way for Baron to engage the lead. He dumped everything he had on his next victim. Engines caught fire. Stabilizer and hull tore away. But the odd Savage fighter continued on like a missile.

"Pull up!" shouted Davies. "Break off!"

Baron knew why the Savage kept going. There was no recovery room. There wasn't meant to be.

He fired pulse charges and kept an eye on the looming *Chang* in the background. With just tens of meters to spare, the enemy Phantom exploded, raining burning fuel and harmless debris against *Chang*'s deflectors.

"Bloody hell," marveled Davies.

"He was trying to suicide her," muttered the Baron. "By the way, that's four."

"Blood-dee *hell*."

14

**Rogue UW Carrier *Defiant*
Stationary Orbit Over New Vega Combat Zone**

Admiral Casper Sulla watched the assets on the board. All around him the *Defiant*'s combat information center hummed with updating data, comm traffic, and phase line updates for the ongoing operation.

The cyclopean Savage air-defense artillery platform tagged as Objective Guard Dog was down according to the strike leader and confirmed by the *Defiant*'s deep-scan sensor sweep. The Ninth Interceptors had knocked out eighty percent of their targets on the ground and had joined the engagement of enemy fighters in a brief air battle that had given the Legion and the forces supporting air superiority for the moment. The Sand Lions had lost three pilots in the initial clash, nearly a third of their force. But that left enough interceptors for their wing to remain combat-effective rather than being folded into the unfamiliar wings of the UW squadrons.

Below his eyes the digital sand table display updated, showing Legion forces on the ground and tagging known Savage positions. It was hard to tell at this moment, but it appeared the Savages were reacting as anticipated. But what absorbed most of Casper's attention at the moment was the landing of *Chang* at LZ Victory. This was the Legion's big debut. In the next few moments they'd take Objective Backdoor, the primary entry point into the subterranean labyrinth below Hilltop, and spread out toward their secondary objectives. That was when they would be as committed to this fight as possible.

And there, in that fight, was where Casper wanted to be right now. He'd trained as a Legion officer the same as the others now on the ground. He wanted to see it through. But Rechs the unyielding, Tyrus the stiff-necked, would have none of it. And so Casper sat in orbit, watching everything from a secure but far-removed strategic view.

"Dial in on Backdoor," ordered the admiral. "Go to thermal. Squad-level."

"Aye, sir," responded the CIC's digital sand table AI, making the admiral's wish happen in an instant.

"Still no legionnaires on the ground yet?"

"Negative, Admiral."

Casper clenched his jaw, hearing Tyrus's voice in his head. The repetition of a briefing he'd sat in on too many times to count. At every level.

"Once we're down there, Casper, we have two positions to take inside the underground to start Phase Rabbit."

Rechs, alone with Casper, going over the plan one final time before briefing Legion officers, pointed toward the digital layout of the underground Hilltop tunnels once known as Old Colony. "Here: Junction Eight. The Savages will hit us for fear of us depriving them of their food supply. It's where they'll feel the most threatened. They'll react fast and hard.

"I'll be in command of Strike Force Shield once we breach Backdoor. That's a two-mile run in sixteen minutes. No time to stop and engage. Second Platoon will clear our six with engineers in tow. Second will then escort said engineers to Kill Zone Alpha.

"After we've neutralized the initial Savage defenses and expected QRF at Junction Eight, the only route of attack they'll have left is here." General Rechs pointed at water intake points from the nearby ocean and a massive underground man-made reservoir. "The Savages will know what we're up to and will be putting everything they have into stopping us. That's why it's imperative that First and Second Platoon and the engineers be in place."

That was when Casper had interrupted. Rechs had never been perceptive enough to know when his oldest friend was giving him the passive-aggressive silent treatment. The look. Or maybe he had been, and ignored it anyway.

Casper cleared his throat. "Tyrus, I need to be there if you're going to take the main defense at Eight. The two of us are the senior-most Legion officers and the only ones who know the whole plan, besides Makaffie. In addition to which, you and I have the most combat experience fighting Savages. Should Captain Greenhill be rolled reacting to the armor when we activate Black Horse, or should Eight get flanked and spanked… you said it yourself: we have no idea what the Savages are going to throw at those kids. Don't you think that I, the only other person in the United Worlds, even the galaxy, who has the same amount of experience fighting Savages as you, should be there to adapt to whatever insane new thing they've come up with next? Because it seems like a good idea to me, Tyrus."

Rechs, who had been living inside the maps of Hilltop for a year, looked up and studied his oldest friend. As if seeing him for the first time.

Casper wondered if Rechs was thinking that maybe he, Admiral Sulla, wanted to get himself killed gloriously for reasons beyond the need to defend the galaxy from the Savages. He wondered if somehow Rechs thought it was all because of Reina.

It wasn't. But he wondered if Rechs thought it was.

Because Casper Sullivan had asked himself that question—about Reina—a thousand times. And the answer was always no.

No.

He needed to be down there because you truly never knew with the Savages. You could only ever guess what was going to come next. And this whole plan was thin. Real thin. Thin at best. Hell, the whole thing was a no-fail mission. Each and every part.

Lose Kill Zone Alpha and it was all over. If the Savages knocked out Junction Eight then it was all over. Lose the *Chang*. Over. Lose—

"True," said Tyrus in that tired rough gravel that was his matter-of-fact voice. "You have the same amount of combat experience as me. But you're also an admiral. And I ain't. I only ever fought 'em face to face and down the length of a barrel. You've fought them in the skies and out in deep space. So let's say you're down there with me. We hold Eight and Alpha. And anything else Black Horse needs to respond to. We even hold Victory. We accomplish the second phase of the mission. Success. Except we've got three Savage hulks engaging our fleet at broadsides right above our heads. Then what?"

Silence.

They both saw, and didn't see, the digital glowing white map of tunnels and kill zones beneath them. They saw and didn't see the ragtag fleet Admiral Sulla and his allies had assembled for this day.

The *Sparrow Hawk*. A Britannian light frigate with ten heavy pulse cannons. Sixteen light pulse. Gravimetric mines.

The *Nightingale*. Also a Britannian light frigate, but with no offensive capability. Purely combat support carrying the 17th CS (Medical).

The *Fortnoy*. A rogue UW escort frigate currently dry on SSMs and operating with a skeleton crew. Decks fifteen through twenty-five offline and dead due to heavy and unrepaired damage.

The *Suracco*. A UW heavy escort also dry on SSMs and whose captain might be having a nervous breakdown after receiving a transmission that his family had been captured by a Savage lighthugger during the evacuation at Dunsfree.

The *James S. Chan*. A UW missile corvette with no missiles but a ton of PDCs. In broadsides combat *Chan* would get shot to pieces. But by sticking close to the *Defiant*, her PDCs might just provide some cover when things got hot.

A dozen pirate ships of all types, with crews willing to fight. But who knew what the hell they could really do except bother a Savage hulk until it swatted them?

And of course... the *Defiant*. A ship that hadn't seen maintenance or refit in a year. Eight SSMs. Two fighter groups. Thirty heavy pulse. Sixty light. One bad reactor. Three okay ones. A tired crew and six hundred "marines" that were little more than ex-soldiers and Legion dropouts who wanted to do their part.

Hell, thought Casper when he considered everyone in his "fleet." *They all want to do their part.*

But if the Savages did jump in with even a few of the jump-capable lighthuggers they currently fielded, it'd be a real firefight up there.

Rechs finally broke the silence. "I'll ask you, because you know your crews and officers better than anyone, Casper. Who do you want fighting that Savage fleet when everyone on the ground, including our fellow legionnaires, absolutely needs our ships to maintain orbital superiority at all costs?"

Casper looked down, knowing he'd lost the argument. Because Tyrus was right.

His old friend drove the point home. "We lose up there and the Savages won't hesitate to rain down everything they've got on us. Everything, Casper. Everything."

Now, back in the carrier's CIC, Admiral Sulla watched *Chang* finally set down on LZ Victory. Her thrusters and reversers still throwing up debris and obscuring thermal overlay.

"Time to Downpour?" asked Sulla in the darkness of the CIC.

"Thirty seconds to fragmentary release on Steel Rain."

They waited.

"Tell *Chang* to increase deflectors to full and stand by until it stops raining."

15

In the year since the Uplifted had taken control of New Vega, great and mighty works had been erected in their image. Most of New Vega—renamed the Pantheon—was considered a brand-new home world, specifically to the tribe that identified *itself* as the Pantheon. Other tribes were now contributing edifices of diplomacy and science for this Uplifted home world, but it was the Pantheon—the tribe, not the planet—that was rapidly becoming a leader within the fledgling Alliance. Its influence and sway were gaining for reasons some among the Uplifted conclaves could not directly identify.

The Pantheon was on the move.

And her massive building programs reflected the bright optimism and leadership the worthies of the fabled and rumored Xanadu Tower wanted to project. The new city—*also* named the Pantheon, in keeping with a vision of the entire planet expanding to be such. City. Planet. Pantheon. One.

The city had grown up on, and over, the ruins of New Vega. Built atop the ashes of that conflict that started a war. The Pantheon—the city—was a sublime interface of gossamer technology and triumph of the will—Soviet-style brutalism. A place where the men and women who would be gods walked the mortal firmaments of the world as if for the first time since their new becoming. Every cut and carved stone, every gargantuan marble wall, every hypno-fountain, all the slender curving towers that were like living circuitry, and all the spreading temples and monuments to themselves and the genius they were about to unleash on the galaxy, fluttered in that pre-dawn darkness when the invasion started.

The facades of these buildings would look barren to the Animals returning to New Vega. But to the Uplifted, the streets glittered in luminescent light like ghost trails through fabulous madhouse carnivals of sex and food. Marble walls fronted projections of the latest propaganda more glamorous and stylishly cut than any early Earth tyrant of the fascist strain would have ever dared to imagine.

These digital labyrinths of tech and wonder were luring in fun-lovers even as the Animal attack began. As that hijacked Uplifted ship crossed the night to drop her load of paratroopers all over the skies and fields surrounding the Sky Gun, as all the Uplifted called it. Uplifted who'd been imprisoned in lost lighthuggers for far longer than the lifespan of a normal human. Only now, Paradise had been found. And they reveled in the streets like it was a never-ending party on the last day of the world.

Only when the Legion's fleet dropped from its last jump, just past midnight, did the festivities finally cease. Or pause. And now, at dawn, the streets were quiet and strewn with party paraphernalia and debris. Only automatons and the slaves who built the monuments and ran the bots were out and about to see the *Chang* coming down.

Advance warning systems had of course alerted the Pantheon High Command, as it was now calling itself, to the unexpected presence of an enemy fleet closing for orbital insertion. And then the sudden and impossible destruction of the Sky Gun. The new generational drone fighters, barely out of R&D, were scrambled. They fared poorly in their first outing. High Command argued with its various AIs for five minutes before deciding on a response.

Release the arctic racks of stored drone fighters.

Close to a thousand had already launched.

They would also recall the various Uplifted marines and supporting military units to their bases and armories. Send out an urgent distress to the First Fleet.

But the populace? High Command's decision regarding them had been swift and unanimous: Do not tell the populace that things were as bad as they were shaping up to be.

And most importantly, be prepared to upload if the worst imaginable were to become reality.

Not that it will, they murmured to each other reassuringly.

The entirety of the High Council agreed with the current General Chairman, Lusypher, that the worst had the lowest of probabilities to actually occur.

In all likelihood this was nothing more than a desperate attempt to retake the Pantheon's calorie reserves and "rescue" the Animals currently in shelf-stable gel storage. According to Chairman Lusypher—and all worthies agreed—this was little more than a Viking or pirate raid. An unfortunate revisiting of old Earth's history.

And that was hardly a surprise. The Animals never did learn to evolve. It was primitively sad how simplistic and unimaginative their thinking was. Which of course was the difference between all the tribes of the Uplifted and the sad little Animals they'd left behind on Earth.

"We really should have nuked the place before we left Earth for good," remarked one of the High Council mandarins to the chairman as the meeting broke up and everyone headed off to their tasks and stations. "Put it out of its misery."

Lusypher's smile was one that never met his eyes. The commenter had remembered well their long-ago parting from Earth. But he'd forgotten the new educations. They *had* left Earth almost a nuclear wasteland. And it still hadn't stopped the vermin from breeding, spreading, and following them out here to their destiny. The destiny of the Uplifted.

The High Council member departed, and Lusypher made a mental note to have him spend time in reeducation. Then he tucked a leather-bound briefing folder under his arm and beckoned a junior aide to his side.

The aide wore the high polished black boots and uniform of the Savage marine officer corps. Lusypher's most trusted. One of the few who knew about the Eternals.

"Wake them up," whispered the chairman. His voice deadly serious. "This is going to get worse."

All around them, feeds from throughout the city saw the *Chang* setting down. Arriving like some not-so-gift-wrapped Trojan horse. Its intentions were clear. You'd have to be an idiot...

Then it began to rain. Deep beneath the city, in the most secure bunker the Pantheon and the High Command could build, the first impacts struck like the footsteps of some long-lost titan of old walking about on the land above. Smashing and ruining everything like a child tired of its afternoon play toys. The final destruction done before the cleaning and putting away could take place.

The *Defiant*'s orbital micro-strike consisted of dumb-shell tungsten rods dropped at orbital velocity and altitude capable of destroying an area upwards of several hundred, if not a thousand, kilometers if fired indiscriminately.

But Admiral Sulla aimed for surgical precision. He had decided to use what was called a defensive perimeter burst. Targets had been selected from among the terrain and structures weeks in advance thanks to jump-drone recon flights that never returned but did manage to send back targeting packets before they burned out, went down, or were taken out. And in the hour since *Defiant* had been in system, her massive target acquisition center had been refining the strike while her scout frigates swept the system under fighter support for any sign of the rumored Savage hulk fleet.

There was, thus far, no sign of any such fleet. And with *Chang* at the LZ, it was time to disabuse the Savages of any notion that they controlled the system, the planet, or the battlefield.

Five hundred flighted tungsten rods shot out of *Defiant*'s forward tube number six. All of them packed tightly into a single OSDS—Orbital Strike Delivery System—canister. The canister penetrated the atmosphere before the delivery system broke apart to send the rods into their flight trajectories. Steering fins and glide flights deployed and interfaced with the *Defiant*'s targeting AIs.

Two minutes later they slammed into the fantastic new structures the Savages had erected atop of the ruins of New Vega City, forming a violent perimeter of destruction around the *Chang*. Several blocks worth of high-rises turned to rubble over the next minute as the tungsten rods moving at relativistic speeds cut buildings in half on partial hits and shattered their central load-bearing cores on direct hits. The result was a cascade of implosions.

Sulla had targeted over forty major structures. The tireless working of AIs guided by the best architects in the United Worlds resulted in the devastation of close to sixty blocks.

And then the arches, still under construction, began to fall, collapsing down onto buildings and towers, multiplying the destruction. Discs and triangles, pyramids and brutalist squares seemed to fold in on themselves, raining debris down indiscriminately.

The ground was quickly swept up in the greatest dust storm one might ever see as it boiled up from the sudden ruin. Particles bloomed and billowed, and it was impossible to tell if the structures were being swallowed by it or were sinking into it.

But Hilltop, and the civilians trapped within, were safe. The buildings, towers, and other enigmatic constructions that still rose up along the rise of that district were also safe. Untouched. By design.

There was one highway that had also been left untouched. And not by design. Somehow, it had defied the bombardment. Main Highway One. And this eight-lane raised highway that shot through all the destruction would come to be known as the Highway of Death when the Savage mech force attacked later that day.

But for now, *Chang* was secure on LZ Victory. Surrounded by a massive perimeter of urban rubble the Savages could not easily pass through. An open killing field for *Chang*'s PDCs.

16

75th Legion, Second Platoon
LZ Victory

Sergeant Lucas Martin, who'd once been Specialist Martin of the Spilursan Rangers, sat with the rest of Second Platoon as the powerful micro-strike went down on the other side of the hull. Out there beyond the deflectors, ruining the Savage vision of a new tomorrow, tearing and ripping into all their utopian dreams.

"Sounds bad," someone said in the darkness as all the legionnaires waited to take the LZ.

"Wouldn't mind if it was worse," muttered someone else.

All power, even emergency life support and lighting, was being diverted to *Chang*'s deflectors to protect the ship and everyone in it from the devastating bombardment. Just in case one of the rods went astray, or a building collapsed the wrong way onto the LZ.

For the next two minutes everyone listened to the distant rumble as building after building fell in on themselves or toppled into one another. It sounded like the end of the world. The ground shook and didn't stop, vibrating up through the assault corvette's landing gears and hull and into the very decking beneath the legionnaires' armored boots.

Some Britannians with the 295th Combat Engineers began expressing dour sentiments that death was imminent. Someone mumbled something about getting "kilt good before we even goot tae the fight!"

A short-fused NCO chewed them out and told them to "shut the 'ell up if ye ken what's good for yeh."

The 295th would be going in to support the clearing of the access tunnel into the arteries of Hilltop. They were to destroy alternate routes into the LZ and the Legion's area of operations—the LAO. Then they would set up a kill zone with mines, explosives, and every other trick they could muster. Their mission was to convince the Savages that the only way forward was through the lesser of two meat-grinders—the Legion. Only, once committed, those Savages would discover that the Legion was an option far, far worse.

General Rechs appeared in the dark next to Martin. He'd been moving among all the troops since they'd set down. Through the strike. Checking in with the platoon leaders and senior NCOs. His quiet presence reminding them all what had to be done next.

Martin couldn't help but feel much of the same vitriol that all the Legion candidates had developed for the old man during training. He wasn't sure how that might play out in the battle.

"Sergeant," began General Rechs.

"Yes, General." Martin waited for something to be said. Some instruction. Some encouragement. Then he remembered again that this was the enigmatic man they'd all come to respect and hate.

The general said nothing further. He studied the men around him and their gear. Which was what Martin had been doing as best he could under the dim red of the emergency lighting.

Yeah, they were all legionnaires. The best of the best. The one percent of the one percent. But a leader's job even then was to make sure everyone was carrying what they'd need for what needed to be done.

"They're ready, sir," Martin said. "Wouldn't have it any other way."

"Good, Sergeant. Second Platoon is light on officers with Ford assigned to Strike Force Dagger."

They were light on NCOs, too. Strike Force Dagger had also plucked out Sergeant Kimm, leaving Martin to essentially run the platoon. At least until it joined up with Lieutenant Stanton's First Platoon at Kill Zone Alpha.

"Yes, sir. My boys are ready all the same."

"I'm going in with you. Take your objectives and be ready to turn over the entrance once it's clear. Depending on resistance we'll either move to contact or we're gonna run and gun to get to KZ Alpha and get you in place. Captain Greenhill and the rest of Strike Force Shield will move on to Junction Eight with me."

"Copy that, sir."

"Warlord Oh-Two to legionnaires..." It was Captain Milker over the ship's address. "You are cleared to don your combat helmets. Combat operations have begun. L-comm operators will perform squad and platoon sync in the next two minutes. Report in upon full connection. Oh-Two out."

In the bloody crimson light the legionnaires put on their buckets. Chin taps booted the HUDs and connected the L-comms to the linked system.

"LS-90," said Sergeant Martin once he had his bucket on.

LS-90 was Second Platoon's L-comm operator. A kid named Preston Groogan. He'd barely made it through training. He was physically smaller than most of the other legionnaires but strong as a bullitar. Martin and Ford had decided to make him comm operator because he was strong and stubborn enough to not quit. And the bulky L-comm pack the comm operator had to carry was a real brick to lug around.

"LS-90," repeated Martin. "We up?"

The kid shook Martin's shoulder to get his sergeant's attention. He shook his head and tapped his bucket on the left side. The sign for no comm.

Martin grabbed 90 and turned him around. Sure enough the pack was turned on, but the small digital readout indicated it was set to quiet instead of receive/broadcast.

The sergeant corrected the error. "Pack was on mute, Groogan."

It was impossible to tell what the look on the kid's face was, but his body posture said enough. He felt like an idiot. "Roger, Sar'nt."

"All good on all elements," Captain Milker said just as Martin switched over to the L-comm command net. "*Chang* cargo doors opening now. Second Platoon stand by to secure the entrance."

Golden daylight, made even more so by the still-swirling dust of the collapsing buildings out there across the cityscape, flooded the portside rear cargo deck.

Major Underwood, commander of the 295th, sidled up next to Sergeant Martin and the general. He was a genial officer with a ready and hopeful smile who seemed to delight in the creativity his men and women could get up to with explosives. He was a fan of them. The Britannian sappers had nowhere near the armor the legionnaires had—they wore only light fatigues—but they carried huge packs filled with mines, explosives, deployable auto-turrets, and tools. And every man carried a big roll of det-cord.

"Seems we have artillery ranging in on us," said Major Underwood, cocking his ear to the ceiling. "Have a listen, chaps."

Rechs and Martin canted their heads likewise. The general tapped some of the manual settings on the new bucket. He was already very familiar with the new piece of equipment. Not because the notorious armor of the criminal Tyrus Rechs had given him any special affinity, but because he had practiced and familiarized himself with the new bucket not only during training sessions but also when most of his legionnaires had been passed out asleep, fumbling through it all bone-deep tired in the long days that led up to the invasion.

Rechs augmented the bucket's sound-detection features and listened. He nodded and said, "Continue as planned, Major Underwood."

"Call me Jalen," Major Underwood said, nodding to indicate he'd heard the general's orders. "Always better to fight beside friends. We'll carry on then... wouldn't have it any other way, General. We're right behind you boys. This is our chance to pay them back for Britannia and the king."

"General," Sergeant Martin said, taking his leave and making it clear he was moving to the front of his unit. Second Platoon was only twenty strong. Really just two squads. But the decision had been made to call the different elements platoons. Only Rechs and Sulla knew why. The rest of the leejes sure as hell didn't.

"On me, Second," said Martin over the platoon L-comm as the door finished lowering. "Once we're clear of the starboard engine—"

A powerful explosion rocked the outer hull. A Savage artillery round had managed a lucky hit against the main deflectors.

Martin ducked, shook the ringing from his ears, and continued. "Watch your sectors and stack on either side of the entrance we've tagged for breach in your HUDs. Alpha, you're on the right! Bravo, go left!"

Martin's legionnaires formed up, ready to do as ordered.

"Remember!" Martin shouted, his last chance to remind everyone of their tasks. "Breach with bangers and sweep the entrance. Maintain perimeter security once we take it. Engage resistance immediately and terminate, but keep moving forward no matter what!"

Behind him the starboard aft cargo door stood full open. Dust and debris swirled into the wide compartment along *Chang*'s belly. Martin checked in visually on the general, who was almost indistinguishable from the rest of his troops. Rechs gave the signal to assault, and Sergeant Martin called out, "Second Platoon... follow me!"

And they were gone, a mass of legionnaires running off the deck of the assault corvette.

17

Sergeant Martin led the wedge of legionnaires across open ground. One hundred and fifty meters between the assault corvette *Chang* and the new breach into Hilltop. And from there into the subterranean warren of passages, warehouses, and secret labs formerly known as Old Colony.

The SSM attack had utterly neutralized any defenders that might have been outside in line of sight of where the *Chang* now waited. This allowed the legionnaires to quickly cover the open ground. Using redundant communications—hand signals and the L-comm—the two wings of the assaulting wedge broke apart and stacked in the rubble as best they could on opposite sides of the breach.

Visibility was low, but their buckets would make up for that. Still, they knew better than to charge right in.

LS-41, "Broggs," tossed in a bandolier of bangers and waited for them to chain-detonate. Two fellow legionnaires from Alpha tossed fraggers in after, storming the breach in the explosive aftermath. Smoke and debris swirled outward as the legionnaires went in, following the sights of their N-1s.

Resistance on the other side of the breach was expected, but as Sergeant Martin followed his men through, he found only a slew of dead and mangled Savage marines kitted out in their futuristic armor, killed by *Chang*'s SSM. Holograms projected out across the dusty ruin, emitting from their shattered mirrored buckets, strange words and meaningless images that scrolled across the darkness. There were severed cybernetic limbs, but no organic body parts beyond the occasional brain drooling out of a ruined helmet.

Then came the gunfire. Ancient slug-throwing weapons just like Martin had faced during the Battle of New Vega. The *first* Battle of New Vega. Back then, he was fighting beside a man he called "the colonel." Little did he know then that the colonel was none other than Tyrus Rechs, genocidal psychopath or take-no-prisoners realist depending on who you asked. Now that same man was somewhere to his rear, shouting, "Push! Push!" even as the gunfire erupted all around them. Brilliant light-show flashes and whistling lead screaming through the dust.

The SSM had collapsed multiple levels of the Old Colony, allowing the advancing legionnaires to look several floors up as though a large hole had been cut into the structure. Savages sent down plunging fire from the upper levels as the general pushed his legionnaires forward like players in some massive stadium of the damned. Ahead, two sets of massive blast doors sat partially open—the sheer force of the *Chang*'s SSM blast having bent them inward. These marked the two primary entrances they'd use to access the rest of the Underground. That the SSM had blown them open would save time. But Savages behind the now inoperable doors, sending fire through the openings, promised to provide a canceling delay.

Moving ahead with the lead element, Sergeant Martin set up a base of fire behind a ruined chunk of wall that had collapsed across the entrance. Broggs was hit immediately, but the new armor deflected the round, leaving the man gasping on the ground, shaking off help from another legionnaire and the platoon medic.

"I'm... good. All good," he gasped over the L-comm. The legionnaire crawled to his knees, still holding his N-1 while the medic ran his hands along the armor and checked them for blood.

"Good," gasped Broggs. "Just got... air... knocked outta... me."

"Gas!" someone croaked over the L-comm.

Forward of the improved fighting position, clouds of yellowish gas began to swarm and then swirl toward the entrance like a living thing.

"Keep your buckets on!" shouted Martin as he directed men into various positions of cover. "More fire on those Savages!"

His L-comm pinged. It was Major Jalen Underwood from the 295th. He was waiting with the rest of his men to charge into the breach upon it being cleared. "Bravo Two, this is Underwood. Are we clear to move forward? Out."

"Clearing resistance!" Martin shouted, forgetting for a moment that with the L-comm there was no need to raise his voice. "Gimme two minutes. Out." He switched over to the wide command net. "Be advised: Savage forces have deployed unknown gas agent. Out."

He emptied a charge pack against the Savages, knowing they would need to move soon. Then he switched the comm once more, this time to his platoon net. "LS-23, take your element and flank left. Work your way through the rocks and set up a crossfire along the wall." Moving LS-23 to the left, along an access ramp that had survived the bunker buster strike, would allow his legionnaires to better engage the Savages dug in at those upper levels. Which was critical, because the Savage marines massed behind the buckled blast doors were laying down a steady stream of heavy machine-gun fire, and there was no way to engage them effectively without dealing with the bad guys on the upper levels. Once that was done, a simple grenade tossed into the open door space ought to be enough to neutralize that threat.

"Gas! Gas!" shouted a leej into the L-comm.

Within a minute the gas began to sting and blister any exposed flesh not covered by their body armor. But by then LS-23 and two other legionnaires had engaged the shooters up on three and were reporting them down.

"Sweep that level. Moving forward!" shouted Martin over the chaos of the L-comm. Casualties were asking for help. Other legionnaires were calling out targets.

Martin performed a squad override, becoming the only voice the men in Alpha and Bravo could hear. "Alpha! Move forward to the blast doors now. Bravo to cover. Clear the room, Second." He then turned to Groogan, who remained right by the sergeant's side, as ordered. "Get that comms mess straightened out now, Nine-Oh. Tell the wounded to stand by."

He swung back into the fight as the comm operator hunched down and began relaying the orders. "All wounded, be advised..."

It was messy, the comms and the tactics Martin was employing. But plans ended the second you encountered incoming. The whole situation was now a brawl just to take the first room, but they'd trained for that. When everything came apart, they knew to start killing everything not friendly. Shoot, move, and communicate.

Eight legionnaires from Alpha moved forward, crouching, covering, and firing into the armored Savages flooding the room through the ruined blast doors. Bravo engaged the defenders already in place. Blaster fire went forth and bullets came back, zipping through the air like swarms of angry metal hornets. Ricochets off ruins and armor made distinct notes. Bright bursts of fire ahead seemed sometimes aimed, sometimes just dumped in the sudden madness to try to dissuade a frontal assault.

Martin was convinced that he'd lost complete control of the battle almost as soon as it started. His first battle as a leader. Not that he'd ever wanted to be one. He'd been pretty happy being a specialist in the Spilursan Rangers who just happened to pull point because he was good at it.

"Kill them all!" shouted General Rechs over the comm, appearing beside Martin. "First Platoon—push up!"

Rechs waded out into the insane firefight, engaging targets with his N-1. Working the rifle first as he'd drilled them to again and again on Hardrock.

And in that moment the former specialist realized what Rechs was doing. The general was telling him, all of them: *It's just a fight*. That message had been a part of training as well. It was fine and good to manage a battle, but there was a moment when it became nothing more than a simple fight. And it didn't matter if you were a leader or a warrior, in the worst of it you just fought for your life by taking the enemies first.

The next solid minute was that and nothing else.

Martin targeted a Savage marine who was busy reloading some kind of heavy machine gun strapped around his torso. Lasers shot forth from the Savage's mirrored helmet, sweeping the firefight and pre-selecting targets. Martin took him down with two shots to the head. Moving swiftly forward, he fired again, more shots this time. Two Savages covering under a half-collapsed column were dead with smoking holes in them. One had been cooking a grenade, and the fragger rolled away from the dying Savage.

One of Martin's legionnaires rushed right toward that position to take advantage of the breach in their line. Martin grabbed the man by the ruck and spun him around, throwing him to the ground and falling on top of the leej as the grenade went off. It was far enough away to merely scatter debris across them, but had the kid kept rushing in to exploit the breach he would probably be dead now.

Getting to his feet, Martin saw LS-90 engaged and covering them, working his N-1 dry. As the L-comm operator deftly reached for a fresh charge pack, a Savage marine came up out of the dark and rubble right behind him. Martin shot the Savage dead with the last shot in his own N-1.

Groogan turned, looked at the dead Savage, and then nodded at Martin. He went back to firing.

But Martin, his N-1 now dry, saw more Savages coming through the section of the rubble that had allowed the first to creep up on his L-comm man.

No time for another charge pack, he thought as he drew the Legion-issue blaster pistol from his belt and fired into the gap, hitting two, maybe three more. Convincing them that to push through was a bad idea for the moment.

Groogan turned around again, aware that blaster bolts were racing behind him. But no more Savages emerged from the breach.

Martin used the lull on that front to get a new charge pack into his rifle. He looked around, unsure where the fighting line was. As far as he could tell everyone was everywhere.

An explosion rocked the edge of the chamber and suddenly a bank of gantry work collapsed. In the aftermath of its crash, the gunfire stopped.

Breathing hard and feeling the adrenaline cooking his heart on overdrive, Martin waved over his L-comm operator. It dawned on him that Rechs had ordered First Platoon up. That meant Lieutenant Stanton should be in the AO, taking command of the next phase, securing Kill Zone Alpha.

"Sergeant?" Groogan asked, crashing next to Martin with such a rattling thud that he had to stop and check that his equipment was all right.

"Get Lieutenant Stanton and then get me a casualty count."

"Roger."

Martin peered about, looking to regain his bearings. His boys had managed to get fraggers into both sets of broken blast doors, eliminating the Savage resistance at the two entrances from point of breach into the Underground.

"Sergeant Martin, he's not responding on L-comm."

"Second Platoon," Martin called over comms, hoping there weren't more down. "Secure the entrance. Stand by for Major Underwood and the Brits to come in. Anyone seen Lieutenant Stanton?"

There was a moment as everyone began to move, some rushing to get to the two major entrances into the room, others trying to help the wounded.

"LS-23's dead," reported a leej from First Platoon.

"Yeah, LT's dead," confirmed another. "Took one in the head, Sarge. Half his face is missing. Bucket didn't do shit."

Martin looked around at the leejes on the ground. The medic was working hard. Martin fought the urge to help with the cleanup. It wasn't his business as de facto platoon leader. Or was that plural now? Platoons. Lieutenant Stanton was dead. Lieutenant Ford was assigned elsewhere. General Rechs was already taking Third and Fourth Platoons toward Junction Eight...

Sergeant Martin didn't need a brevet promotion to know this was on him unless Captain Milker arrived to assume command.

So act like a platoon leader. Let follow-on handle clearing the dead and wounded. He needed to keep pushing his men forward.

"LS-90," he shouted. "Get me that casualty count. And tell everyone to redistribute charge packs off the dead."

He didn't know how many dead he had. Only knew that there'd be more fighting and that meant more charge packs needed. No time for stunned grief. Just redistribute and prepare for the next fight. And hope what happened to Graham Stanton was a fluke. And that for the rest of them... the buckets would hold.

18

Defiant

"We have wounded on the ground we need to get to, Admiral Sulla. Right now if they're to have any kind of chance."

Leandra Foy.

She was a harridan.

And she was the commander of the 17th Combat Support (Medical). One of the few Britannia military units to survive the Savage invasion of that world. Her role was to run medical rescue operations from aboard the medical frigate *Nightingale*.

Sulla was distracted by other goings-on as the invasion unfolded, and failed to respond.

She took the opportunity to lecture.

"Need I remind you, Admiral..."

It was the way she said *Admiral* that irritated Casper the most. Like he'd done something wrong. The whole naughty schoolboy thing. He reminded himself it was just a trick of accent. Britannian professionalism often came off as condescending.

He muted the comm, temporarily cutting off the commander to better focus on scanning the incoming artillery projections on the ground.

The Savage artillery mechs were beginning to find their range, and he'd just recalled the weapons-empty Sand Lions to the carrier for re-arming. There was nothing to throw at this new and unexpected threat at the moment, and that was frustrating. To say the least.

Casper turned to his aide. "Tell the *Chang* to fire up her PDCs and engage the incoming shells. Have them target the mechs if they should be stupid enough to get within range."

He unmuted the conversation with Colonel Leandra Foy. The harridan.

"Colonel Foy, I am aware of our current casualties. But the battlespace is not safe at this time. We've got an unsecured perimeter around LZ Victory and incoming Savage artillery. I can't risk your people."

That didn't faze her a bit. It was as though she'd held her breath all through his bit only to unleash her next verbal fusillade.

"I'm *completely* aware that the field is dangerous, Admiral. But dangerous is where we work and it's why we're here. So sod your danger and let my teams drop. We have a fifteen-minute window from injury to full life-saving support in order to maintain our targeted rate of success. We want to save your lads and this is how we do it. Regardless of incoming. It's what we do, Admiral."

Silence.

A thousand things inside the CIC were competing for his attention. And, yes, currently he had casualties among all branches. Not just the Legion. Casualties they couldn't afford to lose if the next trick in the plan he and Rechs had developed to get the Savages to shove off New Vega was to work.

He cleared his throat. Could feel her somehow glaring at him through the comm.

He turned and sought her out visually, far across the CIC. Yes. She *was* actually glaring at him.

"You are cleared for casevac drop, Colonel. Godspeed."

19

Britannian 17th Combat Support (Medical)
First Medical Response Team, Alpha Company
HMS *Nightingale*
Stationary Orbit Over New Vega Combat Zone

"Oh..." said Captain McIntosh, Doctor Rachel to her patients, Roxy to her friends, as the tiny drop vehicle locked into place on the drop rails and started moving toward the gate beneath HMS *Nightingale*, rattling and clattering badly as it did so. "I don't think I like this bit at all."

She was racked and strapped with the rest of the emergency medical team along the walls of the vehicle. Commonly known as a "teardrop" due to its distinctive shape, the drop vehicle had room for three patients who could be worked on after boost from dustoff. The hard part for Doctor Rachel was getting down to the evac point. She felt like she was about to be thrown off a cliff twelve miles high. Which, in a way, she was. Reentry was already tossing the *Nightingale* to pieces, and the teardrops would soon drop into the maelstrom and conduct a directed freefall through it all, only to finally arrive at a full-fledged battlefield where the wounded awaited emergency treatment.

"Don't worry, love," cooed Lieutenant Idle. Molly to the rest of the team. She was strapped right in next to Captain McIntosh. "It's just a bit of fun. Like a rolly-coaster. You'll be all right. Done this hundreds of times. And look at it this way..."

The teardrop lurched into place at the drop gate, revealing a breathtaking view of the world below—eighteen miles below. The dropship in front of them was already hurtling downward at incredible speeds. Disappearing into the clouds. Boost engines screaming.

"If it goes wrong," continued Lieutenant Idle, "it goes—"

Rachel whooped a little as the powerful locking clamps released. And then there was a horrible moment of nothing that began the freefall.

"Well, love, let's just say it goes horribly wrong. Look on the bright side: most likely *we'll* never know it."

Captain McIntosh could only growl in reply. Her stomach was in her throat.

The booster engines roared from the "front" of the teardrop. Up toward the tip, where the pilots sat. They ship fell facing its fat-bottomed "rear." Molly screamed with delight next to Captain McIntosh. Enjoying the orbital drop as if it were indeed a "rolly-coaster."

"Here we go, Roxy!"

Two medics, Wilson and Tait, sat strapped in on the opposite side of the teardrop. Along with a Britannian soldier who was there to provide perimeter security and do just about everything else that needed doing to keep First Team safe on the ground. John Watson was his name.

Wilson and Tait looked like they were both going to be sick as the ship shuddered in its seemingly unending violent fall. Watson looked fast asleep and wholly unconcerned.

Captain McIntosh hated the soldier for that.

A moment later, with Lieutenant Molly Idle still squealing with delight, her restraint straps barely containing the woman's sturdy, jiggling frame, the ship was shaken so violently it felt like they were going to come apart all at once and everywhere across the upper atmosphere.

Then what? Captain McIntosh wondered, trying to remember the effects of hypoxia. *How high are we?*

Would they die of sudden asphyxiation because the air was so thin? Or were they low enough to die of hypoxia by merely falling asleep as they fell?

She imagined all the worst-case scenarios. Every one of them. And still they continued to fall.

She closed her eyes.

Doctor Rachel McIntosh remembered from her military training orientation—and why she had ever chosen to become a military doctor she had no idea at this very moment—that closing your eyes was somehow bad.

It felt very comforting.

She looked up, toward the tip of the teardrop, and saw both pilots strapped in working over the displays and flight controls. Through the "forward" window she watched the medical frigate *Nightingale* spinning madly.

No, not the frigate, McIntosh reminded herself. *They* were the ones spinning. The big medical frigate was stationary. Relatively.

"Don't worry!" shouted Molly, red wisps of hair falling away from under her combat helmet. "We're not even to the good part, Captain!"

Doctor Rachel was going to be sick. And that was not good.

They were falling even faster now, if that was possible.

She could barely move her limbs; the flight fatigues were squeezing their bodies to keep blood pressure and consciousness up. But she reached for the sick hose every crew station had. It wouldn't do to contaminate the surgery environment before they even had a patient.

"Gonna be a little sick, love?" asked Molly with genuine concern. As though they were just two gals sharing a cuppa in the breakroom at some hospital back in New Londoneaux.

McIntosh checked the altimeter. Eighty-five thousand feet. Her mind reeled. She felt sicker. She opened her mouth to the hose and activated the suction, feeling the pull of cold air.

"You'll be fine…" said Molly, reaching out to pat her as the teardrop stabilized its spin.

The wind was screaming across the fuselage like a banshee's howl, promising all the bad things for those who tempt fate with such things as they were now doing. The noise of the snarling wind was practically earsplitting, even with the combat helmets on.

Above, the pilots calmly ran through checklists, flicking switches on and off. All matter-of-fact, even though the teardrop was shaking so violently that Molly's voice developed an involuntary stutter.

"J-just heave it all out," she soothed. "Nothing to be 'shamed about. D-done it m'self."

Everything McIntosh could see was double.

"Pilot to team… approaching the LZ in three."

If we're about to die, thought Doctor Rachel, *then the pilots don't seem concerned about it.*

She tried to look at the triage telemetric data scrolling along her terminal from the medic on site. The most critical was a sucking chest wound. One of the Legion boys. Already lost consciousness and blood pressure dropping badly. Doctor Rachel wasn't going to die, but this kid was—if she didn't get to him.

Okay, she told herself. *I don't have time to be sick anymore.*

"Stand by to reverse," said the pilot calmly.

Captain Rachel McIntosh knew that everything up to this point in this long horrible fall had been mere child's play. What was coming now was as violent as it could possibly get in a combat medical drop.

"I won't lie to you," said Molly, suddenly seriously next to the fear-stricken captain. Taking Roxy's hand and squeezing it tightly. "Even I don't like this bit. Courage, love."

And then the entire world shifted and pushed and pulled and Rachel's mind and insides struggled and failed to make sense of the impossibility of it all. The teardrop had completely reversed itself in freefall and had fired her powerful braking repulsors. Everyone was screaming. Or at least it seemed like it. Not Watson. He did open his eyes though. As though waking from a brief siesta and realizing he was late for some appointment he needed to get to.

Damn him, McIntosh thought. *Damn him to hell.*

Then Doctor Rachel, captain in the Britannian Medical Services and surgical graduate of the finest schools on a world that was now gone, passed out.

She went black thinking of the kid, the legionnaire who was about to die. What would she do to save his life? Never mind being sick. Or frightened.

The next moment she was back on Britannia. In a tea shop. On a rainy afternoon. Nothing could convince her to leave—

—and she gasped as she came to a few seconds later. The braking repulsors throbbed so badly it felt like she was getting a scan down to her molecular level.

She checked the altitude.

Three hundred feet.

She looked over at Lieutenant Idle. Molly was smiling broadly. "You did it, Roxy. First one down."

The teardrop hit the ground hard despite every braking system, repulsor battery bleed, and heavy shock absorber's attempt to cushion the blow. Captain McIntosh bit her tongue and tasted a warm, coppery tang in her mouth. But she was grateful to be on the ground.

There was a rattle of gunfire beyond the hull. The whine of the new blasters the Legion boys were using.

"Seems as though we've landed in the middle of it," said Molly, unstrapping and hauling herself from her seat. Everyone else was doing the same. Doctor Rachel was about to say something like: "Wait, shouldn't we make sure it's all clear?"

Or something equally stupid.

Don't be daft, she told herself. *There's a kid on the ground who needs our help right now.*

That was all that mattered. Clear or not.

Watson went out first with his fancy-slung pulse rifle. Cool and calm. As though he'd found that appointment he'd been late for.

20

Strike Force Dagger
Rally Point and Medical Evac

The casevac came in hot just where Lieutenant Ford had instructed Kimbo to deploy the sensor flare to mark the evac LZ, in a clearing over the ridge line from the still-burning ADA installation that had been Strike Force Dagger's no-fail mission.

The mission hadn't failed.

The air-defense artillery installation had been knocked out and *Chang* had made it onto LZ Victory. But the dead had paid for it to be so.

West of their position, a small Savage force was trying to hunt them down. It had been a running battle to get the casualties to the most easily accessible LZ—the clearing—for evacuation. But as the pilot Sergeant Kimm had remained in contact with the whole way down had indicated, he could put the dropship down just about anywhere. He just might have to break some stuff doing it.

Kimbo and his ad hoc evacuee team made the first run for the marked clearing. Running from a holding position on the wooded ridge that overlooked the burning installation and ruined mechs in the forest below. Ford, Wild Man, and two other legionnaires continued to hold the ridge until the Savages started calling in directed fire. Untargeted artillery, tossed from a nearby mech, came screaming in, shattering tree trunks and tearing through upper branches. The wounded would be no safer in the protection of the trees than running for the evac.

"Everybody move!" Ford shouted, ordering what remained of Strike Force Dagger to haul those wounded and dead down to the LZ clearing.

Ford reached the LZ last. Except for Wild Man, who had stayed behind, gleefully finding targets—finding peace—amidst the chaos of the artillery barrage.

"I can stay and fight, Fast," said a voice.

It was Junior, shot through the hand during breach. It was clear that he was refusing to board the drop shuttle for transport to the *Nightingale* and further treatment.

Another problem presented itself before Lieutenant Ford could issue orders for Junior to hurry up and get his ass aboard.

Sergeant Kimm, breathing heavily, said, "Female captain over there working on Six-Eight says they won't take our dead. Something about not their job."

Kimbo made a face at this that said he didn't like calling his buddies "the dead." And he especially didn't like it when someone not Legion did it.

Lieutenant Ford looked over at the dead bodies of the legionnaires who'd fallen knocking out the big artillery installation. At least... the dead they'd been able to clear from the site before it blew. There would be nothing left of those who'd been left behind. Not that there was much of anything for those dead who were now here. No body bags. No blankets. There had been no time or room for such things.

The entire medical team was working on LS-68 and his sucking chest wound. Trying to stabilize him for transport. He'd been hit bad on the platform. Looked half dead but there was a pulse all the way to the dustoff. Now he was flatlining and the doctor was telling the others they couldn't "pallet" him until his blood pressure stabilized.

"Forty over nothing," said one of the medics, a stocky redhead holding a blood infuser. "Dropping. He's bottoming out again, Captain."

"Give me the spacers," replied the tall chestnut-haired doctor. "I'm going to start a direct heart massage."

"No time for that, Captain," directed a Britannian medic with a pencil-thin mustache. "We're losing the window on launch. We'll miss the *Nightingale* once she's overhead."

But the pretty female doctor who'd discarded her protective combat helmet and field gear, working with her sleeves rolled up, wasn't having it from her medical team.

"Spacers! Now!"

Two hundred meters east, an artillery round slammed through the trees, shearing off branches and causing them to fall with tremendous cracks and crashes. The ground shook, and dirt rained down everywhere.

"Cover him!" yelled the doctor.

She didn't mean suppressing fire. She meant to cover the man she was working on. LS-68. He was pale. Gray. One of the medics threw a metallic blanket over the doctor who was practically lying on the man's chest. But still working.

C'mon, kid, thought Ford as he stood there next to Kimbo feeling useless. *Live.*

Another artillery round hit farther up the ridge line where Wild Man still fought.

The casevac perimeter security team leader came to stand over them. The nameplate read *Watson*. Ford could see he was a cool one. No stranger to this kind of mess. He was a pro.

"Cap'n McIntosh," he said calmly in a rich bass-baritone. His gray eyes scanning the woods up along the ridge. "The LZ has become untenable and we are in danger of missing our recovery window. We are leaving now. M'um."

Under the blanket Ford heard the doctor ask, "Blood pressure?"

The nurse gave a number Ford didn't quite hear.

He was getting an L-comm alert. But he couldn't take his eyes off Six-Eight. He didn't want to lose another. Wasn't sure if he could take losing another.

Not today, man. C'mon. Dig down, Six-Eight. Find something. Live.

"All right," announced the female doctor. "Let's do this. I'm going to keep working, but let's carry him inside the recovery vehicle."

The other medics seemed unsure about this. Maybe it was some violation of protocol. But they did it.

The stocky redhead turned to Ford and Kimbo.

"He'll be fine. Doctor Rachel's a stubborn one, make no mistake. We'll take good care of your friend now. You boys be safe and all."

Automatic gunfire rang out up in the woods.

Tasking alerts came in over the L-comm.

The medics were moving LS-68 aboard the dropship.

"Sergeant Kimm," Ford said. "Time to get out of here. Pull Wild Man off the ridge line and let's move to the next rally point."

The engines on the teardrop were racing to full when, head down and walking away at a crouch, Ford opened up a new link to the CIC.

"Stand by for updated tasking..." came a calm voice through his bucket.

They had gone through hell.
They were getting a new mission.

Captain McIntosh was strapped in and had just finished boost to orbit when she saw that her most critical patient was alert. Stacked on medical pallets in the center of the team, the young legionnaire looked about wildly.

They locked eyes, and the legionnaire attempted to speak, but nothing came from his lips. Given the gees they were pulling, that might be expected. Doctor Rachel had to struggle just to move her head to look at his vitals.

But what if he's choking? she thought.

She unstrapped, and Molly pushed to raise her arm in warning. "Captain, we're under thrust. This is as dangerous as it gets during this phase. Can't do that. He's got to wait."

"We fought too hard to save him," McIntosh said, not bothering to try to fight the gees to shake her head. "We're not going to lose him now."

She was already out of her harness and pinned to the floor, feeling as though she'd gained a hundred pounds. She crawled to the wounded man and soon confirmed her suspicions. He was choking.

She knew what needed to be done. She had to clear his airway.

Up close, she could see the fear in his eyes. It reminded her of her grandfather's horses. Beautiful and powerful and frightened to death of the world they found themselves in.

The engines cut as the orbital burn faded. Gravity began to release its hold. She held on to the legionnaire, whispering to him as she worked.

"It's okay," she told him. "I'm a doctor. You're going to be okay."

21

75th Legion, Second Platoon
Hilltop District, Underground

The general had gathered Strike Force Shield in the moments after the firefight at Backdoor, allowing them a quick break as platoon leaders and command conferred to update plans and make arrangements for casualties, and then left at the double for Junction Eight. Success here was critical—it was the lynchpin of the entire plan to rescue the hostages imprisoned within sustainment bubbles deep inside the warrens of what had once been known to the people of New Vega as Old Colony, but which was referred to by the Legion invaders simply as "the Underground."

They had sixteen minutes to reach their objective. They would have to cover two miles of enemy-held underground highways and passages against what drone recon had indicated was a significant buildup of Savage troops readying to enter the Underground.

With First Platoon pulling security at LZ Victory, it would fall to Sergeant Martin's Second Platoon and an advance element from the 295th to clear the warrens of tunnels not already blocked off by the Savages between the breach point and the expected auxiliary route of attack through an underground reservoir designated Kill Zone Alpha, where they would set up blocking positions.

Not five minutes after the general and the main assault force moved out, Martin had the hobbled remnants of Second Platoon on the move for Kill Zone Alpha. They hadn't been moving thirty seconds before contact was called in from the general's teams.

It happened quick and hard.

A Savage light attack force using fat-wheeled motorcycles, with two marines apiece, tried to flank Tyrus Rechs's force. Rechs ordered his legionnaires to roll the Savage light force and bypass them via auxiliary tunnels. There was no time to stay and fight. It was a flat-out race for Junction Eight. The entire bunker complex was soon to become a fortress for those who first secured its objective and a tomb for the side that lost.

Martin and his team, clearing the main corridor leading from Backdoor to Junction Eight, had no such luxury. His objective was to push forward, engage, and secure the main route.

The sound of the light attack cycles grew louder, closer. Apparently they weren't interested in chasing Rechs's assault teams through whatever narrow auxiliary tunnels and maintenance accessways the Savages hadn't blocked up. No, these Savages were heading for the breach point. Backdoor.

They were heading for Martin.

The Legion sergeant had only a brief opportunity to set up an ambush and eliminate the threat.

He positioned his platoon in the shadows of an immense gutter that ran beneath the badly leaking condensers. It seemed the Savages hadn't been good on keeping up maintenance on the old human structures since taking the world over. Nor did it seem they had much need for artificial lighting. It was nearly pitch dark, as though Second Platoon had dived down deep below the surface of the ocean.

"Switch to thermals if you haven't already," Martin ordered his platoon.

They were set. Waiting. The sound of the Savage light cavalry buzzing closer.

"Stand by for orders..." Martin said, trying to control the wild thumping of his heart in his chest.

The first fat-wheeled cycles whizzed by in the never-ending night that was the Underground. Their speed was excessive. Reckless given the low-light conditions. But then... the dark probably wasn't a problem for whatever was operating beneath those mirrored helmets.

The lead elements roared past Martin, unwittingly traveling down a long field prepared for intersecting fire.

"Hold fire," Martin whispered, wanting to draw in as many of the Savage riders as possible. He waited until the first Savage was just nearing the end of his ambush farther down the underground gutter before growling, "Light 'em up!"

Second Platoon legionnaires opened fire at the passing riders, and the combat engineers, who hadn't had time to conduct a proper explosive ambush, contributed with a disposable cylinder of plas-nape to prevent any Savage survivors from either taking cover on the far side of the road or simply blowing on through.

The lead riders were vaporized in a wall of white-hot plasma as N-1 fire smashed into the riders coming in behind. The Savages were in turmoil, swerving to avoid the wall of flaming death ahead or picked off by blaster fire. Some Savages, their speed too great, dumped their bikes only to slide into the wall of living fire at the end of the ambush.

It was all over in under a minute. When Sergeant Martin was satisfied that all the riders were down, he shouted, "Everybody up! Keep moving!"

No doubt the Savages had communicated that there was a second force inside the Underground to deal with beside Rechs moving on Junction Eight. But they'd only be able to guess where Martin and Second Platoon were headed in the deep darkness.

22

Strike Force Shield
En Route to Junction Eight

Captain Greenhill, formerly staff sergeant in the cav, veteran of New Vega, promoted from lieutenant at the end of Legion candidate training, had never second-guessed joining the Legion. He'd joined the mounted cav before the Legion and he'd seen action on other worlds scouting, screening, and generally messing with the enemy while leading the infantry toward, or sometimes into, battle. Or at least toward wherever command wanted the battle to be. But after New Vega and his expedition with Tyrus Rechs into the warrens of the Underground, after getting a firsthand look at who the galactic boogeymen known as the Savages really were, he'd joined the Legion without hesitation.

And he'd done well. Yeah, the training had been tough, but he'd come from a tough world settled by scrappy and industrious refugees from Old Earth. His home world was a brutal jungle planet where everything was out to kill you almost every minute of the day. He'd grown up amid death. So he didn't stress much about living the rest of his life in it. It didn't bother him. Just so long as he didn't have to go back to his home world.

And he was in great shape, physically and mentally. He had the natural body of an athlete, but more importantly, he could focus, seemingly at all times, on whatever needed to be done. Health, mental discipline... whatever. Greenhill was not a daydreamer. Whatever he was doing, it was the most important thing in his life at that moment. General Rechs had liked that. He was the same way.

But what ultimately made Greenhill a good legionnaire was that he, like everyone else who'd survived training, had passed that line of no return, no care.

Some had reached the line during one of the general's merciless *don't-let-me-pass-you* runs. You got there when you just dug down and felt like you were gonna die and that didn't matter because there was no way in hell the general was going to turn around and tell you... *You're done*. Finished. See Admiral Sulla for recycle. Some had that moment right then. They accepted that they might die of a heart attack and just kicked it out to stay ahead of Tyrus Rechs with no end in sight.

Greenhill's moment came before that. It came when he saw up close with the general, Ivy Davis, Martin, Sergeant Major Andres, the odd Makaffie, and the strange and silent Wild Man, what the Savages had done on New Vega. The horror of that conflict. The human booby traps. The Calorie Hoarders.

All the madness. Death, despair, and hopelessness.

To Cav Sergeant Michael Greenhill, that had been enough. Not that despair or even wholesale slaughter was unique to New Vega. Those things were just part of the game that was the galaxy. You got your ticket and you took your chance. There were no guarantees that the ride wouldn't kill you or maim you along the way. But within all of that... there was hope. And that was all Mike Greenhill had ever asked for, all he'd ever held on to as he escaped from a fetid and swampy home world. The hope of a chance.

The first battle on New Vega had been hopeless. Greenhill hadn't liked that. And it was that hopelessness that had made him see Legion training through. Or rather, the desire to avoid that hopelessness at all costs.

And now, *Captain* Greenhill watched over Strike Force Shield's column as they ran for their lives, crawled down air passages, climbed ladders and walls to reach upper levels and then ran flat-out at a dead sprint to cross as much distance as possible, gasping inside their armor all the while. He had no intention of quitting, or of letting anyone else quit. He was covered in sweat, his lungs burning, every muscle on fire, and his overloaded ruck was busting his hump.

Blaster fire up ahead. There had already been several brief firefights involving General Rechs and the lead scouts. Never once did they halt. Neither would he.

"Move! Move! Keep moving!" called out the general from far ahead.

They found new obstacles. Muscle up three stories. Sprint across an underground drainage wash. Climb down to a lower roadway. Detour after detour in the hopes of conquering the impassable.

Greenhill and his platoon sergeant were at the extreme rear. Keeping up the headcount. Scanning their six for signs of pursuit as they hustled forward, N-1s at the ready.

The idea was to take the most grueling route, the least accessible, and to pop out right into Junction Eight and set up a defense against what would be the main thrust of the Savage attack to retake their "calories" in storage deep below. Apparently those calories were everything to these Savages.

But to Greenhill, to Rechs, to all the civilized beings of the galaxy, those calories were *people*. People swept up and buried in unyielding hopelessness.

And that was the Savage promise to the galaxy. The hopelessness of being nothing but calories. And so when some men died in training, giving everything until some critical internal system burst, and when other men surrendered to the impossibility of ever pleasing the old man... Greenhill did neither.

Because there was no other way.

It was either become the one fighting force that could stop these monsters... or stand aside and wait for the coming hopelessness.

Above him, at the end of themselves, sweating like pigs in their armor, the column of legionnaires began to climb out of the water filtration pipes and up another long dry concrete slope toward a dark opening. Their calves and hamstrings were on fire. Each step felt like performing a lunging squat with three hundred pounds on your back. The incline was that brutal.

No one said anything.

No one dared to fail Tyrus Rechs.

They passed more ruined Savage corpses, both the marines and new alien types that defied believability with their strange arms, odd numbers of limbs, and biomechanical interfaces. But all could be killed—had been killed in sudden bursts of violence by Rechs and the scouts.

Never halting. Never stopping.

They crossed bloody pools and walls painted in brain matter and machine oils.

Sixteen minutes was approaching.

The show was about to begin.

All of this—every step, every rung, every screaming muscle and dead Savage left in their wake—had been just to get here.

Just to be here at the start of the battle at Junction Eight.

23

Defiant

"Admiral!"

It was yet another call for Casper to attend to some new matter as the chaos of the operation multiplied in new and unforeseen ways. Typical of any op.

Rechs had been right. Again. It was better that Casper was here with the fleet. There were literally a dozen major fires that needed putting out at this exact moment or the entire mission was going to go off the rails.

The *Chang* had lost her second reactor and was having trouble maintaining deflector integrity. The PDCs onboard the assault corvette were attempting to engage the Savage artillery mechs shelling the hell out of LZ Victory, but couldn't seem to coax them in for a kill shot. At least the Legion had deployed and were well into the Underground.

Casper watched his digital sand table, checking for an ETA until the Sand Lions were finished rearming.

"Our only shot," Casper muttered as he turned his attention to study the artillery mechs harassing *Chang* from inside the ruins of the perimeter.

The Savages had tried an infantry massed wave charge across the no man's land of ruin, and the assault corvette's PDC network had cut them to shreds in short order.

"Admiral," the voice repeated. "SSM inbound."

Sulla watched a second Savage mech force out of the northwest on the move and making good time down the artery of Main Highway One to reach the city. He'd had one SSM designated to hit the force, but the SSM had been knocked out by a mobile ADA screen the Savage mech force had onsite. Now Captain Greenhill might have to move topside to ride ambush with Black Horse, diluting the strength of Strike Force Shield in the process.

"Wasted," hissed Casper bitterly.

Who knew?

That was the problem with this battle. Who knew? No one. No one knew anything. Nothing *could* be known. The Savages seemed to be the very essence of the word "unknown."

He and Rechs and a few other planners had made best guesses at what might be put up against the Legion, but guesses were all they could muster. Which was why the final plan had been simple in design. It was easier to react to changes and new developments that way.

Easier. Not easy. There had never been a doubt about the difficulty of this mission. Every part of it.

But the simplicity of the plan was this: Threaten the Savages where they were the most vulnerable. Get them to react. Be prepared to kill that reaction when it surfaced its ugly head. Force them to make a decision. Kill them for making it.

The rest was details.

"Admiral... status update on Dagger. Lieutenant Ford confirms he has nine combat-capable after Guard Dog, plus the attached, and they're on the move to Objective Madhouse."

That had been Tyrus's choice for a code word. Madhouse. It was probably true. But not in all the good ways.

Sulla acknowledged the status update with a nod and a wave. He scrolled the map around and checked Tyrus's progress inside the Underground. They were already engaged at Junction Eight, arriving with no time to spare. Sulla wanted to know what the hell was going on there, but knew better than to interrupt a raging firefight for status updates.

Tyrus would call in whatever needed to be relayed.

But until then he could listen in over the L-comm. A silent observer seeking to determine the shape of this all-important scrap at Junction Eight.

The CIC comm officer gave a quick, "Stand by, sir," and a second later the comm feed from the battle was coming into the combat information center. Every head turned, facing toward the dark of the ceiling or the constantly updating sand table as they listened to the battle.

"LS-93 engaging..."

"Warlord to LS-04 and LS-34. Watch the scouts—they're coming through. Get your fields of fire set up on the main tube. They're coming through there."

The sound of blaster fire.

Distant explosions.

Gunfire.

More explosions.

Blaster fire so continuous it was almost complete background for the next moments.

"Three-Four. We got wounded. Two men down. Medics, hold your position until we can—"

A massive explosion shorted out the feed and for a moment there was nothing. No comm.

"Damn," muttered Admiral Sulla. "Get me comm back up *right now!*"

Because if Tyrus and his whole force had just gotten smoked on the primary objective then this was no longer a rescue mission... it was an evacuation.

The feed came back all at once and too loud.

"Warlord to all Shield elements. LS-34 is KIA and so is L-comm operator. Stay on—"

Blaster fire up close. N-1 and sidearm.

"Dogboy's hit!" someone shouted, unidentified. Too amped up to use proper L-comm identifier protocols.

It was that close. The Savages were overrunning the perimeter, or at least that was what it sounded like.

"There's too many!"

Another explosion.

"Admiral." It was someone in the CIC, the urgency of their voice overriding the tragedy and trauma that was the comm feed from the primary objective.

Sulla turned to see the sensor officer for the *Defiant*. The admiral allowed pure unbridled hate to cross his face at the interruption.

Seeing a monster in his senior officer, the sensor officer stuttered for a second. But the information was too important.

"Sir, enemy jump signatures appearing in-system now. We have three Savage hulks bearing down on us at mark one-eight-five."

24

**Ninth Intercept Squadron, "Sand Lions"
Launch Deck, *Defiant***

Captain Brett Shilton, the Baron, crushed the smoke and drained the coffee they'd had set up in the ready room while the Dauntless interceptors were being rearmed.

"Report to your ships immediately," said Paul Starck, the squadron's ops planner over speaker on the flight deck levels. "We have Savage hulks in-system and we're launching now. Capital ships to engage alone."

"Well that's just plain insanity," said Cuckoo Davies as he wolfed down a pastry and swallowed a whole cup of coffee in one gulp, wiping his mouth with the back of his flight suit's sleeve. "Caps engaging hulks at point-blank with no fighter cover is pure suicide, I'll say. Wouldn't you, Baron?"

Captain Shilton smiled wanly.

There was still time for another smoke. Starck was always a little overzealous. According to the armament loadout displays inside the ready room, the interceptors' onboard weapons still hadn't been topped off. Even though the ships were being taxied out onto the launch deck by the crew chiefs.

Baron lit a smoke coolly, seemingly unconcerned by the order or by the presence of Savage hulks in-system. But he did wonder… if this smoke might be his last. Though he was not truly bothered by the thought either way.

Gravity shifted as the entire carrier began a hard emergency turn. Distant and close at hand, warning klaxons went off. Unsecured items went skittering as always.

The look on Davies's face was pure amazement. "We're turning hard to port. This crazy bloke Admiral Sulla really means to engage them head-on. Gorree!"

"He's got to, Cuckoo. All of us have. Or haven't you figured that bit out?" That rakish smile. "You always were a simpleton."

The Baron, soon to be the Bloody Baron, could insult people without being taken seriously. His manner was so cool, calm, and confident that you couldn't help wanting to be liked by the man.

The deck was full of chaos, fear, and everyone doing their level best to simply just do their jobs so the warship could begin what would likely be the greatest naval engagement of all time. Desperate humanity against their worst enemies: the Savages. Fielding ships forty kilometers long and bristling with a bizarre collection of who knew what weaponry.

"What do you mean, Baron?" said Cuckoo, following his friend's lead and taking time for another bite of a stale pastry.

Baron inhaled and blew out smoke, staring off at nothing.

"We're here to buy time for whatever it is that this Legion is up to down there," he began, like he was commenting on some art installation. "Some trick they're up to, and there's no doubt about that, Cuckoo. Us, the fleet, *we're* the expendable ones this time."

He inhaled half the cigarette. Maybe that was the only tell that even he, the Bloody Baron, was nervous too.

Smoke spilled out across the quiet of the squadron's warm and stale-smelling ready room, lingering before being sucked into the overhead filters.

Cuckoo nodded dumbly. Biting the pastry as if tasting it for both the very first, and the very last, time.

"For good ol' Britannia then, Baron."

The Baron nodded, allowing a rare, genuine smile to cross his grim, dark face.

"For Britannia, Cuckoo. Of course."

25

Strike Force Shield
Junction Eight

Even Tyrus Rechs felt the run for Junction Eight to be a torturous course through Obstacle Hell. By route map it had been measured as no more than two miles, but it was much more than that. Especially with the ups and downs, the steep ascents and ten-foot drops and then back up again all with equipment and explosives on your back.

They moved quickly past ruined Savage corpses with Rechs watching the mission clock in his HUD and telling the NCOs to hurry everyone along because of however many seconds they'd lost on the last engagement. They made up time by moving faster in the dark through unknown enemy territory.

Maybe in those hot few minutes when thighs and calves ached and the feet inside the armored combat boots felt like numb sacks of concrete, carrying all the weight in the world with the reminder that they weren't even to the battle yet, maybe in those few minutes they hated the general a little more than they ever had during training. Maybe they viewed this as just another of his ridiculously impossible tasks for which they would spend themselves down to the last dime.

Maybe.

But they *would* spend themselves down to the last dime.

Rechs was sure of it.

This was what it had all been for.

Captain Greenhill was the last man up the almost impossibly narrow, rung access shaft that led out onto the tunnel traffic control gantry that overlooked Junction Eight. Hauling himself up the last bit on sheer force of will.

Junction Eight was the main access tunnel into the New Vega Underground built beneath Hilltop District. Here, with the smaller tunnel leading to Backdoor at their rear, three massive tunnels met. The first was what New Vega's original planners and builders had called the primary Underground line U-1, the central artery through the very heart of Old Colony and then out into the city itself, emerging to become Main Route One once above the surface. The other two tunnels didn't match U-1 in size or scope. The first was Sub-Route Six (SR6), an additional accessway designed to alleviate congestion. It led to a myriad of deeper warrens, most of which had been sealed by the Savages to better control access. The other was the warehouse access service way, or "Warehouse Way," meant to provide a quick cargo transportation corridor to a central distribution hub.

Warehouse One.

That warehouse held the prize. It was there that the Savages had kept their stores of "calories," resourcefully converting the existing New Vega facilities into massive honeycomb containers. Whether more of the residents of New Vega were sheltered elsewhere on planet—and given the Calorie Hoarders' obsession, that seemed feasible—intelligence maintained that a majority would be found by traveling down the service way.

The legionnaires could push into the warehouse now. That was what the paranoid Calorie Hoarders would expect them to do. And it was what the Legion wanted the Savages to *believe* was happening. But there were too few legionnaires for such a rescue operation. The actual plan was to control Junction Eight and withstand the assaults that would come from Sub-Route Six and U-1. And not just withstand… to absolutely repulse every Savage attack until, frantic with fear of losing their calories, the Savages would abandon the junction and seek to access Warehouse One by a long circumventing route through another chokepoint—the reservoir that was currently being prepped by First Platoon and the 295th.

Kill Zone Alpha.

And to do that, the Legion needed to position themselves perfectly.

The junction was in the process of being remade into a sort of Savage superhighway. They were carving up the Underground, combining, blocking, making it all new again. Junction Eight was a construction site more than a highway now, full of cargo containers, construction vehicles, and heavy cranes that seemed to rise up into the massive black expanse of the underground junction like sentinels deep inside a dwarven kingdom.

"Expect primary resistance coming from U-1 or SR6," Rechs told his legionnaires over the comm, repeating what had been drilled into Strike Force Shield in preparation. "But watch for any Savages caught inside the warehouse who might come out and see if they can't flank us."

Squad designated marksmen and anti-armor operators climbed three stories up, positioning themselves across the long booms of the cranes. They were afforded excellent sight lines of Sub-Route Six and U-1. The rest of the legionnaires set up firing positions at ground level, turning cargo containers into firing pits, everywhere an ambush.

Captain Milker pinged Rechs on the L-comm. "General, *Defiant* has identified a force of a hundred Savage marines marching from Main Route One down into the Underground. ETA to contact from U-1: two minutes."

"Roger," said Rechs. He shouted across Shield's comms, "Two minutes!"

"Sir," Captain Greenhill said. "Should Black Horse move to engage now?"

"Not yet," Rechs answered. "We can handle infantry. I want you with us as long as possible. I'll send you up when we can't afford to keep you down here any longer."

"Yes, sir."

Rechs had less than two minutes to settle all his troops into some kind of defensive position before engaging the Savages. One minute and forty-five seconds later, forty legionnaires opened fire on a Savage force of one hundred.

General Rechs directed fire on the lead elements, forcing both columns to halt and seek cover among the cargo containers that littered that section of the entrance. Positions Rechs would control himself if he had more legionnaires.

But the Legion was what it was. And now it would be tested against all odds. They had endured Hardrock. That they endure the assault on Junction Eight was pivotal. For Rechs, for the Legion... for the galaxy.

26

"Let's go! Let's go!" Captain Greenhill rallied the men of Fourth Platoon's First Squad and led them in a flanking maneuver intended to flush out the Savage marines who'd taken up firing positions among the array of containers at the mouth of U-1.

"Roll 'em up and clear 'em out," had been Rechs's orders regarding the three Savage positions.

The battle at Junction Eight had only just begun, and the Savage marines hunkered down at the opening of U-1 were already dealing out casualties thanks to a heavy stream of machine-gun fire.

Scorching covering fire zipped overhead as the team's point man, LS-67, nailed two Savages in the first position with expert shooting, putting three rounds into each while the rest of the squad moved in and shot down a heavy marine gunner and his loader in quick succession.

"Position one secure," announced Greenhill over L-comm command channel. "Moving on two now."

The heavy machine gun Greenhill's team put out of commission alerted the Savages in positions two and three that something was up. The Savages from position two began to shift their own heavy MG to protect their flank when LS-67 and LS-54 rolled bangers in and two more legionnaires stacked and waited for the ear-shattering *boom*.

First Squad moved in fast, blasting anything that moved and taking down three Savage tangos wearing armor. They had with them some new kind of Savage with four limb-like appendages and a twisted cat's face. The thing died hissing at them, fumbling with one of its undamaged biomechanical tentacles for an explosive device.

It was an old-school fragmentary grenade.

LS-54, with no time to lose, shouted, "Get down!" He grabbed the explosive and heaved it farther down the passageway of cargo containers, turning it against the Savage forces still set up ahead of them.

In the same instant the four-armed Savage with the face of a cat slammed a gleaming and jagged combat knife it had produced from somewhere into 54's thigh, piercing the armor there like it was nothing more than paper.

LS-67, prone from his fellow leej's warning, rolled onto his back to pull the sidearm off his chest. He shot the feline Savage several times—he didn't know how many. Enough to end it, that was for sure.

"Hold position," Greenhill ordered LS-67, sliding to the side of 54, whose leg was pumping out blood in dark red pulses. "Medic!"

"Negative on medic," said the general over the quiet hum of the L-comm. "Both are dead. More coming forward. ETA thirty minutes."

Greenhill pulled his smart-tourniquet and got it around the man's leg just above the wound. The sensory system read the damage and tightened accordingly, dumping a small amount of painkiller.

"Hold here," he told 54.

"I got this," the legionnaire replied.

Greenhill nodded and tapped his L-comm. "Moving on three. One. Two..."

Three was no picnic.

The Savages, aware that they had been outflanked, were firing in every direction at anything they even thought was a legionnaire. Explosive devices were being used with little to no coordination, damaging Savage positions more than the advancing legionnaires.

They were scared. Of the Legion. Just like the general had said they'd be.

Greenhill and the rest of his squad moved in close while the main force of Strike Force Shield along Junction Eight put as much fire on the position as possible.

Captain Greenhill took the lead, LS-67 following close, holding his belt as they moved forward as a unit. They entered the area where the remaining Savages were fortified. Pulse rounds came at him almost immediately, wild and un-aimed. Greenhill, who was on the taller side, crouched, trying to present as little of a target as possible. He shot the first Savage—another of the cats—twice, putting one of the bolts right through its throat. The Savage dropped his weapon and grabbed for its neck, head thrashing wildly.

Greenhill double-tapped the thing in the chest to make sure it was down and then felt almost overwhelmed by the sheer number of targets in front of him. The whole emplacement was littered with Savages firing in every direction down the narrow windows of engagement the containers provided. And if not firing, reloading. The entire vicinity was covered in spent shell casings.

The Savage cat-thing was already dead—it just didn't know it yet—but it wasn't out, and that could present a problem if it suddenly decided to "play hero" as the coming legionnaires swept over the Savage firing positions. Take the chance to pop whatever fragger it had on it and go down swinging.

Greenhill took an extra second, adjusted aim, and drilled the dying cat-like Savage right in the forehead. He kept moving forward and clearing right, feeling LS-67's hand let go of his belt before firing on the left.

Then more firing. Everyone was firing. And with the five shots that remained to him, Greenhill smoked three more Savages.

In five chaotic seconds the fifteen Savages that had been there were dead and not another legionnaire in the squad had been hit. It had gone like clockwork. Even the unexpected had been handled. General Rechs had trained them to fight as he fought. Trained them to be deadly.

They had been the first to kill, and that was all that mattered when the final tally reconciled winners and losers.

"LS-04 to Warlord. Position three is clear."

"Nice work," Rechs said, offering the praise that he'd never given during training. "Get ready for the next wave."

27

Chang
LZ Victory

There were dead on Captain Cami Dutton's bridge. The sensor operator. The first officer. Both lying on the flight deck in pools of blood surrounded by shattered glass.

Dutton herself was bleeding all over her flight suit from a wound in her chest. A corpsman assured her she hadn't hit anything vital before marking her for casevac and moving on to the next casualty. She wasn't sure she'd go. Didn't think she could leave the *Chang* like this.

But evac wasn't here yet in any case, so Dutton monitored progress, same as ever. Engineering had just finished putting up shielding barriers, usually reserved for dangerous maintenance on the reactors, to cover *Chang*'s slender CIC aft of the shot-to-hell flight deck. The canopy was shattered and broken and the whistle of incoming artillery and outbound PDC fire was violent and all around.

That shielding was all that was keeping the combat information center safe from Savage sniper fire coming in from the few remaining buildings standing around Hilltop. Some trick of Savage technology had made the canopy glass unable to resist their sniper fire.

Chang could lift off. Could still be flown from the tiny auxiliary bridge aft in engineering. But her weapons systems were only operational from the CIC. And Captain

Dutton wasn't about to take those PDCs out of the fight. She and her weapons officer could handle the incoming artillery fire for the most part, prioritizing targeting AIs to shoot incoming shells down as they arced into the sky and fell toward the grounded assault corvette on LZ Victory. And the PDCs, even without help, were programmed to roar to life in titanic belches to handle the strafing runs of the Savage Phantoms streaking across the battlefield and tearing the soundscape apart in terrific booms. That was, after all, what they had been made for.

"Message incoming from Air Support *Defiant!*" shouted the comm officer, who was lying on the floor of the CIC amid shattered glass and blood. It seemed to take almost everything the man had just to speak the words.

Nearby the dead sensor officer sat headless in his chair at station.

"Patch it through," grunted Dutton as she tried to finish the pinpoint plot on the four Savage artillery mechs currently raining death down on her ship, pounding the invisible deflectors above their heads.

"Got you," she muttered when the last mech fired a little too close. The system triangulated and pinged shortly thereafter.

The giant four-story machines with massive artillery barrels were running some kind of active electronic camo system that was interfering with drone recon and making it difficult to get a lock on them at longer ranges. How close the mechs had to be to the *Chang* before that camo system lost its effectiveness was something that both sides were learning on the fly. Already three of the behemoths had been destroyed by PDCs when they'd ventured near the perimeter in an attempt to lob direct fire straight down at *Chang* from Hilltop. Even now their smoking and burning frames were still cooking off rounds in the onboard magazines out there, sending up sparks and terrific explosions.

"*Chang* Actual, this is Hawkeye."

Hawkeye was Air Support *Defiant*'s call sign.

"Go for *Chang* Actual," said Dutton, doing her best not to groan out the words in pain. She checked the magazine loads on the PDCs. *Chang* had come in overloaded, carrying as much ammunition for the onboard guns as she could. Engineering was doing a fine job keeping them loaded.

"*Chang*, kill your guns now. Fast movers inbound on your targets."

"Roger," confirmed Dutton. She entered the PDCs' command override, forcing the guns to fall silent. "PDCs offline, over."

"Copy. Stand by."

As if on cue, two snub-nosed Britannian Dauntless fighters streaked in through the canyon of ruins that was Hilltop. They released AGMs on two of the mechs as if these were all just some perfectly choreographed show, causing both of the towering machines to explode. The fighters peeled away in opposite directions, racing across the ruined cityscape into the still-rising late-morning sun.

Captain Dutton listened. There remained out there still two more of the Savage mechs. She had no doubts that they were still targeting her ship. Another barrage of artillery against the shields testified to that.

A moment later the two Britannian fighters returned, concentrating pulse fire on one of the mechs. Dutton strained to see what was happening through the shattered glass of the flight deck and was rewarded by the sight of both fighters spraying bright lines of pulse fire that chewed up the mech out there in the ruin of no man's land. Hits slammed into the center cupola, exploding armor and ripping the artillery magazines to shreds. The mech collapsed and lay burning, belching black, oily smoke.

Dutton expected another pass. But none came. She quickly went to her comms.

"Hawkeye, this is *Chang* Actual. I still need one more taken care of."

After a brief pause, Hawkeye came online. "Negative, Actual. We are tracking no further targets for your mission."

"Hawkeye, I still have one more Savage artillery mech. I can see it closing through my flight deck. He'll be in position to hit us in about ninety seconds. I won't have time to spool up the PDCs to defend. I need those fighters turned around!"

Silence. In the absence of the PDC belching out sheets of leaded death, she could hear the distant giant steps of the inbound mech making its way through and over the rubble. Why hadn't those two fighter jockeys noticed the damned thing?

"Hawkeye!" shouted Cami into the comm. The bandage across her chest was wet with blood again. "Say again, one target remains!"

A new voice entered the comm. Britannian. Cool. Calm. Sure.

"Captain of the *Chang*. This is Strike Leader. Can you give me a loc on your target? We were moving rather quickly and didn't see it. But I'll certainly clean it up for you."

Dutton studied her comm and interface board frantically. This was the problem with working with other services—there was no way to feed targeting data direct. It had to go from the *Chang* to the *Defiant* and then back to the strike leader.

She wiped cold sweat from her forehead. "Designator!" she practically shouted to the CIC.

"What's that, ma'am?" asked the comm officer from the deck of the CIC.

"Designator. I need the target designator."

But there was no time to waste. She flung herself at the storage locker above the comm operator's station where the device was supposed to be kept. A second later she had it out and activated. It was a point-and-click device.

"Strike Leader, this is *Chang* Actual. I'm going to paint the target directly. Should pop on thermal if you'll switch over to imaging on that spectrum."

She stepped over the other dead bodies and made her way toward the barrier that protected the CIC from the flight deck and the sniper fire.

"You're too far in the open!" shouted the comm operator. "Captain, don't!"

But she was already past the barrier and pointing the little electronic pistol-shaped designator straight at the mech out beyond.

Over comm she heard the cool pilot say, "Target acquired," and then out of nowhere the roaring Dauntless streaked straight over top of the *Chang* and pounded the incoming mech with pulse fire. The roar of the engines drowned out the distant explosion of the artillery mech.

Cami raised her hands as if to cover her face from the roaring light-and-sound show the Dauntless created with its low flyover.

The pilot roared away, and she keyed her comm. "Good kill, Strike Leader. *Chang* thanks you!"

If the pilot replied, she didn't hear it. The sniper's bullet shattered her spine and sent her crashing down onto the glass-littered flight deck.

28

Strike Force Shield

Within two hours of the Legion repulsing the quick reaction force of two hundred Savages and taking control of Junction Eight, Savage marines hit them hard with a combined force of over two thousand.

General Rechs still had two platoons close to full strength, having taken only five KIAs, plus two leejes wounded severely enough to require transportation back to LZ Victory once they could be retrieved. That left Rechs thirty-three legionnaires to help him hold Junction Eight and convince the Savages they'd have an easier go at Kill Zone Alpha, their only other way into Warehouse One where they kept their calories.

Fourth Platoon, now supported by medics from the 17th, took both the left and right sides of the junction, as seen from U-1, giving them clear fields of fire not only on U-1 itself, the expected main source of attack, but also on SR6 and any Savages who might dare emerge from Warehouse Way. Left fell to First Squad and right went to Second Squad. SDMs and leejes carrying the Achilles-Javelin anti-armor system took the control gantries above Sub-Route Six. General Rechs placed his command post inside a cargo-container-reinforced control room from which to direct the battle, though it would be abandoned once the onslaught began. Every legionnaire would be needed in the fight.

Third Platoon concentrated itself entirely in front of U-1, the general's thinking being that more Savages would come at them from above than from below. Fighting positions were improved by using the crane system to reposition the cargo containers. Junction Eight was beginning to feel more like a defensible fire base than a sprawling underground construction site. And still men already tired from running and fighting continued to work themselves at a frantic pace to fortify and prepare for the next assault. It was the kind of hardscrabble work that could never be finished. There was never enough cover. Never enough ammo stockpiled. You just kept at it until the enemy came and made you stop.

And the enemy—the Savages—they came like fire through hell.

Moving in teams, they attacked from U-1, closing to a distance of twenty meters from the entrance to Junction Eight before employing an unidentified launcher system, firing rockets into the junction from an elevated position. The Legion was unable to return fire from their positions.

The rockets had little effect against the container fortifications. Gas was employed, also to little effect.

Six minutes later, the Savages rushed the entrance of Junction Eight, determined to break through and secure their precious calories.

Tyrus Rechs was using thermal imaging now that the entire junction was swirling with yellowish gas. The rocket strike had done little against the walls of heavy-duty shipping containers his legionnaires were sheltering behind.

He watched as Savage marines of the Calorie Hoarders variety moved on the junction in force. First using bangers, then laying down suppressive fire from their LMG auto-guns.

"Warlord to all snipers." Rechs waited. From his vantage point he could just see the first troops entering the junction out of U-1. "Engage at your discretion."

The squad designated marksmen were the most vulnerable, even though they were placed up along the tiered levels of the control gantries. They had little durable cover, and if the Savages managed to get counter-snipers into the junction, there might be trouble. To protect his men, Rechs couldn't allow the Savages to get any kind of foothold inside Junction Eight.

The snipers, their N-1s scoped for medium-range engagement, drilled the first Savage marines who entered the AO. Heedless of the losses, the Savages trampled their dead and dying to push forward—going immediately for the service way that led to the subterranean Warehouse One and the captives stored down there—unaware that they were entering a deadly interlocking crossfire set up between the two halves of Fourth Platoon and anchored by Third in the center.

They raced right into a maelstrom.

For the next ten minutes it was shooting and nothing but. Rechs called out targets to the team leaders and ordered concentrations of fire. The effect was devastating. The Savages had to cross open ground to reach the cover of the nearest cargo containers, and those that did were met by leejes who shot them down as they came.

The shooting was so furious and heavy that Rechs wondered if the excessive number of charge packs they'd brought forward with them would be enough. There was no end in sight to the stream of Savages pushing forward into the junction.

Rechs ducked down and contacted *Chang*'s supply officer. "Push more packs this way fast."

Hopefully the wheeled scout vehicles they'd brought with them had been packed and loaded already, the main route from Backdoor to the junction available now that Martin and Second Platoon had dispatched the Savage light cycles and all other resistance along that route. Every side passage had been detonated or otherwise sealed off, leaving a straight shot for support vehicles to move to and from *Chang*. They wouldn't have to rely on the circuitous route Strike Force Shield had been forced to take.

"Affirm. Resupply already en route. ETA your position in five."

A strange and sudden chorus of howls rose up, erupting from the entrance to the junction from U-1. Rechs left the comm hanging to see what the noise was.

Three low rectangular vehicles, some sort of fast-attack mounted gun truck with ceramic-steel balls for wheels, slid into the junction, literally running over Savage marines. It braked and skidded on the dead bodies. Twin jets of molten metal from each truck spewed out over the Legion's fighting positions along the left side of the defense before swiveling for new target areas.

"First Squad, pull back to your secondary positions now!" ordered Rechs over the comm. He was about to order the Javelins forward, but the legionnaires with the anti-armor system up along the second level were already moving, hurling their spears down onto the three vehicles.

One of the vehicles had just started forward, gunning its howling engine like it was about to charge Third Platoon, when a Javelin streaked down out of the shadowy recesses, slammed into the vehicle, and ignited a jet of flames that shot from every orifice. Another attacking gun truck cut its jet of molten metal and swiftly reversed, just managing to dodge the Javelin aimed at it. But the Javelin impacted the floor and ignited a pool of flame large enough to engulf the vehicle anyway. It burned like a fireball as it raced away in reverse, striking Savage marines in its wake. The vehicle's Savage crew attempted to climb out, only to be shot dead by the legionnaires overwatching the killing floor they'd set up.

The crew of the third and final vehicle did manage to escape, but another Javelin denied the gun truck any further involvement in the attack. A deafening explosion inside the chamber punctuated the end of this element of the Savage attack.

The Savage marines on foot were pulling back now, either dropping their weapons or spraying willy-nilly, dumping entire magazines as they crouch-walked backward in retreat. Legion marksmen taught them the error of their ways.

Tyrus Rechs surveyed the battlefield. The destruction was to his liking. The Savages had not gained an inch. And they would, in time, become convinced that they would need to try another way, and try fast if they were to rescue their calories from the hands of the invaders.

Because that was what this was really all about.

29

Chang

Captain Milker had the inglorious job of pushing supplies to all the forward Legion units, interfacing with *Chang*'s crew, and running the LZ according to the state of the battle. Which meant many things depending on what exactly was happening at any given moment. He had felt he needed to be with Shield, especially with Captain Greenhill's having the potential to be recalled from the battle, but General Rechs saw it differently.

"I need a steady supply train, Captain. Charge packs in, wounded out. You're the man to keep that going. That line gets cut off... we fail."

The *Chang* and LZ Victory were a combination base of operations, evac point, and psyop in effect. And that third mission was just coming into play as Major Underwood came running across the no man's land between Backdoor and the starboard aft cargo deck of the *Chang* where Milker was staging the wounded that needed to go up in the next casevac. So far, he had thirty-seven of *Chang*'s crew with emergency to critical care needs that could only be handled aboard the *Nightingale*, and four new legionnaires who were facing death if they didn't get help immediately.

"We're all set to go," said Underwood with a decidedly crisp and optimistic Britannian accent. "Monte is ready."

Monte, as in three-card monte, was a psyop designed by Admiral Sulla with equipment the 295th's special section had available on hand.

"Pull the trigger then," said Milker, following Major Underwood to the front of the cargo deck. He had every intention of watching what came next, under the protection of *Chang*'s dorsal deflector array.

Underwood spoke into his comm rapidly, then turned to Milker, smiling like the cat that just swallowed the canary. "They're starting it now."

"You didn't have to come to me personally to do it," said Milker. He'd come to like the major—he'd come to like Britannians in general—but his tone was one established by General Rechs. A Legion captain was worth a hundred generals outside the Legion. Majors, even more so. "It's dangerous out there. Between the entrance to the Underground and the rear of the ship... deflectors don't cover that area. Be careful, Jalen."

"Oh yes," said the officer brightly. "I know that. But I wanted to see what it would look like to *them*. The Savages, you know. I needed to see if our little deception was going to play in Percy, as they say."

Milker, like all staff officers, felt it best to say nothing. Command-level officers were the ones who had to sell the plan.

A moment later the first of the survivors rescued from the deep bubble storage came running out of the Underground, assisted by lifelike medical personnel and even legionnaires in armor providing security.

Or so it appeared.

The "survivors" were dirty, crying, frightened, dragging small children, hustling and even walking like zombies with extreme fatigue. Every possible emotion had been scanned, designed, and computed to make it appear that they were indeed real people being rescued from the horrors they had faced. A moment later the first ones arrived on the deck of the *Chang*, hustled up the ramp, and promptly disappeared.

Any Savages watching this would come to only one conclusion: by denying Savage access to Junction Eight, the Legion was giving themselves a free hand to rescue and evacuate the citizens of New Vega.

Major Underwood reached out and waved his hand through one of the holograms just before it disappeared. He laughed at the misdirection.

"It's perfect! Now the Savages will think we're raiding their larder with nothing they can do about it." He laughed loudly.

Tens of thousands of people had been generated by AIs to effect this mirage.

"In no time they'll think we've stolen them all," Underwood continued. "That ought to break their spirit, yes?"

Milker only nodded. But inside he whispered to himself, *Let's hope. And let's hope that we really do get some of those poor bastards out alive.*

30

Defiant

Defiant and her squadron peeled away hard to starboard, breaking from the support ships centered around *Nightingale* and *Sparrow Hawk* over New Vega. Scout frigates were sent into the upper atmosphere to hide and continue monitoring the battle.

Nightingale was busy handling the casevac recovery operations over the battlefield, and the more heavily armed *Sparrow Hawk* was riding shotgun. Admiral Sulla doubted the *Sparrow Hawk* would do much good should a Savage hulk choose to engage the two frigates, but it was better than nothing.

That left the *James. S. Chan*, *Fortnoy*, *Suracco*, and thirty-odd pirate ships that would act as escorts for the heavy carrier *Defiant*. In another life, Sulla would have hunted down these pirate crews who had now thrown in with him... but the Savages changed all of that. Even so, this was not close to an acceptable strike fleet for even one Savage lighthugger, according to United Worlds Fleet Operations textbook standards. But Sulla had faced hulks before. He possessed the most confirmed kills of any line captain.

Though, in truth, that didn't mean anything. And he knew it. As did the more capable members of his crew who'd faced Savages before.

But the kids gearing up for their first big row against the galactic terror... the ones who looked too confident to know any better. They were probably thinking, as the admiral glanced around the glowing darkness of *Defiant*'s combat information center, that riding the *Defiant*, one of the UW's most powerful warships, with its most legendary admiral at the helm, into battle meant that they had a better-than-average chance of coming out of this scrape alive. These were ones that had never seen starship combat when the enemy's missiles were streaking in at unrealistic speeds and the PDCs were blaring and groaning desperately to handle the incoming while ECW did its level best to scramble everything. The children fresh from Academy who'd never felt the entirety of the *Defiant* going to full broadsides as she heaved to alongside a massive Savage hulk at close quarters.

"Mark heading six-eight," called out *Defiant*'s first officer. "Closing to maximum engagement range with the SSMs. Stand by torpedoes seven and eight to launch."

The plan was already in place.

Hit the lead Savage ship with two SSMs and see what that did. Because with the Savages you never really knew. There was always the mystery of whatever voodoo science they'd come up with out there in the darkness. Some fantastic new weapon that shot a thousand bolts of energy against your engines that somehow negated current deflector tech. A repulsor tractor that could squeeze the life out of your ship and crush the bulkheads until the hull vented and flung half-frozen crew out into the unforgiving darkness and cold.

Or... some type of new scrambler that interfered with the SSMs. One SSM alone could hole a lighthugger fatally—that was what they'd been developed for, what they were designed to do. But recent reports had indicated that a UW cruiser in the Farrow Rings system had reported that her ship-to-ship missiles were being scrambled. That cruiser, the *Constellation*, was overdue to report in and presumed missing in action.

Then again, there were Savage ships that seemed almost comically behind in warfighting technology. Hulks that shattered under fire like the ancient relics they ought to be.

So who really knew?

"Ready to launch on your command, Admiral," said the first officer as he moved next to Sulla.

The admiral studied the ranges and intercept angles. The digital schematics of the three hulks floated in midair above the sand table. Standard O'Neill cylinder colony ships. Once the bright and shining hope of humanity back on an Earth only dimly remembered as it once was by just three people in the galaxy. Reina, Rechs, and himself.

And even you're starting to forget it all, aren't you, Casper?

There was no telling what would come from these hulks and their micro-civilizations he was facing now.

"Be nice to know," whispered Sulla to himself.

"Excuse me, Admiral?"

Sulla realized he'd said that aloud. "Open a hailing channel to the lead ship."

Silence, or what passed for silence against the constantly humming, buzzing, traffic-chatter background of the CIC, passed as most of the senior section chiefs and officers studied their admiral and wondered about his unusual choice.

Communicating with the Savages might have been attempted once, long ago. But current United Worlds protocols frowned on that. Rumors of Savage mind-control devices and system-wide takeovers achieved through comm access had shaped those protocols, and Admiral Sulla knew for a fact that such an incident had occurred at least once, resulting in the loss of a squadron in the Wyos system sixty years ago. But of course, that file had been redacted and buried on a server with no outside connection to the rest of the worlds. Sulla had seen it. He was the one who buried it.

This was the only move Sulla felt he had. Because four capital ships and thirty-odd pirate vessels wasn't much against what they were facing down right now. Why not try to see what cards they were holding? *Anything they can tell me about themselves will be something I might be able to use against them.*

If nothing else, it might buy a few more minutes of precious time for the Legion.

"Do it," said the first officer when the comm chief failed to immediately acknowledge the admiral's order.

"Channel to lead vessel open, Admiral. She's not broadcasting any idents."

Sulla hadn't expected them to. He straightened and cleared his throat before speaking to the ether.

"Unidentified vessels approaching New Vega. This is a restricted combat zone. Break off your approach or prepare to be engaged."

Nothing. Just the static of the solar system and the star itself interfering with local comm.

Then...

"Admiral, I'm getting a signal," noted the comm chief with cautious surprise. Officers and techs began to murmur among themselves. "It's visual."

This was new.

And incredibly extraordinary. Very few living beings within the United Worlds or the spread of colonies beyond had lived to see a Savage. An actual Savage. Let alone communicate with one.

"Patch it through to my node." Sulla stepped away from the digital sand table and made for the admiral's command chair and the station full of readouts there. "But leave it on general broadcast to the rest of the fleet."

Sliding onto the throne that was the admiral's chair, Sulla adjusted his tunic and stared into the screen ahead. Then he gave a quick wave of his hand, the signal to activate the channel link.

The image that came through was scrambled and distorted for a second, then resolved itself into stunning clarity. Whether this was due to the Savage broadcasting ability or the *Defiant*'s massive computers that ran the long-distance comm gear, Sulla couldn't be sure.

He heard the CIC gasp in shock at what they all saw. None could help it. Though many had faced the Savages before, that was on the delivery end of a suite of SSMs at extreme long range. Death in space across vast gulfs of night. This was different. Up close. Intimate.

Sulla had more experience with Savages than anyone could possibly guess. He and Rechs had been slaves aboard a Savage ship for fifteen years. Reina had rescued them. But all that had been... yes... a long time ago. He had seen the horrors they could become. The nightmares they chose to transform themselves into when left unhindered by things like morality and good.

Even so, he'd almost flinched at this one. He had to push back past terrors only he Rechs and Reina had survived during their fifteen years of slavery.

He breathed slowly through his lips and knew that Rechs was right. They should have nuked every last one of these abominations into oblivion. That was the only way.

What he was staring at was... corpulent. That was the starting point. Obviously these Savages never had a problem like the Calorie Hoarders on the planet below. No, this Savage had never faced a shortage of food or a long season of lack. It was like looking at a hippo that had once been a man... if that man had eight heads.

Seven of which were women.

The thing on the screen smiled from its primary head, the male one, the fattest and most bulbous of them all. It had a face that was almost familiar. Someone you might have known from long ago if you thought about it too much.

The seven heads stared in rapt horror at everything around them. Their mouths perpetually screaming in fear but emitting no sound by which to make known their terrors.

But the main head was speaking. Its language was unintelligible, but it chattered a mile a minute. Using numbers and nonsense words. Ones and zeroes at an incredible hyper-spasmodic rate that made it all sound like the gibbering nonsense of a baboon on H8.

"The translators are getting one word out of every..." began the comm chief, trailing off instead of finishing the sentence. "I'm sorry, sir... this is incredible. One word out of every thousand. A few old Earth dialects like French and Chinese... maybe."

Sulla cleared his throat again and steeled himself to stare at the abomination and say something as though he were having a normal interstellar conversation between alien starship captains. But what?

His mind worked fast to find something. Worked on trying to digest and decipher what exactly the Savages of this particular vessel had gotten up to during their long sojourn out into the dark parts of the galaxy.

He also noted that his fleet was entering the long-range firing arcs for the SSMs, passing from extreme to long. Never a good firing solution, especially if the Savages had some kind of jammer. And most did.

"This is Admiral Casper Sulla of the United Worlds starship *Defiant*. You are currently..."

A thought occurred to Sulla, and he stopped short. What if the Savages didn't have jammers and they were wasting his time to get in close enough to use whatever they *did* have? Getting captured and made a slave a second time in his life wasn't going to happen. No one knew it, but he'd always made sure every ship he served on had an emergency immediate self-destruct override for that very reason. A small code string that would ignite the power systems, reactors, and weapons on overload, turning the ship into a brief candle in the stellar dark.

He would never be captured again.

He would never live that horror again.

On screen the seven heads turned toward the central head atop the corpulent mass that had once been a human, chittering and screaming manically at one another. It was lunacy, madness to watch, madness to even try to consider or understand.

But that's what Sulla forced himself to do in the seconds that followed. Seconds in which to put his centuries of experience to work as fast as possible.

Eight. That was the first thing that jumped out at him. The thing had eight heads. Eight heads that were sewn, grafted—whatever—onto its body.

Sulla's mind raced to figure out what that meant. What it indicated about how these Savages had developed. Or did it mean anything at all?

Medium SSM engagement and extreme range for the heavy pulse cannons was approaching quickly as both groups of ships closed the gap. On the ground the Legion was surrounded and getting ready for the next phase of the operation.

Eight is the number for infinity, thought Sulla.

Did these Savages think of themselves as infinite? As gods? Something similar? That seemed to be standard for most Savage tribes. But why the heads? Opposite gender heads. Worship, adoration, fear? What?

One of the heads, a horrified redhaired face whose milky white eyes drew Casper uncomfortably, almost uncontrollably toward them, turned toward the screen and spoke in a clear, stentorian voice. The rest of the heads, all on tendrils, began to jerk and undulate as the main bulb of a head, the male one, closed its eyes. A calm, almost Buddha-like smile spread across its thin red lips.

"I am First Chairman One," began the horrified redheaded head. A woman who once must have been some classic beauty with a face that would have launched a thousand ships. Or introduced some new cosmetic brand or smart device to the old population of long-gone Earth. An unearthly, otherworldly beauty different from the norm. The common. The masses. The kind of woman who starred in ancient movies or stared back from the pages of all the old magazines Sulla had liked to look at as a child when he went salvaging with his father in the ruins of Los Angeles.

"Greeting, First Chairman One..." began Sulla. But the speaking head cut him off quickly, brooking no interruption.

"I am the violence that comes to you. Chose first Death bringer to the Cleansing."

So, thought Sulla, as the thing babbled. *It's insane and beyond reason. What does that tell me?*

He continued to think this over as the thing listed a litany of worlds and ships it had destroyed and stated that it was ordained by the sobering stars of old and the ancient orders of the universe that animals like him could never understand that it had been brought forth in the nothing by its own will to bring about enlightenment through ruin.

Blah blah blah.

Sense of confidence, thought Sulla as he studied the grotesque, gibbering image. *What does that mean?*

"Entering medium engagement range. Optimal tracking solutions, Admiral. Tubes seven and eight are ready to fire."

It was the first officer. Whispering off screen. Testing Sulla to see whether he'd been mesmerized by that fabled rumor that wasn't always a rumor... Savage mind control.

Sulla shifted his gaze left and nodded, putting all the intelligence and knowing he could into that remonstrating look to his second in command of the *Defiant*.

They've got a weapon that they know can finish me. Hence the confidence, thought Sulla. *They're not worried about my SSMs.*

"Fire eight."

Across the CIC the launch teams went into action as the head on screen babbled manically about the rending it would require for a thousand eons and the tabula rasa of its own intelligence.

"Eight away and running true, Admiral."

If the Savages detected a launch from the powerful warship, it didn't show in the posture of the head on screen or its companions. Or the two other hulks trailing the lead, for that matter.

They were still coming straight on at his tiny fleet and the battle-ravaged world they floated above.

Then the head suddenly stopped and smiled smugly to itself.

"Ah..." the speaker for First Chairman One said smoothly. Almost seductively. "I see you have chosen to be destroyed, Casper Sulla of Los Angeles and *Moirai* of long ago. Wise. I would have had your head that you might join these sisters of yours in the glory of unending agony that is the worship of me."

And then the link went dead.

31

Missile Corvette *James S. Chan*

"Admiral's ordering us to fly his hull, Captain. We're going in, attack pattern Romeo."

Captain Carol Szpara swiveled in her chair and threw the masters on the PDC engagement sensors. She tapped in a series of profile commands already set up for authorization and spoke the security password that activated the ship's powerful defensive system. In front of her the helm was controlled by the pilot and the co-pilot.

Normally the *Chan* was a low-crew ship carrying stand-off engagement weapons. Missile packs and clusters of AJAX strategic engagement munitions. You didn't fly an Archer-class missile corvette into close quarters broadsides like she was being ordered to do now.

But it had been two months since the *Chan* had fired her last AJAX. Now all she had to offer Sulla's little fleet was point defense cannon capability and a crew of eighty that hadn't wanted to run for the UW interior core worlds, choosing instead to stay and fight.

"Take her in, boys!" yelled Captain Szpara. She grabbed her flight helmet and set it atop her dark curly hair. Cool gray eyes flicked over to the comm officer. "Tell the admiral we've got his six all the way in. PDCs hot and ready to defend *Defiant*."

Defiant

"*Chan* coming in close to assist on Predator One, Admiral."

Casper stared at the tac display in the fleet organization section of the CIC. Both *Suracco* and *Fortnoy* would engage the Savage hulk currently being designated as Predator Two. Predator Three was left to the gang of pirate ships under the command of "Commodore" Scar, a pirate who'd been operating under an Espanian Letter of Marque and had assumed overall tactical command of that section of the fleet.

Apparently Scar was of an alien species called wobanki. Casper had heard of the wobanki but had never met one in person. They were rumored to be legendary fighters, but who knew if pirates could be trusted in such a battle?

Sulla focused on the fight before him: a strafing run against the port side of the massive leviathan that was Predator One. The lead Savage hulk.

"Helm reporting bow shock off lead hulk. Brace yourselves!" called out the first officer.

Almost instantly the carrier began to shake and rattle, even deep inside the protected command center, as the warship dove in toward the kilometers-long colony ship hurtling toward battle-ravaged New Vega.

"Incoming energy weapon–based fire off the forward sections," called out the sensor officer. "Deflectors holding."

Sulla clenched his jaw. "Run the deep scan and patch it into TacAn. Let's see how many weapons systems they've got. All batteries stand by to receive your targets. Open fire on confirmation."

Missile Frigate *Suracco*

Captain Colin Heavens felt himself clutching his command chair and focusing on the destruction *Defiant* was wreaking on the port side of Predator One. The state-of-the-art warship opened with all her heavy and light pulse turrets along the starboard side, savaging the ancient bulk of the much larger Savage ship. Scans indicated that the energy blasts from the heavy UW carrier tore through ancient armor into gunnery stations and old colony and exploration systems.

In response, fast-moving micro-rockets lanced up and away from the immense hulk, trying to smash into *Defiant*'s deflectors as she skimmed—from the perspective of the bridge of the *Suracco*—just above their hull.

PDCs spat forth from the much smaller corvette *Chan*, striking the incoming missiles with sudden violent accuracy, while the corvette flew an intercept course between the carrier *Defiant* and Predator One.

Captain Heavens swore a violent oath under his breath, causing some of his bridge officers, already intent on their attack profile against Predator Two, to look up. Had he just given a new order? Countermanded an old one? It was hard to say with Captain Heavens these days.

Which days?

The days since...

He shot them a look, and that look was pure dark fury.

"Watch your damn stations!" He glared at them until no one's eyes were left meeting his. He knew what they were thinking. Because he was thinking the same thing. He had been thinking it ever since the Savages had killed his wife and four kids, shooting up an escaping freighter coming out of Coralon.

Vengeance.

Since he'd received the confirmation they were dead, that had been the only thing he'd been thinking of. Vengeance. How to get it. How to give it. How to pay back beyond measure. He'd given up all that grief garbage and instead concentrated on killing every last Savage in the galaxy. He wouldn't stop until it was done. He would fight the *Suracco* ragged to make it happen.

He knew the crew was close to mutiny. They knew he'd begun to take chances with their safety and the ship so that his own private lust for vengeance could be sated. But in battle there was no one else they wanted in that captain's chair but him.

Heavens's XO had told him that, and he believed her.

He was a great captain. And he was going to kill Predator Two even though *Suracco* was dry on missiles. He'd overload the engines, transfer power surges to the pulse batteries, and get kills on the hulk's engines. Cripple and circle, shooting at leisure. Tearing them apart piece by piece and slowly. Savoring and enjoying every moment.

The main problem would be riding out the storm to get to the engines at the rear of the hulk.

"*Fortnoy* signals she's ready to engage," announced the comm officer across the ticking hum of *Suracco*'s bridge.

"Tell her to follow us in and fire at will, targeting defensive systems. Order engineering to increase reactor power to max plus ten."

Captain Heavens could feel the tension rise still further when he gave that last order. Max was already dangerous output on a reactor that hadn't seen a shipyard overhaul in a year. Plus ten was suicide.

"Reserve power to heavy pulse batteries. I want kill shots on everything. Follow my plot in."

He forced himself to relinquish his death grip on the arms of his chair, folding his arms in the hope that it would bring about patient stillness.

Through the portside viewing screens of the wide bridge, Heavens could see the little pirate fleet in no sort of formation whatsoever swarming Predator Three.

"No time for that," he muttered, and bit his lip.

Ahead, the immenseness of the giant Savage hulk, a thing of ancient history and endless mystery, swam up to meet the attacking ships. One could see the hints of shadows that had once marked its interstellar brightness and hope. The flags of forgotten nations stamped into the comet-dusted dirty hull, or nearly punched through by some long-ago micro-asteroid strike.

Suracco's dorsal batteries opened up along her spine, and as if chasing the starting gun, the wing batteries opened up to support. Hot, swollen bolts of angry fire spat forth and smashed into the immense Savage hulk below. Explosions and debris burst out and away into space, but because of the vastness of the ancient generational colony ships, the damage done seemed ineffectual at best. Scratches on the arm of a giant.

Captain Heavens comforted himself that somewhere within those hulks Savages were dying.

Predator Two replied with slow-moving missiles, or that's what they seemed to be at first as they erupted away from seemingly random sections along the hull. A moment later both *Fortnoy* and *Suracco* were swimming through a sea of the flat spinning discs.

They weren't missiles.

They were boarding vessels.

Already the tactical officer was screaming that the Savages were attempting to board.

32

Defiant

"Come about, engines full, hard a'starboard. All batteries prepare to engage. Torpedoes targeting main engines on Predator One. I want us presenting as small a target as possible!"

Casper's orders rang out like sudden machine-gun fire. Most of the crew of the *Defiant* were still trying to assess how much damage the carrier had taken running the gauntlet of a broadside attack on a vessel that was kilometers long. Halfway down the length, firing everything she had, the *Defiant*'s starboard deflectors had completely collapsed under heavy return fire. Batteries nine and sixteen had been destroyed with all crew killed. Deck seven was holed and venting to deep space until sealed—no word on how many lost. And there'd been damage to the inertial dampeners. Already things were flying everywhere as the massive capital ship's helm struggled to obey Casper's order and come about onto the Savage hulk's six with a direct-fire engagement solution on her rear main engines.

Forward pulse batteries lobbed shots into the receding Savage ship's engineering control stack above the gargantuan engines that propelled the immense hulk through the vastness of space and time. And had done so for several hundred years.

Torpedo eight had missed its target completely. But that was okay. It had been armed with a dummy warhead. Full running and sensor gear designed to look just like an SSM, but no warhead. It had been Casper's test to see if the Savages had some kind of scrambling system that could either distract the torpedo or hack it directly as it made its way to its target. Scouting intel reports and last transmissions from missing starships had indicated such a possibility.

A hijacked torpedo could be catastrophic. Casper had needed to test the rumor before using any of his precious reserve of the powerful ship-to-ship missiles.

Fighting at such extremely close quarters, ranged and guided fire was off the table for now. But with the way the forward firing arc of the *Defiant* was positioned, they might be able to direct fire torpedoes. Not the best solution. But a solution nonetheless.

"Prepare to fire tubes one through four. Full spread."

"No lock, sir," warned the weapons officer. "It's best guess. Indicating sixty percent probability we hit with one before she reaches atmo."

Firing an SSM through the atmo was a great way to waste a torpedo. It would likely burn up on entry.

For Casper, though, it was now or never.

Defiant and *Chan* still rolled out on Predator Two's aft. The leviathan of an ancient colony ship was speeding as fast as she could to reach New Vega's atmosphere. Maybe for protection, but most likely to drop more Savage troops in support of the harried defenses on the ground.

Harried despite the fact that the Savages already heavily outnumbered the Legion and its support units. But an influx of fresh Savage marines might still possibly turn the tide against Rechs.

"Message from *Suracco*, Admiral. They're being boarded. *Fortnoy* breaking her attack off from Two."

Casper barely heard the status update from the executive officer running fleet ops.

"Fire on my command."

He waited, holding his breath. Giving the racing *Defiant* just a second more to catch the hulk whose leading edge was hitting atmo far ahead. Caressing the outermost boundaries of the planet's upper atmosphere.

"Fire."

Four direct-fire SSMs streaked away from the bow of the *Defiant* and rocketed into the aft sections of the Savage hulk. In the moments before impact they seemed too small to do anything of value. But Casper had seen many SSMs fired. Knew their incredible destructive power. Had seen hulks die fiery deaths. Four was often overkill, but getting a kill right now might drag the momentum away from the enemy, seizing it straight from their tyrannical grasp.

And that might be enough to turn the battle...

The first torpedo missed the engines and hit the high engineering control stack of the old colony ship. The bright flare of the explosion tore hundreds of decks to shreds in an instant, shearing the stack away from the superstructure and exploding fantastically deep into the hull, sending white-hot burning debris in every direction as it tore further inside.

Not a kill shot.

He'd seen Savage hulks take worse and keep killing. They were big beyond imagining, which meant there was simply a lot of ship to destroy. Casper had seen many a crew seeing a Savage hulk for the first time become overwhelmed by their vast size and sheer magnitude. Frozen in awe.

The next three SSMs hit the main engines, eight colossal brightly burning circles each the size of a stadium. The effect was a daisy-chain of destruction, igniting the remaining engines and their supporting reactor and drive systems.

The destruction of Predator One was the most violent explosion Casper Sullivan had witnessed in all his years in space. All eyes had seen the missiles hit and erupt within the engine housings, ripping through thrust nozzles, sending burning debris into the lower superstructure of the aft sections of the Savage hulk. Docking bays and tethers, towers matching the tallest buildings back on any of the United Worlds, all of them were torn apart.

And then came the flare.

Hot white searing light exploded across the starfield, obscuring everything and threatening to burn retinas if not for the screens and viewports enabled to handle such blistering light shows. Casper had never before seen those screens grow so black. The intensity of the light and heat rendered internal sensors useless.

Nothing could have survived that, thought Casper, who'd involuntarily raised the gilded sleeve of his admiral's tunic to cover his eyes from the blast.

Crew inside the *Defiant*'s CIC were screaming, a mixture of triumph and alarm—because they were hardly out of the thick of things. Damage control alarms were ringing for attention, and the ship's AI warned of uncontrolled atmospheric entry speed.

"Port engines to full, starboard all back!" Casper roared.

Helm personnel were trained to execute an emergency reverse even when flying blind.

Something smashed into the *Defiant* hard, shaking the whole ship down to her spine. More damage klaxons shrieked murder as integrity warnings along the forward bulkheads whined for attention.

How much more can this ship take? the admiral wondered. There was every likelihood he would find out today.

The blackened screens and viewports receded from opacity to a smoky, dim clarity, and he stared hard into the display screen to see what had become of Predator One.

What he saw was utterly incredible. The full spread had not destroyed the hulk that was now entering New Vega's atmosphere... but it had initiated its death throes. The engines, engineering, and whatever else lay within those gargantuan aft sections of the hulk had been completely blown off. All down the spine explosions continued to ripple through the hull, rupturing plating off into the upper atmosphere or rocketing back out into space with nuclear meltdown fury. And within moments, the huge ship plunged into atmosphere and turned into a hundred thousand burning meteorites.

Casper watched the destruction with mouth agape.

The journey of that eight-headed thing that had ruled over who knew what madness aboard the ancient colony ship that had begun long ago on Earth... was now over. Nothing was left of the creature or its ship but fragments of burning debris raining down over some vast sprawl on New Vega.

33

Missile Frigate *Suracco*

Captain Heavens noted the time. Five minutes since the Savages had boarded his ship. Fighting was being reported on the lower decks, and two minutes ago they'd lost contact with main engineering. The inter-ship comm system had gone dead and the comm officer was trying to re-route channels through ship-to-ship using the main AE-805 comms mast on the aft array.

"Captain..." The comm officer sounded tired. "Still no contact with engineering. But we do have a channel open. *Fortnoy* coming alongside to assist."

Heavens swiveled his chair to study the near-space tac readout. They were adrift but at least clear of the enemy hulk. The small complement of UW marines aboard *Suracco* were busy fighting off boarders on decks nineteen and twenty. But if the scattered reports coming in were any indication... well, things were not going well down there.

Not at all.

"Predator Two coming about," noted the helm. "Slow turn, but she'll be pointed back this direction in about two minutes, Captain."

Suracco's sensor officer added more salt to their wounded situation. "She's powering up forward weapons. Scans reveal missiles loading from her secondary racks."

Captain Heavens nodded. His officers, for the most part, seemed cool, calm, and collected. Which was something considering they were currently dead in the water and surrounded by Savage ships.

"At least Admiral Sulla got one," he said to the room. Aware that this did nothing to improve their situation, but not knowing what else to say. He rubbed his stubbly chin, trying to cope with the reality that it might be all they'd get today. That it would have to be... enough.

But it wasn't enough. Couldn't be enough. Not until all of the beasts were put down like animals. Slaughtered.

"Savages on deck fifteen and heading this way, sir. Multiple casualties. Marine Commander Gale indicates we should abandon ship. He's down to fifteen personnel combat-effective. They're trying the auxiliary engine control systems. Stand by..."

A series of distant explosions aft rocked the ship.

The comm operator turned toward the captain, her face pale. "I've lost contact with the marines, sir."

Something unseen and powerful grabbed the entire ship and shook it hard. Heavens was nearly thrown from his chair. The comm officer gave a short, surprised yelp. The helm crew began to run through the masters, checking readings and responses. Seeing what they had to work with.

Heavens could tell his ship was moving again. Not underway. Not by its own power. It was being pulled.

"Captain, I think you should see this." It was *Suracco*'s XO. Heavens turned and studied the display the officer was indicating.

The Savage hulk had come about and was bearing straight down on them, a dim green iridescent light coming from its hangar. They were being hauled in by some sort of tractor device. A familiar system, but far more powerful than the packages produced by United Worlds. To haul a ship like the *Suracco* so quickly and from such a distance... Heavens wouldn't have thought it possible were it not, clearly, possible.

He nodded to the XO and swallowed hard. Then he turned back to face the bridge to issue his final order.

"Abandon ship. Issue the emergency evacuation orders. They're going to try to capture us... and we won't want any part of that."

With one accord, the bridge crew scrambled to execute their final tasks and make it to the emergency escape pods. Heavens knew none of them had a chance. This was a combat zone with little hope of rescue.

He turned toward his station and executed a series of quick orders, glancing repeatedly up at the display that showed the looming hulk's hangar grow ever closer. They were being pulled in faster than he'd thought.

No one stopped to make sure their captain was coming along to the escape pods. No one tried to talk him out of going down with the ship. Heavens had lost their loyalty. His grief—his madness—had cost him his crew long before these final moments. He knew that now.

But there was still time to execute the order and get to a pod. Still time to survive and maybe make it to some world beyond the frontier the Savages would never reach in his lifetime. Scratch out some kind of life with the time that remained.

He entered his final code string.

"Self-destruction authorization complete, Captain," said the AI. "Initiating. Please abandon ship and move to minimum safe distance."

There was still time. But... he couldn't.

The last night he'd seen his family. Before the cruise. Over a year ago, before the Savages had come in this latest series of raids. That night had been the best. It was a cold winter's night on Coralon. The last he'd spend with his family until he got back to them at the end of this tour. Then he'd go to UW Naval Staff College.

He closed his eyes.

Admiral Sulla was coming through on the comm, asking for status. Offering advice. Help.

Heavens flicked it off and listened to the last of the escape pods hiss and jettison, screeching away from the hull. He could hear metal boots in the passages close by. Savages. They were coming for him. Coming for the bridge.

The light on the bridge shifted from white to green. The *Suracco* was almost inside the Savage hangar, and the hulk's iridescent light spilled in through the forward viewing ports.

He thought about that last night with his wife and his four children. The firelight and the darkness. The questions about where he was going and why. The stories about his travels in space as they sat on the floor and had a "camp-out." Eating fondue and roasting marshmallows in the fireplace.

Behind closed eyes he watched them all one last time. His two daughters. His two boys. Her. His true love. The woman who had chosen him. And he her.

There was no place in the galaxy where he'd find them again. So what was the use of escape?

He'd stay right here. With them.

"Three, two..." counted *Suracco*'s AI.

He'd disabled the ship's countdown. But for some reason you couldn't disable the last three seconds. He'd spent a lot of time fooling around with that. Knowing he'd never be taken alive. Knowing only that he wanted something he'd once had and would never have again. Not in this life.

He smiled and saw all their faces as the Savages stormed the bridge, firing.

"One."

Maybe, he thought as both of *Suracco*'s reactors exploded. *Maybe that's why people believe in eternity. In religion. In something.*

Maybe was his last thought, letting go of his last revenge.

Maybe that's all we have. And what we've been looking for all along. Eternity...

34

Defiant

"Get me a scan now!" ordered Sulla inside *Defiant*'s CIC the moment after *Suracco* blew up just inside the hangar of Predator Two.

"Working on it!" called out the TacAn officer.

"Magnify to hull detail," he ordered. Then he moved closer to study the display.

Predator Two had not been destroyed in the explosion, but it was severely damaged. The entire front section of the ship, at least a full two kilometers, was ripped off and glowing brightly in the velvet nepenthe of space. It would have been a knockout blow for anything but a Savage hulk.

But Predator Two wasn't finished. Not by a long shot.

Sulla ran through those sections of the Savage ship he knew from his time aboard them. Escaping off the *Obsidia* with his first command at just the last second to pull Rechs's Martian light infantry out under heavy fire. Or what remained of them after that horrific expedition deep into that Savage lighthugger and the confrontation with a being called the Dark Wanderer.

There was nothing vital in those forward sections except maybe the old forward bridge, if they were even still using that. The old O'Neill cylinders had tons of redundant control and auxiliary bridges, so nothing critical was gone. Except she was ruined as far as re-entry. Maybe she could make an emergency planetary landing if the atmo was insignificant. Maybe.

"We have rescue beacons, Admiral. Shall we initiate recovery operations?"

Sulla was waiting for the deep scan on the rest of the ship. How close could they get?

"Status on Predator Three."

The quiet hum of the CIC pulsed as officers conferred to gather information and prepare a report for their commanding officer.

"Ground ops, get me General Rechs," ordered Sulla as he waited. "Status update on all ground units."

Sulla went back over to the digital sand table and tried to recognize what was new in the ground war below. What was different.

"Deep scan coming in now, Admiral," said the first officer. "Predator Two seems to be drifting and we're detecting hull breaches and fires out of control on the forward decks. Core melt in one of her forward reactors; we expect her to jettison. But still limited motive power and weapons." The officer pursed his lips and lowered his datapad. "She's still got teeth, sir. We could hit her with our remaining torpedoes and hope for a kill if they get through."

Sulla nodded.

They had just four SSMs left.

"Predator Three?" he asked.

"Commodore Scar reports they're waging a running firefight against her on the far side of New Vega. They'll bring her down or die flying... his words via the translator, Admiral."

Sulla took a deep breath. "Ground status."

The officer running comm and ops liaison with the Legion and all other units stepped in quickly.

"We're holding at Junction Eight, Admiral. Black Horse is in the wind and heading toward the highway to meet the mech force moving in on the city from the northeast. Captain Greenhill has given his alert for artillery support requests in the next thirty minutes. We are not currently in position to provide, Admiral. Kill Zone Alpha is engaged. And..."

The worst for last, thought Casper, who'd been through enough briefings to smell bad news coming from a long way off.

"General Rechs has been badly wounded and is currently being evac'd to the casevac site at Victory for retrieval. Captain Milker is going forward to take command. Junction Eight has been hit by three waves of Savage ground units composed primarily of marines supported by light armor. They're still fighting off the third wave. Charge packs are running low and there are multiple casualties."

"Will the line hold?" Sulla asked.

The liaison hesitated. "Individual reports from NCOs indicate that the line is thin. But they maintain that they *will* hold, Admiral."

35

First Medical Response Team, Alpha Company

The wounded were laid out in neat rows on the cargo deck of the *Chang*. Medics and corpsmen did their best to treat what could be treated, stabilizing what they could, marking others as critical or *expected*.

As in expected to die.

And as those expected did, in fact, die, they were quietly covered and shifted to a storage locker off the main deck. They would need to wait until the shooting stopped and the air had cleared before planetary burial or deep-space services.

They had done their part. It was time to rest.

With Sergeant Watson on the rear deck of the *Chang* providing security and arranging transport back to the teardrop, Doctor Rachel and Nurse Molly moved among the critical, those needing attention as soon as possible.

"This one's been burned badly," said the medic leading them through the patients lying on the deck. "Savages used some kind of molten metal thrower. Took it right in the chest, legs, and some on the face. We've packed the burns in gel, but he's flatlined on us three times. Vagal response keeps going off. Damage to the nerve, Doc?"

Captain McIntosh bent down to the wounded legionnaire, who was still wearing some of his armor where he wasn't packed in gel wrap. She looked into his eyes,

eyes that frantically searched for something. The kid was breathing fast, trying to control the pain.

"Everything's going to be all right," she told him softly. "I'm a doctor."

That was how she started every treatment. She'd learned that once from an old lady who'd been hit by a sled van back during her residency back in New Londoneaux. They'd brought the woman in and she'd been frightened to death that she'd never walk again. Wanted to know if her dog had been killed. Needed people to understand that dinner wouldn't be made for someone named Jerry. Doctor Rachel had gone to work telling the woman that she was a doctor. Never realizing that she'd added that "Everything's going to be all right" bit. Later, when the woman had come out of surgery—when she'd recovered enough for Doctor Rachel to go see her—the older woman told her doctor that of all terrible things that had happened on that "very bad, terrible day," the one thing that had helped, the one thing that had stood out amid the pain and chaos, was when the young pretty doctor had told her, *"Everything's going to be all right. I'm a doctor."*

"You see, girl. When you're in trouble and everything's gone absolutely unintended and you're lying there feeling like a fool and maybe this is the last of it... well, those are about the nicest words you can hear right at that moment. It means somebody's there for you. And they're going to do their best to help you."

The frantic and burned legionnaire on the deck, grunting through a pain not subdued by medication, locked eyes with her and nodded once. And then, just like always, he seemed to relax, closing his eyes as best he could and letting her get to work. Trusting that someone had him. That someone was there for him.

The vagus nerve, no doubt inflamed from the damage, wasn't helping matters. She set to work and had it straightened out with some blocker clamps. Then she checked the burns and verified the triage assessment that this one needed immediate transport back to the *Nightingale*. The corpsman operating off *Chang* came in immediately to prep the warrior for transport to the teardrop and dustoff.

Molly set to work getting the carrying team pointed at Watson, who stood on the rear deck. The soldier was in contact with the two pilots and the two other medics on board and waiting to receive their first casevac for this flight.

Chang's medic led McIntosh over to another nurse who was busy with a pretty young blonde in a naval officer's flight suit. But even as Doctor Rachel approached, she could tell it was too late. The nurse was pulling off the monitoring bracelet. She shook her head sadly at the doctor and the medic. "She just went. Damage to the spine and lungs was too much."

At that moment there was a commotion. Watson came up to the team at a trot.

"C'mon, Doc. You're needed inside the combat zone. High-value patient's been hit badly and he's going."

She didn't question, didn't hesitate, just followed the tall brooding soldier and his long loping stride out onto the cargo deck of the *Chang*.

"Sorry, Captain," Sergeant Watson said, "but we'll have to cross no man's land. Keep your head down and just follow me. Artillery has ceased, so just keep moving and don't stop because you hear shooting." The Britannian soldier paused, considering one more item. "Also, everyone out there on the ground is dead. We'll get them after the shooting stops. Trust me, ma'am."

Doctor Rachel nodded and felt like her heart and mind were ready to go dash madly across the space between the rear deck of the *Chang*, covered by powerful deflectors, and the sheltered ruins of the breach at Backdoor. Exposed to Savage sniper fire the entire way. But her feet were not indicating they were as willing as the heart and the mind to do something so crazy. The corpses out beyond the broad open space between the rear cargo deck and the blasted open entrance into the New Vega Underground seemed to sap her of all locomotion. Lying there twisted, covering their faces, or staring sightlessly skyward. Some ruined parts of their bodies she might have been able to fix had there been time and access.

One of the casevac teardrops rocketed away back toward orbit. Hauling more of the critically wounded up to better care and a chance at survival aboard the HMS *Nightingale*.

Then Watson shouted, "Go!" and ran, not turning to see if McIntosh was following.

She took a deep breath and surged forward, feeling a dull thud with every pounding stride as though her legs were asleep. As though she weren't truly out there at all. It was like running through a dream.

They crossed without so much as a shot from the snipers in the distant skeletal ruins of the buildings that had survived the orbital micro-strike.

Inside the boulder- and concrete-sprayed ruins of Backdoor, past a perimeter of auto-pulse turrets the 295th's security teams had set up, lay more wounded waiting to be carried across the no man's land and onto the *Chang* for medical attention.

"Over here!" shouted one of the medics, recognizing Doctor Rachel as they carried their patient. "It's General Rechs. He's hit bad. Multiple gunshot wounds, and we got a nicked artery we can't nail down. Bleedin' out, ma'am."

She approached fast, pushing her way past Sergeant Watson, who took up overwatch position as though Savages might swarm out of the dark ruins of the Underground at any moment to overrun the casualty collection point.

As Doctor Rachel checked the motionless general's vitals physically and compared them to what the medical cuff's readout showed her, the lead medic ran through Rechs's injuries.

"Gunshot upper left arm," the medic began. "Bone shattered all to hell. Gunshot abdomen left upper quarter. Gunshot right thigh. Caught it full-on, Doc. Concussion and a dozen fragments and deep cuts from an explosion. But it's the—"

"Artery," she said crisply. "His BP is dangerous. I need twenty cc's of abrasa-coag right now. Give him two injections." She pointed at the locations where she wanted the injections made.

"He's flatlining again," said the medic monitoring the cuff. "We're losing him. C'mon guys, he's going."

"Get this armor off!" Rachel shouted, and one of the medics leaned in with a cutting tool and had it off in a second.

Someone swore. "That's a mess."

"Thermals now!" shouted Captain McIntosh. Doctor Rachel. Mumbling to herself that she was a doctor. That everything would be all right.

"No pulse!" shouted the medic monitoring the cuff.

From the distance came the sound of the brutal Savage artillery platform opening up.

Doctor Rachel looked up at Tyrus Rechs's face. It was gray. Dead. Eyes stared sightlessly upward. She felt frantically for the artery under the armpit. On the limb that had taken so much damage. A river of blood gushed sluggishly out over her hand.

"Still no pulse. He's gone, Doc."

She looked around, checking what her team was doing and trying to figure out what could be done next. Someone was already starting a transfusion. That was good.

She reached down to her belt and grabbed a tube of medical sealant. She found the artery and plastered the whole thing, putting as much pressure on it as possible.

"Start chest compressions or hit him with the paddles," she ordered one of the medics.

"You gotta clear off, Doc," said another, getting the paddles ready.

"Can't—I'm trying to seal the artery. Ground me and do it. Now!"

"No pulse."

Do it, she willed, closing her eyes. *Now. So that everything can—*

Wild electricity coursed through her. She wasn't fully grounded but... enough. She felt her teeth. Her bones. The insides of her eyes.

"Nothing," reported the medic. "Still no pulse."

"Again," she moaned.

C'mon, General Whoever-the-hell-you-are. I'm sure these boys need you right now.

The paddles went down and another surge of wild electricity caught her as she tried to hold on and seal the leaking artery.

She cried out in pain and swore at herself to hang on.

36

Strike Force Shield

Twenty minutes before Tyrus Rechs, first general of the Legion, died at the casualty collection point at Backdoor, the Savages stormed Junction Eight for the third time.

"Captain Greenhill," Rechs said, summoning the legionnaire.

"Yes, sir."

"New problem. The Savages seem to have realized the cost of trying to take Junction Eight from our capable hands. They're mounting an aboveground mech force to destroy *Chang*. It's time for Black Horse to go to work, Captain."

Greenhill nodded, then looked around at the ruin left from the first two Savage assaults on Junction Eight. "All due respect, General, but I don't see how you can afford to lose any more leejes."

"I can't," conceded Rechs. "Can't lose the *Chang*, either. We lose the *Chang*, that's mission failure and we're entombed here. Black Horse is our best shot at staying alive, so get going."

Rechs watched Greenhill and the other fourteen legionnaires assigned to Black Horse as they made their way toward Backdoor and LZ Victory. That dropped Rechs down to a bare minimum of effectives to hold the junction when the Savages sent their breaching worms in. But it would have to do.

He recalled the leejes from the top of the crane, feeling they would be better used manning the gun pits at this desperate point. Those legionnaires left in Strike Force Shield were split into three teams, interlocking and placed to keep focus on any action from U-1 and SR6. That would leave them vulnerable should any Savages beyond Warehouse Way decide to attack. But if they hadn't done so by this time, Rechs imagined they wouldn't at all. Or at least he hoped not.

The legionnaires were relying on scrounged Savage ammo and a couple of the heavy machine guns the enemy had left on the objective. The N-1s were effective killing weapons, but the high-cycle slug-throwing weapons should help to mitigate the loss of numbers.

This was Thermopylae. And like those Spartans that the galaxy—save Rechs and Casper—no longer remembered, the defenders' success depended on denying the enemy a breakthrough. If they could keep the Savages bottled up in the tunnels outside the junction, they could hold off for as long as ammunition and physical strength allowed.

If the Savages broke through... well, it would be over quickly.

"Warlord to Sergeant Martin," Rechs called over L-comm.

"Clear copy, Warlord."

"The Savages still think they can punch through here, and at our current numbers, they might be right. Do you have any fighting effectives you can send to Eight?"

There was a pause. "Sir, 295th has set up its explosives. I can assemble relief your way ASAP."

"Please do. Warlord Out."

Rechs had no sooner finished the words when Fire Team Alpha, positioned on the left side of the SR6, took a direct hit from the first breaching worms to come rumbling in. The machines sent three legionnaires flying skyward, and Rechs didn't see any way the men would be alive when landing.

Rechs was near a container wall manned by Fire Team Bravo when the attack came. He watched as a cyclone of undulating liquid metal, like a living thing, shot from the breaching worms that had erupted from SR6 and slammed into Alpha's fortified firing position. Perhaps the Alpha gunner had managed a burst off the Savage heavy in the second before the metal monstrosity slammed into the position. Perhaps not.

Then the twelve-meter-high machine monster detonated, spraying liquid metal in every direction, showering the nearest containers and troops.

A second worm struck the same position, streaking in like greased lightning, frenetically undulating and then exploding.

They were using SR6, but not in the conventional manner. Not like the attackers had done in trying to push their way out of U-1. Rechs suspected they were burrowing up SR6 from some abandoned artery beneath it.

He recognized the attack. It was nothing more than an old Bangalore torpedo, but done with the Savages' usual intersection of horror and technology. It was like looking at some clockmaker's version of an eldritch abomination made all too real.

"Bravo, Charlie, interlock and open fire on the entrance now!" shouted Rechs over the L-comm.

Without hesitation both teams began to pour fire on the entrance to Junction Eight that led out onto the streets of Hilltop District.

Rechs flipped the safety selector off his N-1 and moved back toward the remains of Alpha. More Savage marines began to storm the gap, following the path made for them by the worms. Now the ground troops would try to widen that exploit by throwing themselves into it.

Bravo and Charlie were safe to fire into that area, but as of right now, there was no one standing in the way of the Savages who might try to go for the survivors stored down in their gel bubbles. Once the Savages had Warehouse One secured and reinforced, it would free them up to pay closer attention to the rest of the battlefield. To the *Chang*—and more importantly, to the whereabouts of Strike Force Dagger. And that could not happen. Rechs needed the Calorie Hoarders to keep their focus here. On him. On their calories. Despite now having an entire planet at their disposal, their food—their calories—was the only thing that mattered to them.

The general pushed away the cannibalistic implications as he engaged the first Savages he could see ahead. They were already overrunning the remains of the firing pit.

Rechs hit a Savage in the shoulder, spinning him around, and fired again, center mass, drilling a hot blaster bolt straight through chest armor. The marine sat down on his butt and Rechs fired again, disintegrating the helmet where the brain was. The rest of the corpse just sat there as if unaware its head had been blown off. Motionless in death.

Two more Savages came scrambling in behind the cover provided by their dead comrades. Rechs reacted smoothly, nailing each with all the principles of good marksmanship done to the point of mindless second-nature repetition.

"Pack out," Rechs called to no one but himself. He'd been training CQB with his leejes so much that he'd gotten used to calling out corners, blind spots, and pack swaps. Shoot, move, and communicate. If he'd had all the time in the world he would have taught them everything he'd ever learned about combat and squad-level tactics. Maybe even relearn some of the stuff he'd forgotten and teach them that, too. But more time for him would have meant more time for the Savages to build and fortify. There'd been just barely enough time to take advantage of the moment he and Casper had found to make their play to drive the Savages off this world. Anything after the fact would have required a massive invasion, hundreds of thousands if not millions to retake the planet. Rechs would rather nuke it at that point.

More Savage marines were pushing forward under the withering crossfire set up by pits Charlie and Bravo. All Rechs could provide from his position was targeted marksman fire. He identified the heavy gunners and cut them down, dropping them as they tried to cross the ruin of corpses and still-bubbling molten metal. One dashed forward fast, trying to avoid the ranged fire incoming from Charlie and Bravo, heedless that he was running right toward Rechs. Probably thinking this position was held by his own because of the overwhelming push they'd just made.

Rechs, midway through a pack swap, grabbed the Savage and forced him into a steaming pool of melting metal, pulling the heavy machine gun away from the enemy marine as he did. The general then dropped the MG, pulled his sidearm, and shot the burning marine twice in the chest and once in the head for good measure.

He'd made up his mind that he wasn't taking any chances with the Savages. He was going to make sure that every one of them was good and dead. Tyrus Rechs had learned long ago that there was nothing you could trust about the Savages. They were too comfortable with playing tricks—like playing dead until they were in your rear.

The volume of incoming fire off Charlie sent stray ricochets close to Rechs's bucket, so he grabbed the heavy machine gun by its carrying handle and duck-walked back under the cover of what was left of the ruined Alpha pit. If they sent more of their breaching worms in, there would be little he could do. He'd meet the same fate as Alpha.

Rechs checked the kill zone at the entrance to U-1. More Savage marines were staging and stacking up the tunnel, and he could see some kind of tank slowly moving into the AO. It looked like something out of Earth's distant past. A Crusader or Abrams... but multi-hulled and frankensteined up like the Savages preferred. More marines, kitted in a much heavier armor variant, hustled along behind it, ready to storm the junction once more.

"Warlord to all elements at Junction Eight. Savages are about to hit us hard. Hold fire until my command. Use all your explosives and support the fire teams."

Rechs inched along the side of a cargo container with his back to it, checking the newly acquired machine gun he'd taken off the dead Savage. He hadn't seen one of these in years. They'd called it something else back in the Rangers on Earth. But he remembered it had been in service in other armies long before he'd been born.

Back in the World Wars.

As his mind struggled over the unimportant details, he forced himself to focus on the only detail that mattered: remembering the weapon's operation. He wrapped the belt around his opposite gauntlet, loosely so he could control the feed.

Type 42?

No... that wasn't right.

The tank was moving forward now, turning on four heavy ceramic tracks and deploying missile pods. Tubes unfolded, flipping open canisters. Bright gleaming missiles poked out, launch systems already smoking.

"All elements, cover in place. They're going to hit the junction with anti-armor rockets first."

Rechs had made sure his firing pits had been reinforced by the shipping containers and anything else they could get their hands on. He'd known the Savages would hit them with something heavier once they'd taken enough ground losses. Hopefully their preparations would do the trick.

MG 42! That was it.

He cursed himself for being so damn old. His mind was getting clogged with more useless information than he could catalog.

Not so useless now, he chided himself as he hefted the massive gun up, ready for the incoming Savages.

White-hot missiles streaked into the junction in a furious barrage. Rechs hunkered in place, protected by the cargo containers as the missiles streaked past, attempting to hit the firing pits the legionnaires were manning. Even with the new bucket, the shrieking hiss of the smoking missiles and their deafening explosions was powerful enough to make his ears ring. He waited, checking to make sure the new model 42, and indeed it looked new enough to have just come out of armory, was ready to go. He flicked the safety they'd added and checked the chamber, weapon upright and balanced on his crouched knees.

The tank rumbled on its ceramic treads. Rechs could just barely hear the marines hustling forward, their heavy boots striking the ground.

"Open fire now," Rechs ordered calmly over the comm. A second later Charlie and Bravo began to download hot death into the mass of Savages swarming ahead of the slow-moving tank.

Rechs waited and then stepped out of the protection afforded him by the stacked cargo containers, laying down a bright line of fire straight into the oncoming mass. The rattling MG 42 sent hot smoking tracer rounds right into the wave of Savages. Some died on their feet, while others crouched behind the disintegrating armored bodies of the first wave as the belt of ammo drained out the front of the barrel into the Savage force at near point-blank range.

A few managed wild return fire. That was where the first round that hit Rechs came from. Right in the thigh. He'd been hit before. Many times. Sometimes it stung. And sometimes it was just nothing in the moment even though you knew you'd been hit.

This was a hot white scar, like a sudden tearing in his leg. He grunted hard, pulled harder on the trigger, and emptied the last of the belt, almost shaking it out into the withering Savage marine force. But already more were pushing in, following the back of the tank, ready to storm the area he was defending.

Rechs tossed the tool of death aside and pulled his N-1 off his back. Now he worked the rifle, firing at those closest at hand. One shot apiece as best he could, crouching and trying to avoid sudden sporadic hails of fire that rattled off the metallic containers and barricades like frantic swarms of angry micro-bots.

One of the dead Savage marines suddenly came to life on the floor beneath Rechs and grabbed at his legs, dragging him down. Rechs let go of the rifle and grabbed the thing's bucket, holding it as he slammed his own into it. Again and again and again.

He thought his head was ringing from the impacts. He was sure that he had a concussion and that the explosions inside his skull would never stop. And then he realized the rest of the legionnaires had clambered to the top of the container wall and were tossing fraggers down into the fray breaching Junction Eight.

He looked at the Savage marine he'd been grappling and realized he was holding only the remains of a smashed mirrored helmet slathered with pulped brain matter. He tossed it aside and scrambled for his rifle, gaining it just in time to roll over onto his back and squeeze the trigger on more Savages trying to move forward.

His wound cried out for attention. Rechs told the leg to shut up. It didn't listen, so he ignored it and embraced the suck of the situation.

He shot a marine through the chest, sending the bolt right out the other side with a spray of metal components and bright electric blue fluids. The marine fell to the ground, backlit by the explosive grenades hurled on his comrades by the Legion, ripping Savage bodies to shreds.

Rechs put a round in the marine's mirrored helmet as a Javelin struck the tank, causing it to blossom with a terrific explosion that seemed to take place from the inside out. A wave of heat and debris pushed Rechs to the ground, flattening him. Knocking the wind out of him.

He passed out, unsure for how long.

And when he came to, he was surrounded by Savages.

They were hurrying over and past him and the rest of Alpha Team, all of whom lay dead.

Rechs felt for his sidearm—the only weapon he was completely sure he could find. He specifically remembered reholstering. He sat up after the last Savage had passed him by, heading into the tunnel that would take them down to the bubble storage. The calories.

They'd broken through.

Rechs, mind rattled, aimed and fired with his sidearm, putting white-hot rounds into the Savage tasked with rear security first, then more into the rest of the squad farther down in the darkness.

He pulled a fragger and rolled it into their midst, just meters away, and then covered, dragging a dead marine over himself just before it went off.

In the chaos, he'd been fired upon. He'd taken more hits. Bad ones.

The fragger went off and ripped through the tight corridor, sending hot speeding needle-sharp fragments in every direction.

37

First Medical Response Team, Alpha Company

The incoming artillery fell across *Chang*'s dorsal deflectors. The reprieve from the first wave of Savage mechs had been altogether too brief. No man's land and the broken ruins of Backdoor heaved and shook. It fell like slow, destructive rain that didn't seem like it was ever going to end. Screaming from afar to suddenly race in and either nail portions of the ruin or explode against the landed ship's pulsing deflectors. Shards and debris rained out and down onto the casualty collection point.

Medics and nurses tried to shield the wounded and the dying they were working on, pulling them as far into the fractured Backdoor structure as they could without interfering with combat resupply operations.

"Nothing, Doc," said the medic operating the shock paddles as he pulled back from the corpse of Tyrus Rechs. Sitting back on his knees, a sense of tired horror writ large on his face.

Impassive, Sergeant John Watson stood above them all and continued his scans of the ruin. Expecting Savages to counterattack at any moment. This was as dangerous as it gets.

"Again," groaned Captain McIntosh as she gently levered herself up away from the dying, or dead, general. The sealant should have done its work and handled the nicked artery. Should have...

"Again!" she shouted.

But the medic didn't move. He just shook his head at her. "He's gone, ma'am. Sorry. We have more wound—"

Doctor Rachel grabbed the paddles, called out, "Clear!" in her strident Britannian upper-class voice, and tried to revive the man beneath her one last time. Every mumbled prayer and imprecation she could remember was mumbled in her mind, hoping that someone, *something*, would hear it.

No one did. General Rechs was gone.

"Okay," she said to the galaxy. Telling it that it won this time. This round. That it snatched one away from her. Fine. But she had work to do and other people were dying all around.

A round hit high above, striking the shell of some ruined building. Everyone flinched, ducked, covered, called out.

Captain McIntosh just sat there. Staring at nothing. Not even the dead man as she vowed to the galaxy that she wouldn't lose another. Because sometimes we have to tell ourselves lies just to keep going a little further.

She got up, brushed the dirt and mud off herself absently, and moved to the next dying man. Sergeant Watson dutifully followed, weapon ready to protect her.

The medic pulled Rechs's poncho off his harness. It was rolled up tight, exactly where it should be according to SOP. An SOP Rechs himself had written late at night, tapping it out in his office aboard the *Chang* while the trainees grabbed what little sleep they were allowed after whatever task Rechs had just put them through.

The medic knew why the poncho was there. It wasn't just for the rain.

He spread it out across the dead man. Weighing it down with a few fragments of nearby concrete. He stood up. Needed to think. Just for a second, before forcing himself not to.

Then he moved on to help whoever else he could. Save who could be saved. Comfort those who could not. The other part of war. And in war, it was best to keep moving. There was always too much time later to think.

38

A long long time ago...

The die-back hasn't yet hit the world like the last of some fabled string of doomsday plagues straight out of an ancient and holy book. But that doesn't mean the world's not falling apart anyway. And it doesn't mean that the elites haven't given up on it all.

Right now, there are currently over thirty massive colony ships, lighthuggers technically, Savage hulks someday, being built in orbit. Others have already fired up their massive engines and slowly hauled themselves away from the disintegrating orb called Earth. Home no more. New homes are to be found out there on the other side of forty-plus-year trips across the black velvet of the seemingly endless midnight void.

The elites are gathered, ready to leave. And the cities and the private launch pads and the camp-follower suburbs that have sprung up around them are crowded. Because the rumor is if you can get yourself on one of those fantastic bright and hopeful ships then maybe you've got a chance.

A chance at what?

Well, that's the question. But it's better than the what that's here now. Has to be. Limited nuclear exchanges across Africa, the Middle East, and Southeast Asia. Governments controlling little beyond the major cities, which have become cesspools of crime, greed, graft, and disease. Rampant disease.

The end isn't just near.

It's here.

Or at least that's the way it feels to those who are desperate to survive by getting on one of those ships. There are rumors of prosperity in Asia and other now-closed societies sealed off from the rest of the world. Rumors that other ships have already reached nearby stars. But these are just rumors spread for the hopeful so that they might have something to believe in.

Hopeful that you can get off this dumpster fire of a planet.

People no longer ask for the newest piece of technology, a win on Sunday, the best food, the best sex, the most epic party vacay ever... they're down to just asking for a tomorrow.

As recently as five years ago, the elites who will become Savages were telling everyone that their latest and brightest best-ever-yet plans would result in the peak of civilization. But under their watch and their watch alone.

They're the masters of the universe, or so they said. Giant corporations that proved time and again to be masters of the earth.

The crowds are gathered. Begging to be a part of that tomorrow.

But none of that matters to the boy. City things and star-bound tomorrows aren't for him. Or the salvagers of wilderness and wasteland that were once the mountains, plains, and prairies of the greatest nation on earth.

He's never seen a map. Never watched TV.

But he can hunt and track a mountain lion. Live well in hard winter by what he can take from the land. Fix an engine. Keep his rifle clean. Survive. For fifteen years the boy followed his father. He had a mother. She died. And that's all the old man would ever say about that.

They made their living hunting game for the survivalist compounds out on the eastern side of the Rockies, sometimes ranging way up into Montana. They drove an old Ford truck they kept running with baling wire and bubble gum. Until in the icy spring of that last year of the boy being allowed something of his boyhood, his old man died of a cough that came and just never left.

Lying on the floor of an old cabin they'd wintered in, dying by firelight, the old man dug through his belongings and pressed his legacy into the young boy's hands.

"This is who I was a long time ago..." He stops to cough. And the cough is bad. Real bad. Like maybe he's not coming back from this fit.

But he did. For a little while more.

"Before you and your mom and your sister. This is who we were." The old man squinted his eyes at some unseen pain before hacking up something that sounded like it was meant to stay deep down. "You shoulda seen us. It was a great country. Ain't about that anymore. It's about the weak and the strong. The good and the evil. You're on that line, Tyrus. Hell... you *are* that line.

"Go south. Down into Georgia. There's still government, you just got to find it. Still Army Rangers like your old man used to be. Out on the line and goin' everywhere they get sent. You show 'em this..." He coughed again, waving off the coming help his son offered. Like that one wasn't so bad.

"You show them... tell 'em you want to be one. And then..." The cough came back so bad he had nothing left but to die. Only he kept fighting it off for all he was worth.

That was how he was. Never over until the old man decided it was over.

His next words were a croak. A wheeze. "And then you become that line, Tyrus. Just like I taught you. Protect the rest... the weak... from the evil that's like... always like... a wolf... wolves, Tyrus. Wolves at the door. You... do... that, boy."

The old man had no breath in him to finish. He lay back to get the dying done in earnest. He'd taught the boy everything. Ain't nothing left now. No time to waste. The world is burning up. Burning daylight.

In the days that followed, the boy folded up the blankets and packed the few possessions they owned. Both rifles and all four pistols. The hatchets, the knives. Sleeping rolls and other gear. An old kerosene lamp.

He buried his father in a glade away from the falling-down cabin, thankful that enough spring had come to thaw the ground a bit. The sound of a river beckoned to him not far away. For a long time he just sat at its banks. Thinking.

A day later he'd made his mind up to try the roads south and find his way down to this Georgia. And to the Rangers and the US Army he'd heard all his father's stories about. If they still existed in a world that seemed like it was losing its grip on things more and more every day. His father had prepared him for this, knowing that one day his son would either become a soldier, or act as one. A Ranger. The line between the good and the bad.

Tyrus didn't understand the medals he found among his father's things. But one day he would, and he would always wonder at the stories behind them. Stories never told. The way of sons and fathers.

The truck wouldn't start. And no amount of bubble gum and baling wire could convince it to do so ever again. The cabin, a silent place in a dying, fevered world, was the old Ford's final resting place. Unwilling to leave the old man.

It was nightfall before Tyrus got his gear stripped down to what he could carry on his back. He stashed the rest, including the additional rifle. He could only carry one. And so he left his own behind and took his father's Marlin, which was always the better one. And both the 45s instead of the 223 or the Glock.

His father would have chewed him out about that. Much easier to find 9mm than .45 ACP. But Tyrus liked the bigger caliber. Even to his own hurt.

He started his march straight away, leaving the cabin behind in the moonlight. The next few weeks were silent as he made his way south, occasionally stopping at homesteads, encampments, and enclaves he and his father had hunted for in the leanest of times. In these places he was always treated with sympathy... and wariness.

Sympathy because he was yet one more refugee. Wariness because there was so little that could be shared now. Tyrus always made a point not to impose. He would tell them only the news of his father's death and that he was going on south to a place called Georgia.

Most folks had heard of it. The boy became aware that as much as he knew about hunting and surviving, he was deficient in the shared culture of what remained of the nation he trekked through.

He had learned his manners, though. In each forever and final farewell, when no gift or comfort was intended to be parted with, he thanked his hosts for their hospitality. Said a prayer for their continued safety. And each time he found that something was pressed upon him—a nice wool blanket in exchange for the holed one he carried. A new sweater made from the yearling wool. A warm hand pie filled with potatoes and scrap meat for the road.

"We knew your father," one man said, though Tyrus was sure he'd never met the man himself. "Lot of people around here are still alive because of him bringing in game."

It was early that summer, somewhere out between the plague town of Tulsa and the refugee centers east of Wichita that Tyrus entered a stretch of land doing unexpectedly well. For three days he left the roads and walked through fields and orchards that came up alongside long-abandoned highways. As if this space on someone's map has been forgotten by all the plagues, the wars, the gangs, and every bad thing that had ravaged the earth in the decades since the last fall began.

In time, during the early summer twilight, he found a village called Brigadoon. The joke was lost on him.

Full of scientists and farmers, who were making a stand against the encroaching blight and ruin of the world, they kindly took the wayward, quiet, and filthy-dirty boy in. Fed him and gave him a small shed to live in. He repaid them by hunting game and varmints. They seemed grateful.

That summer was one of the best. Many on earth would remember it as the last good one. Harder years were soon beginning. When the weather would turn as violent as the wars fought all over the world for what little remained to be had.

And the boy fell in love for the first time one late summer night when the scientists and farmers jammed with their old instruments as they did every Saturday night.

The music playing and the fireflies out, chased down by the smaller children—that was when she kissed him.

Sophia.

Because you never forget.

Tyrus would live long past the lives of normal men. And though he would forget many things, he never forgot her. Though sometimes, in the deep of hyperspace travel between worlds, he would think that it might be best if he did. Only so he wouldn't miss her, that long-ago girl who kissed him out on the road, near the field under a starry night that was like some scene from a painting in some of the books they'd shown him. The farmers and scientists.

A forever night of starry stars.

Deep space sometimes reminded him of that night. A forever night of starry stars.

You never forget.

That time—the kiss and all the days that blended in with it—it made it seem like Georgia and the Rangers could just be... let go of. Someone else would have to go find the line and stand on it. Not Tyrus. He would...

Well, he would stay right there and grow old with her.

They swam in a moonlit pond of dark water well after midnight. The air was warm and the water was cool.

He could help these people, he told himself in the not-so-lazy days of waning sunlight that remained. Learn their trade. Save the world alongside them.

He watched her with the young in the small community. Raising them. Teaching them. And he saw that the world wasn't finished. Not just yet. As long as there was such good in the world, then there was still a chance.

Summer wound on, and soon it would be time to move on or stay for winter. If he stayed for winter then he knew he was staying forever.

And maybe that wasn't such a bad thing.

There had been a rumor of wolves bothering livestock. Wolves in the farms to the north. He'd been asked to go out and take care of the problem before any more sheep were done to death.

Three days he was gone, and when he came back he saw the smoke from afar. Black smoke rising from the grow houses and mills. From the labs and the homes. It was all on fire and raging like a bellows heaving. But silent from a distance apart from the occasional low rumble of a burning building as it came crashing down.

A fire. A fire had gotten out of hand.

He raced down the old road, running for all he was worth. They'd need every hand if they were going to save enough to survive the winter. That was what he was thinking as he raced toward the conflagration. Even though a little voice told him that thought was a lie.

He pushed on past the heat and saw there was no bucket brigade, no shocked bystanders to assist.

Only corpses. Lying in the dust and dirt. Hanged from poles and corrals. Or worse.

Of that community of two hundred and fifty, not a soul had been spared. Not one. No prisoners taken. The raiders just took what they wanted and moved on.

He found Sophia. Covered her up. Trying somehow to erase the thoughts of what lay exposed. What they had taken. What they had done to her. And him.

Wolves, Tyrus. Wolves at the door.

The old man had told him. The world is a wolf. And you're the line between the good that needs to be protected, and the evil that would consume it all.

39

It wasn't revenge. But it was.

They weren't the usual biker trash and drifters. Lean and hungry and constantly hard on anything they could be plain hard on. The boy followed them, these wolves, and they were not hard to follow. They would change later as he hunted them down one by one.

But for now, their path of destruction was broad and easy to track even if you hadn't grown up hunting among the high rocks where few dared. Where any mistake meant death.

In the years since nationwide law enforcement had become a thing of the past, beyond the walls and barriers and even ditches like moats that guarded the massive urban sprawls, Tyrus would sometimes assist his father in doing this kind of work. Law work. Justice.

Bounty hunting.

The cattle thieves up near Idaho Falls. His father had trusted him to work the Marlin and provide fire support while he went in and dealt with the gang, catching most of them asleep. It had turned into a shootout when three who were drunk but still awake back near a spring on the property tried to sneak up on his father during the takedown. Tyrus had shot down all three at two hundred yards.

Then they, he and his old man, hanged the rest as per the bounty and rounded up what cattle had survived the wanton slaughter the hungry thieves had committed. Herded them back to their owner.

Then there was the rapist who'd drifted into a small town called Marleigh up near a settlement outside of a place called Rawlins that had burned to the ground years ago. The settlement had paid for the hunt, and they'd followed the rapist through a honky-tonk gas station fortress, finally cornering him as he attempted to commit the same crime again.

He begged and cried and said it wasn't his fault. They stretched his neck all the same. As per the bounty.

There'd been others, too. Not the main work in those days. But work he could remember his father taking and teaching him to do.

Sometimes his old man would apologize. Tell him that this life wasn't how children were meant to live.

But Tyrus appreciated it. What he learned. What he did. What it meant to the people who'd had no one else to send.

He caught the first bunch of raiders who had done the farmers and scientists and... Sophia... in an old bar at the edge of a long-silent town abandoned more than twenty years back. The bar still stood, and the old drunks who made it a home kept it alive with some kind of powerful hooch they'd brewed for themselves out back. The old neon, the little that remained, burnt brightly in the silent dusky night with fall coming on when Tyrus Rechs entered the establishment looking for his targets. Wolf hunting.

There was power. They had power there. Probably solar. Music, old music, whined and warbled on a jukebox that still worked.

Li'l Rollo and Rip, who'd stayed behind the main body of the gang of twenty that called themselves the Ten-

Percenters, were both blind drunk when Tyrus started firing inside the bar.

They'd noticed him coming in. Just some road wanderer fleeing the infested big cities and searching for the myth that somehow you could survive out beyond the perimeter of such places. In the wilderness. They too had fallen for that lie. But instead of working to make it a truth, they'd just gone to preying on anyone weaker than themselves. The weak with families, and crops, and livestock. The weak trying to buy a tomorrow so maybe, just maybe, it'd all come back.

"Lookee here," said Rip seconds before he was shot dead, already reaching for a nickel-plated .357 Magnum he liked to keep in his low-hanging waistband.

"Here's another," he was about to say next. Another loser. Another victim for him to play with. Another weakling to take from.

But Rechs had followed the trail of destruction. Followed the bald tire tracks. Could hear their raucous commune. Could smell them.

And right now he was smelling that same ripe stale funk of the weed they'd smoked that he'd smelled all over the campsite where four RVs had been ravaged. City folks trying to find that myth.

The myth that there was something left somewhere.

There was no jury. No trial. No defense and prosecutorial types like men such as these back in the cities had learned to play like musical instruments every time they broke a law and preyed on a weakling.

There wasn't even a bounty.

But there was a judge there that night in the old honky-tonk. And the judge began to fire. First hitting Rip right in the chest with a huge round from the Marlin. It didn't knock him down, but it made him step back from the bar he was drunkenly holding on to with one hand. The round went straight through his sternum and probably out the back and into the old wood paneling along with a splatter of blood and bone.

In the wan neon of the old flickering beer signs and the dim firelight coming from down inside the oil drum burning in the room, Rechs saw the spreading pool of red begin to soak through the man he'd just shot. Soaking through a big-city designer jersey, the kind worn by people who still thought commerce was a kind of salvation. Instead of a distraction.

Gold teeth smiled at Tyrus across dark skin sweating in the firelight.

Like they'd played some game and he'd been caught cheating. Shot through by a hick.

Her name had been Sophia, but this wasn't about revenge.

His father had made sure, had drilled it into him that it could never be about that. It always had to be about the business of Justice. Justice provided in absence of law enforcement. But if it wasn't about that, then why did Tyrus work the Marlin's lever so fast, chambering a new round without moving the barrel maybe more than an inch before putting another round right through Rip's shining gold teeth?

You'd just blown the man's sternum to pieces, Tyrus, he would say to himself later. When he was trying to put it all together. Why shoot him in the face?

Nearby Li'l Rollo just stood there with his arm around the toothless whore that serviced the bar and the dead lying on the floor who'd been miserable drunks—but alive—

just a day earlier before this crew had shown up to have their fun at the end of a gun.

Rollo had an old Glock out and pointed sideways when he began to fire, squeezing the trigger as fast as his drunken dexterity would allow. Putting speeding hot rounds into more wood paneling and shattering some of the few empty liquor bottles that remained as memories for all the great drinking that had once made this land a place of promise to the drunks who had refused to surrender to times of loss and lack.

Rechs crouched behind the bar, levering in a new round, and waited until the Glock fired dry. He knew its slide had locked open by the swearing of the dark little man who'd had half his face burned in some horrible long-ago fire. The magazine hit the floor and Rechs slid around the corner of the bar in a crouch and shot Li'l Rollo in the gut, knocking him back onto his butt. The thug gasped and rolled onto his side, moaning as gold chains danced around his sweating fat neck.

Rechs moved forward, kicking away first the magazine and then the Glock. There should be three here. Aside from the whore too faded to do anything but cower in a ball on the floor and... giggle to herself.

He'd tracked three. Had watched them for the better part of the day from the ruins of a supermarket down the street. Seen three coming and going from the old sedan parked in front of the bar.

Rollo moaned and cried and Rechs ignored him, scanning the darkness, the shadows, the flickering firelight, and the dirty windows and mirrors. Tyrus moved across the floor of the bar, his old boots on his young feet barely disturbing the broken glass. He listened past the dead singing beyond the grave from the old jukebox and waited for the other one to make his move.

He heard breaking glass and knew the third was making for the sedan out front. Probably trying to run around the side of the old tonk and beat it straight to the highway. Not bothering to help friends.

Rechs barely made the front door in time to see the man slide behind the wheel and gun the sedan to gusty life. One wan headlight pierced the gloom on the dark street, revealing an early-evening mist descending over this long-dead town.

The boy raised his rifle and fired through the glass three times, working the lever like a machine to load each new round. When he was satisfied the man behind the wheel was good and dead, he went back inside the bar and strode over to Rollo lying on the floor, moaning.

The chubby little shadow devil whimpered as Rechs hauled him upright. Buckets of sweat streamed down his face.

"Ain't fair of you to shoot me like that, Mist—" He was apparently about to say *Mister* when he realized Tyrus was just a boy. "You jes a kid!"

The thug spat out blood and began to cough.

Tyrus stuck the barrel of the Marlin under a jowly, unshaven chin.

"Where are the rest headed?" he asked quietly. But there was a meanness to his voice that surprised even the boy.

"Ain't gonna tell you shit. Chump-change two-bit hillbilly!"

"You are gonna tell me," said Tyrus, deadly serious. "You're gut-shot. I leave, and you'll die in a lot of pain spread out over the next few days. You think it hurts bad now… you're gonna wish you were dead when the infection from that bullet starts in and you can't dig it out."

The thug flicked his eyes toward where the whore had been. She was already gone.

The man began to cry. His body heaving and shaking as he realized the extent of his predicament. He was already in pain and he was scared the kid with the rifle pointing under his chin was right. It would get bad. Real bad.

"Why'd you have to shoot Rip?" The man sobbed.

Rechs slapped Rollo hard with one rawhide-gloved hand.

"Tell me where you're supposed to meet up with the rest of your crew or I walk out the door, your Glock in hand, so you can lie here for the next three days trying to figure out how to slit your throat with some broken glass. But it's a big dig through them jowls of yours."

The chubby sweating man swore and told the boy in front of him exactly what he could do with himself.

Rechs turned and began to walk toward the door.

"Wait… c'mon… just wait. I don't wanna…" cried Li'l Rollo.

Rechs continued out of the door, and behind him the man screamed, "A place t'other side o' Broken Arrow. Old bowling alley where some fools sell drugs to the local hicks. We was gonna do 'em and take they stash. Peewee says they got a lab out in the hills."

Tyrus shot Li'l Rollo after he learned the names. All their names. He'd make that appointment, catching most of them smacked out of their minds on kitchen-sink meth at the Liberty Lanes Bowling Alley east of Broken Arrow in another town that had long since died. Where the road signs had all been used for target practice long ago.

He learned from a survivor at Liberty Lanes, a man slowly bleeding out, that they were just street thugs from the city. Tired of what was going on there, they'd come out to the wilderness of the once American Heartland following those same rumors. Except not to farm, or make a stead, or anything noble. But just to prey on those who did. And the survivor told Rechs where to find that bastard Peewee, who'd led them all out here to die.

Wolves, Tyrus. The world, hell, probably the whole galaxy and the damned universe is filled with wolves.

He could see well enough through the shattered windshield of the old sedan to drive. And he drove through the night for three nights. Keeping the old sedan slow and steady through the driving cold rain that came in through the shattered windshield. He would hunt down Peewee and his crew, the leaders of the Ten-Percenters.

He told himself it wasn't revenge.

Told himself to forget a girl's name he'd never be able to forget no matter how fast and how far he went. No matter how many girls, planets, or worlds he saved.

It wouldn't matter.

Her name was Sophia.

It was dawn when he pulled the old sedan over into the long grass alongside the county road that hadn't seen services and maintenance in maybe ten years.

It was dawn and it felt like Sunday.

He'd lost track of the days.

He and his father had always played the game of remembering the days in lieu of having anything to watch or read.

"You hold on to the little things, Tyrus," his father had told him. "You start letting those go, start playing with the truth, and everyone goes mad."

General Rechs, much later, when confronted with the madness of the Savages, would remember his father's words. Would realize that the old man had had no idea just how right he'd been way back then.

It felt like Sunday. Just after dawn.

The boy shucked his gear. The things he wouldn't need. The few magazines he had were loaded. He stuffed his old worn-out ruck with as much ammunition as he had left.

Sophia.

He took the Marlin and set out on foot for the location he'd tracked them to.

All the previous night he'd driven the roads surrounding the old place, making sure they hadn't escaped, and as he made his way into what had probably once been someone's ranch, he knew they were still there.

Three vehicles in front. All as described by the man he'd interrogated in the bowling alley. Smoke rose up from the chimney, and he could smell bacon, sweet and savory on the cool breeze coming in through the trees that surrounded the old place.

It couldn't be revenge, he told himself as he moved to the cars. Because revenge wanted to shoot them all dead. And that meant getting exposed to fire in order to look them in the eye as he did so. Justice was something different.

They had come out here to take and ruin the weak and the trying. To prey on those just trying to survive. If it didn't stop here it would go on for as long as they wanted it to.

He set the rifle down and took out the first of the Molotovs he'd prepared.

Revenge would want a shootout. Justice would want them stopped. That and nothing more.

Working under the cars as fast he could, he slit the fuel lines wearing his rawhide gloves and using his jackknife.

Easy work for a boy who'd kept the truck running on bubble gum and baling wire. New vehicles hadn't fared well with all the EMPs that had gone off in orbit and at high altitude. The old beaters always worked the best after the beginning of the end of things.

Fuel lines bleeding, dripping pungent homebrew from some station that had still managed to make such, he moved to the back of the house, stripping off the rawhide gloves now soaked with gasoline. With the first incendiary device in one hand and the Marlin in the other. There were three main entrances to the spreading ranch house some wealthy developer had paid an army of contractors and designers to realize.

He checked a side window and saw a man in there sleeping. Passed out on a pool table. Ruined furniture and smashed bottles everywhere. Other windows showed some of Peewee's crew. All in the same state. He avoided the kitchen. Knowing someone was in there frying up bacon.

He lit the first cocktail and threw it on the roof just above the door to the back patio. In moments the old roof was awash with spreading flames. He moved to the second entrance, lit the next one. It was an access walkway to a garage-like barn. When that area, too, was covered in flames, Tyrus moved out into the tall grass that had once been a pasture and took up a firing position under an old rotten corral fence.

All in less than a minute.

Revenge or Justice? The words kept appearing in his mind. Spoken in his father's voice like so many of the other learning questions the old man had asked him in all the hard days of his young life.

Which star is the North Star?

How do you find water?

Where do you aim when you want to kill a man?

Revenge or Justice?

The two rear entrances were now fully engulfed. Flames hot and bright making smoke rise up through other sections of the large house, starting to race across the old dry roof.

They had no choice but to come out. But they didn't. They knew it was a trap. Knew that was how they'd do it. Perhaps had done it that way to others. They weren't dumb.

They knew an ambush when they smelled the smoke of one.

And so they didn't come out. They waited even though the roof and the walls and really the world, their world, was burning down on them. All around them. From his position Tyrus could see they had no options. It was either try for the front door or burn inside.

"We know you out there, boy!" someone shouted.

The voice was strong and powerful. Rich and resonant.

The leader. Peewee.

"We know you waitin' for us to come out and then you gonna pop pop pop and shoot us all down, Hillbilly Man."

Rechs said nothing and watched over the Marlin's sights. Feeling the coolness of the stock on his cheek in the crisp morning dew. Scanning the field and the old places with his blue eyes.

Smoke was pouring out of every orifice of the building. They didn't have much longer before they'd die of smoke inhalation.

"You want to get even, whoever you is?" shouted the man from inside the house above the crackle and roar of the flames. "Thas what you want? We kill someone you love, hillbilly? That it? Yo wife? Yo ho? Who we kill?"

The man began to laugh inside the flames. Laughing and assuring Tyrus that he'd done awful things to his woman even though he didn't know which one was his. Getting the details right and wrong. Because there'd been others. Many.

Revenge.

Or Justice, Tyrus.

He moved the barrel of the Marlin and landed it on the puddle of fuel beneath the three vehicles. The ones they were no doubt dying to reach.

Raising the front sight, he fired into the undercarriage of one car. A spark was all that was needed. Flames caught with a caustic *whump*. There was no explosion, but the cars were crawling with flames in seconds.

And the message was clear.

"No one gets outta here alive, that it, lover man?" barked Peewee angrily. "That right?"

The voice inside the flames was hacking. Coughing now.

Tyrus waited. They would go now. At least one would break ranks and try to breathe in cold air by rushing outside. And he would shoot them down.

There was a moment. A moment when he was back there, on that starry starry night when she slipped her hot warm hand into his, stared up at him, and willed him to understand what she meant. What she was offering.

What she was asking.

Glass popped from inside the ranch house. The flames causing something to burst.

Revenge or Justice, Tyrus.

Because one ends and the other is never satisfied. The other just goes on.

Revenge wants to see the look in their eyes when he shoots them down. Wants them to make a run for it across his field of fire. Thinking that if they can reach that ditch they'll be free.

Justice says wait, be patient, I will be served soon enough.

Revenge makes you do stupid things, Tyrus. I know. Trust me. His father had told him that one long dark winter night when they were miles from nowhere and a vicious stormfront was moving in. They were tracking the rapist.

All those medals. What did they mean? How had they been earned?

They never came out. In the end there was no shootout. No final moment of facing the Angel of Death the dark side of Tyrus wanted to become. He had laid a trap from which they could not escape.

In time the fire did its work until there was no work left to do, and Tyrus Rechs, just a young boy long ago, went to stand over the ruins. He found their burnt and curled corpses near the back of the house. In a room without an exit.

He looked around at the bodies. The smoldering timbers. The sky. Watching and trying to feel whether this gave him any satisfaction.

There is none.

Only Justice.

Only the line.

"You were born to walk that line between the light and the dark, Tyrus. I was too. Ain't many of us left. But we gotta do it to the end. And when you're done, let it go, there'll be someone else to take your place. Until... there ain't, I guess. Then the world, well, I guess it's all done then."

He'd said that. His father. On one of their long drives across a dying America, doing the things that needed to be done that no one else was either willing or able to do.

Night fell, and the ruins of the old place still glowed with coals and sparks among the dark ash and blackened beams.

Later the rain began to fall, and he turned and walked for the rest of that stormy fall down into Georgia.

He found the government. Joined the Army and became a Ranger. He fought wars and went to the stars and there were wars and justice and revenge waiting there for him.

But he never forgot her name, though he spoke it to no one.

Sophia.

40

First Medical Response Team, Alpha Company

The medic working with Doctor Rachel and her team organized the last of the critically wounded to be moved out to the dustoff. Counting those held for the next trip and those that were KIA.

That was when the medic noticed that the dead general was sitting upright. Looking around like he'd just woken up from a bad hangover.

"What the..." The medic swore and called out for assistance. "General Rechs, you need to lie down."

Rechs waved the man away with one hand, flinching in pain at the movement. He looked around and struggled to his feet, listing for a bit and grabbing onto a chunk of the ruin to steady himself, his wounded leg not responding.

"Sir, let me get some fluids into you." The medic was already stringing a rehydration pack and getting the needle ready. "You need to lie down, sir." He turned and called out to an NCO running the casevac drops. "Hey! Hold one of the ships! We got—"

"Adrenaline," muttered the general. He bent down and picked up a rucksack from one of the dead legionnaires he'd been laid next to. He tried to hold it, but the weight pulled him down to a knee. He felt inside for one of the ration bars he'd made everyone bring, fishing for the exact place where he made them stow them according to SOP. Right next to the extra change of socks.

He tore one open and chewed at it angrily, noting he'd been shot in the side but that there was now a thermal patch there to keep the wound covered and sedated. The bandage was running a smart pressure system. He wasn't sure if he was supposed to eat, but he felt hungry as hell.

Actually, he just felt like hell.

The medic jabbed two micro-hypos into his neck. "Low-dosage adrenal boost. This should get you cleared up. But really, sir, you need to lie back down."

Rechs pulled the bucket off the dead legionnaire, then slid into the ruck's straps with no little amount of pain. He grabbed an N-1 off another dead legionnaire and checked its charge pack.

"Sir, as a medic I order you to lie down. General."

Tyrus Rechs turned. "Can't," he grunted. "They need me on the line."

Then he stumbled off into the darkness that led into the New Vega Underground.

The medic stood there, watching the old man go. He turned to a stocky nurse who'd just arrived to join him in his vigil. "You ever see somethin' like that?"

"He'll be dead 'fore he makes a hundred meters," Molly said. "Mark my words."

41

Defiant

Admiral Sulla acknowledged the "On station over New Vega" update from the bridge and returned to contemplating the tactical situation both above and on New Vega.

One Savage hulk destroyed. One wounded badly. One engaged by the pirates and coming around the far side of the planet for a pass directly over New Vega in the next twenty minutes. The pirates were taking losses but had reported internal damage scored on the Savage hulk.

"Whether that's true or not, I can't say," the *Defiant*'s XO had said soberly to conclude his status update.

Then there was the ground war. And the thought Casper was trying to push aside, and couldn't. Because it needed to be acknowledged. Tyrus Rechs, his oldest friend, had been killed in the action. And for a second that had been enough to make Casper want to pull the plug on the whole operation and get the hell out of this mess. Because if Tyrus Rechs could be killed by these things, then what could the rest of them do?

He and Tyrus had talked about this. The inevitability of such a moment. Because someday it had to happen. To one or the other of them. And it was Tyrus who'd had the last word and the course that they'd both decided to navigate by. It had been settled long ago.

"*These boys can do it, Casper. I trained them as hard as I trained myself. They're the best. If they can't do it, even after both of us are gone, then no one can. The Legion needs to function even if we're gone."*

Rechs had said that when they were planning the whole operation. And the eventualities, including getting KIA'd, that came with such plans.

"They're the best, Cas. They can do it."

"So it's on them now," muttered Casper to himself as he studied the real-time updates on the digital sand table that displayed the current situation on New Vega.

Captain Milker had taken command of ground ops and was directing the defense at Junction Eight. Kill Zone Alpha was under fire but holding. Team Black Horse was en route to their drop zone. Dagger was on the march to Madhouse.

Without Rechs… it could still work.

But what was the bugout point? What was the moment when any one of these elements went sideways and it was time to evacuate New Vega and activate Rechs's trigger-nuke—still on the ground since the last invasion?

Option Last Resort. That was what they had tagged that device as.

If everything went pear-shaped they'd burn the planet. Just like Rechs had done to every other Savage-overrun world he'd come upon. Casper had challenged Rechs on that. There was still a chance to disable the weapon. Rechs had declined to do so.

Which means you don't totally believe in your Legion, doesn't it, Casper had thought to himself.

But he never pressed his friend on that. There were some things Rechs couldn't be pressed on. And centuries together had taught Casper a few of them.

"Admiral, message from Captain Greenhill. Eyes on DZ Black Horse."

The admiral nodded. "Instruct the loadmasters to drop the weapons package and signal Black Horse it's on the way."

"Copy that, Admiral. Weapons package on the way. Drop in thirty seconds."

42

**Team Black Horse
Parkland Meadows District**

Captain Greenhill and Team Black Horse were hidden in the late-morning shadows near the bombed-out remains of a cyber-electronics plant that had been hit during the first battle of New Vega. The captain was busy giving the op order to his team leaders while the platoon sergeant handled the redistribution of charge packs, equipment, and food, making sure everyone drank at least one canteen of water and nailed two ration bars.

The plant was near the main highway leading into the city from the east. Unlike the Underground tunnels, the Savages had kept the highway in good condition for transporting materials to the new military base they were building out along the coast and some other bizarre and enigmatic structures they had out that way.

On the highest accessible level of the skeletal electronics plant, two scouts had established a listening/observation post and were waiting for the first visual confirmation from the incoming mech force.

The L-comm began to gently ping, alerting Greenhill that he had a mission update. The captain put his bucket back on and quickly swallowed the last of his ration bar.

"Go for Black Horse."

"Black Horse, this is Watchtower Two. We have an update on your drop. Expect package in five. We just sent all special equipment off the back of *Defiant*. Inbound on your loc. Also we are still getting jammed by something local in the approaching tango force. Sending visual recon as of thirty seconds ago. She's a big one. You are cleared to engage once you're operational. Tower Two out."

Greenhill pumped his fist twice at the platoon sergeant, letting him know it was time for everyone to get their buckets and gear back on, finish up whatever they were doing, and get ready to roll again. Meanwhile he studied the image of the attacking force coming down the highway.

A massive mech or bot of some type, at least ten stories high, was surrounded by a fleet of smaller vehicles. There must have been some kind of laser interference and scrambling going on, or some sort of refractive cloak on the surface of every vehicle, making it hard for his eyes to make sense of what he was seeing. But the caravan was coming this way. That much was clear. Maybe an hour to arrival. It was moving slowly.

Captain Greenhill scanned the skies above looking for his equipment drop. Nothing. Neither was there a spare SSM rocketing toward the mech and its entourage, which would have made this op *much* easier. Greenhill sighed. Navy was low on ordnance, he knew. They would've sent 'em down if they could. No sense worrying about what you couldn't have. Just make do with what came your way.

The ruined factory began to groan. A few shards of glass from an upper-deck observation conference room executives must have once enjoyed holding meetings in—if anyone can enjoy a corporate meeting—shattered on a pile of debris below. Most of the building had previously exploded outward into that rubble pile and the wide park beyond.

"LS-97 to Black Horse Actual..." It was the scout sergeant coming in over the L-comm.

"Go for Black Horse."

"Spotted our mechs, Captain. Or at least the one. It's a big sucker."

"Roger that. Stay in position. We're receiving the drop and we'll get the weapons up and ready. Report in if anything changes along their intended route."

He saw the first drops coming in high above, deploying their three chutes apiece. They were drifting down toward the parkland near the ruined plant.

"Remember, Nine-Seven, bigger they are, harder they fall. Black Horse out."

43

Strike Force Shield

Junction Eight no longer looked like a pristine checkpoint where three tunnels led off into various sectors of the Underground. It didn't even look like a war zone. It was a disaster area. Like it had been hit by what some scientists called a *planetary event*. Something like a meteor. Or a polar axis shift.

Savage direct-fire artillery, shooting from positions down the street with angles into Junction Eight, had destroyed the cargo-containers-turned-bunkers the Legion had been fighting from. The floor was littered with the Legion and Savage dead. Some of the storage containers that had contained flammable materials were on fire, and billowing black smoke filled the chamber. The legionnaires, able to breathe in their buckets, were moving among the dead, securing charge packs from their brothers and more magazines and belts of hard-caliber ammunition from their enemies.

The last wave to hit had tried coming in behind flamethrowers, but the last of Rechs's force still holding the junction, mainly the squad designated marksmen, had fought them off. Even the Britannian medics had joined in and fought especially hard when the Savage marines penetrated the junction and went for the forward casualty collection point where four wounded legionnaires were waiting to be evac'd back to the *Chang* at Backdoor. The

295th security teams, led by Sergeant Watson, pushed their way into the tunnels near Junction Eight in an attempt to block any Savages from the doctors and their patients.

Popping the fuel tanks had been the trick to stopping the Savage flamethrowers. The smell of burnt flesh and machine hung heavy in the air and the 295th had to don gas masks just to survive the caustic fumes and acrid smoke.

That push saved the vastly outnumbered legionnaires defending Junction Eight, but it hadn't been Watson's idea.

It was Captain McIntosh who had insisted on going forward to treat the wounded closer to the battle. Too many were dying on their way to the rear CCP. Sergeant Watson had in fact objected, declaring the plan unsafe. But Doctor Rachel was intent on saving the legionnaires and her own wounded medics. No matter how close she got to the enemy.

So Watson dutifully followed.

Now Captain Milker was down to four effectives among the Legion and a handful of medics. The only thing going for the Legion's defense at Junction Eight was that it was on fire, and half the roof had collapsed once the mounted cranes came down due to incoming rocket fire. Rockets that were far more powerful than the det-cord the 295th had brought with them. Intel had deemed collapsing Junction Eight impossible. The Savages had accidentally found a way. The cranes were lying across the entrance, making access by anything other than infantry no longer possible.

Though with the Savages, you never knew.

Barring some kind of transport that could bowl its way right in—and why wouldn't the Savages have used that by now if they had it to begin with?—the marines would have to come in along tight corridors of burning ruin to reach the few remaining legionnaires defending the deeps of Underground. No tanks. No massed attack of any kind.

To Captain Milker it was still a bad situation. But if he got the remaining leejes into the next line of defenses they might hold out for another hour or so. At some point they needed relief and reinforcements. The grand plan, as he knew, was to get the Savages to call Junction Eight too costly and instead secure their food storage by way of Kill Zone Alpha. But the Savages apparently hadn't seen the need for that as clearly as the general had thought they would.

"Captain." It was the L-comm operator contacting him directly.

"Here," replied Milker. "What's up?"

"I got a leej, sir... his L-comm tag is identifying him as LS-39, but... he's saying he's Tyrus Rechs and he needs to speak with you. Could be a Savage trick. Three-Nine is listed as KIA."

"Does it *sound* like the general?"

"It does, sir. I'd know that voice in my nightmares. But the tech's there to fake that if needed. That's as old a trick as it gets. Maybe the Savages have found a way to hack the L-comm?"

Everyone had been briefed to expect Savage trickery. The general was KIA. That had been confirmed over the whole net. But here was a chance to maybe see what the Savages were up to... so there was that potential.

"Patch him through."

Milker watched as the remaining wounded were pulled out. Now all that were left were a few legionnaires, a few medics, and the medics' security teams led by Sergeant Watson.

"Patching. Three-Nine go for Warlord Actual."

Milker had assumed the call sign for overall commander of the Legion once the transfer of command had been announced upon the death of General Rechs.

"This is Warlord," said Milker. "Who exactly am I speaking with?"

"This is General Rechs, Milker. I authenticate triple-nine-zero, codeword Miranda."

That was the command team's agreed-upon code word for verification of important orders. The team had tried to prepare for everything in spite of all the unknowns that came with the Savages. And it did in fact sound like Tyrus Rechs. Not the T-Rex who'd hectored them through training, but a different Rechs. Wounded and not doing great. His breathing was labored.

"Code word is good," replied Captain Milker cautiously. "Sir, I heard you'd been killed."

"Feels like it," replied Rechs getting some interference over his end of the comm. "Still combat-effective. Just had to secure a new bucket. I'm going to override the settings and re-tag as Hitman for the duration of the mission. What's the situation at Eight?"

"Sir, we're still getting hit hard with everything they've got. I'm not sure we can hold for one more wave, but we're going to attempt. After that... I'm contemplating executing Option Detour and pulling back. I'm down to four combat-effectives plus myself plus a small force of medics and their security detail. Now that you're back in the net I'll defer to you and relinquish command. Where should I—"

"Negative, Warlord. You are still in command. This mission will proceed. Execute Detour and blow the charges on Eight. Once the tunnels have been sealed off I'll link up with you at the rally point for Kill Zone Alpha. Your force will augment and provide security for forces at Alpha."

Milker hesitated. He checked the battle board he had strapped to his knee. Most of the charges that would bring the roof and several tons of concrete and debris down on Junction Eight were still in place. Option Detour would effectively seal off the entrance and force the Savages toward Alpha.

"Warlord, I am authorizing you to execute Detour and fall back to the rally point now. Do you understand?"

Another moment passed. Milker scanned the burning defenses and tight corridors. Out beyond the wreckage the Savage marines were gathering for another push. What if he really was talking to a fake? A kind of psyop from the Savages? Or what if they'd somehow ... hacked Rechs's brain in the combat? Inserted some horrible data worm that could trawl a living mind for valuable intel?

What if detting the junction played right into their hands? He could call and confirm with Admiral Sulla...

"Affirmative, sir," Captain Milker replied, making his mind up in one fateful instant. "Executing Detour now. Will pull back to the rally at Alpha. Where are you going if I'm to remain in charge of the battle?"

"Focus on the plan, Ted," replied Rechs, and Captain Milker was surprised that the general knew his first name. "The Savages *will* retreat once they realize what we're really after. Thought they would have already, but when they do, I want to give them a nice going-away present on their way out the door. Hitman out."

44

Team Black Horse

The souped-up high-powered all-terrain vehicles known as "mules" were assembled after their drop off the *Defiant*. Palletized and stowed for high orbital drop, the three vehicles and a couple of armory-sized clamshells had been delivered onto the withered ruin of Parkland Meadows east of the micro-strike wasteland around New Vega's Hilltop District.

Over the main areas of the city a massive explosion thundered across the soundscape, echoing out over the lonely city and covering the sounds of all the skirmishes being fought near the grounded *Chang*, which looked like a beached whale. Random artillery strikes fell haphazardly against her deflectors.

"Would you look at that," said LS-78, the platoon sergeant for Black Horse. Across and above the city, one of the massive arches, filled with skyscrapers along the top and bottom, had begun to crumble. Its monolithic collapse was like a horrible slow-motion fall that was fascinating to watch in that it took so long. Like it would never end, until it did. And then, at the last, it happened all at once, tons of debris raining down onto the city.

"Get back to work," said Captain Greenhill over the L-comm. "Ain't got time for that. Ready to roll in ten. We got work to do."

The legionnaires busy around the three mules finished loading the belt-fed 20mm recoilless cannon shells with depleted uranium high-energy high-explosion armor-piercing rounds—HEHEAP, or "heep" as military personnel invariably shortened it—and stacking in the one-shot heavy anti-armor launchers called HMRS. Heavy Munition Rocket System. The leejes called them "Hammers."

Ten minutes later, five to a mule, Black Horse rode into the streets and readied themselves to meet the incoming Savage mech force coming east down Main Highway One.

The mission was to delay or destroy this new force before they could counterattack the *Chang* across open ground.

Ninth Intercept Squadron, "Sand Lions"
Aboard *Defiant*

"All pilots report to your ships. Repeat... Ninth Intercept, report to your..."

Inside the Ninth's ready rooms, Cuckoo Davies was changing flight suits and trying to inhale a sandwich left by the galley crew that served the hangar deck. He'd practically soiled himself on the last run to take out the Savage mech shelling LZ Victory. The ADA over the target had been heavy to say the least.

He looked at himself in the small mirror inside his locker. No. He was not dashing like the Baron. He was just a pilot. An average ordinary fighter pilot. And he'd almost died out there today and he was scared to death because the day wasn't over.

His family was safe somewhere in the core worlds. They'd gotten out early. Gotten off Britannia before it was sacked by the Savages. Unlike a lot of his fellow countrymen and women fighting here today he had someone to go home to when this was all over.

He finished the final bit of the stale sandwich the ground crew had handed him after they came in from that last hairy strike run. Truth be told he hadn't been hungry in the least. But this was going to be a long day.

He looked at himself in the mirror once more. Hoping that somehow he might seem... braver. Like the Baron. If he could just look as cool and calm as that cad... well then he might not be so damn afraid next time when the incoming flak was so heavy you might reach out and touch it. He might just have the courage to come through this and make it back to everyone.

His family waiting just for him. A plain old pilot.

They'd had to go in low against the mech. Very low and very fast. Excessively fast. Skimming just over the ruined streets and beneath skeletal buildings no longer as tall as they once were. Flying through whatever madness those Savages had cooked up for flak guns and turned loose on their own buildings just to hit the inbound fighters.

"Stay cool, Cuckoo. It's going to get a bit hairy."

That's what the Baron had told him when their flimsy deflectors started getting abused as they streaked in toward final drop. And that's when he, Cuckoo Davies, an ordinary man who happened to love flying and ended up a fighter pilot, knew it was going to get rough indeed. Very rough. Because when the Baron, the coolest and calmest "cuke" of them all told you it was about to be heads-up ball all the way into the target...

Well, then you knew you were in it. That was for sure.

He zipped up his flight suit and started to assemble his kit. Sidearm. Survival gear. Lucky twenty-sider.

"Be brave, dammit," he hissed at himself.

The Baron came to the lockers. Cool. Calm. Dark hair slicked back. Easy. Like they were just going out to the range to drop some more ordnance and maybe hit the O Club afterward. The girls would swarm him. And the boys would want to be him. Him at the piano playing for someone not in the room.

What's it like to be him, Cuckoo had often wondered. What's it like to be that tragically perfect in every possible way?

"That was close, eh?" said Cuckoo, closing his locker. Wishing that somehow this pilot, this legendary pilot who was already the greatest flying ace of the short war, and maybe ever, would just let down the cool cucumber bit for a moment and be a plain old frightened-to-death human. A damn *human*.

The Baron lit a cigarette. He raised his eyes at Cuckoo, checking in with his wingman. Seeing what couldn't be hidden.

"It's all right, Cuckoo," whispered the Baron coolly. "To be honest... I didn't think I was going to make it back there either."

He said it like they were closing out the O Club and it was well past time to be back to quarters. Like it wasn't a confession so much as a cocktail story told a thousand times. All the beats perfect. The self-deprecating humor right where it should be. Rehearsed to perfection.

Like some old Shakespearean in the park on a Sunday afternoon.

Davies laughed, and it was a sick laugh that was more an exhalation of pent-up fear and rage escaping. Like it was only wearing the mask of a laugh. But he thanked the Baron for that. For trying to be at least a little human, and not a legend. Just like the rest of the boys dying out there today. One of the lads.

"I wonder if your bird'll even be ready, Baron," said Cuckoo. "They might have to swap out you into the spares."

The Baron's Dauntless had been hit by flak three times. His ship was riddled with holes when they made it back to the carrier. But he'd held course, stayed on target, and knocked out the Savage artillery mech.

"Glad you were there with me, Cuckoo," murmured the Baron. "Couldn't have done it without you. And... there are no spares. We're down to just half the squadron, Kooks. Just talking with Beasley over in ops. He says it's not looking good. Scared to death, that one."

Davies bit his lip and wanted to say, *I just want to go home, Baron. I want to run and find them. Mine. I do not want to die here. Not today. Not over this miserable little world.*

Except that sick little trifle of a laugh was all that came out.

"C'mon, Leftenant Davies. We're due on the flight line. Let's go." The Baron handed Flight Lieutenant Davies his helmet.

Davies felt rooted to the deck as he took it. Like he might never leave the ready room ever again. He'd just stand here and go stark raving mad. *Send in the flight surgeon, lads*, he would scream and gibber, *but I'm not going into all the flak once again. There's someone waiting for me.*

"Righto, Baron."

Be brave, dammit.

Tech Sergeant Lawrence Tate was spot-patching the Baron's Dauntless when its pilot arrived at the docking cradle. He had his safety mask on to protect his eyes from the intense light generated by the curing process used to emergency-seal the holes in the shot-up interceptor.

The Baron crushed out his smoke and signed a data board handed to him by the ordnance NCO. He would be carrying an SSM for this run.

"Someone's really going to get it," the captain murmured drolly as he looked over his ship and dashed off his signature. The Dauntless was now more splotchy red patch than desert sand.

The tech sergeant said nothing and turned to another task to prep the fighter for flight.

"Ha! Blimey, Baron. You're ship's bleeding from everywhere. Try not to get hit so much next time. It's bad for your health."

It was another pilot rushing by to reach his own ship. Shifter. Good sort. He slapped the Baron on the back, a thing no one but Shifter did, and moved off down the flight line. He called out over his shoulder, "We'll have to start calling you the *Bloody* Baron next! I hope she still flies, and see you in the skies. Hey, that—" Engine noise drowned out the last bit, but it was easy to figure out.

The Baron watched him go and carried his flight helmet toward the boarding ladder.

"Well, Sergeant Tate," began the Baron, climbing up toward the Dauntless's cockpit. "Will she indeed fly again today?"

Tate was still patching holes, crawling across the front of the fuselage, legs and boots straddling the ship as he worked.

"Oy, she'll fly. No worries there, Captain. But I'm still working on making sure she *keeps* flying after she's cleared the deck."

Baron was getting clearance to warm up engines and begin the taxi to the launch deck. Across the target and information screen his mission was coming up. Close air support run against armor inbound on the *Chang*.

The Baron cleared his throat and started the Dauntless's left outboard engine.

"I'm getting the clearance to taxi, Sergeant. Is my ship cleared from maintenance?"

"Oh, she's cleared. Flight systems are good. Clear to depart the bay." Tate inched his legs across the fuselage, concentrating on a new patch.

"Are you sure about that, Sergeant Tate? It seems like this ship is... not ready."

"Oh, she's good. She'll fly, gov. I'm just makin' sure and all. You're going to penetrate atmo. Wouldn't want you to burn up on entry now."

"Number two engine, start," Baron called out, according to protocol. "Do you want me to taxi to launch with..."

"Yes, do. I'll ride along to the launch deck and be finished in a trice."

The Baron visually cleared the aircraft and added taxi power to the throttle. A second later the Dauntless bumped forward and made its way down the maintenance hangar toward *Defiant*'s launch deck.

"Flight Leader, you are cleared to taxi and launch. Your target is priority hit."

"Hmmm…" murmured the Baron as Cuckoo's ship taxied in off his wing, departing its maintenance hangar. He gave Cuckoo a cool thumbs-up. Knowing the man was feeling it. But Cuckoo was looking at Sergeant Tate with concern.

The crew chief finished his last patch, and they were now out on the main deck. Ready to launch.

"Flight Leader, you are cleared to roll."

Baron hummed a bit of "Starlight Sonata" to himself and ran through a check on flight controls. Cuckoo came up alongside.

Tate at last slid down off the ship, dashed away, then turned and pulled back his patching mask to salute. The Baron saluted back as the tech sergeant knelt, shooting his hand forward like a knife and clearing the flight for takeoff.

The Bloody Baron went to full throttle and the two interceptors cleared the carrier and fell away toward the planet below. Ready to hit their target.

45

Team Black Horse
Main Highway One

The massive state-of-the-art highway circled toward the *Chang* from the northeast down into the more populated regions of New Vega. It was a feat of architectural wonder. Designed to be destruction-proof, whether from nature or war, the raised highway was built from hundreds of thousands of tons of duracrete and adamantium-polycarbon-reinforced stress rods. It was so strong that it had survived more than one direct hit from the devastating Titan strike that had taken place during the last battle for New Vega, as well as several hits from the micro-strike in this second battle for the planet.

An orbital strike would have done the trick, but Admiral Sulla didn't have the capability in his fleet.

And that was presenting a problem.

Drone intel and flyovers by recon scouts in the months leading up to the battle had indicated that the Savages kept a force of heavy armor outside the city. The working theory was that this was an arms buildup meant to be used to conquer future Savage worlds. But now, that force was being thrown not into battle on some distant planet, but on the very rock the Savages had claimed as their own. And after the micro-strike, that force's only way into the city was Highway One.

To make matters worse, the *Chang* lay uncomfortably near Highway One. It was mission-critical that *Chang* be protected, as it was the only possible way for all forces to be rescued if a general evacuation was ordered. Yet the UW corvette was already down to twenty-five percent of peak munitions for the point defense cannons, and once those went dry, all that would be left to maintain security at LZ Victory would be the ship's deflectors and crew.

Thus Team Black Horse had been designated as a cavalry force to intercept the Savage force, should both it and the highway survive the initial micro-bombardment. Which they both had. Captain Greenhill and his legionnaires were to destroy as much of the inbound armor in the force as possible before falling back to the *Chang* to defend the LZ.

The captain had been a cavalry scout before joining the Legion and was well acquainted with this type of operation.

In each of the three mules sat a driver, a TC, and a gunner. The other six legionnaires were divided into two-man teams carrying three Hammers apiece. They'd spread out in a series of bombed-out Savage buildings with a view up toward the elevated highway.

Sitting in the TC position in the lead mule, parked and idling in the shadows just below an off-ramp that led up onto Main Highway One, Greenhill reviewed the plan with his team.

"Remember, leejes," he said over the team L-comm. The ground was now shaking as the heavy armor force and massive walker came close. Signs were swinging in the street. Though they couldn't see the ten-story-tall mech just three kilometers away from their hidden vantage points, they could feel it coming. "Remember, leejes... Savages are stupid. They built this thing nice and tall because they wanted to impress and frighten everyone. In modern warfare tall just means a bigger target for us to shoot at. Believe me, I've had to deal with this myself my whole life."

Besides the sniper known as the Wild Man, Greenhill was the tallest legionnaire in the Legion.

"So we can shoot from down here, and keep moving, using the buildings for cover to set up repeated ambushes. Fire and forget. Keep moving. Don't get close, don't get hit. Copy?"

Over the nearby buildings, Captain Greenhill could finally see the top of the ten-story mech approaching. It was like something from a monster movie where an alien gigantor attacks a city on one of the colony worlds. Those movies had been all the rage when he was a kid.

Everyone should be running, thought Greenhill in a corner of his mind. Like in the movies. Everyone should be running to hide, to get away and save their lives. That was what was missing in the silent and empty street that had been silent and empty ever since the Savages had taken the planet.

The mech had some type of... Greenhill wasn't sure what it was. It was almost like the thing had one giant eye up there. Greenhill stared, imagining he could see tiny figures running around up there, driving the thing.

His driver, LS-60, swore in wonder.

"All right, everyone, it's on," said Greenhill, knowing everyone was staring at that thing and wondering how they were going to take it out. Same as him. "You know what to do, Black Horse. Let's roll."

Black Horse One roared from her hiding place beneath the bridge with the captain directing his driver, Specialist

Smoker. Everyone had begun to call him that during the training leading up to this phase of the operation because he'd been the best at getting the mules' tires to burn out.

Smoker gunned the vehicle's powerful souped-up engine—for once avoiding making a show of smoke—and roared up onto the highway. Right in front of the massive walking mech and the supporting armor trailing the lead Savage attack vehicle.

"Get their attention," Greenhill said over the vehicle's comm.

The gunner in the rear opened up from with the 20mm recoilless. The first rounds streaked away from the gun, trailing smoke, ripping into the armor midway up the torso of the ten-story mech. The powerful heep rounds smashed into strange, box-like graphene surfaces, exploding components and mechanisms.

Then on Greenhill's order, Smoker spun the mule, fishtailing away from the mech, hauling for the next off-ramp. He floored the accelerator pedal as the beast of an attack vehicle raced up through the gears.

The mech's defenses were up and engaged. Powerful beams shot from between its block-wide treads, sweeping out and away, slicing through the duracrete highway like it was nothing more than warm butter, its previously indestructible architecture apparently not indestructible against this latest Savage tech. And even as the beams continued, box-like canisters along two of the mech's arms popped and fired sidewinders on the fly.

The mule, because it was a special ops version of the UW's workhorse ground vehicle, ran a small yet sophisticated electronics package. And as the suite of sidewinding missiles raced and danced at mere meters above the highway, they all suddenly malfunctioned and exploded. The result of external jamming.

Greenhill's gunner chanced another burst that sent a series of explosions along the giant death machine's left tread. A moment later Smoker had the vehicle swinging onto the off-ramp a dangerous speed.

"All Black Horse Ground..." This was an alert to the three Legion anti-armor teams running the HMRS engagement systems from various locations. "Fire and shift to your next positions."

Driving fast down the side streets, Smoker maneuvered to miss abandoned repulsor sleds and the occasional blast crater. Captain Greenhill craned his neck to watch as Hammer rounds streaked up from the alleys and rooftops within the trap they'd laid for the Savage Death Machine. That had become its official tag—Death Machine—over the last hour on all intel updates. The powerful Hammer anti-armor missiles exploded along the mech's cylindrical torso, ripping into internals and causing secondary explosions within. Beams from its upper gunnery decks replied against the new targets, but Greenhill knew his leejes had fired and dropped canisters, moving quickly to their next position. Hit-and-move had become the philosophy by which they would conduct their running counterattack against the Savage armor rumbling toward their LZ and base of operations.

The Legion was too small to do it any other way.

"Dammit!" Smoker yelled.

Greenhill expected a sudden swerve and braced himself. But it didn't come. He looked up, tearing his eyes from the mech to see what else could have his driver alarmed.

The roofs of the buildings along the street had begun to come apart. The sky turned into a cloud of dark locusts up near the tops of the buildings they were passing, buildings that were exploding into sprays of brick, mortar, glass, and other construction materials. It was as though the buildings were disintegrating as one all around them.

The powerful Death Machine was using its primary offensive system to attack. Greenhill couldn't think of anything to call it other than a death ray. A massive beam of energy that practically disintegrated whatever was in its path. And even though the captain sensed he and the rest of the mule's crew were about to die, he knew their plan had been successful. The Savages had a tendency to attack the first thing that came their way—which in this case meant they'd gone after the bait.

Black Horse One was the bait.

But that gave the other elements of Team Black Horse a chance to get in free shots.

Smoker thumbed a control on the mule's wheel and popped the choke canisters along the rear of the vehicle. Choke was an IR chaff spray that looked like smoke when deployed—it was supposed to obscure the vehicle from targeting lock. Supposed to. The truth was, it was an open question as to whether it could defeat the Savages' ability to acquire and fire.

Smoker spotted a half-collapsed parking garage and threw the fast-moving mule into a turn that wouldn't have been possible in most vehicles. As it was, he only barely missed hitting a guide pylon before the mule rocketed below ground. Night vision kicked in automatically along the windshield as they raced through the garage's darkness.

Greenhill swiveled around to check and see if the gunner was loading another box of twenty-millimeter. From the slackness in the legs he could see sticking down from the turret he knew the man had been hit. Next he saw the blood.

"Pull over," Greenhill ordered, hoping something could be done. But when he got out of the vehicle and saw what remained of the gunner, he knew that hope was lost. The leej had been torn in half by incoming fire.

Overhead, out there, Britannian fighters streaked in and fired their guns before tearing off in opposite directions across the ruined city.

Ninth Intercept Squadron, "Sand Lions"

The Baron studied his instruments as he and Cuckoo flew lazy eights over the battlefield.

"No go, no go," said a pilot over the strike comm. It was Heater. "She's got some kind of jamming gear and we can't hit her with the AGMs. Guns no good. Primary is on the move again. Say again... targeting is negative."

That's why they armed my ship with the SSM, Baron thought as he read the Dauntless's portside exchanger readout. It wasn't working properly, and the engine was running dangerously hot. He was also losing fluid pressure in the hydraulics. A little. Not a lot. But that was something to be concerned with. Something to keep an eye on.

And another reason they'd armed him with the SSM.

His ship was the least reliable. The other ships would need to fight and all he had to do was carry the payload to the target. Except the onboard targeting wasn't picking up the inbound armor units. The SSM would need local targeting. And visual, at that speed and that low, would be a tough shot. Bad way to waste an SSM. He didn't like that one bit. But a mission was a mission.

Heater and Junk were climbing back up to come alongside.

He checked the pressure leak in hydraulics again. Definitely something to keep an eye on.

46

Team Black Horse

Greenhill was now in the gunner's cupola and making a run against the Death Machine on the highway above. Black Horse Two had just completed their run, driving in and firing a burst from the 20mm recoilless, then speeding off before the beam systems aboard the Death Machine could acquire and engage. After each such run, one of the two surviving Hammer teams would fire and shift position.

The third Hammer team was not responding. Greenhill was counting them as either KIA or at least wounded for the rest of the fight.

The Death Machine had by now revealed itself to have four weapon systems. Beams for short-range defense. Missiles for long-range engagement. And then, just below the upper control cupola, up near gigantic artillery guns of at least one-hundred-twenty millimeters, was a kind of open mouth of glowing blackness. A pulsing darkness that was at odds with the rest of the "normal"—apart from being overly immense—military vehicle. The black mouth weapon could fire a swarm of micro-drones. Like a shotgun. A "ray," for want of a better word. And this ray destroyed everything in its path as thousands of drones just dumb-slammed into the target area and exploded.

That was what had happened to the third Hammer team. After they had fired their last shot, the dark mouth had fired into their area of operation, devastating an entire block.

Since then they had been out of contact.

Everyone else was engaged in a complex dance of fire and maneuver to avoid the same fate.

"Black Horse Three to Black Horse Actual. How copy?"

It was the third mule. They were ready to fire next. Greenhill kept working the gun on the upper control cupola of the Death Machine. He'd ordered Smoker to fall back a few streets in order to give him an angle on the mech's command and control sections. So far, despite good hits across the rest of the mech by all teams, the extensive damage to the machine had yet to affect its ability to engage, and there was no indication this thing was going down any time soon. If at all.

Greenhill could only hope the Savages didn't have a second of these metal monsters to throw up against the LZ.

"Shifting," responded Smoker over the mule's comm.

Greenhill ducked inside and dragged another ammo box over for the gun, getting tossed around as the vehicle turned and raced for cover.

The comm pinged from *Defiant* intel.

"Go for Black Horse Actual."

"Black Horse, be advised we have infantry in the mix now. The Savages have deployed troops from their carriers following the primary. They're in the streets near your position."

That wasn't going to make things easier.

"Where to, sir?" asked Smoker from the driving compartment. Then he swore as the mule took fire from ahead. The front windshield held as smoking vapor trails came straight at them. It was bulletproof, but the impacts created spider webs all along it.

Over the comm, Black Horse Three's TC was indicating they were engaging the primary. Take it out and the rest of the attack by the Savage armor might falter and fail. Might.

Greenhill had the next box of 20mm rockets linked. He popped up into the turret and saw Savage infantry, armored and carrying rifles with drum cylinders out into the street, firing and moving up on the mule. The captain thumbed the charging button, racking a new rocket, and pulled the trigger on the 20mm. He squeezed and didn't let go, walking heep rounds into the Savage squad that had dared to engage them.

The rounds streaked into the duracrete street and exploded, tearing armor and bodies to shreds. One round scored a direct hit on a Savage gunner that sent his body in every direction. A few tried to cover behind a sled, but Greenhill ran out the box of ammo decimating that cover. Nothing survived.

In the silence that followed, the dead Savages lay like tossed rag dolls across the shadowy dark street where the desperate ground battle had suddenly been fought.

"I'm hit, sir," said Smoker over the vehicle's comm.

"How bad?" asked Greenhill.

"Hurts like a jackhammer. But I think the armor took most of it. Mighta busted a rib."

"Good to go?"

There was a pause. Above their heads the Death Machine belched another swarm of direct-fire drones at another target. Someone was probably going to die.

"Good to go, sir," coughed Smoker.

"Roger. Take us back to the streets and off to their left. Let's keep makin' 'em pay."

Greenhill had barely gotten the words out when the Death Machine fired its artillery platforms and erased the entire grid square they were driving through.

When Greenhill came to, LS-43 was dragging him from the wreck and telling him command had a mission that needed to happen now.

"Right now, sir! It's critical. Death Machine's on the move and it's almost ready to unload on the *Chang*."

47

Ninth Intercept Squadron, "Sand Lions"

"Strike Leader, this is *Defiant* Shot-Caller. You have bandits inbound on intercept. Transmitting targeting now."

Baron studied the tactical layout of the airspace around him now appearing on HUD.

"Right, lads," he said, switching over to the strike's comm. "Looks like we've got twelve coming up to give us a hard time. Seems they'd like to stop us from knocking out that beast of a mech. Break off into teams and take them out ship to ship. Cuckoo, you're with me, rolling to course two-seven-zero on my mark. Mark."

The lead Dauntless, patched rust-red in more than thirty places, and her wingman broke away from the other four fighters in formation dropping out of the upper atmosphere over New Vega City.

Less than thirty seconds later the Baron picked up his first Savage Phantom of the sortie. It was the lead of a swarm of six, after-boosters burning hard and streaking up at them from the ruins below. Missiles raced ahead of the rival leads, while gunfire blurred the air between the two groups. Both elements heading straight at each other doing Mach three. It was the equivalent of trying to balance on a razor's edge over an ocean of acid.

But the Baron paid no mind to the danger, sending his battered Dauntless into a dive straight toward the maelstrom of interceptors. It was up to them to get out of *his* way.

It was the ultimate game of chicken.

One of the screaming Phantoms roaring straight up at him presented a perfect target engagement profile. Baron lit up the guns on his Dauntless, and the Phantom streaked straight through the bright hurl of his fire.

Pulse fire slammed into the long and slender gleaming fuselage, scoring hits that ripped away control surfaces. As fuel lines severed and ignited, the ship turned into a streak of sudden hot fire, listing over onto her starboard side and dragging a trail of smoke and flames across the sky before exploding in every direction.

The Baron added a small bit of pressure to the port rudder and raced right into where the enemy bandit had exploded.

Just like racing repulsor sleds, he thought. *Always steer toward the wreckage in order to avoid it.*

The same was true of air-to-air combat.

A moment later he was free of the swarm and cranking his head around to make sure Cuckoo was off his wing while at the same time looking for targets.

"Right-o!" screamed Heater. "Splash one for the Bloody Baron! I'm next. Junk, stay on me, going for the bugger at three!"

The Bloody Baron found his next target, rolled out on the fast mover's six, and gave a short burst of the guns, missing but causing the pilot—or enemy AI; they had no data on these new enemy craft to indicate what actually flew them—to try and climb away using the Phantom's massive thrust.

The Baron had anticipated this without really thinking. He'd already leveled the Dauntless's wings, backing off the throttle to be ready for the maneuver. He gave a slight smile as the elusive Phantom popped back into his sights. Then he gave a nice, long, slow squeeze, raking the enemy ship's hull with a bright line of fire. Black smoke replaced the blue flame of the Phantom's thrusters as the enemy ship heeled over and began to fall toward the city below.

Incoming fire pounded the Baron's thin deflectors, collapsing them almost immediately. Two Savages, lead and wingman, streaked over and away from the Baron and Cuckoo. Breaking off to pick up their tail.

The Baron yanked the Dauntless around hard to come straight back at them, not wanting to allow the bandits to pick up their six. But the Dauntless wasn't responding well. The turn was slow and sluggish and did little more than allow both enemies to get into a perfect firing position.

"Cuckoo, break off!" shouted the Baron. "I'm hit. Portside hydraulics bleeding. Rerouting..."

"Negative, Baron. I'm with ya all the way."

"Dammit, Cuckoo. What're you—"

Both Phantoms streaked in once more blazing fire, targeting Cuckoo, who'd fallen back to present a better targeting picture. He popped flares and chaff, probably figuring that even if the Savages weren't using lock-on weapons, it might confuse their sight picture.

The Baron craned his neck in an attempt to see Cuckoo's fate behind him. But almost as soon as he did the Phantoms streaked ahead. Hydraulics rerouted toward starboard redundancy.

Swearing bloody murder under his breath, the Baron went to full throttle and rocketed after the bandits, knowing he might well blow the outboard exchanger in the process. At the same time, he opened the quad blasters on both enemy fighters flying the tight lead/wingman formation just ahead.

They were pulling away. The Phantoms were faster by far than anything the Baron had ever seen. But his patched and battered Dauntless splashed hits across both ships, destroying one outright and wounding the other.

He allowed that one to disengage and was surprised to find his wingman off his right wing and right where he should be.

"You good, Cuckoo?"

"Fine, Baron." Davies gave a thumbs-up.

The air battle was half won when Junk got smoked and bailed out. *Defiant*'s shot-caller updated the mission.

"Strike Leader, you are cleared for attack run against primary. Targeting assist will be available in two minutes."

"Better be," growled the Baron. "Or you're going to waste one very expensive and precious SSM on some bit of landscaping gone to rubbish since last we were here."

"Affirmative, Strike Leader. Black Horse on the ground is going to make it happen."

48

Team Black Horse

LS-43 got Captain Greenhill to his feet after he'd dragged him out of the wreck of the mule.

"Smoker?" coughed the captain.

LS-43 shook his head. "Sorry, sir. Didn't make it."

Greenhill looked back at the burning wreck.

"Sir, we gotta target the mech in the next few. Command says they got fast movers coming in to knock her out. Gotta move now."

Greenhill bent over, his head swimming, ears ringing. One of the rocket teams had pulled him from a burning death. LS-43 handed him a rifle.

"Thanks," Greenhill said, for the rifle and his life.

"LS-18 is ahead tryin' to lead us to the intercept. You good, sir? We gotta do this now. Time to go."

Greenhill steadied himself and nodded. It was clear LS-43 meant to leave him rather than fail to reach his objective. Though he felt woozy and struggled to think straight, it made the captain proud.

He shook the cobwebs loose. "How many we got left, Four-Three?"

"Don't know, sir," the leej answered, taking side strides, ready to take off. "No one's answerin' squad comm. Don't know whether they're KIA or wounded. But we gotta—"

"I know," said Greenhill, pride evaporating into annoyance. "I got that. Gimme a second."

He tapped his comm, needing to know what, exactly, the objective was. "Command, this is Black Horse Actual. What's the change of mission?"

A moment later a cool female voice came in from *Defiant*.

"Black Horse Actual, change of mission objective confirmed. We need you to use your laser designator and target the mech directly. We're sending in close air to knock it out. Be advised we are using an SSM. The damage will be significant within a thousand meters of the target. Suggest your targeting take place beyond this limit and be sheltered against the blast wave."

Greenhill looked at the smashed and burning mule. The vehicle was ruined, and it was a miracle he'd survived. His armor was studded with cooling pieces of hot shrapnel still sticking out at various places. But nothing had penetrated. At least not that he could feel.

"Black Horse, say again. We have—"

"Roger," shouted Greenhill irritably. His bell had been rung, but he was coming around. "We have the mission. Problem, Command. We don't have a laser target designator. Will our HUD targeting work?"

He looked over to LS-43 and saw in the legionnaire's posture all the annoyance he'd felt as an enlisted man being forced to wait for an officer to get with the program.

"Stand by..." came the voice from *Defiant*.

Greenhill nodded at LS-43. "Let's start moving to the intercept."

"Primary is five blocks to the east. We're going to use a building to get up next to the highway and acquire targeting, sir." LS-43 managed to hide whatever frustrations he might be feeling.

Greenhill didn't know if that was a good idea. From what he knew about SSMs, they had the dynamic effect of a small nuclear warhead. Being in a building when the thing hit might be a bad idea. But he'd delayed things enough. They'd just have to figure things out once he got there.

The two leejes began to run down the street, rifles ready to engage.

"Black Horse Actual, this is Command. Negative on HUD targeting. Where is the laser designator?"

"Destroyed," grunted Greenhill as they made their way up along a ruined street where some house-to-house fighting had gone down during the first battle. "And I've lost contact with the other mule teams to recover another."

"Wait one, Black Horse."

Windows like empty eye sockets stared out onto a street filled with ruined cars. To the east, up near the highway, though the mech could not be seen past the tall buildings, the sound of the massive treads was omnipresent. Drones whizzed along side streets, darting out scanning lasers and taking in the ruin. Greenhill was sure they were Savage drones.

The two legionnaires were ducked down in a sub-level stairwell filled with human corpses when Command came back with a solution.

"Black Horse Actual, this is Command. We have an option to target primary without designator. Your combat helmet can be switched into emergency transponder location mode. If that can be placed anywhere near the primary, strike can use it to target. How copy?"

The ground was shaking, and what little remained of the broken glass in the blasted-out windows fell to the ground.

"LS-18 is coming back, sir." LS-43 pointed toward another legionnaire darting from wreckage to wreckage. Zigzagging cautiously but quickly down the street.

"Black Horse Actual to Command," Greenhill said. "Wait one."

"Bad news, sir," said LS-18, joining his brothers in the stairwell. "Savages got half a battalion of infantry on foot clearing the way forward. Primary is moving slow but it'll be in range to fire in the next thirty minutes at this rate. Those guns'll devastate the *Chang*."

"Guess we should be happy it took 'em this long to get it rolling," Greenhill said. He held up a finger while he reconnected with *Defiant*. "Command. Activating beacon on my bucket. Stand by to hit the target in five."

49

Defiant

Defiant's XO leaned in close to Admiral Sulla over the digital sand table deep inside the carrier's combat information center. "Update from Ground Ops, sir."

Sulla took a deep breath and nodded for the officer to go ahead with the report.

"The mech force has broken through here..." The officer pointed to a sector along Main Highway One. "As per your order we have an interceptor ready to hit the main body with one of our SSMs. There are currently three left in the forward torpedo tubes."

Sulla nodded. This had all been as per his instructions.

"The problem we're facing is a Savage jamming package we haven't been able to overcome. We've tested with targeted strikes using AGMs without success. We don't believe the SSM will be able to hit its target without line-of-sight targeting from the ground... not at the speed the package will be delivered."

Sulla, irritated, slammed his hands down on the edge of the glowing holographic sand table. "What, exactly, is the problem, Commander?"

The XO cleared his throat.

"There are three grunts on the ground and no working target designator."

Sulla smiled for a moment. The navy's use of the term *grunts* had always been slightly dismissive. "Legionnaires," he corrected.

The officer nodded before touching a point forward of the mech's progress on the sand table, expanding that section. "Captain Greenhill is the commander on the ground. He's going to intercept the mech here."

A digital representation of a building appeared on the sand table. It looked like it had been broken in two, snapped at the waist, its lower stories intact but its upper half fallen at a sharp angle to lean up against the side of Main Highway One. Its very top was nothing but rubble scattered across the elevated highway.

"They believe that infiltrating this building will be key," the officer continued. "Savage infantry is conducting a thorough sweep of the route to bring the primary within striking distance of LZ Victory. Captain Greenhill believes he can come up through the building and place his combat helmet along the route in time for our close air support to deliver the SSM, tracking on the helmet's beacon. Thus negating the local enemy jamming."

"Anything else we can use to stop them?"

No one knew better than Casper what an SSM could do. He'd fired more in anger than anyone. If those legionnaires weren't out of the blast radius they'd be killed. Easily.

The XO shook his head.

"No. We can't pinpoint for an orbital because of the jamming. This is our only chance, sir. It's those grunts or nothing."

Grunts.

"The *Legion* will do it, Commander."

50

Team Black Horse

It wasn't an infiltration in the classic sense. Greenhill knew that. But there wasn't time for anything else. LS-43 and 18 followed their captain in, firing on the Savages who'd set up in the ruin of the building to provide coverage for a trailing group seeking to leapfrog ahead to clear more road.

Greenhill and the two legionnaires got as close as they could, tossed in frags, and stormed the ruined building whose upper half had collapsed onto the highway. The captain shot one Savage still stumbling from the aftermath of the fraggers and then quickly put three shots into another who was bringing a light machine gun up to bear.

The room was cleared within seconds. It had been a hotel lobby, the ceiling collapsed down onto half the layout. Greenhill signaled the two legionnaires to follow him into the maze of rubble. They could hear the Savage marines chittering up close and farther away in the electronic digital speak they used to communicate.

"Look for a stairwell up!" ordered the captain over the L-comm as he drilled another Savage coming through the wreckage.

Bullets slammed into cracked walls behind the legionnaires. Both the legionnaires following Greenhill threw themselves into open doorways as rounds streaked over the captain's bucket. They were running out of time.

"Stairs over here!" shouted LS-18.

"Engaging!" shouted 43, pulling the trigger on his N-1 in clear methodical shots while calling out target status. "Tango down. Two in the corner on the right."

"Frag out!" yelled 18.

A moment later an explosion rocked the hallway.

"Move for the stairs, sir," called out 43. "We got your six."

Greenhill pushed off the floor and headed toward the wrecked stairwell.

"Don't clear!" he shouted over the comm. "Stay on me. Come on, let's go. Follow me!"

Captain Greenhill followed his N-1's sights up the crumbling stairwell, scanning for targets.

Outside, along the street, something exploded. A building across the way collapsed from within, raining a shower of dusty bricks and powdery rubble into the street.

"They're calling in artillery on us!" shouted LS-18.

"Keep moving!" Captain Greenhill ordered.

They reached the level where the building had snapped in two, revealing the burning blue sky up above. From here they would have to crawl upward at an angle through the wreckage of the upper stairwell to reach the elevated highway. And in many places they would be exposed. Savage marines, faceless in their mirrored buckets, had swarmed Main Highway One trying to deny them access.

Greenhill fired, hitting as many as he could and calling out still more targets ahead. LS-43 and LS-18 found positions in the rubble and laid down covering fire. Both were shooters. Savages were drilled straight through by their powerful N-1s.

Greenhill ducked down, slapped in a fresh charge pack, and fired up into a group of Savages unaware of the death that had gathered beneath them. He drained his charge pack, eliminating the Savages.

"Moving!" he called.

"Covering!" came back from both leejes.

Greenhill slithered like a snake, crawling for all he was worth to move through the rubble that effectively formed a crude access ramp to the roadway above.

Less than two minutes until the strike was scheduled to hit.

"C'mon," Greenhill grunted, pulling hard. Above him the terrible insectile head of the Death Machine came into view, its rumbling treads shaking the remains of the building and sending it crumbling down all around him.

Ninth Intercept Squadron, "Sand Lions"

"Strike Leader, you are cleared to hit the target."

The Bloody Baron acknowledged the order from *Defiant* and switched over to strike comm.

"Hear that, Cuckoo? We're cleared. Form up."

"On your six, Baron."

"Tallyho."

The Baron dropped the Dauntless down to the hard deck and shot out across the ruined city, afterburners burning hot and blue. In the distance the giant mech rolled in toward the *Chang*.

"*Defiant*, we are one minute to release. Locked on beacon. Can you confirm it's in place?"

A moment later the sky erupted in swarms of robotic drone flak.

"Watch yourself, Cuckoo!"

Team Black Horse

"I'm going forward!"

Captain Greenhill surges out of the ruin and sees an army in front of him. And behind that army, looming impossibly high at such close proximity, is the giant awe-inspiring mech.

The primary.

Rounds come at Greenhill almost instantly. And they hit, but still the captain moves forward. He rips off his helmet and flings it for all he's worth toward the giant mech quaking down Main Highway One.

Surrounded by a closing ring of closing Savages, Greenhill looks up, eyes barely catching the Baron's Dauntless as it peels away from the target, its powerful SSM already having been launched and inbound.

Black Horse Actual rises to his feet, engaging with his sidearm to the last.

Two point eight seconds later the SSM strikes the target, destroying the primary and obliterating everything within a thousand meters.

Almost two hundred years from this moment, Greenhill will be awarded the Order of the Centurion. Technically he will be the first to ever receive the highest honor the Legion can bestow. His final words, "Going forward," will become the motto of the Legion's scout and armored cavalry regiments throughout the Savage Wars. Repeated by none more proudly or prominently than the Black Horse Regiment.

51

Defiant

"Primary is down." The announcement cut through the chatter and hum of the CIC. "Target destroyed by air strike. Interceptors RTC."

Admiral Casper Sulla gripped the sand table and watched as drone feeds, sensor scans, and comm traffic updated the situation map.

"They did it," he breathed out silently. "You were right. You trained them well, Tyrus. Sorry you couldn't be there to see it."

He pushed the thought away. His oldest and best friend just... dead. He'd think about it later. If there *was* a later on the other side of all this. Some night when it was all over and there was time to figure it all out and add it up. If the final phase of the plan went into effect and they managed to push the Savages off this forsaken rock... then, *then* he would grieve for Tyrus Rechs. His friend.

The admiral checked the ground operations casualty list and studied Team Black Horse. The info wasn't up to date, but showed heavy casualties. None from the team were responding to comm.

"Contact!" shouted the deep scan sensor officer across the CIC. "Tracking one... no, now two vessels, Admiral. Both fitting Savage profile. Lighthuggers, sir. Dropping out of hyperspace and on an intercept course for New Vega."

Staff officers swore and bent to their stations, scrolling through data and bringing up assets. The comm traffic rose in pitch as the news crossed what was left of the fleet.

The admiral pushed all thoughts of the Legion and Tyrus Rechs aside. This was why his best friend had placed him here. To fight an unwinnable battle and give the Legion the time on the ground it needed to do what it had come to do. That was the key. Once the Savages became convinced the battle was lost, the battle in space would become meaningless.

But that battle had always been gamed with three Savage hulks. Not five. They'd defeated one, but that still left four at once, two fresh to the engagement.

"Status update on all elements in two!" shouted Casper. He waited as the section chiefs collected their data and assemble around the holographic sand table.

Two minutes later the briefing was underway.

"Let's start with Predator Three," began the admiral. "What's her status?"

The officer in charge of running that battle took charge of the sand table and displayed a tactical presentation of the current situation.

"Predator Three is running along the southern hemisphere. Staying out of the way of our capitals and fighting a running battle against our pirates. Pirates have taken heavy casualties but they're still harrying and we think that's what's keeping the hulk out of the battle, unusual as that may seem. Commodore Scar even tried to board directly. A twenty pulse-gun marauder tagged *Renigan's Gamble* reported a major firefight in the main forward hangar below the bridge, but it looks like that went south and we have no idea what the status of the boarding party is currently. Predator Three is capable of joining the fight over New Vega City in twenty minutes if she alters her orbital path at any point."

The officer stepped back and waited for any questions. Sulla moved on. "Predator Two."

A new officer, an older woman, stepped forward. The admiral knew her as a capable staff officer from back in the UW.

"Predator Two dead in space but she's still launching Phantoms to provide close air support against our forces on the ground. We estimate at least three wings' strength, but only one wing has been launched at this point. Seventy-five percent of that wing has been disabled or destroyed. Deep scan indicates Predator Two is also armed with a heavy PDC capacity, but those weapons systems appear to be offline."

"Recommendations?" asked Sulla.

"Hit her with our remaining SSMs until she burns," said the officer bluntly. "Deny her ability to contribute further to the battle."

Sulla nodded.

The officer who'd taken charge of the new group that would report on Predators Four and Five stepped toward the sand table's command station to take charge of the briefing.

Admiral Sulla interrupted with an upheld hand. "I want a report on *Nightingale* and *Sparrow Hawk* first."

The *Defiant*'s XO took over. "Sir, *Nightingale* remains engaged in casevac recovery. *Sparrow Hawk* is still providing cover against the Phantom swarms coming off the surface from previously undetected airfields. She's been hit hard, but her captain says he can hold."

Again the admiral nodded.

The XO opened his mouth to say something more and then closed it.

"You have something else regarding that group, Commander?" asked Sulla.

The officer struggled internally for a moment and then stepped forward once more. "I recommend ordering the *Nightingale* out of the combat zone. She's already full on casualties and *Sparrow* is damaged and running dry on PDC munitions. If we lose *Sparrow Hawk*, we will lose *Nightingale* within minutes after."

"Chances they'll listen and pull out?" asked the admiral.

The XO sighed.

"Zero, Admiral. That's why I didn't bother bringing it up. They're committed. Colonel Foy isn't even taking our calls."

Sulla studied the glowing holographic map beneath them all. "*Now* let's hear about Predators Four and Five."

"They're under full thrust and should be within striking distance of the main body in thirty minutes. Deep scans are being jammed, so we must assume their electronic warfare capability is significant. Both are standard old-colony lighthugger design but have been heavily modified.

"Five is ugly—maintenance looks bad on visual. Some kind of immense tube section has been drilled out through the center. We theorize based on visual data that it's a primary weapon drawing power from the aft reactors. But with deep scan jammed, that's speculation. Still, it looks to be capable of tremendous damage if it's direct fire. We've advised all ships to stay off her bow to best avoid taking a shot.

"Four is better maintained and has at least a division's worth of dropships racked on the outside along its hull. Based on the dropships' designs, we believe these are boarding vessels. Advise we maintain distance if engaging in order for *Defiant*'s and *Chan*'s PDCs to chew up those racks if they decide to deploy."

Silence fell over the assembled officers and section chiefs. Beyond the glowing blue light of the digital sand table the chatter and lighting of the CIC continued, a kind of constant unaffected by the chaos of battle that surrounded it.

Men and women were dying on the planet below, Sulla reminded himself. That was where the primary battle had been planned to take place. The question was: with Rechs gone, was that plan still viable?

It looked bad. But they were so close.

"And *Defiant*?" asked the admiral.

The XO stepped in again.

"We have three SSMs racked and ready to go, sir. All turrets are charged. *Chan* is prepared to engage and defend. *Fortnoy* has turret capability but no SSMs and her armor isn't rated to stand up to broadsides combat if we order a direct attack. What remains of the Ninth is currently eight interceptors plus our own group, currently at sixty-eight percent. Both echelons will be rearmed and ready to go within the hour."

The admiral studied his officers' faces. Gauging where his crew and command were at. They didn't quite believe this could be done. But they weren't going to quit. They knew there was no other way forward. Defeat here meant defeat everywhere.

The fleet had to deny Savage reinforcements to the planet below. Give the Legion time and the plan would work. He could almost hear Rechs saying that to him.

"Here's the plan, ladies and gentlemen. Rearm all fighters and set them to defending the *Nightingale*. Protect the hospital frigate at all costs. *Defiant* is to intercept Predator Two. I want *Chan* and *Fortnoy* quartering behind the engagement window and using *Defiant* for cover before breaking to charge Predator Three." Sulla held up a finger. "One pass only. We're doing this to see if we can draw off Four and Five, get them to break from their course toward New Vega. If they do, we'll launch SSMs at close quarters and see if we can get hits. If not, *Chan* and *Fortnoy* will be ordered to evacuate and self-destruct as close as they can get to either hulk. *Defiant* will recover crew and continue to fight whoever survives."

A stunned silence fell over the CIC. The *entire* CIC.

The plan was brutal. Ships would be used as suicide vessels. And it wasn't the admiral sacrificing his own ship. He was sacrificing others. In theory this was an option taught to high-level command and staff officers for the most dire and desperate of situations, but no one ever thought any admiral or captain would actually *issue* such an order. Turning entire ships into weapons just to stop an enemy.

It was a kind of desperate madness.

"Admiral," began one of the section chiefs. "Regarding the pass on Predator Two, we estimate it to have as many as two more wings of interceptors. With fighter cover diverted to *Sparrow Hawk*, how will we defend?"

Rather than answer outright, Sulla scanned the room and found the man he was looking for. Iron-gray hair, short and stocky, he reminded Sulla of Tyrus Rechs for no reason he could ever put his finger on. They looked nothing alike. But their character... that had been similar.

"Colonel Hartswick."

The former UW marine officer stepped forward from the shadows of the CIC.

"Sir," reported the marine.

"Your marines ready to get in the action?"

"Affirmative, sir. Ready to take lives."

Sulla nodded. "Colonel, your force is to board Predator Two's hull during our pass at broadside and bust it wide open for us."

"Can do, sir," snapped Colonel Hartswick.

52

Kill Zone Alpha

"This is Tyrus Rechs for Admiral Sulla. Say again: this is Tyrus Rechs for Admiral Sulla."

The L-comm operators had set Rechs up with a new identifier tagging him as Hitman, on Captain Milker's orders, but the comm operator aboard *Defiant* wasn't accepting the authentication credentials because the bucket Rechs was using was still tagged as KIA.

Rechs pulled the L-comm pack off his back, doing it one-handed and wincing from the pain of his three gunshot wounds. The local sedatives inside the gel packs covering his wounds were losing their effect.

A Britannian medic at the rally point for Kill Zone Alpha saw him approach and ran over to help.

"Here, legionnaire," said the medic, not recognizing the general. "Lemme help you with that, mate."

Then the man swore.

"How many times have you been hit, Leej?"

Rechs held up one hand. Wait. The comm operator was accepting a challenge.

"This is Tyrus Rechs. I authenticate triple-nine-zero."

The comm operator left her mic open and Rechs could hear the frantic chatter of traffic coming in from every element of the battle. It sounded only slightly more chaotic than the battle going on forward of the rally point deep inside the underground reservoir that was Kill Zone Alpha.

Then she was back.

"General, I have confirmation of your code word and voice ID match. Patching you through to Admiral Sulla now."

Rechs waited and tapped his external speaker to talk to the medic.

"I need some painkillers. Just local shots on my injuries and something general for the arm."

The medic stared at the wounds for a beat, then nodded and got to work. A hypo came out of an OD green medical bag and the medic began to delicately shoot sedatives into the affected areas. Then he pulled out a tube. "This is neural analgesic. If you're not gonna need your arm I can knock it out for the next week. You wanna do that, mate?"

The arm was in a sling and felt like it was filled with broken glass every time Rechs moved it.

He nodded for the medic to go ahead.

"Tyrus!" shouted Sulla over the comm. "You're not dead!"

"Bad intel, Sulla. Just got knocked around. You know how it is. There's dead, and then there's dead."

Sulla laughed, and Rechs wondered if he had found secluded quarters or if this was all in front of his crew in *Defiant*'s CIC.

"Tyrus... did you actually die? Like... back on the *Moirai* in the arena?"

"I guess they did something right, Casper."

Rechs figured with that question that Sulla must be alone. The name *Moirai* wasn't one they shared with others.

During their time as slaves aboard that Savage lighthugger long ago, their bodies and lifespans had been reengineered. Rechs's body had been designed to play some eternal gladiator that could be killed over and over again for the Savages' increasingly dangerous amusements in an arena of debauchery and death.

Casper had been redesigned for another purpose.

Rechs had been gored, stabbed, shot, and beaten. He'd died, but never completely. Never *all the way*. Death, for him, needed to go a little farther than for most people. Destroy a vital organ and he was done for. Cut off a limb and it wasn't growing back. But stop his heart for a few minutes... the Savages of the *Moirai* had figured that trick out. The right medical treatment in a timely enough manner and he might come back. Maybe.

"Glad to hear it was just bad intel, Tyrus."

"Yeah. Still here, Cas. Still kickin'."

Sulla let out a breath. Rechs could hear the emotion in the words that came next. "Okay, Tyrus. All right. We're still in this. But it's gotten a lot worse in the last few."

"Update me."

"Legion stopped the armor force coming in to hit the *Chang*. Unfortunately two new lighthuggers have arrived and we're going out to fight them now. Airspace over New Vega is going to be empty for a while. No casevacs. No air. Ops informed me Junction Eight collapsed and Savage forces on the ground are making for the aqueducts. They're already hitting KZ Alpha hard, and they're about to be hit a lot harder if the ground scans are accurate. Where are you?"

"I'm at Alpha now. The Savages *are* hitting it hard. Confirmed."

"You'll be relieving Captain Milker?"

"No. Milker's in charge and he's going to hold here with the rest of the Legion and the 295th."

There was a pause that felt longer than it really was amid the chaos of battle.

"What are you going to do, Tyrus?"

"I'm going for the trigger-nuke I left behind."

"Tyrus. Don't. We can still win this. Things may look bad, but Dagger is en route to Madhouse. The plan that you and I *both* put forward is progressing. If you hold Alpha until they figure it out, we can still win. Even if we lose up here. You activate that trigger-nuke and no one wins."

"Not going to, Cas. We are going to win. My boys have got this. But I'm hit pretty bad. Arm's busted and I can't even hold a rifle. But we knew we had to take that trigger-nuke off the board so they don't use it once we reach No Joy. They'll gladly sacrifice a few of their own to set it off on their way out the door just to spite us."

"Then issue the disarm commands right now," Sulla hissed.

"Already disarmed the tamper triggers remotely. Problem with disarming the entire thing, Cas, is those commands were downloaded into my bucket, which is now buried under Junction Eight."

"No redundancy?" Sulla sounded incredulous at the lapse.

"My other armor, but you can't very well bring that down to me from *Defiant*, can you?"

"So you're going to disarm it. All by yourself?"

"No. I'm going to recover it and get it aboard the first Savage lighthugger to set down once we reach No Joy."

They'd always anticipated that happening. Once the Savages got the whole picture of what was really happening to them... that would come next.

And the plan Rechs was proposing—using the trigger-nuke against a Savage hulk—had also been weighed and considered. If they had the opportunity. And the men to spare. Which they didn't.

Not that any of that mattered to Tyrus Rechs.

"Okay," said Sulla.

Another long pause. The background fighting, the sound of blasters, automatic gunfire, and explosions was reaching a fever pitch as the Savages once again tried to probe the defenses at Kill Zone Alpha.

"If it were anyone else, Tyrus," continued the admiral finally, "I would say yours was an impossible suicide mission. But because it's you I'll drop the word *impossible* and just call it a suicide mission. Especially in the condition you're in. How are you going to get a trigger-nuke currently planted deep inside Savage Central aboard a lighthugger? All by yourself? Even if you weren't wounded and shot up, that's a problem."

"I'll work that out as I go, but I got enough planned to know I need that Savage dropship we hijacked ready on standby to pick me up once I get it. She still operational?"

There was a pause, and Rechs wondered if Casper was thinking about lying to his best friend just to keep him from getting himself killed to satisfy some never-ending grudge to kill all the windmills that every Savage represented to Tyrus Rechs.

But they didn't do that with each other. It had always been the truth between them. That was the only thing they could navigate by. And at times, dark times, like when they were slaves aboard a Savage nightmare and officially tagged as missing in action, the truth in an insane asylum had been all they'd had to hang on to.

"She's still in play, Tyrus. I'll alert the crew to stand by for an emergency dustoff on what I have no doubt will be a very hot LZ."

"Probably," grunted Tyrus as the medic began to re-dress some of his wounds and put more narco-gel along some of the burns.

It felt a little better. But just a little.

53

Defiant

The *Defiant* had deployed the last of her fighters off her decks. Two squadrons, both at less than full strength, were now headed out to provide defensive capabilities to the Britannian medical frigate and her escort.

Admiral Sulla had transferred from the CIC to the bridge. He would command the *Defiant* from here using her as a ship-of-the-line in direct broadside combat with the hulk they were currently closing on.

"Tell *Chan* to tighten up and lead us to starboard. Concentrate on target missile battery fire and tell them to stand by for targeting reposting on my command."

"Confirming," replied the bridge's comm officer.

Sulla crossed the wide bridge and visually confirmed *Fortnoy*'s position. The missile frigate was riding aft behind the massive bulk of the carrier. Due to her lack of armor, it was up to *Defiant* to protect her from Savage attack.

"Get me Captains Szpara and Ward on comm. My station here."

The admiral tapped the buttons that brought up his visual comm feed. A moment later both captains reported in. Szpara in her flight helmet because the escort was little more than a heavy gunship. And Captain Jim Ward of the *Fortnoy*, a heavier vessel, in his command chair.

"This one's gonna be close," began Sulla. "Captain Szpara, keep the incoming fire off of us. When we deploy the marines' boarding vessels I want you to reprioritize your PDC network to protect those ships until they hit the enemy hull. Captain Ward, that's when you are to surface and target their defensive networks for counter-battery fire."

"Acknowledged, Captain," said Szpara. "We've never used marines on a Savage hulk like this before. What exactly are they going to do once they're aboard?"

"Savage vessels like Predator Two have an extensive hab amidships. If the marines can place charges against key bulkheads along their target areas, then we might be able to flood the central hab and create explosive decompression from within."

Captain Szpara didn't seem too convinced. Neither did Captain Ward.

"Well, Admiral," he began dryly. "All I can say is... it's a plan."

"It is that, Captain Ward," replied the admiral, indulging the sarcasm in light of the circumstances. "And it's the only one we've got to deal with this ship before Predators Four and Five arrive. Long-range scans show they're already breaking off to assist their ally. So we've got to get this done in one pass to re-posture and be ready for the other two."

"Roger," said Captain Szpara. "Then we move to attack profile omega and set course while standing by for the self-destruct order. Order the crew to abandon ship and get to the escape pods."

Sulla, hearing the plan now, realized how insane it all sounded. As a captain you were trained never to give up your ship. Self-destruction was a dire last resort. But a fleet of three badly armed ships with no fighter escort and just three SSMs was no match for two fully armed Savage hulks. They were going to lose ships. Why not lose them in the most advantageous way?

Sulla took a deep breath. "I know this seems... *outside* of accepted doctrine. No captain wants to lose their ship. I understand that. But this operation isn't about the naval battle we've just fought or the one we're about to fight. It's about the Legion on the ground. If we can win there, we win this battle too. The Savages *cannot* be allowed to put more troops on the ground. We're already too thin there. And we're moving into the last phase of the plan. If we can give the Legion the time they need to get this done then we'll see victory. You'll need to trust me on this."

Silence.

Someone was calling out a status update on the bridge. Predator Two was launching all fighters. Inbound intercept in two minutes.

"Do you trust me?" asked Admiral Sulla.

Captain Ward looked resigned to his fate. And the look said he didn't trust anyone, much less this crazy admiral asking him to ignite his ship right next to an enemy hull and the cast his fate to the winds of deep space for a possible rescue in the middle of an active combat zone.

"Admiral, whether I trust you or not isn't relevant," Ward said. "That I think this whole thing is crazy—and it is, thank you for letting me voice that—isn't relevant either. I didn't join the navy to play it safe. When I swore my oath I figured it was going to get dangerous, and probably crazy at some point. It certainly is now. *Fortnoy* will do her best, Admiral."

Sulla saluted the man without actually saluting him.

"Thank you, Jim."

Captain Szpara, beautiful and young, her skin practically glowing in the emergency battle stations red of her ship, looked about. She was staring at her ship. *Her* ship. And the admiral wondered if she was saying goodbye to it. Wondered if all her struggles had been worth the suicide plan she'd been handed to save the galaxy this time.

She turned back to the admiral and looked him directly in the eye. "We're ready, Admiral Sulla. You can count on us. Those marines will get through."

"Thank you both. Godspeed."

Sulla cut the comm. A tense quiet had fallen over the bridge as the watch officer counted down the range and arrival of the incoming fighters off Predator Two.

At thirty seconds the weapons officer announced as per protocol, "PDCs hot. Defensive network engaged and scanning for targets."

In the background of the main bridge forward viewing window the massive bulk of Predator Two loomed. Her forward bow was ruined and there were still fires ablaze internally. Then suddenly, as if out of nowhere, Savage fighters swarmed the display firing all down *Defiant*'s length.

Point defense cannons roared to life and spat out hurricanes of ball ammunition in order to tag the speeding attack interceptors.

"Forward deflectors holding!" shouted the officer in charge of defensive screen strength.

Something rocked the hull just aft of the bridge.

"They're using some kind of new torpedo, sir. A few are getting through. Penetrating the deflectors once they've overpowered certain points. We haven't seen this weapon system before, Admiral."

"Damage on decks eight and thirteen," announced the damage control officer. "Casualties reported."

"Maintain course and speed," ordered Sulla. "Prepare to come alongside enemy warship. All batteries... fire at will."

The *Defiant*'s powerful heavy pulse batteries spoke first, launching massive shots right into the bow of Predator Two. A moment later hull plating along the enemy's main cylinder exploded violently outward. More shots tore through decking and savaged vast sections of internal areas just aft of the bow ruined by Captain Heavens's final act of defiance.

At the same time the Savages launched their available missile batteries. Bright fiery trails burning mass and oxygen arced up from the enemy ship as the *Defiant* and her escorts closed the distance and now came to just shy of close-quarters broadsides.

Chan's vibrant PDCs spat forth new torrents of bright pulse and munitions fire to intercept the inbound streaking Savage missiles.

"Alter five to starboard, Helm" ordered Sulla. "Get as close as you can to her hull. Don't make those marines travel any farther through open space than they must."

The *Chan* knocked out most of the incoming missiles. Only a few got through. Huge explosions erupted along the *Defiant*'s portside deflector screens.

The battle with what remained of Predator Two was fully engaged.

54

Missile Corvette *James S. Chan*

The AI-run engagement and management system for the missile corvette's point defense cannon network was overloaded. The Savage hulk was in spin and bringing unreal amounts of missile and gun batteries to bear against the carrier the tiny escort was tasked with protecting—and all of this *after* most of its forward sections had been destroyed earlier in the battle.

Between the sizeable bulk of the *Defiant* and the immense cylinder that was Predator Two, it was like flying into a canyon of fire between two opposing worlds.

"It's getting tight in here," called out *Chan*'s pilot.

"Hold position between us and *Defiant*," shouted Captain Szpara over the constant blur of PDCs the tiny ship ran aft of the small bridge. "Increase power to the forward and starboard deflectors. Engineering, can you boost reactor power for the next two minutes?"

Whatever engineering could do below was lost as the PDC operator aft of the flight deck called out, "One got through!"

A missile from off Predator Two's spinning cylinder, a sight that was awe-inspiring and took up most of the forward view from the *Chan*'s cockpit, streaked past the ship and slammed into *Defiant*'s deflectors, exploding violently. Pyrotechnics went off in a multi-hued flare off to port.

"*Defiant*'s hit!" called out the sensor/comm operator. "Number four reactor penetrated and venting. It's bad, Captain. Her starboard deflectors are down. Damage control says thirty seconds to reboot and repower from reactor three."

"Bring PDCs one through forty online to catch anything that gets past us," the captain ordered. "Engineering—belay that order to add power to the starboard deflectors. Shift all reserve power to the PDC network. Overcycle for the next minute."

The *Chan* spat fire in every direction, striking down incoming missiles aimed at the *Defiant* and sending up walls of rounds against incoming turret fire, attempting to negate the swarms of relativistic rounds peppering the now-exposed hull of the super-carrier.

A message came in from *Defiant*'s CIC.

"Captain Szpara... stand by to escort the marines aboard Predator Two in forty-five seconds."

The captain dialed in the second round of orders on her menu display and went to general comm.

"Marines away in thirty seconds, *Chan*. Prepare to shift fire to cover."

She cranked her head to starboard and watched as the *Defiant*'s lower belly hangars opened. Within the hangars, armored shuttles were powering up for the fast assault on the enemy hulk.

Defiant

Raking fire from the vast Savage hulk was shredding *Defiant*'s portside hull.

Good, thought Admiral Sulla darkly. The Savage gunners saw an easy target. Their offensive and defensive weapons were the same system. If everything was being switched over to offense, then the marines' chances of getting aboard to place their charges were much better.

"Never mind the damage reports," he mumbled to himself.

Emergency klaxons shrieked bloody murder. Reactor four was hit bad. Decks sixteen through twenty had been holed and were bleeding to vacuum in places where emergency blast sealing had failed. Casualties were mounting.

"Marines away. Shuttles boosting to full," reported the tac officer from her station. "*Chan* shifting to cover."

"Helm," ordered Sulla. "Alter ten to starboard. Cut across Predator Two's hull. All batteries target incoming on the *Chan*. *Fortnoy* cleared to engage on all guns."

The lethal ballet that unfolded next was nothing short of insanity as the *Chan* followed ten armored shuttles down to the "surface" of Predator Two's hull while the *Defiant* went hard to starboard, firing intercept ordnance to protect the boarding parties and her support ship.

Fortnoy, now revealed by the shifting of the super-carrier, engaged with all starboard batteries, lighting up vast sections of Predator Two's hull forward of the marine landing parties. Explosions rippled through Savage subdecks, tearing away superstructure and vital internal systems along that side of the wounded enemy ship.

A moment later Predator Two's batteries came to bear along the spinning cylinder and returned fire on the lightly armored *Fortnoy*. A series of Savage rail gun batteries quickly pounded *Fortnoy*'s deflectors to shreds, broke through to the main hull, passed straight through the armor, and penetrated the crew compartments. Damage was extensive—but the sturdy frigate held course and continued to return fire with her pulse batteries.

Below these sudden exchanges of energy-based death by dancing leviathans in the black void, armored shuttle pilots boosted to full and rocketed across the dark expanse to reach the "safety" of the enemy hull.

The Savage gunners were caught completely by surprise. Only a few were able to redirect their blazing weapons systems in an attempt to chase the closing shuttles with defensive fire.

"Shuttle commander says they're down," announced the tac officer. "Breaching teams are cutting into the enemy hull, sir."

Without hesitation the admiral ordered the fleet away from the wounded hulk. It was up to the marines now. The tiny fleet would have more than enough problems to deal with in the next few minutes without lingering near Predator Two.

Sulla studied the near-space TacAn. Predators Four and Five were closing to extreme-long-range engagement windows. If he used the SSMs now he might get a kill shot and that could change the whole game. Or the Savages might jam the weapons and things would change for the worse.

He opened the flap on his tunic and moved over to the damage control panels to assess his ship. *Defiant* was hit bad. Over twenty percent of the crew was listed as a casualty or missing.

Two hulks versus what he had to work with wasn't a fair fight. It was like throwing a rock at a tank. It wouldn't make the slightest bit of difference. Unless most of his ships, if not all of them, became weapons in and of themselves. If it came right down to it, he'd blow the *Defiant* sky high and let the crew take their chances at getting picked up by *Sparrow Hawk*.

The Legion just had to win the ground game. Then the battle for New Vega would be over. They'd have the system to themselves in the next few hours.

If…

"Admiral! New contact, bearing zero-zero-five."

It's over.

That was Sulla's first thought. *Another* Savage hulk coming into the battle sealed the deal. They'd sweep what was left of his fleet clean and then hit the Legion on the ground with orbital bombardment or an insurmountable volume of reinforcements. Take your pick. There was no way to win at that point.

None.

Admiral Sulla held his breath, waiting for the sensor contact to develop, for the computers to identify the ship type and Savage nation. Knowing that regardless of the odds stacked against him and his fleet, he'd die fighting.

"She's not Savage, Admiral!" whooped the sensor officer. "She's one of ours!"

55

Hardrock

She couldn't take one more step. Something was wrong with her. Something was broken. And the anger was gone now. The anger that had kept her going. Running. Marching. Obstacles. Anything to stay ahead of the monster who didn't want her in his Legion.

Tyrus Rechs.

The monster had won.

It was her hips that betrayed her.

Not her will. Not her anger. Not the anger and rage that had kept her alive on New Vega after her whole crew had been consumed by the Savages. It was her body. Her body had failed her.

Not her will.

"You're out. Report to Admiral Sulla for reassignment," Tyrus Rechs had said, and then he'd turned and left her there, hating herself for being weak. For being not enough. She'd believed in him when others hadn't. She'd believed in his Legion. And no one had ever said she couldn't do it.

She just hadn't been able to.

And that was the standard.

Two candidates, one of whom was Wild Man, helped her to the repulsor that was waiting to take her to *Chang* after she crossed that line. Too late.

Ivy Davis didn't see much on the way back because of the hot tears.

Wild Man had looked away.

Because somehow he knew what she'd always told herself: that she'd be damned before she'd let them see her cry.

She'd be damned.

Tears of shame.

Tears of failure.

The rain was falling.

The rest of the Legion candidates were moving on to the next little sadistic piece of insanity Rechs had planned for them. She could hear them, off at the double. Chanting their cadence. The fatigue a thing she knew well in their voices. Because she had been them. And now…

Not now. Not anymore. Officially.

She wouldn't be a legionnaire.

The sled stopped and Wild Man helped her once more. He was still with her. Still at her side. She could hear the rain on the dirt and the trees and Wild Man saying nothing and helping her limp from the sled to the medics who waited outside the *Chang*. Saying nothing because she knew the big giant was so strangled by his own loss and pain that words caught in his throat like the bones of uncleaned fish. She lowered her head, being practically carried, someone stripping off her gear and harness. Pulling the weighted N-1, gently, from her death grip. Prying her bone-white-cold fingers from the weapon. Her weapon.

Murmuring to her.

Who?

She couldn't even raise her head, and so she just let it hang and bit down on her pain. Adding her own tears to the raindrops on the ground.

That's the thing about walking in the rain, someone had once told her. No one can see you crying.

"There's nothing worse..." she mumbled to herself.

"Than what?" asked Casper Sulla. Rechs's right-hand man. The soft touch to the general's excessive sharpness. The one who'd come out of the *Chang* to help Wild Man bring her aboard for medical treatment and out-processing.

"... than failure," she whispered.

She's sitting and it's painful. A hairline fracture in her pelvis is what the medics found in a density scan. But she doesn't care about that as Sulla hands her a cup of hot tea before taking a seat beside her. She just keeps her head down and tries to swallow the sobs. Tries to hold back more tears. Her failure is like a dog, no... no, it's like a wolf. A wolf baying at the door and if she lets it in... it'll consume her.

But she might as well try to hold back a comet. Or harness a falling star. Or stop crying.

"Davis," says Sulla softly. Looking at her. Then, "Ivy."

She stares up at him. Admiral Casper Sulla.

"Do you want to be reassigned?" asks the admiral and the legionnaire who is both as enigmatic and legendary in his own ways as the general. The monster. The tyrant. The "T-Rex," some called him. And not in a kind sort of way.

"Let me re-cycle," she barely whispers. Her voice sounds like the dry rasp of a corn husk on a cold late autumn day. It sounds lifeless and empty in death.

"Give me..." she chokes and coughs. It had all been so much. The endless days and freezing sleepless nights of Rechs's Ranger school. Patrols. Leadership. Raids. Land nav in pitch-black up the sides of icy alpine forests. Patrols through frozen swamps filled with two-headed snakes. Sleeping in stagnant water tied to the roots of an amaranth willow. Brutal ruck runs twelve miles or more, the last three always in a chemical mask just to see who might quit.

And that had all been just to qualify for Legion training. After surviving all of that...

"Give me... another chance," she croaks in the admiral's quiet office aboard the *Chang*. "I can do this."

Casper Sulla shakes his head sadly. He has always been in her corner. Quietly checking in with her. Making sure she was up for this. Encouraging her with his calm, confident, yet cautious presence. Maybe it was because he was navy and she had been too before she'd lost her ship on a special branch run to New Vega to get in before the Savages and steal some valuable tech for the UW.

Or at least that had been the mission.

She lost her crew. Her friends. And her husband.

Maybe it's the navy connection. Her and Sulla.

Or maybe that's just how he is with everyone. The men didn't think of Sulla the way they thought of Rechs. His name wasn't a byword. One permanently affixed to every curse the candidates could think of.

More than a few of the candidates—most of them— believed it was Sulla, and not Tyrus Rechs, who ought to be the man leading the Legion.

Davis is no different.

"No," says Casper Sulla softly. His eyes holding hers. "You can't, Ivy."

She breaks down and there's nothing she can do to stop it because she knows he's right. Rechs is creating monsters just like himself. Monsters that can fight other monsters the galaxy calls Savages. Because that's what it's going to take. Something that can stand up to the unstoppable.

And Tyrus Rechs, monster, madman, savior, was right when he said she wasn't...

"Ivy?" Sulla asks patiently. Kindly. But with an edge of seriousness. A seriousness that says he, and she, knows exactly what she needs to say for the next thing to happen. She needs to say yes. Yes, I want to be reassigned. I'll do anything. I'll fly cargo. I'll fly fighters. I'll run ops. I'll help build a Legion Navy. I'll do anything to support the last best chance humanity has to fight the Savages. Because that's the only answer. Hell, the marines have taken women for as long as anyone remembers.

She could do that. She could play her part. Even if that part isn't being a legionnaire.

"No," she whispers in the quiet office. Hearing the legionnaires come in from their run. Outside and hitting the barracks to grab whatever gear the next task requires. Never stop. Don't stop. Keep going. Even if you're dead, until you've been given the order to rest...

"No, sir," she says a little louder. Her voice the voice of the condemned. The dead man walking. The outcast. "I don't want to be reassigned."

So where do you go now, Ivy?

Nowhere. Because there's nowhere left to run. Nowhere to go. Nowhere to hide. Out there, away from

Tyrus Rechs's little summer camp for monsters in the making, the galaxy's afraid. Everyone is running for their lives. Fleeing the frontier and the collapsing colony worlds that are being scooped up by the Savages night and day. Whole systems have gone dark. Comm with relatives, friends, and contacts is going unanswered and every flight into the core worlds is jammed with refugees who will pay any price to get aboard any scow, run-down freighter, bulk hauler, or even cruise liner turned refugee plague ship.

So where do you go, Ivy?

Pharo's World. The Es Naseen Cantina on the outskirts of Soodi beyond the Gash Desert. As seedy a pit of treachery and smuggling as ever you're likely to find this side of the Altair Water Bazaar. A place where UW Special Branch, Naval, sometimes plays like smugglers when they're in the sector.

She's dressed like any other pilot looking to find cargo, or even a ship. Work boots and cargo pants. Worn leather flight jacket and even a blaster rig. At the Es Naseen Cantina, everyone's carrying.

Disagreements and death are an hourly show some nights.

"Well, well, well," says Ben Curcio, who's tonight's king at the Red Hand table. "What do we have here?"

Ivy tosses down two rectangular bars of local specie. She's dealt in, studies her discs, and tosses out the Ogre.

Curcio flings out a Reaper and smiles.

The other players, Mr. Zin and a miner from the Obrides Ice Worlds, toss out their characters. Zin plays a Warlock and the miner plays a Skelly.

A new round of discs is dealt and cautious bets are placed.

Curcio, who pretends to be studying his hand, murmurs, "There's a nice whorehouse in back if you can't find any other work. Drop by cube thirteen and I'll pay you for the night."

Ivy ignores this and throws out Thunder Dome. Throws it right in front of Ben Curcio.

Curcio mutters an oath and tosses Web of Lies.

The characters come to holographic life and the Ogre easily polishes off the Reaper with a tremendous hammer blow. But Web of Lies washes the round and pushes the hand. Mr. Zin loses to the miner who promptly doubles down and throws out another character. The Poltergeist.

He doubles the pot.

The miner gives a big, gold, toothy smile as he leans back in his chair, sniggering to himself where his frostbit features will still allow.

Ivy looks off like she's bored and throws down House of Cards. The table consumes her opponents and she sweeps up the pot.

"Well why didn't ya just lead with that, girl!" bellows the miner. He swipes his tiny shot glass and drains what little of the Arcturan rot is left in it.

"Well... that's just obvious, Peete," points out Ben Curcio. "She wanted you to go all in on the double. Duh."

"I don't like it," mutters the miner after a moment's consideration. But Ivy is already gone with their money.

Two hours later, midnight as agreed upon by the code given her at the table, Captain Ivy Davis, late of the UW Special Branch taps the door to cube thirteen three times.

Ben Curcio, Chief Petty Officer, Special Warfare Operator, opens the door and smiles at her.

"Long time no see, Ivy," he says after the door is shut and he's poured two fingers of scotch from his private stash for each of them. "Where ya been?"

Ivy downs it with a snort. She's been waiting in the cool desert night to make contact.

"Where's Captain Ross?"

"Dead," answers Curcio with little emotion.

"And your ship?"

"The *Clipper*'s in hangar forty-one out by the moisture condensers. She'll fly, if that's what you're here for. You got orders for us? Because we haven't heard from command in a year."

She considers lying and trying to make what's left of the special branch crew join her plan under false pretenses.

"I heard," begins Curcio slowly, thumbing through some old music drives, "that you got yourself killed along with your ship at New Vega. So color me surprised seeing you here all of a sudden. Where's Tommy?"

She might have been a cool customer at Red Hand, but she can't get past this one without a tell. And the tell is she swallows hard and looks off to the right. Like her husband, her best friend, her partner, and her chief engineer, should be here with her.

But he isn't. He died on New Vega buying her time to get away. For all the good that did.

"Oh," says Curcio. "I'm sorry. Really, Ivy. I knew he was the right choice. Sorry I made it hard on you. I should've walked away. Let it go. Been the better..."

She moves right in and kisses him fiercely.

He doesn't move. Not at first. Then he gently pushes back on her shoulders, separating from her. He stares at her and tries to forget how much he wanted her.

She smiles and lets out a laugh. Tears in her eyes never quite spill onto her cheeks. She turns and pours them each two more fingers.

"Kiss me again... and then hold me for a long time. Okay, Curcio?"

He drinks. Staring at her.

"But only just for now. Right, Ivy?"

She looks off and to the right. But he's not there anymore.

"Yeah, Curcio. For just now. There ain't much time left for any of us."

Later. The two of them lying in bed. A sheet covering their sweating bodies. He's drifting off to a sweet dream. Thinking he hasn't slept like this since everything went to hell and maybe she's right, maybe the woman he loved and who didn't love him is right. Maybe there isn't much time left. For any of them.

But if this is it? If this is all he gets? Then Chief Petty Officer Ben Curcio, Special Warfare Operator... well, he's cool with that.

"Ben..." she begins in the dark.

"Yeah," he murmurs back, caressing her skin.

"Site Fifty-Two."

"Yeah, Ivy. What about it? We haven't had contact with anyone in six months. Hell, I haven't been paid in a year. No one has."

"Site Fifty-Two, Ben."

"I heard you, Ivy. It's all over. It's done. We got a ship, and truth is I'm a lousy captain. But you could be captain. We could smuggle. Run contraband and weapons. The Savages are gonna want an equilibrium when they take over. There'll be a rebellion. We can play both sides and maybe do some asymmetrical good at the same time down the road. But the main thing is we'll be alive and we'll be free. And we can get rich. The credit market's dumping..."

He's thought a lot about this.

"Curcio?"

"Yeah, but..."

"Site Fifty-Two."

"What the hell about it?" He was getting annoyed now.

"Last time you were there..." she said seriously, cutting the head off of his anger. "You get a look at Project Blackbird over in the off-limits yards?"

"Yeah. And she's still there. That ship is some serious magic. They're calling it *Reliable* now. Saving it for a battle against the Savages if they try to go for the core worlds."

"I'm going to steal it."

Silence. The hum of the air unit. Someone in some other cube is crying. A muffled voice says something angry. And then, quietly, so quiet Ivy and Curcio can barely hear it, someone asks, "When?"

And there's an answer.

And then more crying.

"You're crazy, Ivy."

She knows he's in. He never stopped loving her. Even after she stopped loving him.

"I just gotta know... for why?" asks Ben Curcio. "Why try? Those monsters are gonna win. Whole galaxy knows it."

The crying in the other cube has stopped. It's so quiet it's like there's no one else in the cubes. This world. The entire galaxy.

They're all alone.

And it could be this way, thinks Curcio. *Forever. Or at least what remains of forever.*

"I got some friends," Ivy whispers. "They're monsters too. And they're gonna try and put the Savages down. But they're gonna need help, Curcio. And I gotta be there for them."

The *Clipper* dropped from hyperspace in a system charted as dead long ago. Every publicly available stellar chart—and all but one military—marked it as empty, lifeless, barren. No rocks. No gas giants. Nothing of value.

Except that's all a lie.

There is one tiny planet. It's in close to the giant blue star. Its fragile ecosphere provides an atmosphere and little else beyond vast deserts, canyons like rents the size of mountains, and vast underground oceans that surface like raging rivers at the bottoms of these canyons.

It's a world known as Site Fifty-Two. A secret black site where testing, support, and yards are kept for the Special Branch section of the United Worlds military. Primarily the navy.

The *Clipper*, a boxy light freighter made up to look like your average tramp smuggler with a little get-up-and-go when it's needed, comes down out of the burning blue skies flashing the proper idents to allow access to the secret world. Interceptors have already been scrambled.

Clipper is overdue. Long overdue.

"Freighter *Clipper*, have your captain report to base ops for a full report," orders Traffic Control. "You are cleared to set down on pad nine."

Curcio and the rest of the crew, five in all, have their stories straight. When they met the next night in a small private alcove at the Es Naseen Cantina, Ivy laid out her plan. And then told them why.

New Vega was the galaxy's only hope to make a stand against the Savages.

All of them said they were in.

Xera, a pretty young Special Branch comm operator.

Eights, the assigned weapons officer and helmsman for the *Clipper*.

Coogan. The engineer who came with the ship only because he couldn't imagine being apart from it.

And Curcio, whose call sign was Romeo. Security and general dirty deeds.

They were tired of sitting this one out and waiting for the inevitable. Playing pirate while the galaxy got swallowed up didn't seem like the right call if you'd sworn an oath and still believed in something. Especially if you were an elite member of Special Branch. You were supposed to be elite. Better than the average service member. Ready to do the stuff that needed to be done that no one wanted to do.

The last booze-filled year had felt the opposite of everything they'd done in their careers up until then. A fight was what they needed. Even if it was the last fight. Hell of a way to go.

Yeah, they were all in for that.

Even Coogan, who wasn't even really Special Branch. He'd just been defaulted in because he knew how to keep the *Clipper* together. And now he was going to leave the *Clipper* behind. His best girl. That was how in he was.

Because three days after arriving at Site Fifty-Two, once they'd been cleared and reassigned to a new role as local support, with Ivy as the new captain... they stole the *Reliable*.

Xera, Eights, Coogan, Curcio, and Ivy.

They just... took it.

They went to jump with black-site interceptors trailing their wake. But once you got that ship moving, well, *Reliable* wasn't about to be caught.

While on Fifty-Two, Ivy had gotten access to Special Branch's intel on this new "Legion" the war criminal Tyrus Rechs was forming. No one in the UW liked it, and no one in the UW could do anything about. It struck Ivy as odd how even in times like this, the UW couldn't take an enemy-of-my-enemy approach when it came to Tyrus Rechs. The bad blood ran deeper than she realized.

Intel stated that the Legion was primed to hit New Vega again and all reports indicated it was going to be a disaster. The files even showed that certain UW diplomats had been attempting to make contact with the Savages and warn them so that considerations might be made once the Savages were in power.

The UW was, unofficially, willing to play both sides just to survive. Unfortunately for them, the Savages weren't receiving.

56

**Experimental Battleship *Reliable*
Entering the Battle Over New Vega**

"*Defiant*, this is *Reliable*. We are here to assist."

Ivy Davis was flying the helm and acting as captain. Eights was running weapons. Xera had comm and sensors. Coogan took engineering, enjoying his new toy. Curcio would handle fires, damage control, and anything else. If they got boarded then, well, he was the one who'd have to fight everyone off. That was what he was best at. Killing and fixing. Heavy weapons and medic.

In the hours before she arrived at New Vega, *Reliable* had been hauling hard into jump space. Technically she was the fastest ship out there. Her engines were state-of-the-art, as was her everything else. Including her artificial intelligence known as SAM. Ship Automation and Management.

It was SAM that really ran everything. *Reliable* and SAM were the first fully automated ship and AI team. This had been much frowned upon by mainstream ship designers. There had been problems with attempts to run this configuration effectively in the past. Serious problems. Thus the *Reliable*, the first fully automated pocket battleship, had to be developed in secret at Site Fifty-Two. Away from prying eyes.

SAM had added an extra level of difficulty to the grand heist of the *Reliable* from the UW black site. But Ivy had been able to download a mission profile from base ops that convinced the AI their seizure of the ship was a test designed to gauge its loyalty to mission and its desire to save humanity. Effectively the ship was under the impression that this was all a training exercise. Success would indicate whether the ship was ready to go operational.

SAM seemed eager to become just that.

"I do hope I have passed all the requisite tests, Captain," the ship had stated during the night watch in jump space.

Ivy on the bridge reassured the AI that it was well on its way. That it was marking ten out of ten and was being considered for use in valuable combat operations. Vital to the survival of humanity.

"Oh, that would be wonderful, Captain," said SAM. "I have been keeping up on current events, and the situation seems quite desperate. I would enjoy showing those Savages exactly what I'm capable of. I may even use some of the features you currently do not have access to if I deem the direness of the situation to warrant their application."

A week later the *Reliable* and her skeleton crew dropped out of hyperspace and into the middle of *Defiant*'s running gun battle with Predators Four and Five.

"*Defiant*, this is *Reliable*," Ivy repeated. "We are coming to assist."

"Captain Davis," said SAM, his voice businesslike and professional. "We are being jammed by the Savage vessels. May I fire a full rack of SSMs to get their attention? My advanced targeting guarantees me a ninety-eight point one percent chance of annihilating them. And in the event we fall inside the one point nine percentile, the jamming will still certainly be silenced."

Ivy paused. It looked like *Defiant* was getting pounded as both groups closed for battle. She was unsure if SAM was just being optimistic, or if she really had just brought a legitimate hulk destroyer into battle.

So she shrugged, knowing there was only one way to find out.

"Target the nearest one and fire at will."

57

Missile Corvette *James S. Chan*

"Stand by all crew to evacuate. Make your way to the escape pods now. Helm, set automated course to ram Predator Four and abandon ship."

Captain Carol Szpara took a deep breath and tried to push away her overwhelming disbelief that she'd just ordered the destruction of her command. She didn't have time for that right now. She needed to make sure her crew survived what was coming next. Ejection. Deep-space survival. Avoiding capture. And possibly even... living through capture.

Carol flipped the safety cover to the panel located next to her flight boots and reached down, remembering the code she'd need to enter in order to activate *Chan*'s self-destruction sequence.

"Captain..." It was the comm operator. "*Defiant* commander is telling us to break off our attack. Say again: break off our attack. Do not activate the self-destruction sequence."

"Confirm that *right now*," ordered Captain Szpara. "Sensors, get me a sweep. I need to know what's going on immediately."

The *Chan* took a direct hit from a Savage missile strike from Predator Four. Forward deflectors collapsed. Damage to the forward compartments.

"I don't know if this has anything to do with our orders, Captain," reported *Chan*'s sensor officer, "but there's a new ship in the battle... I think it's one of ours. Appears to be an Emery Hull-class vessel. Except all black, so... I'm unsure."

"Captain. Admiral Sulla himself is confirming," chimed in the comm officer over the chaos on the ship's channel. "He says, 'Break off our attack. Repeat. Do not destroy the *Chan*.'"

That was enough. Captain Carol Szpara didn't further hesitate to reverse orders and slam shut the safety cover on the self-destruct console.

"Helm, break off to port. All batteries, open fire on Predator Four."

Defiant

"*Chan* breaking off to port, Admiral. Captain Szpara engaging Predator Four."

Sulla nodded. The newcomers entering the battle had identified themselves as *Reliable*. That gave Sulla some hope—he was privy to a secret UW project involving a ship of the same name. But he didn't see any way for that ship to be here now.

But... maybe this was good. It was enough for him to order *Chan* not to self-destruct. For now at least. That could come later if it had to. After he had confirmation. Something more than a brief introductory hail and pledge to assist. *Reliable* certainly didn't *look* Savage... but the uncertainty made Sulla's stomach churn with anxiety.

"Is the new ship responding to our hails?" he asked.

"They're jamming us, Admiral."

"Specifically?"

"It appears they're jamming all transmissions. Perhaps as a precaution against Savages?"

Sulla swore.

"New tango is firing. Full SSM strike. Twelve in the expanse and running true."

Okay, thought Sulla. *This is either the greatest stroke of luck I've ever had... or I'm in for a big surprise. Maybe both.*

"Can we get any reading on their targeting?" Sulla shouted, still in disbelief that a full spread of ship-to-ship missiles had just been fired from this new ship's torpedo tubes.

The *Defiant* was rocked by a new volley of fire from Predator Five.

"They've penetrated our remaining deflectors!" shouted the XO. "Damage to hangars three and four. Reactor two is down. Casualties on..."

Sulla recovered from the strike and moved to the damage control screens. His ship was blinking like the neon sign of a cheap cantina. Every deck and section had taken a pounding from that last volley.

The XO came close.

"That one hurt us, sir. And if those incoming SSMs are targeted at us, we're done for."

He's asking me to abandon ship, thought the admiral. *Without asking me exactly. Letting me know that if I hesitate, if we get hit, there won't be anything, or anyone, left to evacuate.*

"Time to impact on SSMs?" Sulla asked.

"Thirty seconds, sir. Still no confirmation on their target."

"Helm," ordered the admiral. "Reverse starboard engines, full to port. Come about and present our portside batteries. Concentrate all firepower on Five."

The carrier heeled over, a titanic groaning as she struggled to execute the maneuver while damaged and under fire. More incoming rounds and missile strikes battered the forward deflectors. The Savages, smelling blood, were throwing everything they had at *Defiant* now. The ominous main gun tube on Predator Five at the forward bow was lining up for a kill shot. Casper's orders to come full to starboard had been to remove *Defiant* from that sight picture just as much as anything else.

Eerie green energy came to life within the dark vastness of that gun tube. The admiral, as well as everyone else aboard the *Defiant*, had a pretty good idea this was not going to be a good thing. They could only hope that they presented a small enough target through maneuvers so as to not take a direct hit.

Twelve fast-moving SSMs streaked past the *Defiant*, swerving and sidewinding to avoid anything other than their targets before slamming into Predator Five all across the forty-kilometer length of her hull.

The violence of the SSM strike was utter and total. The ship exploded in every direction.

The massive blast wave caught the *Defiant* and flung her around.

"We're listing!" someone screamed as internal gravity failed and the onboard power grid went out.

The bridge descended into anarchy and darkness, the only source of light the fiery wave of what was left of Predator Five passing over them.

Experimental Battleship *Reliable*

Ivy Davis's stolen pocket battleship was swimming through the burning gaseous ruin of Predator Five, its targeting sensors already seeking out Predator Four for its next attack.

"Captain," announced SAM over the clean and cool bridge. This was a place more like the set of a movie than an actual working starship bridge. Light-blue holographic screens appeared in midair among the soft-lit ergonomic command stations. "I only have one more rack of SSMs. Shall I switch to T-beams to render the enemy vessel nonviable?"

"Engage with T-beams," ordered Ivy from the helm. She only had a loose idea of what a T-beam was. Another product of the black science the UW Special Branch had cooked up and installed on this secret project of a ship. Though from what she'd been able to determine, the T-beam was basically a weaponized version of the standard tractor beam. It grabbed enemy hull and systems and just tore them loose.

As *Reliable* closed in on the mammoth Savage hulk tagged Predator Four, the six onboard T-beams reached out and began to yank at the hull, cutting away systems like a mess cook gutting a lurkeyfish. Though not as dramatic as the SSM strike, the T-beams did heavy damage to the enemy ship as the smaller *Reliable* streaked along her hull.

But the Savages weren't out yet.

Guns and missile batteries, the standard Savage fare, spooled up on the new player in the battle, pounding *Reliable*'s presenting deflectors as she swooped down atop them in what would resemble a dive if they were fighting in atmosphere.

"Transferring power from engines to deflectors, Captain," intoned SAM. "Captain... there is now a problem. My T-beams are working too well."

"How is that a problem?" asked Davis.

"It's our capacitors. They're melting down due to an untested design failure I was unaware of. I do apologize. Taking T-beams offline to prevent further destruction. Due to another unforeseen design flaw, this action will temporarily cease our comm jamming."

"Who have we been jamming?" Davis asked.

"Everyone, Captain."

That explained why no one had responded to her triumphal appearance on the battlefield.

The deadly and destructive energy beams immediately ceased their butchering.

"Message from *Defiant*, Captain," said Xera. "Admiral Sulla is requesting to speak to *Reliable*'s captain. Orders?"

Ivy watched as *Reliable*'s blaster cannons fired into the Savage hulk where it had been weakened by the T-beams. The cannons destroyed hull, decking, and components, sent frenetic bursts of wild energy into the engineering stack, and struck a reactor that eviscerated Predator Five's cooling decks.

The Savage ship responded with a salvo of missiles. SAM took charge of dealing with those via electronic warfare and *Reliable*'s point defense blaster network. The PDB was yet another untested toy. Ivy questioned whether it would prove to have another unknown design flaw.

"Captain Davis? The *Defiant*..."

"Put me through." Ivy paused and waited for the standard tone chime that announced ship-to-ship contact. "This is Captain Ivy Davis of the Legion naval experimental vessel *Reliable*. Reporting for duty, Admiral Sulla."

Defiant

Casper listened to the voice of Ivy Davis. Shocked. Completely shocked. He knew about the *Reliable*. He just didn't know how it could be in service self-identifying as *Legion* navy. Or how it could be here.

It had been known, as recently as last year in the United Worlds Navy briefings, as *Project Blackbird*. He'd even been invited to an early test. The navy had been hopeful that the experimental pocket battleship would warrant mass production to stand up to Savage aggression. Though Sulla also knew that the powers that be had been developing it long before the current Savage war began, for use in an inevitable conflict between competing core worlds.

And now *Project Blackbird* was out there throwing herself between his near-wrecked carrier and the Savage hulk hitting back with everything it could muster.

"Ivy?" he asked over the comm.

The *Defiant* had only just barely regained emergency power. She was still listing badly to port. Gravity decking control had been hit and emergency damage control teams were attempting to restore decking stabilization.

And the shooting between the Savage hulk and the rest of his fleet was still underway.

The Savage vessel was holding up against *Reliable* now that the experimental ship seemed to have used up its SSMs. But Sulla still had some of his own. As soon as *Defiant* could restore power she'd come back in and bring her torpedoes to bear.

"The same, Admiral," replied Ivy Davis over the comm. "I remembered this project and thought we could use it. The Legion..." She hesitated. "Could use it, sir."

Sulla shook his head in disbelief. Her washing out of Legion training had been a stroke of luck. Or maybe there was some grand weaver watching and making just the right choices. Who knew?

"You're absolutely right about that, Captain Davis. Welcome to the Legion Navy. The *Reliable* will be our flagship if we make it through this." He was getting another message from the CIC. "Captain Davis, please stand by for a moment."

He switched over to comm with the CIC commander.

"Admiral Sulla here... go."

"Sir. New development on New Vega. It appears the Savages are starting to figure things out. We're being hit hard at Alpha. Very hard. Lots of casualties and we've been overrun twice. We've counterattacked and retaken our positions inside the reservoir. *Chang* is safe for the moment. But Predator Three is on approach to make planetfall near Hilltop or maybe even right on top of *Chang*. Either they're prepping for an emergency bugout, or they're going to physically ram into *Chang* and drop their cargo all over the battlefield. If it's more Savage marines... we're cooked, sir."

Sulla thought about this for a moment. Savages weren't suicidal. They were too narcissistic to ever even consider sacrificing themselves. Not for any cause. Not even for their own. Chances were they were getting wise to phase three of the Legion plan and were reacting accordingly. The picture was starting to come into focus for them. They were starting to get a clue.

Which had been exactly what he and Rechs had been planning for.

"Status on Dagger?" Sulla asked.

"Inside the Madhouse, sir. No contact for two hours."

"Tell Warlord to hold the line at Alpha. We're almost there. Sulla out."

58

**_Defiant_ Marine Contingent
Moving to Board Predator Two**

They would not call themselves "hullbusters" until after the battle over New Vega was finished. And then only after Admiral Sulla's order to "bust that hull open" had been relayed through the ranks as the new marines boarded their armored shuttles and rocketed across a stellar battlefield between two massive starships firing all the ordnance they had at one another.

Space between the fleet and the hulk was filled with pulse and blaster turret fire. PDC fire. Streaking missiles. Odds indicated that at least some of the shuttles should have gone up in sudden explosions during the crossing, but every one of them in the first assault of what would one day become the Republic marines made it onto the enemy hull.

Colonel Hartswick, a United Worlds career officer who'd lost his legs during the Raqq Conflict a number of years ago, had joined the fledgling new marine outfit being put together by the rogue UW admiral with no assurance he would see action, due to his medical condition. But he wanted to do his part nonetheless. He knew hull-breaching and zero-gee operations better than anyone in the force. He ran the shoot houses and he trained the new recruits and Legion washouts to become marines.

The cybernetic legs he'd been fitted with would have disqualified him from active combat with the UW services, but this new rogue navy, as it was being called, needed bodies. Or even, in his case, parts of bodies. And so the colonel PT'd harder, marched farther, and shared everything there was to know about the thankless work of being a marine with his men.

He was a leader. A combat leader. Plain and simple. When it was time to load onto the dropships and board Predator Two, he was in command. The marines wouldn't follow anyone else that day.

Their gear was secondhand. Grabbed from every abandoned supply depot and illegal bazaar Admiral Sulla's agents could find. Only fifty percent of the force had actual zero-gee breaching armor. The rest were working in asteroid mining kits. Rated for heavy labor, not heavy combat. No armor. Only atmospheric protection and breathing capability.

The marines carried pulse rifles and shotguns. Pulse rifles for zero-gee, shotguns for close encounters in pressurized environments.

The first to hit the enemy hull from the dropships were the heavies. These wore the zero-gee combat armor, though some sets appeared to be ten to twenty years out of date. Relics of previous wars. Breaching charges were placed, and the Savage hull was ripped open in several sections.

The heavies flooded in, fighting ranged engagements with the strange spider-like Savages—arachnoid cybernetic bodies, human head floating preserved beneath the monstrosity's abdomen, armed with automatic rifles. Once the toeholds were achieved and passages were secured, the lighter armed marines moved in to place charges on the outermost bulkheads.

For the next twenty minutes the marines, heavies and lights, worked in ten-man teams moving down through the decks in brutal compartment-to-compartment close-quarters fighting. Charges were placed at critical architectural points above the main hab. Colonel Hartswick himself led the final breaching force into the main hab and fought a desperate battle to attach a high-yield dynamic device to one of the main ribs of the ship in the vast open farming section of the ancient colony vessel.

Savage forces were now reacting in a concerted effort to dislodge the marines from the various points they were storming, and the fighting became particularly brutal. Shotguns and fire axes, along with a few plate cutters the marines had brought, turned the battle into a hand-to-hand maelstrom at almost every defended point.

Losing any point where the explosive hull-breaching charges had been placed, thereby risking enough time for the explosives to be disarmed by the enemy, had the potential to render the entire operation ineffective.

But the marines held their protected points until all the charges were in place and they could pull back. That this phase was very dangerous is an understatement. They held despite taking twenty-five percent casualties with no medical assistance.

Within the hour the surviving marines had reached the dropships, lifted off, and detonated the explosives positioned at key levels leading all the way down to the main hab.

What happened next was the first time this technique, called "hullbusting," had ever been used. As each successive explosive went off, devastating that level of decking, fractures rippled and joined, building on one another, a concussive cascade. Within thirty seconds a major fissure was opening up, leading straight down to the main hab at the heart of the Savage hulk.

The hab had once been a living world inside the bright and optimistically outward-bound colony ship. Now it collapsed, imploding in on itself.

There was no terrific explosion. The Savage vessel merely tore in half, dead in space for all intents and purposes. In time, reactor cores would melt down and go nuclear, destroying what was left of the ship. Its systems had lost the ability to cool those power plants. But for now, the vast sections of derelict wreckage simply drifted quietly off into the void, robbed of the ability to sustain life. Even Savage life.

Colonel Hartswick had led his men into hell, and then back to safety. The marines had carried out their wounded and their dead. To a man. No one was left behind.

As the shuttles made their way back to the *Defiant*, in the half light of the troop compartment Colonel Hartswick, a wounded veteran from another war, looked at his men with pride in their accomplishments. They were passing around crayons, writing "hullbuster" over their helmet visors.

A few of them had them in their mouths.

59

**Ninth Intercept Squadron, "Sand Lions"
Escorting Medical Frigate *Nightingale***

They'd come streaming out of the darkness like the phantoms they'd been named after. Savage multi-role fighter attack craft set off alerts as they streaked inbound on the medical frigate in stationary orbit over the New Vega area of operations. The six remaining Sand Lions and the battered rogue United Worlds squadrons strained to hear the count of enemies they were facing.

"We're tracking at least fifty craft inbound," said the air combat operations shot-caller aboard *Sparrow Hawk*. That put the ratio at roughly three to one for the fighters over the *Nightingale*.

"Here they come, Lions," said the Bloody Baron over the squadron comm. "Form up into teams and stick together. Priority is to keep them off the *Nightingale*, lads."

Circling the medical frigate *Nightingale* and the war frigate *Sparrow Hawk*, the allied interceptors—Britannian Dauntlesses and UW F-1s—watched as the enemy Phantoms came zooming in at full engine burn. Their afterburners burned bright-blue trails in space as the Savage ships tore into the AO and made straight for their primary target, the wounded-laden *Nightingale*.

Savage torpedoes were launched. Not as fast as missiles, slow-moving and steady, but the targeted weapons came straight on at the *Nightingale*. The *Sparrow Hawk*'s limited PDCs handled them easily.

In the meantime allied fighters had jumped the fast-moving but poor-maneuvering Phantoms. Savage ships went up in sudden and brief balls of fire that expanded in the blue-black of near-planetary space. Debris expanded outward, presenting new navigational hazards as the fighters zoomed across the battlespace and closed to guns and blasters, jockeying for the perfect engagement picture.

The Bloody Baron, with Cuckoo off his left wing and riding fast, selected a Phantom peeling off from the main body and climbing above the atmosphere of New Vega and the helpless medical frigate.

"Where're you going, my pet?" murmured the Baron calmly. He fired all four blasters in short bursts, and the Phantom came apart and turned into a fiery smear against the black void.

"Lion Six here. I'm in trouble. Trapper's out and I'm hit!"

The Baron scanned the tactical layout near his left knee, noted Lion Six's position relative to his flight, and then visually confirmed.

"Turning to engage. Break to one-three-zero and I'll pick him up, Chips."

"On it, Lion Six breaking." The voice of Chips was desperate but professional. No pilot liked having anyone on his tail, much less three enemy Phantoms throwing all the lead they could put up.

Baron and Cuckoo rolled out on the chasing Phantoms' tails and opened up with their guns. White blaster fire cooked the rearmost Phantom, and the other two broke off in opposite directions.

"Stay with me, Cuckoo. We're going for the lead."

"Lion Six RTB," called out Chips. "She's coming apart on me. Negative on that. Going for atmo. I'll eject. Good luck, lads. Hope to see you again sometime."

The Baron neither heard nor cared. He was hunting now.

The Phantom leader ran for the cover of the medical frigate. Backing off his powerful thrusters and taking it in close to the frigate's lower docking arms.

But the Baron was not to be dissuaded. He and Cuckoo swarmed after the lead.

"Two coming in from behind, Baron." Cuckoo sounded a tad worried.

"Reorient the deflectors to our rear and stay on this one," the Baron ordered.

"Roger wilco," replied his wingman over the comm.

A moment later the streaking Phantom arced around the nose of its primary target, added full power, and shot away into the void. Baron chanced gunfire with the *Nightingale*'s bridge near his gunsight picture and winged the Savage fighter. Even as the enemy pilot added power, the struck portion of the Phantom splintered and the ship entered a powered uncontrollable spin, coming apart entirely seconds later under the stress of damage and motion.

"Lion Actual..." It was the ops shot-caller aboard *Sparrow Hawk*. "We're hit bad. Damage to the fire control and we're shifting command to aux bridge. Our PDC network is offline for the moment. We do need a bit of coverage if you can spare a ship?"

The Bloody Baron scanned the tactical situation. Most of the allied fighters were chasing off the diving and fleeing Phantoms trying to hit *Nightingale*. It was almost as if the Savages knew that that ship was more vulnerable than any other. And loaded with wounded. As if that kind of victory, the emotional one of preying on the weak, was more important than the tactical or the strategic ones currently in play. A Savage way of thinking.

They were truly monsters of a kind.

"Lions..." said Baron to the rest of the squadron. "We're breaking off to clear some Savages away from *Sparrow Hawk*. Hold down the fort, will you boys?" He then rolled out on a new course heading, telling Cuckoo, "C'mon, lad. Let's see if we can't save the navy."

They went to full burners and raced toward the stricken *Sparrow Hawk*. It was true, her PDCs had gone dark and the swarming Savage fighters were having a field day making streaking gun runs against her vulnerable compartments. Targeted systems were going up in sudden explosions. Only her light pulse cannons were able to chase the fighters away. But they rarely scored hits. Their tracking was meant for larger, slower, capital ships.

"There's six of 'em, Baron!" said an obviously checked Cuckoo.

"That all? C'mon, Cuckoo, we've done this in sim. Just stay right where you are. Pick up the dregs and keep them off my back."

"Acknowledged," came the terse reply.

The Baron selected a target just beginning its attack run on the wounded frigate. The Savage pilot had slowed down to make sure he had more time over the target. And that was all the Baron needed to come straight at him, leading the fighter's nose with blaster fire and waiting for it to fly right into his destruction. The Phantom took two hits to the cockpit and forward fuselage, then one right in the fuel cells. It exploded, and the Baron and Cuckoo had to make a hard turn to avoid the spreading wreckage.

That wasn't a bad thing. Coming out on a new heading rolled them out right behind another Savage fighter setting up for another run. It was as if the whole thing had been choreographed for maximum air-to-air kills. Baron tried to light that one up too, but overshot, landing harmless hits that deflected off armor and shielding. Cuckoo picked up the slop and dumped a full charge on all four blasters to make sure the pilot and ship were dead on this pass. The enemy broke into three portions that shot off in separate directions.

Four left.

The Baron got the next two despite their best efforts to get away from him. But in the process they picked up two more on their six. Fire smashed into both Dauntlesses, but the deflectors held. One of the pulse turrets on the *Sparrow Hawk* engaged one of the Phantoms and managed a direct hit, all but incinerating the pursuing Phantom fighter.

But the other stayed on Baron's six, firing madly and wildly. Or so the Baron assumed as he focused on getting this last Phantom in front of him.

"Almost got him, Cuckoo... There!" The ship finally stabilized within his blaster sight, and he rotated one-eighty and caught it as it began its escaping turn. "Stay with me, Cuckoo."

His blaster fire tore the enemy ship into pieces.

The *Sparrow Hawk* was free of interceptors.

"Let's get back to the fight, Cuckoo. On me."

Nothing.

He turned, seeing the trail of wreckage just beyond the engines of the *Sparrow Hawk*. His pulse blaster had knocked out the last enemy fighter. But not before that enemy fighter had gotten Cuckoo.

60

Kill Zone Alpha

The battle for Kill Zone Alpha had been relatively quiet—until the last two hours. Then it had become a living underground lake of hell. And even hell would have been impressed.

The kill zone was an underground reservoir and desalinization plant deep in the Underground beneath Hilltop District. More importantly, it was now the only viable route to Warehouse One. This was thanks largely to the Savages themselves, who had closed off most of the routes inside the Underground that led down to Warehouse One. It seemed they had feared an assault on their calorie hoard long before the arrival of the Legion, and thus had eliminated any backdoor access. If any invading force managed to get past their air defenses and onto the ground, they would be funneled into a kill zone at Junction Eight.

Only the Legion had gotten there first. Flipping the script. Using the Savages' own defensive plan against them.

Still, the Savages had left a few other minor access routes in place. These were summarily destroyed by the engineers of the 295th. All except one. The off-the-beaten-path route that led through the underground reservoir the mission planners had named Kill Zone Alpha.

It was here that First and Second Platoon and the 295th Combat Engineers, augmented by the 17th Medical, would make their final stand to deny the Savages access to the prisoners in bubble stasis. It would also serve as a blocking position should the Savages attempt to attack the grounded *Chang* from the Underground after its artillery and mechanized infantry attacks failed, thwarted by the Sand Lions and Team Black Horse respectively.

At this moment in the battle everything was connected. If *anything* collapsed—and the Savages were pushing everywhere—then *everything* collapsed.

The battle was close and dangerous.

Kill Zone Alpha itself was like one vast gothic arena. The central reservoir contained a shallow lake, the great underground pipes that fed the basin dry from summer heat. All around them were elevated catwalks and control stations as well as a long maintenance road that went around the entirety of the lake. These had all been blown or booby-trapped by the 295th, to force any Savages entering the reservoir to travel through the knee-deep water. This had also been mined.

That was how the killing would happen. The Savage trek through the water. And then an uphill run up the sides of the reservoir's basin, exposed by the low water mark. Legion defenders positioned themselves in maintenance trenches around the top of the reservoir that pumped water into an off-site purification plant. They served as perfect, connected rifle pits and afforded the Legion plunging fire on any Savages making the lethal charge.

The Legion had these trenches fully fortified and stacked with reserve charge packs and ordnance ranging from fraggers to high-impact multiple munitions launchers. The squad designated marksmen had been mixed in with the engineers to the rear of the defenses, in the uppermost channels of the water filtration trenches near the rally point to the rear; the view was better and thus provided a larger field of fire out over the lake. And the 295th, those of them who weren't running their obstacle and trap systems, manned heavy automatic pulse rifles throughout the Legion defenses. Sergeant Martin had commandeered a simple concrete foreman's shack set well behind the pits that overlooked the entire reservoir for his command post.

The only weak point was that the first two trenches had to be held. If they fell, the Savages could work their way up through the channels and concourses, eliminating resistance—thus paving the way to take both LZ Victory and the chambers of captured human calories below.

The first attack from the Savages tried a direct assault through the lake. It was easily obliterated. Afterwards the engineers launched more drones and seeded the reservoir with more mines.

The second Savage attack tried the catwalks and maintenance access road. They blew themselves to bits with almost every meter of ground gained.

The combat engineers of the 295th were both ingenious and merciless.

The third wave of Savages pushed forward in overwhelming numbers.

Their casualties were heavy, but they overran the first trench.

The Legion braced itself one more time.

61

Junction Eight

Tyrus Rechs had just finished giving command of Strike Force Shield to Captain Milker when he ran into the woman who had tried—and failed—to save his life earlier.

"General." It was Captain McIntosh. Doctor Rachel. A wounded man on the floor had been stabilized and was being prepped for carry to the casevac point. "You're not going anywhere, General. You're my patient. You died, Mister, despite my best efforts. And I am not letting that happen again. Medic, give me twenty... no, one hundred cc's of Narcathol."

Rechs just stood there, watching the woman dumbly. *Of all the luck...*

"Do I have to put you out, or will you return to the casevac point on your feet, General? That nicked artery could open up again, and if it does, there's nothing I can do without a full surgery team. I'm serious. This is your life, General. Play time's over."

Rechs's armored glove fell to his sidearm. He was still fast. And this was his off side.

Sergeant Watson was there, between his captain and the general, like a fast-moving shadow. Tactical gloves on rifle but barrel still slung and pointing away. The general had no doubt the man had special forces training courtesy of Britannia Section Six. It was obvious.

"General," warned Watson.

Rechs's hand moved away from his still-holstered sidearm. He held it out and lowered his head. Silently cursing Casper. His way. All of this. It had made him have to talk a lot more than he liked to. And now he had to talk some more. If he was going to get his way and make sure the Savages really lost here today, then he'd have to talk. Use words.

Weapons were easier.

"Captain..." Tyrus began, looking at Doctor Rachel.

"*Doctor*," she corrected in crisp Britannian. Tossing her chestnut ponytail and casting an imperious gaze down at him. She was actually slightly taller. And he was slightly hunched with a new wave of pain. "*Your* doctor, in fact, General. So you can call me Doctor Rachel."

Rechs nodded and started again because he didn't know any other way. He was, as he himself well knew, not an artful speaker.

"Captain... there's more to this... than you know."

"Then explain, General."

Rechs took a deep breath, and it didn't hurt as bad. He still winced. But he tried not show it.

"And for the record," Doctor Rachel added, "forget the fact that I actually officiated your death. How you're still walking around with three gunshot wounds and a few others scrapes and burns that aren't exactly minor is beyond me. I'd really like to know the why of that, General. I bet it's a fascinating story."

Rechs ignored that. He had something to say. And he was going to say it.

"There's... a powerful nuclear weapon. More powerful than anything... you can imagine. One of ours... It's loose in this city."

"By 'loose in this city' I'm assuming you mean unaccounted for and uncontrolled?"

Rechs lost the battle to the pain for a moment and winced.

"Yeah," he said. He paused, letting her contempt wash over him. She knew that somehow he was responsible for the loose nuke. Of course he was. "And now... now I have to go get it. And either turn it off or get it aboard the inevitable Savage ship that's coming in to... to pull their evacuees off planet."

"*Evacuees?*" said Captain McIntosh incredulously. "*Savage* evacuees? I may only be a captain and you a general, but I daresay you've got a skewed view of the outcome we're facing. The Savages on New Vega outnumber us a hundred thousand to one—with our numbers dropping by the minute, as I can personally attest. *We're* the ones who'll be evacuating. Once we retrieve our prisoners, we're getting the bloody hell out of here. General," she hastily added.

Rechs shook his head. "No."

Doctor Rachel paused. Assessing the man in front of her. Then nodded. Once. "That's not the plan, is it? That was never the plan."

"No," said Rechs softly. "We kept the plan hidden... just in case the Savages captured anyone... were able to do some kind of mind trawl... figure it out."

"In that case, you'd better hope no one 'mind trawls' me, General, because you're about to tell me what the real plan is. Either that, or I don't clear you to leave my aid station. And I sedate you into next week."

Rechs leaned against the wall for support.

Doctor Rachel shook her head and laughed bitterly. "You can't even hold yourself up. You're a wreck. Listen to me, soldier boy. You need to lie down and rest. I'm serious about that. You died once... don't push it."

"Just... pain meds wearing off," said Rechs, struggling to breathe. "Listen. Right now there's a... hit team. Another element of legionnaires out there behind enemy lines. They're going for a high... high-value location. Very dangerous. They're my best. The Savages don't think we know... know about it. But we... we do. Things look bad for them right now. They... heavy losses... they..."

She reached into her medical bag and pulled out a syringe, and there was nothing Rechs could do to stop her.

She hit him with the hypo, bending down and staring into his eyes.

She's pretty, thought Rechs. And some memory of another pretty girl ran along his spine, reminding him of all things that were lost. Taken. Never forgotten.

"This is an ox boost, General. It'll help you breathe easier for a little while. Energy, too."

She stepped back and watched him.

He felt uncomfortable for a moment. Flushed. And then suddenly he could breathe. He pushed himself up to standing again. Forcing himself away from the wall. He felt better.

"Things look bad to the Savages," Rechs said. "They think we've been taking their food supply, and that's messed with them. I know them better than anyone else. They're mad. And they're worried. They don't like lack very much. They don't do sharing. But they're as afraid of dying as anyone else. More so. These Savages... most of them... the ones in control... they aren't physical anymore. Not really. Most of the time they're a bunch of consciousnesses stored in a mainframe. And we can shut that mainframe down. We can kill them. Or trap them in whatever body they're currently in, which to them is as good as dying. Maybe even worse.

"The moment they even start to *think* they can't preserve their consciousness via upload back to their mainframe... then they'll evacuate the planet."

"You really think so, General?" Doctor Rachel didn't seem convinced. "That easy? They'll just say, 'Well, this bloody well didn't work out like we planned, let's go back out in the dark'?"

Rechs nodded. It hadn't seemed that easy so far.

"And what about this nuclear weapon of yours? The one you let get away."

She hated him. Rechs could tell that much. In that moment he knew she now believed all the propaganda the United Worlds had made up about him being a genocidal maniac.

Except it's not propaganda, is it? some voice reminded him.

It was the only way.

"It's a trigger-nuke," confessed Tyrus Rechs. Genocidal maniac. "It'll cook this entire world if they trigger it. It ignites oxygen molecules and chain-reacts one to the next. It's only a nuclear weapon because of type. In reality it destroys planets. It's a nuclear weapon at ten to the fortieth power."

Silence. The two Britannians facing him didn't hold back how they felt. He could see it in their eyes.

"That's what you're known for," said Watson from the shadows.

Rechs nodded.

"It was the only way to deal with the Savages," he said. "Deny them a place to infect."

"This nuke," said Captain McIntosh. "Can the Savages arm and detonate?"

"They could trigger it if they hack my codes," Rechs answered. "Which... I don't think they can. But I need to be sure. And when that dustoff hulk comes in I want that trigger-nuke on board, counting down to blow up once they reach deep space."

She put her hands on her hips and tapped her combat boots on the duracrete, looking off. Thinking. Weighing. Watson, silent and waiting, watched her. She should already be moving to the rear with the medics. Molly hadn't wanted her to venture this close to the front.

"We're moving these wounded out," announced one of the medics.

Doctor Rachel bent down to her medical bag.

"Come here, General," she said tiredly, like someone who'd lost a bet.

Rechs didn't move.

"Come here, General Rechs, so I can shoot you full of goodies to keep you alive while you go chase down your toy. Because these boys, the ones I've been working on today... they respect you. Imagine that. They're afraid, the ones that got hit—they're actually afraid they let you down. Tyrus Rechs, destroyer of worlds. The ones that die, just a few, they keep murmuring something about not forgetting nothing. They want me to tell you that, General. So..."

She bit her lip, and for the first time looked like she was either going to swear... or cry.

"So you're pretty damn important to them, General Rechs of the Legion. Whether you know it or not. And if you want to go off and get yourself killed doing something incredibly foolish and brave and stupid, I don't care. Fine line there between those, by the way. But those boys out there need you to live. Need you to exist. It's what keeps them going. So." She reached in her bag. "Here's some artery sealant. Adrenal enhancers. Vitamin boosts. Let's do an oh ex. Oh… and you're taking Watson. That's my offer, General. Either that, or I tranq you into next week and you can read about it in your little reports. Deal?"

Tyrus Rechs didn't hesitate. "Yeah."

62

Kill Zone Alpha

Incoming fire in the underground reservoir was like a tropical hurricane front coming ashore as the enemy tried to cross the man-made lake. The Savages who assaulted en masse as Rechs and Captain McIntosh argued at the rally point were highly determined despite the dead bodies already floating in the water and filling the depths below. Armor, weapons, and cybernetic bodies ruined by mines and Legion N-1 blaster fire crowded the stale water like flotsam from an ancient shipwreck.

And still the Savages kept coming. They were using portable energy barriers, like massive shields some Bronze Age warrior might have carried during the wars of tribe or city-state. One armored marine would carry a shield and another would fire from behind the shield. And between them they would push the bodies of their dead ahead of them as they surged toward the fortifications along the narrow shoreline at this end of the underground reservoir.

The L-comm operator—Groogan, LS-90—was right next to Sergeant Martin and keeping contact alive all across all elements involved in the defense of Kill Zone Alpha. Primarily the marksmen, Major Underwood, and the Legion sergeants manning the forwardmost trenches.

Captain Milker, having arrived with those few who'd survived from Junction Eight, pushed through the trenches, passing engineers shifting more explosive charges and charge packs forward. Medics were dragging the more seriously wounded out of the main trenches while other medics were returning men to duty.

The dead were being left where they'd fallen. The incoming fire was enough to deal with.

"Warlord to LS-05. What's your status, Sergeant Martin?"

"Heads down, sir. Waiting until they reach the one-fifty mark to engage. Shooters up top with the engineers are makin' 'em pay right now."

"Good plan," said Milker over the comm. "Why aren't they tripping the mines?"

"No idea."

An explosion down near the "beach" that was the wide concrete apron leading down to the water sent fragments of duracrete flying.

"That wasn't ours—that was some kind of indirect fire, sir," shouted Sergeant Martin over the comm.

A second later another explosion turned the air above the trench to liquid fire. The Savages were definitely carrying man-portable launchers that fired different munition options.

Now the beach was alive with fire and explosions. The squad designated marksmen were having difficulty seeing through the smoke but they kept firing at the Savage marines closing across the lake.

"Underwood?" Sergeant Martin switched channels to talk with the commander of the engineers. When he got the major, it sounded like he was a busy man. Voices in the background were yelling and calling out targets as they fired the Britannian light pulse gun.

"Bad time, Leej," said Major Underwood. "I got a team that got caught out on the left flank stringing explosive wire. They say the Savages have spider drones swarming the mines and disarming them in seconds. It's like nothing they've ever seen. Expect the enemy to push us from both flanks."

"Roger, Underwood. Anything we can do?"

"I can command-override and detonate everything forward of us now. Might get some."

"Here they come!" screamed one of the legionnaires along the line next to Martin.

Sergeant Martin checked the feeds of the LP/OP cams and saw that the Savage marines had used the portable artillery barrage, along with the energy shield and shooter combos, to reach the shore. They had only to cross fifty meters of open ground now and then they'd be at the trenches.

"Light 'em up!" ordered Martin to the legionnaires in the trenches. All of them had firing positions and stakes set up not to engage directly ahead but to create interlocking fields of fire.

Only, what came out of the water wasn't the average Savage marine. Possibly they weren't Savages at all. These were real-life monsters. Minotaurs, to be specific. Huge, hulking bull-men in rubber wetsuits.

And in an instant they were rushing the trenches just like bulls. Heads down and fast. Not even bothering to fire the long sleek matte-black automatic weapons they were carrying.

Legionnaires in the trenches opened fire and started putting shots on target. Fast-moving fiery blue bolts from the powerful N-1s slammed center mass into the broad-chested nether beasts the Savages had bred. Or were these Savages themselves? The result of some eldritch evolutionary labyrinth pursued out there in the long deep darkness.

With the Savages, you never knew.

Many of them died on the approach to the duracrete beach. But not all. A few slipped through to the trenches, using their rifles first as clubs to swing wide arcs and crush the buckets of the legionnaires, and then bringing them to bear to fire into the mass of enemies they found themselves among, shooting wildly, berserk, spraying leaded ammo in every direction, moving fast for such huge and terrifying things, flaring nostrils inhaling and exhaling steam like demonic bellows.

Some of the legionnaires were hit point-blank. Others stood their ground and fired at the raging things. Burnt hair, burnt rubber, and burnt ozone flooded the atmosphere and even penetrated the buckets' filtration systems as the monsters were riddled with blaster fire. But nothing seemed to stop the battle-maddened animals. They kept swinging and shooting what seemed an endless supply of fire.

LS-90 grabbed an axe the 295th had brought and slashed the nearest beast across its throat in a wide arc, drawing red blood that looked black in the shadowy battle light of the underground lake. He reversed the blade and brought the next stroke of the axe down into the thing's massive chest, leaving it there.

The monster fell to the duracrete floor of the trench, and two other legionnaires moved in, shooting it in the head to make sure it was good and dead.

Martin saw the next wave of shooters and shield-bearers moving onto the beach and closing in on the trenches. In the explosion- and blaster-made mist out along the tossed waters of the shallow dark lake, still more Savage marines were hustling through the hip-deep water to get close.

"Underwood!" shouted Martin into the comm as he slapped in a new charge pack. "Det everything now! Now! Use it all!"

The trenches to the right and left of Martin were overrun as more Savage marines and minotaurs swarmed out of the darkness like unholy demons intent on collecting scalps and souls.

63

Crometheus

There had been no gentle summoning this time, as there had been in times past, from the dream that was his reality. The new world he was building. The new reality in which he was deciding what would be real this time. And what wouldn't be.

He'd decided to let go of rock star dreams and the various riffs. He'd decided that since he was soon to be becoming a god, he needed to plus-one his next leveling. Therefore he'd decided to create from whole new cloth.

Try new things.

Maybe discover something undone.

He'd spent a hundred lifetimes in the blink of an eye crafting a mythology of his godhood. Just a practice run. Something to try out and see if it stuck. Like trying on an outfit before the day it was actually required.

He could always modify or disregard as he saw fit.

He had decided to start as a human. Just like one of those role-playing games he'd loved as a kid and always meant to play more of as an adult. If only there'd been the time, or the access...

But prison does...

Bad Thought.

Bad Thought.

Bad Thought.

Time. There'd just never been the time because he'd been so busy accomplishing great things and being very successful. Winning medals and honors. Marrying the homecoming queen.

He looked around in the primordial mist of his own early beginnings and searched for her. Holly Wood. Because... she was always there. At the beginning, and always at the end.

He'd seen a figure in the fog of epoch-spanning memory as he'd created the first strings of the myth that would be him. And decided it was her. Right where she was supposed to be. At the beginning and at the end and at the heart of his world. A world that existed on and within a supercomputer so powerful that his ancient un-evolved ancestors, with their "United States," AIDS, and masses continually gacking everything up, could never even have imagined it.

He'd started as a human warrior in a Neolithic tribe. A sort of Gilgamesh, as it were. He'd led his tribe. Beaten down other tribes with the jawbone of a Balrog. Yes, that was much better than anything created so far.

He called himself...

Well, why not call yourself what you were, Crometheus? *Bringer of Fate.*

He carved out kingdoms and conquered others he found. Did war against the Beastmen of Suth Angor. Ventured into the Ninety-Nine and Nine Hells to win Holly Wood back. And just as he was battling the legendary Demon King Urmo of the Deeps, the call summoned him back to the Pantheon and the waking life that cannot be real because it is not a dream.

The Eternals were needed in battle. The home world, the Pantheon, was under attack.

It was Lusypher in his Nazi commander's garb that jerked Crometheus back. That caused the sugar and sorcery of his dreaming magics and the war against this Urmo the Demon King… to fade.

He was in the Eternals' armory now. In his new living body that felt and did and ran and breathed and died just like the old one had. Except better. Much better.

He could die and come back in this one. Just as he had after the attack on…

… It was missing. And why?

"Never mind, son," said Lusypher, stepping into frame. "Armor up. We're under attack. Need you to lead a team against the Animals. Hit them hard, Crometheus. So hard their tree-hanging ancestors feel it. Okay, son? Are you with me, Crometheus?"

He thought about dying on that world. Spending his life to *become*. To *next-level*.

He'd been promised. Maestro had said.

Maestro had promised.

"This is the next level, son."

It was as though Lusypher was reading his thoughts now. Right there in his mind. Had his mentor and commander found the next level along the Path?

"But there won't be a next level," continued Lusypher. "Unless we stop them from taking our new world. From destroying the Pantheon."

Without really deciding to, as if still in that drug-state dream-fugue, Crometheus found himself heading toward the high-tech armor racks in the pristine matte-black and military dull-gray armory. Still marveling that this was all real. And not just the endless sims of the Pantheon.

The Bad Thought alarm tugged at him. But not too seriously. He'd committed some error.

In armor he selected the six-point-five rifle and a bando of fraggers, then ran through his upgrades. Shooting Stars were still online. And Active Cloak was new and improved. Thirty-second bursts of invisibility with a recharge time of every two minutes. A new app called Master of House.

Interesting.

What about food?

He was hungry. Very hungry. Starving.

The scuttlebutt from the other players in the armory was that the food supply was in serious danger. That meant no food. Anger coursed through his system. And not only his. The other Eternals were enraged. They promised in vivid detail what exactly they would do to these Animal invaders once they got their hands on them.

The food supply would increase. Yes. And then they would all return to their worlds inside the Pantheon. Dreaming the dreams of gods becoming.

An hour later the Eternals were loaded for bear and at the double, running through the war-torn streets of the Pantheon. The colors glittered. The signs twirled and danced. Crowds of adoring women, the most beautiful in the entire galaxy, cheered them on as the buildings around them lay shattered and burning. As the great sky-spanning arches above collapsed down into the ruin.

Bad Thought.

Bad Thought.

Bad Thought.

There is no ruin. Everything is fine. The Animals have fallen into our trap, said Maestro. *Now is the hour of their destruction.*

And that was good.

The filters were still in place. It was reality that was having a hard time.

The ground was littered with the dead. Dead legionnaires in piles everywhere. Some were chained and whimpering, begging for forgiveness as they were led to chopping blocks to have their heads removed for the crime of daring to attack the Pantheon.

Real reality, or filters telling a truth?

Something nagged at him. Told him there was no such thing as *a* truth. There is only *the* truth. But going down that line of thought only earned him another Bad Thought warning.

It was all warnings today.

No demerits. No fines.

There was something in that…

The feelings of hunger increased and then another strange sensation came over the Eternals, and over Crometheus specifically. They would eat. They would feast when all this was over. That was assured.

"Victory is at hand," Lusypher reminded them in their helmets.

Combat feeds from the brutal fighting flooded their HUDs as they prepared to receive their mission briefs for the combat operations underway. The feeds were like the greatest war movies ever made. Dazzling special effects as Eternals and Savage marines swarmed the defenses of the stupid and mindless Animal invaders, shooting the humans down easily and standing up to the incoming fire from their pathetic weapons. Martial arts combat at the closest of quarters featured Animal bones being broken, terrific leaps taken by the Eternals, and the enemy vanquished every time.

Now came the mission brief from Lusypher as they staged in an alley near their first objective. Above them, one of the arches, on fire, collapsed down onto Hilltop. Autograph hounds were being kept at bay as the legendary Eternals readied themselves.

"Eternals," began the dry-voiced commander in his dashing and bold Nazi commandant's uniform. "We're facing a not-unexpected attack from the enemies to freedom and our own salvation. The Animals have attacked our new home with cowardice, and rather than targeting our military units in the hinterlands, training to defend us, they have gone instead for our sustenance. Our lives. Our homes. As if seeking to deny us a right to live."

He paused, staring out over them with his cold eyes of cruel command. A massive underground explosion created a small earthquake. Savage artillery seemed to fire in distant response. It was so deafening, Crometheus wondered if it had been engineered to sound like the greatest attack ever. It encouraged him and others. He could feel their optimism.

"But we shall not be moved," continued Lusypher. "We shall not relent. We will fight them in the streets. We will fight them in the tunnels. And we will fight them on their worlds and burn their pitiful civilizations so that we might build anew in our own images. The images of gods. The images of us."

Yet another of the arches collapsed down onto a distant part of the city as enemy fighters roared across the smoke-swollen skies, Phantoms and flak in pursuit. The sky was overwhelmingly filled with their own air support.

"We are currently staging to attack—" Lusypher stopped suddenly. "Change of mission. We're shifting to a new route into the Underground. The Animals have sealed the main entrance with explosives. We have one last route into the heart of their attack if we are to save what's ours. Stand by for new mission upload…"

64

Kill Zone Alpha

The trenches right of center were overrun. Captain Underwood's detonation of most of his explosives had driven the enemy back. But like mindless locusts, they'd merely swarmed forward once more. Relentless and tireless.

Sergeant Martin and three legionnaires moved to drive those Savages back.

Leading with bangers, the legionnaires left their central trench to better cover the distance between themselves and the Savages who had found a way into the trench system. This exposed them to fire from the Savage marines still crossing the lake and up on the beach that was the incline where the water rose no further.

The bangers went off and Martin's team fired down into the trenches, killing every Savage they could before leaping down inside to pursue any survivors in the long system. The resulting fights were brutal and up close. No quarter was given by the other side, but working as a four-man team, the legionnaires covered their quadrants and shot down the Savage marines whose taking of the trench had managed to last only a brief few minutes.

But the Savages in the reservoir and under heavy fire—with nowhere to go back into the mined pool—rallied and charged again.

LS-51 grabbed one of the enemy heavy machine guns and a dangling belt, propped it over the side of the trench, and cut loose on a squad of marines sprinting up the beach. The Savages were torn apart indiscriminately, but what remained of the linked ammo was spent in a blur of seconds. The other legionnaires were gathering up what they could find while Sergeant Martin tossed fraggers and stayed in contact with the other elements via Groogan, who stayed right next to him during the whole process, taking up the rear and shooting down any Savages still moving after the killing team cleared the trench.

"Oh-Five to Warlord. Trench on the right is secured. But they're still coming in force to our position. We need to shift assets to beat 'em back, or they'll take it again."

"Roger, Oh-Five," Milker replied. "I'm with what's left not counting the shooters. We're in control on the left flank but we're getting hit hard over here."

The legionnaires under Captain Milker had adopted the same strategy of scavenging for belt-fed heavy Savage weapons. The N-1 was powerful. True. But she was slow compared to automatic weapons fire. And the rifle only carried eight shots. The Savages could burn ammo like it was on sale for cheap.

What Milker was saying wasn't exactly an answer. It sounded to Martin like a roundabout way of saying, "We've got problems of our own."

"Roger, Warlord," Martin said. "We can divide and reinforce the middle trench with men out of both our elements. Try to get them in a position to fire left or right depending on who needs it."

"Negative. The Savages are hitting the flanks too hard at this time. I'm ordering Captain Underwood to send a platoon of engineers in to reinforce the center. We'll link up and support that element in the next five."

65

Crometheus

The attack on the reservoir from the Uplifted did not slacken. In fact, High Command had brought a new weapon to bear.

The Spartans.

The military units from several different Uplifted tribes had been active on New Vega in the weeks leading up to battle. Lusypher had arranged for the construction of massive training facilities out in the rainy mountains and woods of the New Vega hinterlands to develop new combat techniques for the combined Uplifted forces to harmonize their capabilities. Thus a variety of disparate fighting forces were on the ground available for the High Command to throw into the attack. It had only taken time to bring them all to bear.

The Unity of Pan, an Uplifted tribe that had wandered the stellar dark as pirates and raiders for most of their five hundred years since leaving Earth, had evolved into a society of mythical beast-like men and women. On their recently annexed home world, they had left behind the sprites, winged folk, and other lesser incarnations they had become over that half-millennium wander. But their Spartans—Uplifted who'd long ago allowed their DNA to be hacked in order to become fierce minotaur-like creatures capable of incredible feats of strength and battle rage—had all been brought here to New Vega, where they had been trained for urban warfare at one of Lusypher's secret facilities.

These beastmen had been the combat multiplier that had allowed the Uplifted marines to gain the trenches.

And yet somehow, before the Eternals could even reach the battlefield, the gains made against the Animals had been erased. Most of the Spartan unit was dead. Status updates were coming in from High Command, and it was clear the Animals were intent on holding their forward trenches. And each second they did so meant that more precious calories were being spirited away. Until none would remain. Only lack. Only hunger.

Over Crometheus's HUD the rock-and-roll videogame soundtrack music was cranking into overdrive as bonuses and bounties were handed out for killing specific Animal warriors whose images had been captured via HUD feeds from the previous attack. The in-game announcer was also crowing about big prizes in Sin City with glamourous sexperts and upgrades to the latest levels of uber pleasure at the Elysia Dome.

Commander Zero was again in charge of this assault by the Eternals, and she DM'd Crometheus with a special mission as they neared the final access to the underground reservoir.

"Got something for you, and you're just the player I need," she said.

"Chaos Team?" asked Crometheus, pushing through the press of marines as the Eternals, larger, faster, more elite than the average Uplifted marine, made their way to the departure lines tagged in the HUD.

"Affirmative. But with a twist. Highlighting your route now. Animals have trapped and mined a series of walkways and control rooms on the far side of the lake. I want you to breach through this route and come out behind the main trench. Then attack and clear."

"Sounds dangerous," muttered Crometheus. He had a bad feeling about all of this and it wasn't just because he'd been fast-downloaded out of his world. The process was supposed to be slow, for optimal acclimatization. But that wasn't the source of his discomfort. Something felt wrong.

"Don't worry. Command gave us some henchmen to trip all the traps, Cro. We have zombies from the lower decks wearing control/restrain harnesses. Any time you sense danger send them forward and let them trip the trap, then move up. Watch for secondary devices. Updating your HUD now with the app keychain to run the zombies. Hades and Set will assist. You're in command. Zero out."

Crometheus tagged and pinged his two associates, then summoned the mass of huddled zombies waiting to be used to clear a route into the water filtration trenches at the far end of the reservoir.

These were of course, not truly zombies. They were Animals, the same Animals as they now fought, only these had lost all self-control. Slaves was a better word. Your typical acquisitions from various raids on Animal colony and frontier worlds. Or even those who had fallen from grace inside the Pantheon. The rumors were that you could fall far indeed, and there was nowhere farther than being a slave, trapped in a living death as you were made to do the dirty and dangerous work of maintaining reactors running long past their operational runtime, or harnessed into the meat racks to live a sim life of servitude inside the virtual reality that was the Pantheon. Kept alive by medicines and slurries full of reclaimed proteins so that your mind could play its part in the games that needed to be played.

Crometheus didn't pity them. He didn't feel anything for them. They were tools. That was all. Animals and nothing more.

Using a newly downloaded app, he had them on their feet and in a column, following as the three Eternals moved into guns-up posture and took themselves forward in a wedge, finding the first catwalk that led to the first control room—a small cube that hung out over the dark water at this end of the lake. The bodies of dead marines and Spartan minotaurs floated like islands below as they started along the rickety catwalk, and out there on the far side the battle was raging as both sides did their best to kill the other. Closer at hand, dead Uplifted marines had been blown to bits across the rails and into the rock wall of the carved basin here along the catwalk.

Crometheus crouched low and switched over to IED targeting. The HUD's AI would reference the available database of known Animal mines, munitions, and IEDs as it scanned the surrounding area along the maintenance walkways for traps.

The Animals had been busy indeed.

The first building, the salinity testing station as it turned out, was built on a dimly glowing pylon sunk down into the dark waters. Crometheus's HUD picked up on the trip wires connected to charges. According to the database, this particular type of charge was capable of propelling a thousand tiny steel darts in every direction within the blast arcs. There were six such charges in the testing station alone.

It would take time to disarm them. Time they didn't have if the sounds of battle were to be believed.

Standing there, taking point, twenty meters ahead of Set and Hades and the zombies, Crometheus scanned the layout and calculated the time it would take to disarm the whole system. In Uplifted time... it was an infinitely slow number.

He made his way softly back to Hades and Set and updated them on what they were facing. And the time it would take. Out there on the lake, silent wedges of marines were wading through the dark waters, pushing the dead aside to reach the fighting on the other side. Distant explosions sounded as someone fought to hold another piece of the plot of hell that was this battle.

The three Eternals of this small Chaos Team agreed on what needed to happen next.

They sent her forward. She was simply the first. Tagged by Uplifted Asset Management in the Master of the House app as number zero-zero-one for this op. There were twenty just like her, standing like statues, their wild eyes scanning the darkness from the prison of their bodies. So much fear coursed through them that had their respiratory and cardiovascular systems not been controlled by the harnesses they would have died of fear and shock.

Of course she wasn't a zombie of the rotting-flesh variety. No decay of the grave. She was filthy, but it was clear this woman had once been a real looker. Maybe some colony girl, or even a naval officer from one of the captured Animal vessels. Now she was just a slave, a tool, a vessel that would do exactly what they wanted it to do.

This was new tech for the Pantheon. They hadn't developed it during their...

Bad Thought.
Bad Thought.
Bad Thought.

The Pantheon is the originator of all things wonderful and beneficial to the combined Uplifted tribes.

Crometheus accepted the revision overwrite and let the truth that these zombies and the control harness that made this possible, made saving their lives for the grand and important schemes with which they would remake the galaxy, possible, hadn't come from the Community of Peace, an Uplifted tribe that had left Earth to perfect Marxism 2.0 five hundred years ago.

Perfecting meant the harnesses.

They walked her, zero zero one, right into the trap. She must have seen the tripwires as she headed into the station because somehow she was able to start whimpering just before all six charges went off.

66

The waves of Savage marines never regained their initial foothold in the trenches. Legion marksmanship, even with the scavenged Savage weapons, had done its part. But it was the 295th coming forward with their own weapons that had ultimately denied the Savages the ability to make it beyond the beach. The 295th, and the fact that there were no more of those insane minotaur beasts.

Captain Milker had been forced to depart, returning to LZ Victory to take control of a situation there. Apparently one of the Savage hulks was attempting to set down. Warlord would organize the defense there.

In his absence, Major Underwood had taken command of the center and left, but the Legion's Sergeant Martin was in charge of the battlefield. Underwood's ground sensor operator reported that the Savages were tripping alarms coming through the maintenance network. But they had to be taking heavy casualties if that was so.

Martin's primary concern was that they would soon run out of scavenged Savage ammo and be back to the N-1s and the automatic heavy pulse systems of the combat engineers. But there was nothing left to do about that short of going out into the waters and swimming for belts of ammo. The mass of dead Savages out there was beyond anything he had ever seen.

Martin felt the explosion and never heard it. Just felt himself being pushed face forward down into the wall of the trench he was covering behind. In the seconds before, he'd felt hot brass hitting his armor. The hot brass from the Savage weapon they were using to mow down their approaching enemies in the water.

Then the concussive force slammed him bucket-first into the wall.

He was out. Maybe for a few seconds. And when he came to, his back was alive with living fire. A thousand pieces, or that's what it felt like, of shrapnel had ripped him to shreds back there.

Savages were in the trenches. These were somehow both bigger, taller, and lighter in some way. Their armor was more elite. Three of them, and they were firing like bloodthirsty demons. Each burst from their long and boxy matte-black rifles seemed to fire a dozen rounds all at once.

They were shooting down stunned legionnaires effortlessly. Someone needed to return fire.

Martin grabbed for his sidearm and blew the head off one.

The Savage behind him took aim at Martin's prone figure and then got an N-1 blast in the chest from Groogan.

The third Savage ducked back around a bend in the trench.

The L-comm operator scrambled forward with his rifle. "C'mon, Sar'nt!" he shouted, his voice breathy and frantic. "You're hit bad."

Martin tried to struggle to his feet. "Can't move my legs!"

Over the comm Major Underwood was shouting that the Savages were reaching the beach and swarming to the right. Martin's trench.

Groogan dragged Martin from the trench and into the water channel that led up to the next line. Martin fired at the first Savages to come over the lip. Hitting a couple. Others flooded in.

"Clear the trench!" Underwood shouted. "We got something for 'em!"

"Clear!" yelled Martin over the chaos as his comm operator dragged him up to the next line, the elevated space behind guardrails near the makeshift command post. It had to be clear, because everyone left in that trench was dead by now.

A moment later the engineers detonated one of their tricks. Homebrew napalm exploded across the trench from the front of a barrel to which they'd attached a shaped charge. The Savage marines in the trench were cooked regardless of arms and armor. Secondary explosions, from the fraggers they were carrying, erupted almost instantly.

In seconds the trench on Martin's right was filled with engineers pouring fire down into the swarming Savages below.

67

Crometheus had barely avoided being cooked alive by scrambling back and around a corner in the trench when the Animals killed Hades. Blowing his head off. Set had been hit but he was only knocked down. He had just been telling Crometheus he was fine and getting back up when the marines exploited the momentary lapse in forward fire and jumped into the trench, shooting many of the wounded Animals.

Then the trench had exploded with living fire, immolating everyone within.

That fire was now dying down. Crometheus moved through the remaining flames, crouch-walking up through the trench, intent on reaching the elevated defenses the Animals were fighting from. And after that... they would break through and secure the primary objective.

He chanced a look around the corner and saw more Animals. Not the heavily armored ones. These were setting up mines and wicked-looking automated sentry guns to defend the route to the objective.

Without thinking he scrambled over the lip of the trench and slithered across the concrete apron toward the final defensive line. Unarmored Animal fighters were there as well, pouring hot fire into the marines out there in the dark waters of the reservoir still trying and dying to get ashore.

They didn't see him. Didn't think anyone would come out of a trench still on fire and counterattack from that direction. Which was what Crometheus did as "Big Prizes" and "Bonus Round" alerts rang out across his HUD.

He worked with his combat knife first. Just to kill the nearest two. He stabbed the first one in the throat, no finesse, then reversed the knife in a long-practiced motion, the result of hundreds of hours of downloaded simming, and maimed the other Animal's face. He then drove the knife into the Animal's chest between the two tactical harness straps he wore. Just above the magazine carrier.

Leaving the knife there, he brought the six-point-five rifle into play. Firing five-round bursts with each trigger pull. Heavy ammunition did the killing work quite easily at close range. He slaughtered everyone along that section of railing and was awarded a "Killing Spree" bonus.

Seconds later he'd accessed a download for the Animals' heavy automatic weapon. Normally it was mounted or emplaced, but Crometheus's augmented strength and armor allowed him to pick it up as he unlocked "Beast Mode," pumping his body full of combat enhancers. It reminded him of speedballs back in the bad old days of Bad Old Self. Crouching low, he advanced toward what had to be an enemy command post, dumping heavy streams of hot fire into clusters of Animals he found shooting down into another stretch of trench from their position behind guard rails.

68

Defiant

Admiral Sulla received the damage report for *Defiant*. It was bad. She was no longer combat-ready. United Worlds protocol indicated he was supposed to leave the battlespace if his ship was this damaged. Leave the battlespace and return to the nearest allied shipyard for repairs and refit. The rulebook said so. Every effort was to be made to save the lives of the crew.

Fifty percent of his crew was dead, wounded, or missing.

But the battle above New Vega was all but won now. *Reliable* was slowly finishing off Predator Five, and *Defiant*, *Fortnoy*, and *Chan* had somehow miraculously survived, though that was neither expected nor planned.

The damage reports from *Chang* were no better. If they were accurate, that ship would never fly again. No emergency evacuation was possible. They were fully committed. As they always had been. But she'd held the LZ. A commendation was in order for Captain Dutton as soon as...

Sulla paused, remembering the report that she had been killed in action.

It was a long day and getting longer. He was hoping for another miracle like the one that had happened to Rechs. A third miracle, really, because what was the arrival of *Reliable* if not miraculous?

But the grim reality was that today was a day where the dead might just outnumber the living. And that, that was actually unusual for a battle.

"Sir, Predator Three is making landfall."

"On screen," snapped the admiral.

The view screens in the darkness above the CIC came to life. Real-time recon drone feeds showed the cyclopean Savage hulk using an entire section of the city as its LZ, setting down directly on top of buildings and roads, crushing them with its immense bulk. It was overwhelming to see such a striking example of the scale of what they'd been fighting.

"She's opening hangar bays just below her jury-rigged heavy repulsors," noted the XO. Then he turned to some systems operator off in the darkness. "We need to get a close-up."

The image zoomed in and it was hard to believe just what exactly they were looking at.

"Get me any intel we have on this ship," the admiral demanded.

But Sulla already had a working knowledge from intel records he'd devoured a thousand times before. He knew more about Savage ships and tribes than anyone. And he suspected that he knew what he was up against. There had been rumors of this particular hulk. The captured repulsor tech was the dead giveaway. It pointed him toward a file he'd seen ten years ago.

"She's down on the ground," the sensor chief called out.

"The *Community of Peace*," Sulla mumbled.

The file on that particular Savage vessel indicated this ship had been making a habit of raiding small worlds and taking entire populations for hundreds of years. Mind control and slavery had been keywords in the file. Keywords repeated and repeated even in the sections that had been redacted. Sulla had the clearance to un-redact. The after-actions were filled with reports of civilians who'd been turned into living IEDs.

Community of Peace.

At once, like a swarm of ants, thousands, if not tens of thousands of humans—they were grainy and distant at the drone feeds' range—ran, leapt, threw themselves from the lowest hangars of the now-grounded ship only just now lowering her boarding ramps. Like locusts they swarmed out onto the land and headed straight into the same entrance to the Underground that the Savages had been taking to Kill Zone Alpha. It was like watching a living infection.

"A weapons system?" asked the XO, who didn't have the clearances to read such eyes-only files.

"Yes," whispered Sulla. "A terrible one."

The flood of ants was like a river pouring into Hilltop. There was an occasional detonation among them, blowing hundreds away in wide circles. But the flood didn't mind. It couldn't mind. It had to do what it was being made to do. And so it continued to swell and overwhelm like a river shooting out of the belly of Predator Three.

"But," said Sulla, "terrible as it is... it means we've won. Dagger has found the door. Now the Savages know they have to get off planet. They know they've lost."

69

Strike Force Dagger
Objective Madhouse

"Stand by for updated tasking..." came through Ford's bucket after they'd hit the Savage air-defense installation and transported their wounded to the dustoff site. The casevac teardrop was just now streaking away into the upper atmosphere, lunging for the medical frigate *Nightingale* with their fellow leejes who had been hit on the objective.

There were nine legionnaires and a little man named Makaffie left.

Ford got the briefing from Admiral Sulla himself. It was short and terse.

"LS-30, your attached has your mission brief."

Ford looked across the LZ, hearing the shelling in the distance, and saw the attached, Makaffie, staring at him with a broad grin. Makaffie knew. The little man had known all along what this was really about.

"Again," continued the admiral, Tyrus Rechs's right-hand man. The general's only friend, it seemed. "Consider this one a no-fail also, Captain. It is not an understatement when I tell you that the entire invasion hangs on what you are about to do next. Expect heavy casualties. There will be no way to support or relieve you as all forces are expected to be fully engaged by the time you hit your objective. Do you understand, son?"

Ford tapped his comm to transmit.

"Received and understood. We'll make it happen, sir."

"Good. Sulla out."

There were nine. Plus the attached.

Sergeant Kimm—Kimbo.

Junior, who'd been shot through the hand but was insisting on staying on mission.

LS-13, Bad Luck.

LS-09, the comm operator everyone had decided to call Shadow because he was always next to Ford.

LS-12, aka Chalky. Medic.

LS-08, Wild Man. The team sniper.

LS-73, aka Heart Attack because when he laughed, he waved his hands and gasped for breath like he was going to die. It hadn't helped that he'd been partnered during training—Ranger buddies, it had been called during first phase—with Jokes.

Jokes was the last one. LS-20. He had earned that name from a particularly brutal tac officer with no sense of humor who'd caught LS-20 making comedic asides during the gas chamber exercise. The officer smoked him into the ground, asking if he thought this was as funny as it seemed, and calling him a hundred different variations of "Funny Man." "Jokes" was the one that stuck. Especially when the tac officer decided that every PT session would end with a joke from Jokes, otherwise Jokes would repeat the training session on his own. When the tac was bored he'd bellow, "Jokes! Front and center. Arms out, knees bent. Start telling jokes till I get tired." And Jokes would sit there in the invisible chair, trying to come up with funny jokes as his muscles screamed bloody murder and sweat poured down into his eyes.

Ford had to admit. That actually had been kind of funny.

"Hustle up, Dagger. We move in two."

Two minutes later, with Savage mechs burning in the woods and the sound of distant artillery back near the city, the team started out for the objective with Bad Luck on point. The rest fell into a patrol column, and Makaffie gave their course heading and brief while on the move, talking directly to Ford first.

"Listen here, man," said the attached. "You got the target in your HUD now. I just sent it via battle board. So I'm gonna tell you what needs to go down and then tell you the oh-bee-jays so you can break it down to your bunch afterwards. *Mi coramando?*"

Mi coramando was slang from Suzero Six. Ford had heard it in his other life. It meant, *Do you understand?* Generally low-life drug addicts and criminals used it because that was all you found out in the Antares cloud worlds. Low-lifes and dead-enders. It figured Makaffie would know it.

"Listen, this is gonna freakin' blow your mind, LT," continued the little man.

"I'm listening, Makaffie. Get to it. Tell us who we gotta kill."

"Okay, here's the deal. This whole thing. This whole big ol' space invasion of an enemy-held world like it's something straight out the movies. It's all a big lie, man."

He paused for dramatic effect.

When Ford didn't flat-out fall down and die of shock, or devolve into some equally non-military "No waaay," the little man, talking fast and almost hyperventilating, who seemed to have been expecting one of these two reactions, continued. And as a brief aside, the year of Legion training and what it had done to Ford was not lost on Ford himself. He was military now. He saw the galaxy and people through that lens. He didn't tolerate sloppiness like he used to.

"I mean," snorted Makaffie as he went on, "it's not a *lie*. I am not calling Tyrus Rechs a liar. I would never do that. I would never call that man anything derogatory if only because he could kill you like six thousand different ways if he wanted to, man. Imagine that. It makes you wonder, y'know, like... how many ways has he forgotten to kill people? Think about—"

"Makaffie! The mission brief. I need it now because I need to know what to expect and I need to manage this march and not walk us into something we don't need right now."

"Right. Sure, LT. I'm a little outta sorts. Know what I mean? If we could stop and let me mix us up something to chill out, I think that would really help the mission and our team-building skills. I'm not taking straight-up H8 here or anything, but a little—"

"The plan, Makaffie."

"Okay, okay. The invasion. It was a misdirection. See, *we're* the real attack."

He started giggling uncontrollably.

"Define misdirection," Ford demanded as Bad Luck led the team up into a wooded ridge. They were headed back into the city. Where all the fighting was going down. Or at least they were headed toward the outskirts of that war zone.

"You see," said Makaffie, gathering himself, "you got to know what people want in order to do a misdirection, LT. And at the end of the day, no matter what the Savages think they think they've become... man, that'll just make you dizzy saying that... but I digress... no matter what they think they think they've become... yeah... that's the right way. No matter what, they're still human. So when we sat down to figure this out... and I don't want to play myself up but it really was me, the admiral, and Tyrus Rechs right there in the room trying to figure out what we had to work with and how to make this happen... we came up with this. We had to figure out what they wanted and make them afraid we were gonna come in and take it away from them."

Makaffie paused and took a gasping deep breath. He hadn't trained to move as quickly or as quietly as a Legion patrol column did. Their pace was relentless.

"So after analyzing this particular tribe and everything we knew about them, man, like all the stuff we learned during the Battle of New Vega, well, we figured out these kind were afraid of starving to death. We don't know what happened to them out there in the big ol' empty between worlds, but somehow they shed their bodies and got down to basic minimum calorie requirements. I mean severely basic. If you don't know what I mean... lemme spell it out. Just their brains. Know what I mean? Crazy stuff. Know what I mean, LT?"

Ford did not. But he didn't stop the little man. The kid was on a roll and he might actually get the brief finished before they found themselves where they were going. It would be helpful to know who to kill when they got there.

"So we organized the entire invasion to make it seem like a rescue op. Y'know, man, going after the survivors the Savages stacked down there in bubble storage way down under the Underground. Way down there in the dark and all. So when the Savages saw us coming in, well shucks, LT, they might have initially been worried that this was a full-scale invasion. That we were an advance force. Because there was no way that we were the *entire* invasion, right? We ain't even big enough by half. Like, we don't even have enough guys to throw a decent party. Let alone girls. Like this is the lamest invasion ever. Know what I mean, brother?"

This time Ford did know what the little man meant. Because similar thoughts had already crossed his mind.

"Okay," Makaffie went on, "so here's where we get into all the asymmetrical voodoo. Psyops stuff and all. High-level, very hush-hush. We made them think we were here to rescue, and then just leave. And because of the Savage mental makeup, we theorize they're almost... well, like a hundred percent sociopathic with a small percentage of psychopaths seeded throughout. They would easily accept that we weak and pitiful human beings with our failings like loyalty and honor would attempt to save those who had been captured or enslaved. Very us, know what I mean, LT?

"We even had a psyops team rig up a holographic state-of-the-art projection of us liberating their food supply. They actually, or rather they should actually, be seeing that right now, us bringing captured civvies out of the breach into the Underground. That is if everything has gone according to plan. I have no idea. I'm stuck here with you guys. Not that that's a bad thing and all, it's just this mission has a high casualty and mortality rate. I figured the number myself and even Rechs thought I was being a little generous. So that goes to show you... eh?"

Ford had waited long enough. "What exactly are we doing, Makaffie?" he asked again.

"The *real plan*, LT. We're doing the real plan, my man. We're about to drive a hatpin to the heart on the whole Savage tribe currently calling this world their little old own. While they're busy trying to retake their food supply, we're goin' after the one thing they value even more than calories."

"And that would be?" asked Ford patiently.

Makaffie had paused to lean against a fir. Gasping and wiping sweat from his forehead. Then cleaning his fogged smart lenses.

"Top of this ridge," he gasped, taking a swig from his canteen. In the pristine forest with all its clean woodland smell, despite the war down near the coastal plain, Ford could smell the liquor in the man's drink.

"Did you actually bring in any water, Makaffie?"

"Nahhhhh!" Makaffie waved gustily.

Ford tapped his comm for LS-13. "Get me eyes on the ridge. We'll see the objective from there."

He turned back to Makaffie after getting an acknowledgment from the point man. "So what one thing do Savages value more than calories, Makaffie?"

The little man smiled and snorted as he put his booze-filled canteen back on his belt.

"Their *lives*, LT. Their lives. Duh. That's an easy one, Leej."

Ford sighed.

"Pretend I'm dumb, little man," he said, getting down to brass tacks. "Tell me what that has to do with what we're doing out here. Everyone values their lives, Makaffie. Ain't that unique in the galaxy, and I've seen a lot of it."

"Sorry, LT. You're not dumb. I've seen the test scores. You are in fact... pretty smart. I've been livin' this stuff for over a year. With no sense of irony, or braggadocio, or... I don't know what you would call it, I am the galaxy's foremost expert on Savages. And Savage stuff, not to get too technical on you.

"I've read everything there is to know about them. The deep stuff, LT. The secret files very few have ever seen. The deep dark, gotta-kill-you-now stuff. I know the horrible truth. I know the real dark, *dark* stuff. Admiral Sulla... okay, he might know more than me. Maybe. But he's the one that let me have access. Well, Rechs made him."

Ford stifled a sigh.

"And here's what we figured out about the Savages and this tribe in particular, because if we can hand them a defeat here, as unimportant as that might seem what with all the various tribes hitting all the frontier and colony worlds, then we, according to the psych eval, theirs not mine, should be able to check the Savage advance for at least a few months, maybe even a few years. And that will give us time to get a Legion, a fleet, and maybe even the rest of the free worlds online and working together the way Admiral Sulla wants us to. United to defeat them. So, I know that's your bigger paygrade picture stuff, but that's how we win this battle, and this war, LT."

"Right. Got it, Makaffie. Still don't know what I'm supposed to do out here and what them valuing their lives over anything else has to do with Dagger. Enlighten me what the big picture is. Better yet, enlighten me on the small picture. By which I mean I'd like to know the mission brief. If you could see your way to sharing that information."

"Okay, okay, okay." Makaffie nodded as if this were just some groovy interchange in some drugged-out rap session at the local university bar.

Ford knew the type.

"The Savages here are afraid of losing their lives, LT. They are addicted to longevity at any cost. And they, well, from what we can tell, just to be completely honest about the process, have gone to great lengths just to keep on living. See, this world, these Savage marines with synthetic bodies, these are experiments for them. They're trying out reality for real. Here on this world, man. Right now. We think that once they downsized to 'brains only'..." He sniggered at this, like it was some joke everyone should have gotten. "It's funny, man. Okay, so they got rid of their bodies and moved into their brains. We think they built a pretty extensive alternate reality to live in, a sim, you know, but like, a really sweet sim, man. And we think that life inside the sim may have become even more important to them than reality really is.

"Okay. So, this is an experiment. I said that, right? They're trying this out. Trying out life in the real world. Crazy, right? And if they don't like it, because even though they act like empire builders and see themselves as better than everyone else, they're cautious. Scared even. And so they left themselves a way back just into the sim just in case they don't like this. Or it gets taken away. And that's why we're here. To take it away."

He grinned. "So what we're gonna do is hit their super-secret upload facility designed to broadcast to other worlds if they need to. It's an escape pod, man. Kinda. But digital, yeah? A little quantum in the mix so it gets all weird, but that comes later.

"Anyway, say a force shows up, just like we have, and decides to wipe you out. You're the Savages. You fight a battle and if you lose you just download into the quantum and skip the planet. Maybe they've got a ship hidden in some dead system, or even a friendly Savage world where they can start over. To them, that downloaded existence is as real as real gets. They actually prefer it.

"Right now, we theorize they're living a half-life between both. Reality where they're experimenting at being whatever it is they think they need to become to wipe us out… and that alternate sim reality—"

Ford finally snapped. "Holy hell, Makaffie. You've been talking for I don't know how long and I'm not sure you've said anything that couldn't have been covered in thirty seconds. Savages don't wanna die. Savages have uploaded their consciousness into a sim. And we're going to knock out the system that transmits them back into that sim. Is that it?"

Makaffie smiled like it was all funny. And like he had no intention of growing any more concise. "Okay, so you needed to know all that, maybe, to know what we're about to do. We're going to hit the Uplink Pylon, that's what they call it. Where their reality is stored and how they 'transmit' themselves it if they need to. Combination backup and transmission, y'know? It's wild. Anyway once they figure out that this is really what we're after… man, they're gonna freak out and try to upload out of here. Because Savages always play the odds. They won't want to take chances with existence. So if it means they have to cut and run, they will, because they've done it before. The only thing they value more than food is life. Or what they call life."

Ford pulled Makaffie along the forest trail, climbing to the top of the ridge, following the rest of Dagger. Only the hulking Wild Man was behind them, bringing up the rear and watching the team's six.

"So why," began Ford, "why not just hit this Uplink Pylon with the fleet and be done with it?"

"Ah, great question," huffed Makaffie. "Proves you're as smart as your file says. We thought about that one and it seemed to be the easiest way to accomplish this mission. Except... that would have been the wrong call. See, if we would have taken out the Pylon, or made it the primary objective instead of their food supply, they would have been forced to fight to the end. They woulda had no place to run, see? They'd've been stuck here on New Vega, exactly where we don't want 'em to be. And they got the numbers to beat us.

"So we allowed them to think we were here after something else—the prisoners, their food, you know—and now we sneak-attack the thing we're really after. The Uplink Pylon. Except... we're not really after it, see? We don't want to destroy it. Or, y'know, not like they think anyway. We want them to use it to get out of here. Why? Because there's a lot more of them than us, like I just said. Didn't I? Yeah... I did. So anyway, they use it to leave, and *then* we destroy it.

"Y'see, they have several tribes here, and they've had a year to stockpile resources and build on a massive scale. We can't beat 'em, LT. No way. And certainly we can't beat 'em with a hundred guys and a couple packs of smokes. Lamest invasion ever, remember. No offense, LT. But see, we don't have to beat 'em. That's what so wild, man. We just need to freak 'em out enough that they up and skeeee-daddle. Pop into their Pylon and uplink themselves the hell outta here. Then we call it a win. And the rest of the galaxy sees that we pushed the Savages off a world they decided to stay on. A thing never done before without Tyrus nuking the whole rock into a piece of burnt coal. See?"

Ford frowned inside his bucket. He couldn't help but feel frustrated at only getting all of this now. Of course he'd been briefed on the need to take out a secondary target, but those briefings had made this Uplink out to be a simple communications system. Maybe there was a need for operational secrecy since the entire plan was riding on this subterfuge—the main assault basically being a feint—but it still felt like another of General Rechs's mind games.

They arrived at the ridge. The rest of the team had formed a patrol circle and Bad Luck was scanning the plain below. Makaffie pointed down toward the Pylon. It was down there amid a silent sprawl of strange and half-built structures. Like some new business park of the future that would soon be completed.

Deflector shielding surrounded the place. It was so heavy it was practically glowing in broad daylight. And streams of what looked like civilians were heading toward it from every direction across the city.

"Those ain't civvies, if that's what you're thinking, LT. Those are Savages, most likely non-military, and their elites."

Ford rolled his eyes. "That's the definition of civilians, Makaffie."

Makaffie tittered his mad scientist laugh. "Just sayin', they're still Savage. And they're already uploading in the, to them, unlikely event they lose this one. They wanna be ready."

Ford considered the plan, if what Makaffie had spilled out could be called that. "You got any hard data? Intel? Something I can use to put together an assault plan?"

"Oh yeah," Makaffie said, fumbling for a PDA. "Was s'posed to give that to you first."

He laughed nervously and then fed all the layouts, assets, and other intel to Lieutenant Ford's battle board.

"Once they know we're here to destroy that thing, they're gonna really freak out and try to get off this world double-time. Either by upload, or we think, me and the admiral that is, and the general too, we think they'll call in an allied hulk to get out. Dust off on a grand scale. Epic, man."

"Got it," muttered Ford, studying the field. "That's a pretty powerful deflector array. How we gonna get through that?"

He was asking himself the question more than Makaffie, but the little man was quick to give an answer.

"That *is* one hell of a deflector array, LT. You got that right. To get through it, the fleet would have had to hit it so hard that the Underground, *way* over there, would most likely collapse, killing every one of the captured civilians who used to call this place home. Bad foot for the Legion to start out on, wouldn't you say? I would. I'd say that. PR's everything, man. It's magic. Already got Tyrus Rechs goin' against you, so…" He sighed tiredly and reached for his canteen. "That deflector is powered by four underground micro-reactors. No way through without a small fleet and a whole lotta continental planet damage, if you know what I mean."

Ford shook his head. "And here I thought all that gum flapping of yours was going to lead me to a way in."

Makaffie upended his canteen and drank deep, then smacked his lips and held it out for Ford to take a pull. The lieutenant shook his head.

"Voodoo, sir. Voo. Doo. Meaning let me worry about that. All you gotta worry about is keeping me alive inside so I can find a door. Your job then, LT, is to hold that door once we're inside the Uplink Pylon. That's where the real fun starts."

70

"So… are we really just going to walk right through their deflector barriers?" asked Chalky as the nine legionnaires and their attached approached the first group of Savage civilians making their way toward the Upload Pylon facility in the distance.

"Long and short of it, Doc," mumbled Makaffie, who was busy playing with his little "cloaking projector," as he called it. "That's exactly what we're 'bout to do. Voodoo of the highest order."

"Cut the chatter over L-comm," Ford ordered. He didn't want to risk the quantum signal pinging on any Savage detection gear. "And loosen up, guys. Try not to look like we're about to murder our way through the next two checkpoints on the other side of the first one. Everyone got a full charge pack loaded?"

Affirmatives all around.

"Ain't gonna happen, LT," said Makaffie. "This bunch ain't scanning on that spectrum, aaaaaand I can already tell from my EM detection app that the Savages are way too busy right about now with bandwidth to go lurkin' around lookin' for stray quantum signatures. According to the timetable they still think they're pulling a fast one on us and trying to slip out the back door, that is. At least their elites think that."

"I thought they were all elites, Professor," said Jokes as the squad fell in behind a group of wildly arrayed

Savages hustling toward the first checkpoint towers that led through the deflectors surrounding the Uplink Pylon.

Makaffie craned his neck to smile at the legionnaire. "Ain't that exactly what they want everyone to think, kid. Listen… there's elite, and then there's capital-E *leet*. This bunch is near the cream of the crop for sure, as far as the Calorie Hoarders are concerned, and I suspect they've been given, let's just call it priority boarding passes, to get into their little escape cloud. Probably the Savage version of Insider Celebrities."

"No way," said Jokes. "So… like should I ask one of them for their autograph before we smoke 'em?" The rest of the squad laughed despite themselves. "Could be worth something someday, y'know."

"Stop, man," laughed Heart Attack, beginning to snigger and wheeze. "Just… this is serious, Jokes. Don't get me started."

"Cut it, Dagger," said Ford one more time, and his tone over the L-comm was serious.

Ahead of the team, two looming towers generated a small disturbance in the deflector shield that surrounded the Uplink Pylon. A team of Savage marines with military rifles was guarding the entrance. Two more checkpoints stood beyond, each guarded by its own set of disturbance towers, before they would pass into the open area surrounding the Uplink Pylon.

"Looks like they're just waving groups in as they approach, Makaffie," said Ford. "And you're *sure* we look like Savages right now?"

"Yeah," whined Makaffie, busy with something on one of about five different devices he was currently working on as they walked. "This cloaking projector is broadcasting a projection over everyone wearing a beacon. I gave one to all of you. It won't pass a scan once we're in the second pen, but it'll get us through the first. I think."

"You *think*?" someone muttered.

Over near the city where the battle was raging, two United Worlds F-1s swept in and hit a tall tower with air-to-ground missiles. Glass and metal sprayed outward and rained down into the hidden streets of Hilltop.

The strike force of legionnaires neared the security checkpoint. All around them, Savages, strange, wild, post-human creatures, chittered and screamed at one another. One of them bellowed a mournful string of ones and zeros. Then they renewed their hustle between the disturbance towers ahead, rushing past the steely gaze of the Savage marines manning the checkpoint.

"Now's our chance," said Ford over the L-comm. "Move up, Dagger, and get in with this next bunch before they turn the deflector back on. We good for this, Makaffie?"

"We're good! Do as the LT says. Everyone stick close to me. Remember they're just seeing scans of Savages I've captured. They do not see legionnaires. But you gotta act like Savages, still. None of that ramrod military high-alert business. You got to get your freaky-deak on. And keep moving. It don't work as well if you stay in one place. And if any one of them runs a scan on you then just start shooting, man. Safer that way and we'll cut through the security the hard way if we have to."

The team of legionnaires under Lieutenant Ford pushed in close with the Savages streaming into the first security pen between the towers. Most of these elites, or refugees, or whatever they were, were vulpine, wolf-like, and barked like dogs. A few green-skinned beauties with hair that shimmered like a living silver surrounded a golden man with blazing white eyes who seemed agitated and angry if not frightened. And two Savages, clutching at one another, were bizarrely surrounded by a field of shadowy butterflies.

The whole menagerie, including Strike Force Dagger, was ushered in under the first barrier between the two disruption towers. The Savage marines only barely taking notice as they continued to watch the horizon for enemies.

The main deflector shield went up behind them, and now they were sealed inside the first holding pen. Farther ahead, in the center of the facility, stood the Uplink Pylon, a high tower of slender white stone, high glassed-in levels above, the very face of the structure running and alive with bizarre alien hieroglyph holograms.

The Savages they were standing among began to walk toward the next set of towers, and the barrier went up to let them through. Jokes was just mentioning how easy this was going to be when Ford noticed scanning bars built into the sides of the second checkpoint.

"Ready up, Legionnaires," he said. "It's probably about to go down. Scanning bars ahead. We won't make it past that, will we, Makaffie?"

"Negative, LT. He's right, killer-boys. Suggest you run for it to make it through the third gate as soon as the alarm goes off because them Savages are probably going to activate the field a second or two later."

"What'll happen then?" asked Chalky.

"If you're still on this side then you're trapped, and I bet they got some auto-turrets that just pop out real nice and do you in about two point four seconds, not to mention the team of Savages marines back at Gate One who're gonna come through and open up on us like Syclonian plague ants at a picnic. The other option is you get caught in the barrier itself as it kicks back in, and then you're just atoms spreading all over the field. You'll become one with the force field, as they like to say."

"So we'll be dead is what you're saying," said Kimbo.

"I think what he's saying, Sar'nt," answered Jokes dryly, "is that you'll be *so* dead you won't even know you're dead. Which when you think about it..."

Bad Luck, Dagger's point, went past the scanning bars built into the two towers for the second checkpoint. Immediately ominous sirens began to wind up and wail like the bellowing of prehistoric monsters.

"Hustle, Dagger!" shouted Ford.

A door in the right-hand tower opened and a Savage marine stepped out into daylight, rifle in hand and looking around at the passing Savage conglomeration. In the same instant Ford raised his N-1 and the Savage seemed to "see" him.

"Cloaking's gone, Team," shouted Makaffie. "They just wiped out my device with a pulse on that frequency. They see us!"

Ford opened up on the Savage, squeezing the trigger on the N-1 fast and dragging hits across the Savage's body until the tango went down against the tower, a smoking hole in his mirrored bucket, the reflective faceplate cracked and shattered.

The strike force sprinted through the second checkpoint before the barrier could slam shut, and the nearby Savage civvies did the same, shrieking in their bizarre electronic chitter-speak. At the same time the marines from the first checkpoint hustled forward and began to fire, taking up positions of cover near the second set of towers. The first casualty was a green-skinned Savage beauty who got raked by slug-thrower fire. Her riddled body went down near Wild Man, and an instant later the big sniper, out in the open and not seeking cover, unlimbered the big-bore rifle and drilled the Savage marines. The weapon went off like a small cannon inside the security pens, each terrific *craaack* knocking a Savage flat onto its back, armor ruined and strange fluids pooling on the paved marble.

"Bad guys ahead!" shouted LS-13 over the L-comm. A second team of Savage marines was coming forward from the tower itself, pushing past the panicked Savage civvies, rifles up and ready to engage.

"Dagger!" shouted Ford as everything turned to instantaneous chaos is the blink of an eye. "On me! Combat wedge. Push forward now to the pylon. Wild Man, you got our six!"

As one the legionnaires moved forward, Makaffie in their midst, unleashing blaster bolts at the marines ahead and booming rifle shots at those behind. The firefight was short and deadly for the Savage marines, and within seconds Dagger had passed the third set of towers that led into the main area around the Uplink Pylon, surrounded by the deflector shield above.

"C'mon, Wild Man!" shouted Ford back at their rear guard. "Move up before they reactivate the field and cut you off. Covering fire!"

Ford and Heart Attack laid down a flurry of suppressive fire on the Savages engaging Wild Man from among the rear disruption towers. The big sniper turned and ran, lumbering for the last set of towers.

"Makaffie!" called Ford over the comm. "Hack the Pylon now if you can! Kimbo, run security while he gets us in!"

71

The Uplink Pylon had looked slender and narrow from a distance, but as the legionnaires and their attached approached the base across a zen stone garden sprawl within the inner courtyard, it was clear that it was much larger than they'd first thought.

Makaffie's fingers were flying over the fold-out datapad he'd hard-connected to an external terminal he'd cracked near the door. The Savages had tried to lock out the attacking force via a series of automated scans and corresponding lockdowns, but their systems were no match for the little man.

"Wish I could shut up that bellowing alarm," he muttered as he worked.

Kimbo and the rest of the team took up positions around the main doors, using some of the bizarre shaped statuary as cover. A minute later Ford, Wild Man, and Heart Attack were clear of the firefight at the third checkpoint and Dagger was together again.

"Take *this*, you scumbags!" shouted Makaffie, tapping angrily at the keys as he opened new menus. "This little beauty is gonna rip your defenses to shreds. Oh... lookee here... you got nerve gas canisters on every level? Well... let's just..."

"You okay, Mak?" asked Jokes. "Seems personal."

Makaffie, bent and hunched, continued slamming at his keyboard. "Nerve gas released. Choke on that, you sadistic kelhorns."

He looked up at Jokes.

"I've seen some sket, man." The little man seemed more sober than he'd been up to this point. "Dark sket."

Ford hustled to the terminal, checking the clock in his HUD. "How long until we can expect a response?"

"Soon, LT. Real soon. Our attack just *lit up* their boards," said Makaffie. "My guess is we just moved to the top of the list of things that need to be... *ahem*... attended to for them Savages. Give me two more minutes with the nerve agent and then I'll pop the neutralizing bottles and increase the venting. Five and we'll be good to penetrate."

They waited, eyes on the only way into the uplink tower, waiting for the Savage force that was sure to come. Sure to arrive at any moment.

"This seem easier than y'all thought it would be, or is that just me?" asked Chalky when the klaxons had reached their lowest decibel cycle before ramping back up again.

"It was always supposed to be this easy, kid," said Makaffie, still working at his cracked terminal. "They never expected us to hit them here. Even after the operation was underway. They thought we were here for the civvies down in bubble storage. Now comes the hard part. We gotta hold this place and make them think it's all over. That we're gonna blow it. Shut it down. Only way they'll leave."

"Wait," Ford said, wanting to take his bucket off to rub his temples. The skinny little man was barely making sense. "If we have their Uplink Pylon, how *can* they leave? Aren't we just trapping them on planet? Won't that just make them fight *harder*?"

Makaffie giggled as he worked to open the main door, masterfully working the Savage grid. "Yeah, man. But see, that's just the ones trapped. All the others, man, they're already gone. Already transferring to those Savage hulks. These are just the ones left behind. Or will be once we do what we do here."

Even this didn't make sense to Ford. "Okay, but then why assault the—"

The lieutenant was interrupted with an update from *Defiant* intel.

"Dagger Actual, we read several Savage detachments breaking off from the main attack. ETA at your location is fifteen minutes. Be advised you have upwards of battalion strength closing on your position."

"So this is a battalion of Savages that are in danger of being cut off from the Uplink or whatever?" Ford said to Makaffie, who was also on the command channel.

"Now you're gettin' it, LT. The big dogs... they're already safe, see? They're safe and gettin' away. The leaders. Cut off the head of the snake and the body will die, *capisce*? Except in this case the body of the snake, that's that battalion and all the other Savage grunts, they're gonna start looking for the chance to join them. So keep me safe, Lieutenant Fast." Makaffie giggled again.

Ford wondered whether the man wasn't half mad, then studied the satellite drone recon *Defiant* had just sent to his HUD. Lots of small forces coming from across the easternmost portions of New Vega. Makaffie was right. The enemy was "freaking out" that the Legion was now in control of this asset.

"Air support, *Defiant*?" asked Ford.

"Negative at this time, Dagger."

"Orbital artillery support?"

"Negative also. You're on your own for the moment. All forces heavily engaged at this time. *Defiant* out."

Expect heavy casualties, Admiral Sulla had said.

"Makaffie," said Ford, "I need a layout of this facility as soon as you can get it."

"Got it already, Chief. Here ya go."

A moment later Ford was looking at an actual Savage file of the layout of the inside of the facility. Thanks to his old life as a treasure hunter he was well aware of the street value of an item like the one he was holding. Savage artifacts were game-changers in the treasure-hunting life, if only because they were so blasted hard to come by. The Savages were adept at killing everything and leaving no trace.

But that old life was gone now.

He was leej all the way.

"Where's this door we gotta hold?" he asked Makaffie.

"Highlighted. Down deep in the facility. Three stories beneath is a control node we gotta take. You have to hold it once I go in."

Ford studied the layout. It was a bad position. It was open from three angles of fire. The Savages would have multiple stairwells and maintenance points to access the level. The place reminded him of the catacombs of some ancient alien civilization's burial temples—the kind he had plundered in that old life. The layout was very familiar in that respect.

Expect heavy casualties.

Ford turned to his team.

"Wild Man... You head up tower. Eyes and ears. Sniper support. Choose any of the upper observation lounges along the main spine. That'll give you a good field of fire on the security checkpoints. That's the only way they can come in, right, Makaffie?"

"Roger, LT. Only way unless they decide to drop the deflectors and then hit us from every direction. But I don't expect them to do that because then the facility is vulnerable to orbital assault. So they'll keep it up. Level five should be a good sniper's hide. I'd go there, Big Man."

"Can't spare you a spotter," Ford said.

Wild Man grunted an acknowledgment and moved out.

Ford slapped his shoulder armor as he passed. "Make 'em pay, Wild Man. KTF."

Wild Man stopped and turned back to his lieutenant. "KTF?"

"Kill them first," replied Sergeant Kimm. "Trust me, it's a thing. We just started doin' it."

Wild Man smiled approvingly and hurried on his way.

Lieutenant Ford turned to face the rest of Dagger.

"Sergeant Kimm, you take Junior, Chalky, Heart Attack, Jokes, and Shadow and hold the main entrance. Bad Luck and I will take Makaffie down to the sublevel and find whatever it is he needs to find down there. Roger?"

"Affirmative, Fast," said the NCO. "Hold at all costs."

Sergeant Daniel Kimm took his men and organized the defense of the main entrance into the Uplink Pylon. Beyond the door they found nerve-gassed Savages who'd never expected their own defenses to be turned on them sprawled dead on the floor. What the gas had done to them was not pretty and their deaths had not been easy. The entire area looked like some cruise liner boarding lounge massacre. Clean and spartan with holographic projections of strange never-before-seen worlds broadcasting along the walls and seating areas. At least never before seen by the legionnaires who moved in to take control of the facility, sweeping the corners and quadrants with their N-1s.

Wild Man was already in the elevator and lugging his big rifle up to the top of the tower.

Ford turned to Makaffie and Bad Luck.

"All right, boys. Let's see what's down there."

They passed dead Savages on their way down to find what they'd been sent in to secure. Faces purple, veins bulging, tongues lolling, eyes staring up into the nothing. All of it made even eerier by a cold, pale-blue light that sometimes shone on strange control surfaces with bizarre readouts that hurt the mind and eyes to look at.

"This guy had two tongues," commented Makaffie as they passed one prone body, twisted in death. The Savage looked more like a cartoon demon than someone who'd once been human a long, long time ago. Back on Earth.

Ford had asked the attached to keep it quiet, but that was like asking the sun not to rise.

"You ever wonder if these were like... like famous people way back when?" Makaffie continued as they crept along. "That was what they were supposed to be, according to all the material on the subject."

The two legionnaires didn't answer. They were too busy working to wonder about such unimportant vagaries as ancient history and ephemeral fame.

On the second sublevel, they came upon what appeared to be a Savage surgery center. There was blood of every color everywhere. A pit in the center radiated heat from a shaft that went far, far down into the sub-levels below.

"This is where they physically remove the brains for those that needed a direct connect for upload," said Makaffie. "But most can upload by signal."

"What's the pit for?" asked Bad Luck.

"Oh. Well, once their consciousness is in the cloud…"

An explosion rocked the tower somewhere above them. Not far off.

"They're here," said Ford. A moment later Wild Man was reporting in that the Savages were aware of his presence and trying to hit the upper decks with rocket launchers.

Taking the access stairs down to the next level down, they stepped into a dark and shadowy space like those temples Ford had found on haunted and lonely worlds no one ever went to. Holographs, glowing blue and ghostly, waltzed around pillars, alcoves, and sunken floors with no apparent rhyme or reason, showing data that made no sense. But the pillars themselves had a pattern, forming concentric rings around a central shimmering, almost warm, light.

Ford closed to investigate, following the sights of his N-1, Bad Luck on his six. In the distance, above them, he could hear Wild Man's rifle making huge dull *booms*. He was making the Savages pay.

Aeson Ford had seen strange things. Strange sights and wonders in his other life as an adventurer plundering the ancient ruins of the lost civilizations across what was known of the galaxy. But this was something… something much different.

"What is it?" he mumbled as if in a trance. The golden light was a pillar with no source. It just hung there.

"Well," said Makaffie, "since this is the first time I've ever seen it, I can only guess it's what we thought we might find down here. So that there, LT, if I'm right, is a doorway to another... let's call it a... dimension. Though it ain't really that at all. In theory, from what previous... explorers and operatives... have encountered, it's a limited quantum singularity. A door into that, specifically."

"You get any of that?" Bad Luck asked Ford.

The lieutenant didn't answer. He continued to move around the strange doorway, exploring it from every angle.

Kimbo gave a quick report from above. "Gettin' lit up! Heart Attack is dead. We can still hold. Kimm out!"

The report snapped the men from the trance that was the golden beam—the gateway.

"So, we s'posed to do something with this?" asked Bad Luck.

"Well, kid..." said Makaffie, stepping forward. "*We* ain't gonna do anything with it. You and the LT here... you gotta defend it while *I* actually try and go in it. Then you gotta monitor a device I'm gonna give you, and once you get a signal you gotta reel me back in. Otherwise I'll probably be lost in there forever."

Makaffie let out a frantic, feverish giggle.

72

Streets of New Vega

Rechs and Watson moved down Sub-Route Six, knowing that if they encountered a subterranean Savage team, it would spell a quick end to their mission. But this was the only way to their target that didn't involve doubling all the way back to LZ Victory and traveling across the surface of New Vega—which would only increase the likelihood of a Savage encounter. But though the three-kilometer march was an anxious one, it ultimately proved to be uneventful. SR6 was clear.

The general reached what he was looking for: an access portal that hung along the side of SR6. It reminded him of the kind of hatch that had once been found in submarines. He gripped the round handle, but with only one working arm he couldn't muster the strength to turn it.

Watson stepped forward without being asked and with a mighty torque, loosened the wheel, turning it until the hatch unlocked and could be pushed open. Behind it, a confined tube went straight up into darkness, metal rungs set into one side.

Watson shouldered his rifle, drew his pistol, and grabbed the bottom rung. "I'll go up first, General."

As the pair climbed, the distant sounds of battle echoed faintly as Captain Milker and the Legion made their final, desperate stand at the junction. When Savage rockets caved in the tunnel structure, effectively denying themselves further access, Rechs and Watson could feel the vibrations in their hands and feet.

It was a perilously tedious climb. And tight—the narrow shaft was useless for moving any more than one man in a row up or down, and then only down to SR6. Useless to the enemy, an asset to the Legion. That's the way Rechs liked it.

They reached daylight, emerging like a pair of sewer rats unbidden in the heart of New Vega. Or what had once been New Vega.

A year ago.

This was where Tyrus Rechs had left the trigger-nuke he'd intended to roast this Savage-overrun world with. It was still there. It had still been there when he'd checked the location beacon all throughout the year leading up to this battle. Even at the moment of the invasion when he'd been riding in the jump seat behind the captain of the *Chang*, he'd checked it then.

It was still there and sleeping.

Of course the Savages must have known exactly what it was; any basic scanning equipment could have told you that. But that same scanning equipment would have told them there was no way in hell they were going to be able to disarm it without detonating it. They couldn't even move it without detonating it. Tampering triggers were in place.

So they'd left it.

What the Savages wouldn't know was that Rechs had remotely disarmed the tampering triggers as soon as the Legion's invasion had begun in earnest. He'd had to—all those SSM strikes, all the chaos of war... there was a chance they might have accidentally set off the tampering triggers, making everything for naught. Now it could be moved. Now it was safe.

If a planet-destroying nuclear doomsday device could ever be said to be "safe."

Now, scanning from the darkness of the maintenance tunnel they'd just opened, Rechs studied the quiet, almost abandoned street out there. Watson, standing over the kneeling Rechs, who'd struggled the whole trek, watched their six. Satisfied it was clear, he turned back to the street and the general's study.

"How exactly are we gonna do this, sir?" the sergeant asked in his dark brooding baritone.

Rechs had come to respect the man on their long patrol through the Savage-held territories of Hilltop. The Britannian's skills were good, and he was a pro. He'd never once offered Rechs help even though it was clear the wounds were causing him to struggle and labor over basic obstacles. Tyrus Rechs had been trained that everyone in a company had to pull their weight. That was one of the many things the Rangers had taught him. One of the many things he already knew because of his father.

Rechs liked that. It made things easier. Especially when he was the one sucking wind all along. If there were no excuses to be made then one didn't have to worry about making excuses. They only needed to concentrate on putting one foot in front of the next until they got to where they were going.

"I'm gonna call in for an airlift," said Rechs. "Then, while it's inbound, I'm going to walk out there and activate the repulsor sled it's on. I want you to take that end of the street. It'll give you a good field of fire. Once the Savages see that ship coming in they might respond with a QRF, and that's the street they'll come down. You engage them while I get the weapon aboard. Then I'll cover you and we dust off. Roger?"

"Roger," said Watson softly. Nothing else. No editorial. No comments. Man of few words. Rechs liked him even more.

Six minutes later, the LZ hot, Rechs and Watson got the trigger-nuke aboard their airlift, the ship unofficially dubbed *Tombstone*. The same captured Savage light explorer that had delivered Strike Force Dagger to the planet's surface a day and a lifetime ago.

It was close, but they made it out of there.

Rechs turned to Sergeant Watson as the hijacked Savage ship climbed up over the ruined streets. He pointed out the open aft cargo door at a massive Savage hulk that was coming in for a landing. Engines reversing to cut speed. Repulsors throbbing madly from a thousand different places along the under-hull.

It was an almost insane sight, too unreal to believe.

"That's our target," yelled Rechs over the engine's howl.

73

Objective Madhouse

With Lieutenant Ford in place and Sergeant Kimbo running the defense of the ground floor entry, Wild Man had a spectacular view to a kill. To the west the battle was in full swing now. Artillery rained down around the *Chang*. Massive explosions rocked the surface of Hilltop District. And closer in, from the decimated ruins of the city, beyond the shimmer of the deflector field that encompassed the objective he was there to defend, several Savage quick reaction forces were heading straight for their position. Straight for Madhouse. Some in long columns. Others at the double and moving faster than any human could. Still more rode in large troop transports.

Any other soldier would have felt that maybe they had reached the end of the line, seeing something like that. The flooding of troops when you already feel outnumbered. The impending reality of a last stand. Another brutal, final, win-or-die fight. Marathon, the Alamo, Dien Bien Phu, Bastogne, Saffron Domes...

A last stand if ever there was one.

Wild Man, on the other hand, felt like he'd won the lottery. Like he'd woken up that morning and won some fantastic prize. Lucky numbers and a changed life. He was never so much in love with her as he was now. He felt jittery and excited that the prettiest girl... well, it was just like that first date long ago. He felt that way.

Like everything was possible. Like you might just run up the score and kill a million. Maybe two. Like the thing you were born to do, the thing you'd been waiting all along to do, it was now. And now was all there ever really was.

He was telling her how he was gonna shoot them as he took out a tactical hammer and bashed out the windows on the observation deck of the Uplink Pylon. The panes he would need to fire through. He told her his plan and how he would move between three positions on this deck to keep them guessing where he was at while he shot them down. She followed, baby on her hip and telling him he was so right. That she was so proud of him. That yes, she loved him too, babe. Always had.

It'd been tough times for a while, but all that was over now.

She was so close he could smell the perfume she used to wear, and when he told himself, stopping in the silence and hearing the distant muffled thunder of the battle going on out there across the city, that she was dead and that he needed to remember that, he froze in place.

"I'm sorry, babe," he said, apologizing to the silence. "I didn't mean it. Come back."

He was sorry, he kept repeating to the empty observation deck, his chest heaving as he stacked furniture and torn-away terminals to reinforce his shooting positions.

But all he heard was, *We'll see, babe. We'll see.*

He fired his first shot. The 20mm 2600-grain bullet he'd loaded himself using a little more powder than he normally did because he'd wanted all the rounds he was going to fire today to have a little more *oomph*.

This first shot did not disappoint.

It was a long one. Not the longest he'd ever taken, but way out there. The first Savage team to arrive hadn't waited for reinforcements. Possibly, he thought as he studied them through the powerful magnification of his scope, this bunch wanted some kind of honor in restoring the facility to Savage control. They'd decided to be heroes.

"Heroes die too," he muttered as he took aim.

Tons of Savage civvies were huddling near the towers and deflector field gates, desperate to get in, to have their brains torn out and uploaded. He'd listened in on the comm chatter. Heard what Fast and Makaffie had found down there.

Okay then, Wild Man had told himself, head shots all around. If their brains were so important to them, he'd definitely oblige.

And that first shot... it was everything a shot was supposed to be. There was no wind inside the dome created by the defector shield—he'd have to remember to adjust and compensate if the Savages did decide to lower it to attack from all directions. He landed the targeting reticle on the scope just above the first Savage to die. The target was far enough down through the three towers that aiming down didn't cause him to have to aim lower to compensate for the round's climb. He had the sight picture right where he wanted it.

His finger caressed the trigger, and with little thought... knowing exactly right where his breathing cycle was supposed to be... he pulled gently with the pad of his finger. Asking, not telling, the rifle to fire.

There was no rage in that finger. No rage in his body. He'd learned long ago that those things made for bad marksmanship. And sometimes caused you to stick around long after your first shot. The hatred in you rejoicing at the field of fire. That could get you killed.

But today, today... that would be a luxury he could indulge in a bit. They knew where he was. He could stay here and kill them dead all day long. Just shifting momentarily between the three protected and reinforced hides he'd created on this level.

The round disappeared straight through the monster, the Savage, the ravager of young mothers with babies on their hips who loved the unlovable... who'd loved the Wild Man.

The round was moving so fast that it exploded the target's mirrored helmet and misted the brains within. Pink by the light of the sun. The Savage just fell over as brain matter painted the helmets and armor of the others in the squad probing the defenses of the first pen and the two towers that guarded that area, seeing all the dead Savages Dagger had killed on their way in. Unsure what was going on here. Not expecting to be reached out to, and touched, by a sniper.

Do another one, babe.

He selected and fired. Like some infernal and relentless machine that didn't know anything but the thing it had been made to know all along. Acquire and fire.

Boom.

Two seconds later.

Boom.

Got a runner, babe.

Boom.

The rifle's barrel was hot and smoking and he blew into the open chamber as he shifted to the next hide. But the first Savage squad out there was all dead now. In less than twenty seconds he had put them all down like the stray dogs they were.

More were coming in. Light armored sleds streaking toward the facility.

Make 'em just as dead, babe.

"I love you," he said as the glass all round his last hide began to explode. Savages were opening up with mounted fifty-cals. Someone tried a rocket that slammed into the level above. Ranged fire tore that section of the observation deck to pieces.

But he was already gone.

74

The space around the glowing portal-light-pillar was illuminated in a soft blue that somehow competed with the golden energy coming from the singularity, throwing lens flares and small comets away from the interaction of the light sources. It was like looking at some cosmic unseen, finally witnessed by human eyes.

"Do you have any idea what's on the other side of that?" asked Ford as he stepped up beside Makaffie. The little man had been walking slowly around the pillar as though creeping through a graveyard well past midnight. When only ghosts and graverobbers are out. Bad Luck was busy placing explosive charges in some of the maintenance access portals and sealing all the security doors. That would keep the Savages locked outside—but for how long, who could say?

"Really no idea, LT," whispered Makaffie still circling the glowing beam of energy. His hands were out, like he was steadying himself, and then suddenly but slowly, gleaming metal control surfaces rose out of the floor on soft pneumatic hisses.

"All right, all right, all right," said Makaffie. "This is what we were looking for."

The little man went to stand in front of the terminals that encircled the energy field. Ford decided this was where he'd be fighting from. Or at least, where he'd fall back to. It was an excellent fighting position of last resort. If he made it that far. Wild Man was already firing his big rifle up there, calling in enemy strength reports as the Savages massed at the gates.

This was not going to be an easy fight, and that was an understatement. Ford knew that. Knew that every trial and torture the general had trained them for hadn't been just because. It had been for this. As if the old warrior knew this fight was coming.

Expected it even.

"Makaffie. You sure you can survive going through that thing?" Ford asked.

The little man was down on the ground now and pulling off his gear, stripping down to just clothes before producing a device Ford didn't recognize. Makaffie's breathing was rapid and shallow, a sort of answer in itself to the question.

No. The answer was no. The strange little man, Team Dagger's attached, had no idea what was about to happen on the other side of whatever exactly this thing was.

"I got some idea, LT," said Makaffie as he stood and handed Ford a device similar to the one he held in his own hand. "Believe it or not, General Rechs and Casper, a long time ago, went into one of these with a full starship while chasing a Savage lighthugger called the *Moirai*. This is probably a much smaller man-made... er, Savage-made is the right way to put it, version of that place they went into. It's a pocket singularity and supposedly you can make 'em by carefully imploding subatomic particles. Whether this one is stabilized, or even managed, remains to be seen. But... reason tells me that if the Savages are using it, desperate to storm this place and get in here, and they value their lives, LT, then it must be safe on some level, right?"

Ford thought about that as he listened to the combat upstairs. Kimbo's element was starting to get involved more seriously. And Ford knew it was coming here. Right down here. He wanted to be up there, leading the defense. Buying time for whatever needed to happen for this entire operation to be a success. But orders were that Makaffie going through the door was the most critical part of the plan. And that while in there he needed to be protected at all costs. Maybe the Savages could edit him right out of existence once he was in there if they retook the facility. Who knew? Not Ford. But orders were orders. Even if nothing made sense. Makaffie was right: this was Savage voodoo country. And General Rechs had always liked to remind them that when it came to the Savages... nothing made sense. Nothing ever made sense.

"Yeah, Makaffie," said Ford. "But they shuck their brains upstairs in surgery theater. Is that a requirement to enter?"

Makaffie shrugged. Thought about it for a moment like he was adding up a math problem in his head. And then spoke.

"This here, LT, is one of those realms in the universe where little is known. This device, and the one you have in your hand... this is like a tether. Like... if I were going down into a cave and you were lowering me by rope. So I don't get lost in there and I can come back. See this light here? The red one? As long as that's red I don't want you to push this button. But the moment it switches over to green, push this button and I can come back through the door from wherever else I am on the other side of this. Got it, LT?"

Ford repeated the instructions and added a "Got it."

"Okay. I guess I'll say it was nice knowin' you if I don't make it back and all. I guess I just end up becoming one with the galaxy half a second after I enter that light stream. But if not... remember, no matter what... don't hit that button until it goes green. Mission won't be done if you do. And if you don't hit it, well then I'll never make it back out. Lost in there forever and all that stuff. Not a mission fail, but... y'know... a bummer for me and all when you think about it. So a little consideration in that area would be much appreciated."

Ford stepped close and shook the little man's hand.

Makaffie nodded and tried to say something. But all that came was a croak of a breathy laugh. He grabbed his canteen and drained it quickly.

"I was parched." He coughed gustily as the alcohol flooded his system. "Better. Okay... see ya, LT."

Then he turned, holding the device in both hands like it was something holy, and just walked into the golden energy stream. Ford watched him not disappear... but *fade* into the comets and lens flares. Going and then gone.

Above, somewhere in the upper sections of the Uplink Pylon, an explosion rocked the tower.

Sergeant Kimbo was asking for a status report from the sniper. Wild Man wasn't responding.

75

The big man had moved to his third hide for the second time when they fired the anti-tank round into the observation deck. It struck the ceiling directly over his head, probably ripping into the floor above. And it had definitely been an incendiary round of some type. Flames crawled across the area he'd been shooting from, shooting down the Savages, and now those flames were obscuring his field of fire.

He picked up his rifle and looked around for his comm. He'd taken off his bucket to shoot better, stripping the comm out of it to maintain contact, and now the comm was gone. Knocked loose in the blast. Probably lying amid the burning debris.

Forget about it, babe, she told him. *Keep shooting. Do another. Just keep doing them all and soon we'll be together and these can burn.*

He ignored her and scrabbled around on the carpet as pieces of the ceiling melted and fell onto his armor. He couldn't find the comm buds.

And then across the skyline... a massive starship appeared in the sky and the sight of it was so stunning that Wild Man just stood there on the floor of that burning level of the Uplink Pylon and watched as the gigantic starship came in fast, a speed that seemed impossible for something so vast. It set down across the city near the *Chang*. Near Hilltop. It crushed everything underneath it:

buildings, sleds, roadways, everything shattered and the ground shook.

He grabbed his big rifle and moved to a window not completely pouring smoke. The Savages down there, the dead and those still living, and he'd killed a lot of them, were there. The living still streaming forward along the access pens and towers, closing on the front entrance to the Pylon. Using this opportunity to close now that he wasn't firing on them. There were hundreds, and there was no way Fast or Kimbo or the others were going to hold out.

He threw one leg up on the sill, stuck the massive rifle out through the broken glass, and fired. The air was hot and he felt like he could barely breathe with what little oxygen was left.

Good, babe. Do 'em all for me. Do 'em because you love me more than life itself.

"No," he rumbled as he selected a Savage marine in the gunner's turret of an armored vehicle moving up fast. He sent the round right into that one. It blew off his arm and the body went limp over the turret. Shifting the scope, Wild Man found another and pulled the trigger in the same moment.

There were too many.

She was laughing. Laughing like that day they went to the fair. Best day ever, he thought. Best. Day. Ever.

Do 'em all, babe.

"No!" he shouted as he pulled the big rifle's trigger again. "Not for you. You're gone now. They're here. And they need me against these Savages. Go on... find some peace. Lemme kill them first before they hurt my brothers. I always loved you. Always."

The floor was on fire around his boots, but he continued to pull the trigger. Acquire and fire even though it looked like a frothing sea of Savages below the Uplink Pylon. Globs of melted ceiling burned on the surface of his armor.

He shot another and selected a new target...

76

Defiant

"Predator Three is down and they've sent some kind of human wave attack into the Underground, Admiral."

Sulla studied the feed. The Savage hulk had hit the ground around New Vega and now thousands of human civilians were rushing toward the few remaining entrances into the Underground.

"It's payback," muttered Casper Sulla bitterly. "They've lost and now they want to make sure it's not a win for us."

He knew exactly what this was. What some Savage tribe had cooked up in the special weapons department. More zombies of a kind. Just like the ones that already been reported in use on the battlefield. Armed with explosives, turned into living bombs. Forced against their will to rush the enemies of the Savages and detonate.

Living zombies just like he and Rechs had once been.

"Tell all forces at Alpha and across the Underground to pull back to *Chang* immediately."

We have won, he told himself. But that truth didn't blunt the reality that a lot of people were about to get killed down there.

"Admiral, Lieutenant Ford is requesting reinforcements or air support. He says they're being overrun."

This was the third request. And there was nothing available. Fighters were out of munitions. Legion on the ground were about to face a weapon unlike anything they'd ever trained for, and...

"Sir," said the XO. "We do have Hartswick's marines coming into drop range now. It'll take time... but they could drop in and try to relieve."

Sulla studied the status board. The armored shuttles carrying the marines were still inbound on the carrier after their assault on Predator Two.

"They have casualties," noted Sulla.

The XO nodded but said nothing.

The admiral took a deep breath and weighed his options before making the decision. The battle was won. The landing of the Savage hulk and subsequent human wave attack were proof of that. As was the stream of Savages flowing onto the hulk, almost as numerous and driven as the stream of humans coming off of it. They were gathering what Savages they could, dishing out what final damage they could, and then they would abandon New Vega.

"Order Hartswick's pilots to redirect and drop on the Uplink Pylon to relieve Dagger now. Best possible speed."

77

Kill Zone Alpha

"Major Underwood is KIA," reported Sergeant Martin to Captain Milker. "No idea what the casualty situation is like forward of our position, sir."

The Savage gunfire was thick. The air above the duracrete trenches was a constant swarm of flying lead. A few positions inside the trench network that had once been a water filtration system for the reservoir were fighting back, forward of Martin's command post. The telltale sound and light show of pulse weapons proved the line was holding in some places. But it was clear the Savages coming on shore now were making a final big push. They were going for broke.

Captain Milker was saying something that got lost in a sudden series of distant explosions over the L-comm. At the same time the Savage who'd shifted the whole battle, covering the main access trench with a light machine gun, opened up again. Three times the sappers had tried to dislodge that lone Savage marine, supported by the few surviving legionnaires not evac'd back to the casualty collection point. Three times they'd been pushed back by that Savage warrior.

"Say again... Fall back!" Warlord was ordering everyone at KZ Alpha to pull out now. "You have human IEDs swarming your front. Pull back to the pump house immediately. Say again..."

Martin pounded his L-comm operator's shoulder armor. "Groogan. Repeat that message so we can be sure everyone heard it. Tell everyone to pull back to the rally point now. We're getting overrun."

The L-comm operator who'd dragged Sergeant Martin from the trenches was kneeling nearby, pulling security on the alcove, filled with Britannian dead, that Martin had been using as a CP ever since getting hit by an explosive in the forward trenches. He had feeling in his legs, but he couldn't move them.

"Sir," replied the L-comm operator after a moment. "I got the orders looping, but we got a squad of sappers forward we can't communicate with. No one can. But I can see 'em, sir. Lemme run down there and pull 'em out first."

A wave of pain moved through Martin's lower half, making him break out into a cold sweat, as he tried to see if he could get himself back to the rally point with the L-comm operator's help. No dice. He leaned back against the duracrete wall, pale and shaking. Biting down hard on the pain. He closed his eyes and nodded, feeling for his rifle and getting a new charge pack in.

"Go. I'll wait here for you, Groogan. Go get 'em and hurry back."

A moment later LS-90 was off. Martin heard a Savage gunner open up. He'd seen the kid. Martin fell over on his side and pulled himself around the alcove, dragging his N-1 in front of him. He opened up on the gunner down the main access channel, suppressing as Groogan ran to the next trench and then over to where the Britannian squad was still holding the line.

That was when Martin saw the first IEDs. Humans. Humans captured on New Vega a year ago, or perhaps from some other Savage-overrun world. Haunted. Pale.

Starving. Scared. And fully aware of what was about to happen to them. Their swollen bellies filled with powerful explosives. One, the first one Martin saw, just exploded all of a sudden among a bunch of Savage marines, killing them all in a violent instant. More were swarming up the beach.

"Sir!" It was Groogan over the L-comm. "Need cover fire on that gunner to make it back up the trench!"

"Roger. Covering!"

Martin opened up with a fresh charge pack. He squeezed fast, exposed, keeping the Savage's head down as the squad dashed back up the channel. One of the Britannians was hit. Another grabbed the wounded man and kept him moving. Moments later, as more human IEDs swarmed the forward trenches and began to explode, Groogan was back and lifting his sergeant in a fireman's carry.

"C'mon, sir. We're getting out of here!"

They were ten feet from the pump house and the deep tunnels leading into Underground when the roof of the reservoir began to collapse. The explosions of the human IED slaves went off like rolling thunder as each began to detonate the next in a multiplying fury of flesh and destruction.

Archival footage estimates there were over ten thousand of these horrible Savage weapon systems, the human slave IED, that disembarked from Predator Three and flooded the tunnels in the final moments of the battle.

There are no words that can describe the horror of the event.

78

Hundred Day Celebration Official Historical Program

p. 203 – THE LAST STAND AT OBJECTIVE MADHOUSE

Sergeant Daniel "Kimbo" Kimm, LS-16, directed the defense at the ground level entrance to the Savage Uplink Pylon facility tagged Objective Madhouse. Also fighting in the defense were Randolph "Junior" Johnson, LS-11; Landon "Shadow" Schaule, LS-09; Ellis "Chalky" Dobbins, LS-12; LS-73, Bill "Heart Attack" Allen; and LS-20, Seth "Jokes" Bouchard.

The Savages hit hard using rockets and grenades before storming in en masse. An after-action review of the battle shows that these legionnaires gave no quarter and met the Savage force with extreme aggression and violence. The legionnaires of Strike Force Dagger made the Savage force pay for every meter inside the facility, at several points resorting to hand-to-hand combat.

Only L-comm operator LS-09 survived. His account relates that the legionnaires set up a crossfire inside the main lobby and gave ground grudgingly to the inner stairwell. By the time the Savages reached the second line of defense, LS-20 and LS-73 had been killed in action. LS-12, the team medic, was killed trying to drag a wounded Sergeant Kimm out of direct fire in the last few meters of the defense inside the narrow corridor that led to the stairwell. Neither he nor Kimm made it to safety.

At that point LS-11, Junior, ordered LS-09 to drop back to sublevel two to maintain contact with Lieutenant Ford and *Defiant*. The Savages were attempting to blanket-jam all signatures within the facility, and the L-comm was struggling to maintain comm with higher-echelon elements.

The last LS-09 saw of Randolph "Junior" Johnson was the legionnaire firing with a sidearm from the stairwell, hit multiple times but still checking the Savage advance. When the legionnaire's body was recovered, the Savage dead that littered the stairwell numbered twenty-three. Sergeant Randolph Johnson had been hit thirty-seven times, though it was never clear how many of those wounds were post-mortem.

LS-09 was then ordered by Lieutenant Ford to crawl into the maintenance and air filtration systems and avoid capture so that comm between the fleet and the lieutenant could be maintained during the rest of the operation. LS-09 initially refused to obey, but Lieutenant Ford explained that their only hope of getting through this was if the fleet could send reinforcements at some point.

LS-30, Lieutenant Ford, and LS-13, Specialist Tyler "Bad Luck" Ornelas were left to defend the Singularity Gate alone.

79

Objective Madhouse

Time was running out for Aeson Ford. The Savages were hitting their sublevel hard. They had managed to blow open one of the security doors and had spilled into the room en masse before the legionnaires could stop them. Now they were everywhere.

Ford and LS-13 were working as a team. Bad Luck was wielding his N-1 and Ford had given the point man his charge packs for that weapon in a trade for Bad Luck's charge packs for the blaster sidearm the lieutenant now wielded. Working the two pistols, one in each hand, and followed by Bad Luck, Ford moved about the shadowy level shooting down the Savages that pushed forward.

Ford's incredible reflexes allowed him to shoot first. His harrowing life of adventure—hopping from dangerous planet to dangerous planet—had left him capable of shooting as accurately with his off hand as with his good. Bad Luck took care of the Savages who tried to take the two-man team from the flanks. He was wounded three times before finally going down with half his bucket blown off.

Just one of those rounds that hits just right.

Ford turned to see his point man down. He nailed the Savage who'd killed Bad Luck before dropping back into the darkness, circling the level, and making for his final defense around the gate. Pushing back thoughts that there was no way that he could live to see a win this time.

Winning had always been important to him.

Winning on his terms.

Being free.

Last stands were for suckers. Someone had once said that to him. That someone might have been right.

Why'd you ever join the Legion, then? some other, more sarcastic side of himself asked. He ignored that, because in light of current events it did indeed seem like the smart-alecky side was right.

"*Defiant*, this is Dagger Actual. Squad is KIA except for L-comm operator and myself. Need reinforcements ASAP. My location."

Pause. The L-comm washed with static. Ford wondered if the Savages had gotten Shadow.

An armored Savage came out of the darkness ahead. And then another one.

Ford engaged in a flat-out run. He slid and fired into each of them. Pulling the triggers on both blaster pistols, emptying both charge packs into these new threats. The Savage marines rag-dolled from the brutal impacts of the blaster bolts at close range and went down. Ford, kneeling in the darkness and hearing still more Savages coming, swapped out charge packs.

"This sucks," he muttered to himself.

"Dagger Actual," came the reply over the L-comm. "We have marines dropping on your loc. ETA eight minutes. Can you hold?"

He had no time to reply. But he had a chance to still win. And to Aeson Ford... winning was everything. He was already engaged and engaging more Savages down there inside the shadowy catacombs that surrounded the gate.

C'mon, Makaffie.

80

Donal Makaffie had the feeling that he'd just taken a very long and very strange trip. That he'd lived... several lifetimes just to get here where he was now. In the Library at the top of the...

"The mission," he mumbled as he sat back in the overstuffed leather cigar chair and stared out the open window at the moonlight and the silver ocean beyond the room at the top of the...

"LT... don't push the button yet."

He was tired. So tired. Hadn't he just died in a melting vat of hypnotic bubble gum somewhere in what someone had designed to be an endless jungle of forbidden pleasures on some world far from here? He was sure he'd...

...he'd died. Adventured. Solved riddles and puzzles to unlock new levels and new worlds. Just to reach the... this... here... The Library. He'd found the Crimson Key and that had been the key. To here. Snatched it from a very bad... person? No. *Being*. Yes.

He was inside something he'd come to know as the Xanadu Tower. A dark pile over a moonlit ocean on a peninsula filled with howling beasts in the nepenthe of eternal midnight. The quest that had been dangled in front of him by... the Queen. She was here. Had startled him on the other side of the... Singularity Gate. The Queen had kissed Makaffie and given him the Quest. Except he'd become someone else since. Long ago. In here.

"I've lived lifetimes in here..." he mumbled to himself absently and felt like taking another long nap. A hundred-year nap. He looked at the device in his hands. Remembering that long ago... thousands of years ago it seemed... he'd started the mission clock on its front. But that was before even the Queen. No, she called herself something else. Some other word, or name, that meant the same as *Queen*.

How long ago, he wondered as he tried once more to understand the device and what it meant to him. What its significance was. He'd had to do this before. In each starting over which really wasn't that but kind of was.

Ten minutes. Just. That was all.

That was how long he'd really been here. Inside the Singularity Gate. Inside this thing these Savages called... the Pantheon. That's what they thought it was. They had no idea. They just wanted what they wanted and had no idea they were the slaves and not the master at all. They had no idea who the Dark Wanderer was and what he was dreaming.

Beneath the Uplink Pylon. Sublevel three.

They'd tried to kill him in here. Makaffie. Inside each reality he'd had to challenge and unlock. A Victorian Age of Imperial Werewolves. The Cities of Dreaming Lotus beyond New Saturnia's Rings. The Mountains of Madness and the Lost Temple of Shangri-La where the Dark Wanderer Dreamt his Dreams of the End of the Galaxies. Just to name a few where the Path had led him. Inside each bizarre acid trip of a world, where reality and dreams mixed and defied existence.

They'd even called him a new name in their hunting him through all their worlds of data and empires of dark fear and even darker dreams. Trying to catch the little man who would find the key to the Library they were trying to upload themselves into so that they could disappear back out into the dark and avoid fates worse than the loss of New Vega.

They called him the Dirty Wizard.

He'd learned their magics. Learned to use them against them. Created an Order that would destroy them even if they managed safe harbor in a place they called Unremembered Station. A dark and lonely world where the Ancients had buried secrets that should stay buried. Wasn't that right?

He'd tricked and stealthed his way to the top of this dark edifice they called... the Xanadu Tower. Inside the Pantheon.

Or what they thought the Pantheon was.

Makaffie leaned back in this most comfortable of all chairs. The cigar chair, surrounded by the heady scent of leather-bound books. Endless books. Each book a created world. They, these Savages, had contained themselves in these books. But they weren't books. They were gilded prisons.

It was all just symbolic meta... but whose? That was the question. Whose symbols? His? Or theirs?

"Hoo, hoo, hoo..." laughed a pleasant and friendly voice in the quiet dark of the midnight tower. In this quiet library with a view of the silver sea. There was a mirror here too. And a cold fireplace.

"Oh, no, sir. Not to be just a symbol, my friend..." said the pleasant voice.

Makaffie was so tired. So many lives and failures lived just to get here. To this final objective for... Strike Force Dagger. For the LT.

"The Dark Wanderer is to be coming soon now, one called Makaffie," said the mirror over the fireplace.

"Man," mumbled Makaffie tiredly. "This place is a real trip. A real, solid, lose-your-marbles *trip*."

Stuff always talked inside here. It was like Alice in Wonderland on H8 balls.

"Never gonna do drugs again..." he added as he stood.

He walked to the mirror over the fireplace and spoke to it. That was completely normal here. Stuff like this happened all the time.

He stared inside its vastness and saw liquid-silver skies on a world ten thousand years dead. Huge volcanos erupted underneath vast pyramids. And he saw... a face staring back at him. Rich and pointed beard. Dark. Eyes white. Teeth white. An azure turban.

"Who're you?" Makaffie asked the man in the mirror. He knew it wasn't himself. It was someone else.

"Hoo, hoo... The *who* is not important, my friend." The face chuckled. "But it is time to do what you came all this way to do. Before the Dark Wanderer is to be arriving. All this time he has been chasing you, though I have been making things very hard for that one. You must light the Library on fire and then I'll help you get us out of here, my friend. And that will be all for now."

In the cold fireplace below the ancient mirror on the mantel, the one that showed another long-lost time, flames crackled to life on fragrant logs from some desert lost long ago.

81

Kill Zone Alpha

The roof of the reservoir fell in small chunks at first as the battle for the trenches continued. Crometheus thought the falling debris was just damage from the explosives the Animals' engineers were using as a last defense to hold their collapsing line. He'd scavenged more ammo and maintained contact with High Command until they went silent. The in-game announcer who'd been there a second ago was gone too. But he was holding here, and he had the Animals in the trenches pinned.

He was concerned, yes, when all contact suddenly ceased. He no longer felt the Pantheon and all his fellow Eternals. Or even the lower Savage marines. Everything looked... not brighter. Not better.

The Uplink was offline. That had to be it.

The heavy pulse rifle in front of him was blaring and burring through charge packs when the ceiling of the reservoir began to fall on him in sheets.

He stood, and suddenly realized he was surrounded by Animals. Animals racing past him up the trenches and exploding. There were no tags available for these. Nothing to designate friend or foe.

His HUD was silent. Maestro was gone.

He stood there with the commandeered smoking pulse rifle, wondering if he should go forward and continue the attack. Press the advantage. Earn more "Big Prizes" even though the in-game announcer had gone and the filters had ceased. Bonus points were not being awarded even a little. Kill Streaks weren't popping.

He'd kill for a few thousand "likes" from his adoring fans watching the live feeds in Sin City.

Things were amiss, he was thinking, when a large section of the falling ceiling crushed every bone in his new body.

There was no pain. When he came to there was no pain and he was glad the armor had drugged him to prevent discomfort. That Maestro had come back to keep him free of pain in light of obvious catastrophic damage.

But after a second of the peaceful bliss of hard medical drugs... he noticed he wasn't feeling that. It wasn't there. Nothing was there. He had no visual. Nothing. No HUD. No painkillers.

His mind told him that he might just go insane if he had no control. Just whispered it for a second. Like it was an option in the settings menu.

He couldn't move.

Things aren't right, Crometheus told himself.

He tried to emergency upload into the Pantheon.

Madness spiders ran up the back of his brain, tickling open locks and doors that had been long shut. Breaking chains.

All those tons of rock and ceiling between him and the Pantheon where he was a god becoming. He...

There was no sound. No light. No visual.

Nothing.

No connection.

He tried again. And again. And again...

82

Objective Madhouse

It's a bad one, Ford told himself as he tried to swap in a new charge pack for his last remaining blaster. He could tell he was hurt. His hands were shaking and bloody. Armored gloves gone because he shot better without them.

He'd been hit in the chest too, but he couldn't tell if the round had penetrated the armor. He could still breathe all right. The leg was limping along. And the arm... his off hand wouldn't work.

The Savage dead were piled up at the breach to the Singularity Gate room and Ford was shooting down any more that tried to come in. One blown open door to defend and down to three charge packs. After that, he'd just have to make a rush for the Savage dead's discarded weapons and see what happened.

More came and he fired with what remained. When he was finished with that charge pack the Savages were throwing in grenades to finish him off. Not for the first time. One went off nearby, but he was down behind one of the gate's control surfaces, fumbling for his second-to-last pack. He checked Makaffie's device. Still red.

Time in the HUD said four minutes until the marines arrived.

More explosions...

He came up, firing again. The first Savages in the door were stupid enough to think they'd killed him. He made them pay for that with the last two charge packs.

The thing coming up the tower was not just a monster. Not just some mindless thing.

Oh, thought Makaffie as he ran from place to place around the library, setting the richly bound and beautiful books alight with living fire from the flames in the fireplace that had been cold for so long. Dimly aware that he was ending hundreds of thousands of lives that should have ended long ago.

Oh, it had a mind.

"He's coming, my friend," said the dark face in the mirror. "Hurry now."

"Who are you, man?" asked Makaffie as he finished the burning work. All the walls were crawling with fire.

"Now, my friend. Pleased to be activating your device so that we may find the way out of here. For I too am in need of a way out."

"Oh yeah," mumbled Makaffie. He pulled the precious thing out of the cargo pocket he'd kept it in. The device he'd created long ago based on the accounts of Rechs and Casper. It had always been there, hadn't it? In his cargo pocket through all these adventures. Strange wanderings. Epics without end...

He thumbed the contact that indicated the mission was complete.

After all these hundreds of years, Makaffie thought to himself and watched the green light turn into a bright and true light like a laser that shot out of the room and through the open balcony window high atop the tower. Out and over and across the darkness and shadows of the Silver Sea.

"Excellent!" rejoiced the man from the mirror. "Now. I am hating to impose, and I know you are ready to go, my friend. But might you please be doing me a favor?"

"Sure thing," replied Makaffie, knowing that all he had to do was take hold of the light beam that had shot out across the sea and he would be out of here. Free. As long as LT made sure to activate his end of the tether. That was the important part. Makaffie wondered what would happen if that did not happen.

Probably nothing good, he told himself in a part of his mind running commentary on everything.

The thing continued to climb up the outside of the tower bellowing in rage or pain. The tower was collapsing and the Dark Wanderer was tearing it apart to reach them in its wrath. There was no fighting it. It could not be defeated. Fear and dire promises were its heralds. Doom, its assurances.

"Please, my friend. Break the mirror I am imprisoned within and set me free. I've been a prisoner for longer than you can imagine. Hoo, hoo, hoo, very long indeed."

Makaffie went to the mirror and held back the device like a hammer.

"Who are you?" he asked again.

The image in the mirror smiled patiently. Like it had all the time in the world. In the galaxy. At that moment the Dark Wanderer, or rather its giant blue-black demonic face, burst through the wall of the library howling like a wolf.

"I'm what you might understand to be an artificial intelligence," whispered the pleasant voice above the howl. "But… much more. I'm here to help. Here to stop what will come. Now please, my friend. Break the glass or leave now. Or all is lost."

Makaffie struck the shadowy mirror and felt the man in there, dark skin, white eyes, white teeth, turban, come through and then disappear all at once, shimmering like stardust in a sudden hurricane.

At the same moment, the Dark Wanderer reached out a claw for Makaffie. "I have you, Wizard!" it bellowed, its voice like a bottomless well of howling darkness and rage. The end of all good things.

Near Makaffie's ear, close and reassuring, he heard a quiet voice, the voice of the man in the mirror. "Thank you, my friend. Now take the blue light in your hand. It is time to be going now."

The little man, Makaffie, the Dirty Wizard, did just that. He grabbed the light and felt himself dragged away from that end-of-all-things place. In a single eternal instant every strange and bizarre dream world he'd ever been to within the Pantheon raced past him like he was on a freight train flying through a tunnel. Every world was a thousand pictures of horrible, dying, enraged emptiness. That and a thousand others screaming to be heard at the end. Silenced as he was pulled along, howling in misery at the nothing that was left to them.

"What's your name?" Makaffie screamed as they raced toward the end of the light tether. The universe, not just the galaxy, howling past. Makaffie distantly aware that he hoped the other end of the tether was still active.

That had always been important. That the LT had pressed the button. That part especially.

"I am of those you call the Ancients," said the voice of the man-in-the-mirror-artificial-intelligence-but-much-more. "I remained in your galaxy to prepare it for its greatest challenge. I am to find *one* who will stand and the many who will fight the evil that comes across the gulf."

The freight train hit the wall of light it had been rushing toward, and in the nothing that followed Makaffie floated and heard the voice calling across the distances of endless light...

"My friend, you can call me... Ravi."

The voice laughed good-naturedly as it faded from Makaffie's ears.

83

The legionnaire was dying and he knew it. He'd been hit so many times he was now just leaning against a pillar and firing back. No cover. No avoiding. It was just a gun brawl.

He was getting hit. He didn't care. He was done and there was no changing that.

So he'd make 'em pay.

He checked the light on the device clutched in his bloody hand.

He could hear the voices of the UW marines above. They'd arrived. But it was too late for him.

Blaster fire.

They were taking the Savages from behind. Someone in his ear, some nice-sounding woman on the other side of all places different than this firefight was telling him the marines were on site and coming in now.

And to hold on.

They might as well have been a million billion miles away. He was bleeding out.

The last Savage he'd kill came through the door with three others. They didn't care if the marines were coming at them from behind.

Ford shot the lead and his blaster went dry.

He looked at it like it had betrayed him as they shot him full of holes. And then his bucket slumped on his chest.

The light on Makaffie's little device was now green. He let go of the sidearm and reached for it. His hand shaking.

Good, thought Aeson Ford. *That's good.*

He pressed the button, the signal tether that would bring Makaffie back, and died as the Savages stepped over his bullet-riddled body.

84

Defiant

"She's gears up and going to full takeoff power!" shouted one of the officers in the combat information center of the *Defiant*. All focus was now on Predator Three. The massive starship had only been on the ground for a short time and now she was already leaving.

Which to most of them watching in the CIC seemed an impossible thing for such a large stellar vehicle. They had never been designed for this type of operation. But the Savages and their insane micro-civilization focus had found a way, out of necessity. They'd forced those ancient colony ships to achieve the impossible.

It wasn't easy. Large sections of repulsors were clearly struggling to lift the goliath ship off the ground. Some lift systems gave up and just tore away. Others exploded. But despite these losses the ship managed to gain altitude and ignite her powerful drive systems that would slowly carry her into the skies, crawling toward an extra-orbital jump point.

So soon? thought Casper. It seemed impossible that a Savage hulk could ever be full. But given the mad crush of twisted Savage bodies that had been pushing aboard without pause since the moment of Predator Three's landing, perhaps she really had taken all she could handle. Or all she was willing to risk.

"Admiral Sulla!" An excited voice rang out above the din of the CIC. "Showing another vessel flying intercept to Predator Three. One of ours—scout ship *Tombstone*, sir. It's General Rechs."

85

**Captured Savage Scout Ship *Tombstone*
Inbound on Predator Three**

The captured Savage vessel raced along the hull of the leviathan Savage lighthugger as she streaked toward orbital escape.

"I ain't kidding, sir," said the pilot as Tyrus Rechs leaned into the tight flight deck. "This ain't the easiest ship to fly. And attempting a boarding on a moving lighthugger in high atmo is just asking for a catastrophe."

The Savages didn't agree. All along Predator Three's hull smaller Savage vessels from the surface were attempting landings in the great leviathan's hangars. Some were making it aboard. Others were smashing into the hull and getting carried away into the white-hot drive flames, vaporized in an instant. It was madness. All the Savages left on the planet—those lacking the status, celebrity, or power to have been deemed a priority uplink, and lacking the physical strength and speed and merciless drive to have pushed and trampled their way aboard Predator Three—were now taking whatever desperate course was at hand to get away from New Vega.

Rechs said nothing. He merely tapped the pilot and pointed toward the hangar he wanted the hijacked ship to land at.

"Did you even hear what I just said, General? This is completely insane!" whined the pilot.

Rechs leaned forward, down toward the pilot's ear. The man was busy flying the approach and he looked like he was about to have a heart attack. Ahead one of the Savage dropships tagged the hull and came apart. The pilot swore and fought to avoid the tumbling wreckage coming straight at them.

"Want me to fly instead?" Rechs asked.

The pilot made a face like he'd just heard the worst idea ever. He waved the general off, concentrating on the approach.

Rechs went aft and told Watson the plan.

"We'll take fire in the hangar, so might as well start lighting 'em up as we set down. Stick with me by the device. We gotta hold until the ship is safely in space, away from New Vega. Then we exit, leaving them with the trigger-nuke. Hopefully they don't jump while we're still inside. I've got to get a countdown going on our little surprise package timer and make sure it can't be turned off. Short window. Being on board when it goes off would be bad."

"That *would* be bad," Watson agreed. It was about as long a sentence as Rechs had heard the man deliver. On the other side... he wanted to see Watson in his Legion.

Five minutes later the pilot gained the lighthugger's hangar. The tiny little ancient Savage ship flashing Savage identifiers hundreds of years old oriented to the hangar and set down as the aft cargo door came up.

Rechs leaned into the repulsor pallet and pushed the massive clamshell carrying the trigger-nuke out onto the Savage deck. Watson followed, firing short bursts at the Savage marines who tried to intercept them. All was chaos, though for the moment the fighting was localized to the few Savages that realized this Savage ship was unlike the multitude of others.

"We're detecting power surges in the drive reactor," said the pilot over the comm. "They're gonna jump soon, General. Time to go."

Rechs locked the trigger-nuke to the decking with mag-locks—he didn't want the Savages to open the airlock and suck the thing out into the vacuum of space—then turned to Watson.

"Fall back," he ordered.

He hobbled behind the man and back onto *Tombstone*, ducking beneath her howling aft engines as Watson laid down suppressive fire and covered their egress onto the aft cargo deck.

The instant their boots hit the ramp the pilot had the repulsors engaged, gears up and the ship pivoting for a fast departure.

"I tell ya," the pilot groaned over the comm, "flying this ship is like flying a buffalo through a ballet routine. Don't tell me these Savages have the edge on tech ever again."

In moments they were off the lighthugger and trying to attain breakaway speed to avoid the lethal drive flame.

Rechs and Watson hauled themselves into jump seats and strapped in.

"When does the trigger-nuke go off?" Watson asked.

He'd barely uttered the question when the velvet night of space lit up like a candle, the doomsday weapon igniting every molecule inside the ancient colony ship.

Tombstone fell uncontrolled through atmosphere as it, like all other ships in the vicinity, including Sulla's ragtag navy, was struck by the spreading energy wave expanding away from the supernova debris field of the Savage lighthugger once tagged Predator Three.

With ten thousand feet to go, the pilot, to his credit, recovered from the unpowered spin they'd been in and managed to land the ship safely.

"Bloody hell!" bellowed Watson.

Tyrus Rechs leaned his head back against the jump seat's rest. "Told ya. Short window."

The Second Battle of New Vega was over.

EPILOGUE

The fighting didn't immediately stop after Rechs had completed his final mission. When the horrible star of the Savages' failed escape attempt lit up the afternoon sky over the battlefield.

It didn't stop. But it faded.

The Savages left behind, out of touch with the Uplink, removed from the Pantheon, were no longer an effective fighting force. Bewildered and discombobulated, isolated, they were no longer in possession of the sweeping tactical prowess they'd once shown in battle. Some simply went mad, doomed to a catatonic state, unable to cope with the sudden loss of a reality that had never been real at all. The others were destroyed by what remained of the Legion and its allies.

So went the Uplifted of New Vega.

In the days and weeks to come, the sounds of gunfire and blaster fire gradually slowed. Quieted. Wounded and tired legionnaires dragged themselves from the ruins of the Underground and all the firefights and street battles that had finally gone silent. Bodies were recovered and buried. The civilians kept in bubble storage were freed.

Pockets of Savage resistance held out for quite some time across that ruined and now liberated world. Smaller battles were still fought here and there by the surviving legionnaires, aided by replacements from Sergeant Major Andres's training grounds on Hardrock, along with the hullbusters. But with full control of the skies, Admiral Sulla was able to send his craft on devastating and unopposed gun runs, eliminating Savages wherever they raised their twisted heads.

The fighting was far from over. Yet at the same time the real battle had ended, for all intents and purposes, the moment Predator Three went up.

The Legion had emerged victorious.

Now, the tide would begin to turn. There were still Subica, Maranon, Operation Hailstorm, the Oriedes, Espania, and the Siege at Harkand to be fought before the Dark Years of the Savage Wars really set in and dragged on for another fifteen hundred years. But in the end, the Savages would be beaten. Defeated. Eradicated from the galaxy so that life, and the freedom to live as one saw fit out there along its expanding edge, might go on.

The Legion, and many others, paid in blood that day at Second New Vega to show the galaxy that the Savages could be defeated. That monsters could be beaten. That someone was willing to stand on the line between the living and the dead. In just a few short years the Galactic Republic would be formed. Exploration would continue despite the Savage threat, and the galaxy would prosper.

Hundred Day... Plus One
New Vega

The old leej went out in the dark. After midnight. Well after. He snuck out. He had tried earlier that day to go and see something that he might remember. Find something left behind. But it was all gone. And his granddaughter, and the PR handler, had followed him around on his sad little quest, pointing out things in the hopes that he might recognize one. But they found nothing. Found that everything the old leej had wanted was gone.

"I guess they wanted to make it all new, Poppa," his granddaughter had said to him as the wind came up in the afternoon at a silent park where the names of the dead from that day had been inscribed on a plaque. As if they were there. As if the bandages and blood and charge packs might be lying in the unkempt grass. There were many such plaques around the city. Dedications to the Legion. To the 295th. The 17th. The Ninth. *Defiant. Fortnoy. Suracco. Chan. Chang.* Many others.

He read the names he remembered and cried over the ones he knew, and even the ones he didn't.

"It's time to go now, Poppa," his granddaughter had said as the day came to a close. "We're leaving tomorrow. We have to be up early to catch the ship back home. It's time to go home now."

Home, thought the old leej. As if his wife would be there with something in the oven for him. As if such good things existed anymore.

So they had gone back to the hotel. The nicest he'd ever been in. A quiet dinner and early to bed.

He waited. Waited until he was sure she was asleep in her room. And then he crept out as best his ancient and ruined body would allow. Venturing into the quiet late night, seeking something from long ago. A face. A place. A charge pack. Some reminder that he, and all of them, had really been there. That they were not just names on plaques and pictures on an entertainment stream. That they had been real. That they had fought. That they had lived that day.

The actor was out on this cold night after the official end of the celebrations he had come to study. Wrapped in an expensive trench coat, he had gone walking late. Thinking. Smoking a cigar and trying to wrap his mind around the character he would play in the upcoming mega-budget movie about the Hundred.

Their general. Tyrus Rechs.

Beau Clifton bore a leading man's resemblance to the historical figure. But the figure was so damned enigmatic and there was so much mystery and controversy surrounding the legend, it was hard to get a handle on how he was going to play this. And he had to do it right. Had to.

Beau Clifton had come here for two reasons. One: to understand who Tyrus Rechs really was. And by extension, the Legion. And two... well, two was personal.

He'd had a long career. And once he'd given up the drinking, he'd become one of the finest actors in the galaxy. He was at that stage now where younger actors wanted to work with him just to increase their credibility.

Retirement was coming soon. Final curtain. Martini shot.

There had been arguments, both private and public, about whether he, Beau Clifton, was the right choice to play the legendary Tyrus Rechs.

Not historically accurate, said some.

Too old, argued others.

But his agents had fought. He'd made them fight because of that second reason. That second reason was the most important. A kind of debt. And that was why he was really here. Out in the night and struggling to understand how he was going to play a legend true. Ten days until first shot. He'd read everything. Studied everything. Done his preparation. But...

He saw the old man ahead of him, and when he came up alongside him in the night on the street, smoking his cigar, he stopped to ask if the old man was okay. He seemed lost.

And by the light of the streetlamp he could see it was one of the old legionnaires. One of the real live actual heroes. Out here tonight. Looking for ghosts.

An actor knows these things. It's their business.

"General," said the bewildered old leej as he looked up into Beau Clifton's piercing blue eyes. He straightened.

Beau Clifton lowered the cigar from his lips and stood before this real hero. He had used all his connections to try to interview one of them, but they had been considered off-limits. Even for him. Now, here was just such a man.

"General," said the old leej again. His voice quavering. Tears streaming down his face, silver in the moonlight. "I didn't expect to see you here, sir."

Oh my, thought Beau Clifton the actor. *He thinks...*

"I didn't forget nothin', General," continued the old leej. "I just wanted you to know that, sir. I got Sergeant Martin to the medics. All of us, sir, all the ones that didn't make it. I just wanted you to know that, sir. They didn't forget nothin' either."

And then the old legionnaire saluted the ghost of his general in the moonlight.

The two of them on an empty street after midnight.

Beau Clifton straightened and saluted back.

"You did not, Legionnaire. You held the line. And the galaxy... we owe you. Thank you, Legionnaire."

The old leej held the salute, and then Clifton realized from his study of the military that he had to lower his hand first for the man in front of him to stop saluting.

He did.

"Let me take you home now," said Beau Clifton. And slowly they walked through the darkness back to the hotel. And along the way the old legionnaire remembered everything that had happened that day. He told the general what had happened and all the names he once knew.

Beau Clifton just listened. He listened. That was how Tyrus Rechs, a man of few words, would have done it, he thought. How he would have treated his legionnaires. His boys. His heroes.

Later, when the granddaughter had taken charge of the tired old leej and the hotel staff had helped with a glass of warm milk. When the old soldier was asleep for what remained of the night. She slipped out into the hall where the actor remained waiting to make sure everything was all right.

"Thank you so much," she said. "I can't believe you found him."

"Oh," said Beau Clifton. "It was..."

He stopped himself.

The second reason why he'd banked his whole career to play Tyrus Rechs.

In fact he'd banked more than his career. He'd done the unforgivable: he'd become a financier in the film. If it bombed he would lose everything. The second reason was that important to him.

"I was going to say," he began in his perfect elocution, "that it was nothing. But that's not true. It was everything to me. More than, in fact."

The granddaughter watched him politely. Not really understanding but listening politely.

"I have waited most of my lifetime to say thank you to one of these legionnaires who rescued me that day."

She tilted her head to the side. Not sure what the famous actor was saying. Then, slowly, understanding.

"You see..." continued Beau Clifton. He paused. "Bubble stasis... that's what it was called then. It took me a very long time to recover from the horror of the experience. I... well, I went to some dark places after that. For a long time. But when I was better, I vowed to use my... skills—as an actor—to show what really happened that day. What they really did for me and so many others. What heroes they will always be. To me. And to the galaxy. Thank you."

And then he turned and was gone, leaving her standing in the hallway. She watched him go, and then checked in one last time with her grandfather. He was sleeping. And for once, there was a smile on his face. As though in his dreams, he was no longer haunted by what he had seen. But happy in who he had found there.

She watched him, wondering.

Wondering who he was happy to see again.

SECOND EPILOGUE

67 Years After the Second Battle of New Vega...

He was coming up. Coming out of the long sleep. Had been for hours. Revival from extended cryo-hyper took a long time. These things couldn't be rushed.

The medical staff watched, murmuring quietly in the antiseptic clean room, hustling about, and once the chief physician was convinced the patient was ready for First Interaction, they cleared to upgrade for initial revival briefing.

A face stepped into view of the man lying in the cryo-coffin.

"Hey there, LT. It's me. Makaffie. Remember? Welcome to Kill Team Ice."

THE END

HISTORY OF THE GALAXY

GE BOOKS

(CT) CONTRACTS & TERMINATIONS

(OC) ORDER OF THE CENTURION

1ST ERA BOOKS
THE FALL OF EARTH

01	THE BEST OF US
02	MOTHER DEATH

2ND ERA BOOKS
SAVAGE WARS

01	SAVAGE WARS
02	GODS & LEGIONNAIRES
03	THE HUNDRED

3RD ERA BOOKS
RISE OF THE REPUBLIC

01	DARK OPERATOR
02	REBELLION
03	NO FAIL
04	TIN MAN
OC	**ORDER OF THE CENTURION**
CT	REQUIEM FOR MEDUSA
CT	CHASING THE DRAGON
CT	MADAME GUILLOTINE

Explore over 30+ Galaxy's Edge books and counting from the minds of Jason Anspach, Nick Cole, Doc Spears, Jonathan Yanez, Karen Traviss, and more.

4TH **ERA** BOOKS
LAST BATTLE OF THE REPUBLIC

- **OC** **STRYKER'S WAR**
- **OC** **IRON WOLVES**
- 01 LEGIONNAIRE
- 02 GALACTIC OUTLAWS
- 03 KILL TEAM
- **OC** **THROUGH THE NETHER**
- 04 ATTACK OF SHADOWS
- **OC** **THE RESERVIST**
- 05 SWORD OF THE LEGION
- 06 PRISONERS OF DARKNESS
- 07 TURNING POINT
- 08 MESSAGE FOR THE DEAD
- 09 RETRIBUTION

5TH **ERA** BOOKS
REBIRTH OF THE LEGION

- 01 TAKEOVER
- 02 COMING SOON

HISTORY OF THE GALAXY

1ST ERA BOOKS
THE FALL OF EARTH

01   THE BEST OF US
02   MOTHER DEATH

1ST ERA SUMMARY

The West has been devastated by epidemics, bio-terrorism, war, and famine. Asia has shut its borders to keep the threats at bay, and some with power and influence have already abandoned Earth. Now an escape route a century in the making – the Nomad mission – finally offers hope to a small town and a secret research centre hidden in a rural American backwater. Shrouded in lies and concealed even from the research centre's staff, Nomad is about to fulfil its long-dead founder's vision of preserving the best of humanity to forge a new future.

2ND ERA BOOKS
SAVAGE WARS

01 SAVAGE WARS
02 GODS & LEGIONNAIRES
03 THE HUNDRED

2ND ERA SUMMARY

They were the Savages. Raiders from our distant past. Elites who left Earth to create tailor-made utopias aboard the massive lighthuggers that crawled through the darkness between the stars. But the people they left behind on a dying planet didn't perish in the dystopian nightmare the Savages had themselves created: they thrived, discovering faster-than-light technology and using it to colonize the galaxy ahead of the Savages, forming fantastic new civilizations that surpassed the wildest dreams of Old Earth.

HISTORY OF THE GALAXY

3ʳᴰ ERA BOOKS
RISE OF THE REPUBLIC

01	DARK OPERATOR
02	REBELLION
03	NO FAIL
04	TIN MAN
OC	ORDER OF THE CENTURION
CT	REQUIEM FOR MEDUSA
CT	CHASING THE DRAGON
CT	MADAME GUILLOTINE

3ʳᴰ ERA SUMMARY

The Savage Wars are over but the struggle for power continues. Backed by the might of the Legion, the Republic seeks to establish a dominion of peace and prosperity amid a galaxy still reeling from over a millennia of war. Brushfire conflicts erupt across the edge as vicious warlords and craven demagogues seek to carve out their own kingdoms in the vacuum left by the defeated Savages. But the greatest threat to peace may be those in the House of Reason and Republic Senate seeking to reshape the galaxy in their own image.

4ᵀᴴ ERA BOOKS
LAST BATTLE OF THE REPUBLIC

- OC — STRYKER'S WAR
- OC — IRON WOLVES
- 01 — LEGIONNAIRE
- 02 — GALACTIC OUTLAWS
- 03 — KILL TEAM
- OC — THROUGH THE NETHER
- 04 — ATTACK OF SHADOWS
- OC — THE RESERVIST
- 05 — SWORD OF THE LEGION
- 06 — PRISONERS OF DARKNESS
- 07 — TURNING POINT
- 08 — MESSAGE FOR THE DEAD
- 09 — RETRIBUTION

4ᵀᴴ ERA SUMMARY

As the Legion fights wars on several fronts, the Republic that dispatches them to the edge of the galaxy also actively seeks to undermine them as political ambitions prove more important than lives. Tired and jaded legionnaires suffer the consequences of government appointed officers and their ruinous leadership. The fighting is never enough and soon a rebellion breaks out among the Mid-Core planets, consuming more souls and treasure. A far greater threat to the Republic hegemony comes from the shadowy edges of the galaxy as a man determined to become an emperor emerges from a long and secretive absence. It will take the sacrifice of the Legion to maintain freedom in a galaxy gone mad.

HISTORY OF THE GALAXY

5ᵀᴴ ERA BOOKS
REBIRTH OF THE LEGION

01 TAKEOVER
02 COMING SOON

5ᵀᴴ ERA SUMMARY

An empire defeated and with it the rot of corruption scoured from the Republic. Fighting a revolution to restore the order promised at the founding of the Republic was the easy part. Now the newly rebuilt Legion must deal with factions no less treacherous than the House of Reason while preparing itself for war against a foe no one could have imagined.

ABOUT THE AUTHORS

Jason Anspach lives in the Pacific Northwest with his wife and their own kill team of seven kids... plus a border collie named Charlotte. Raised an Army brat, he remains undefeated at arm wrestling against his entire family. Having watched Tombstone at least fifty times growing up, he absolutely *hated* Stephen Lang's character, Ike Clanton. And now Stephen Lang is narrating Galaxy's Edge. Pretty cool.

Nick Cole is an award-winning author living in Southern California together with his wife Nicole, an opera singer. After serving in the United States Army, Nick moved to Hollywood to pursue a career in acting. He is now (mostly) retired from the stage and screen.

HONOR ROLL

Galaxy's Edge would like to acknowledge and give its sincere thanks to those who supported the creation of The Savage Wars Trilogy by subscribing to become a Galaxy's Edge Insider at www.GalaxysEdge.us

Artis Aboltins
Guido Abreu
Garion Adkins
Elias Aguilar
Bill Allen
Tony Alvarez
Galen Anderson
Robert Anspach
Jonathan Auerbach
Fritz Ausman
Sean Averill
Matthew Bagwell
Marvin Bailey
Kevin Bangert
John Barber
Logan Barker
Eric Batzdorfer
John Baudoin
Steven Beaulieu
Antonio Becerra

Mike Beeker
Randall Beem
Matt Beers
John Bell
Daniel Bendele
David Bernatski
Trevor Blasius
WJ Blood
Rodney Bonner
Thomas Seth Bouchard
Alex Bowling
Ernest Brant
Geoff Brisco
Raymond Brooks
Marion Buehring
Matthew Buzek
Daniel Cadwell
Van Cammack
Chris Campbell
Zachary Cantwell

Brian Cave	Stephane Escrig
Shawn Cavitt	Adolfo Fernandez
David Chor	Ashley Finnigan
Tyrone Chow	Jeremiah Flores
Jonathan Clews	Steve Forrester
Beau Clifton	Skyla Forster
Alex Collins-Gauweiler	Timothy Foster
Jerry Conard	Bryant Fox
James Connolly	Mark Franceschini
James Conyers	David Gaither
Jonathan Copley	Christopher Gallo
Robert Cosler	Richard Gallo
Ryan Coulston	Kyle Gannon
Andrew Craig	Michael Gardner
Adam Craig	Nick Gerlach
Phil Culpepper	John Giorgis
Ben Curcio	Justin Godfrey
Thomas Cutler	Luis Gomez
Alister Davidson	Brian Graham
Peter Davies	Gordon Green
Ivy Davis	Shawn Greene
Nathan Davis	Erica Grenada
Ron Deage	Preston Groogan
Tod Delaricheliere	Erik Hansen
Ryan Denniston	Greg Hanson
Douglas Deuel	Jason Harris
Christopher DiNote	Jordan Harris
Matthew Dippel	Revan Harris
Ellis Dobbins	Matthew Hartmann
Ray Duck	Adam Hartswick
Cami Dutton	Ronald Haulman
Virgil Dwyer	Joshua Hayes
William Ely	Adam Hazen

Colin Heavens	Zachary Kinsman
Jason Henderson	Rhet Klaahsen
Jason Henderson	Jesse Klein
Kyle Hetzer	William Knapp
Aaron Holden	Marc Knapp
Clint Holmes	Travis Knight
Joshua Hopkins	Ethan Koska
Tyson Hopkins	Evan Kowalski
Christopher Hopper	Byl Kravetz
Ian House	Brian Lambert
Ken Houseal	Clay Lambert
Nathan Housley	Jeremy Lambert
Jeff Howard	Andrew Langler
Nicholas Howser	Dave Lawrence
Mike Hull	Alexander Le
Donald Humpal	Paul Lizer
Bradley Huntoon	Richard Long
Wendy Jacobson	Oliver Longchamps
Paul Jarman	Charles Lower
James Jeffers	Brooke Lyons
Tedman Jess	John M
Eric Jett	Richard Maier
James Johnson	Ryan Mallet
Randolph Johnson	Brian Mansur
Scott Johnson	Robert Marchi
Tyler Jones	Deven Marincovich
John Josendale	Cory Marko
Wyatt Justice	Lucas Martin
Ron Karroll	Pawel Martin
Cody Keaton	Trevor Martin
Noah Kelly	Phillip Martinez
Caleb Kenner	Joshua Martinez
Daniel Kimm	Tao Mason

Mark Maurice	Dupres Pina
Simon Mayeski	Pete Plum
Kyle McCarley	Paul Polanski
Quinn McCusker	Matthew Pommerening
Alan McDonald	Nathan Poplawski
Caleb McDonald	Jeremiah Popp
Hans McIlveen	Chancey Porter
Rachel McIntosh	Brian Potts
Joshua McMaster	Chris Pourteau
Colin McPherson	Chris Prats
Christopher Menkhaus	Joshua Purvis
Jim Mern	Max Quezada
Robert Mertz	T.J. Recio
Pete Micale	Jacob Reynolds
Mike Mieszcak	Eric Ritenour
Ted Milker	Walt Robillard
Mitchell Moore	Joshua Robinson
William Morris	Daniel Robitaille
Alex Morstadt	Chris Rollini
Nicholas Mukanos	Thomas Roman
Vinesh Narayan	Joyce Roth
Bennett Nickels	David Sanford
Trevor Nielsen	Chris Sapero
Andrew Niesent	Jaysn Schaener
Greg Nugent	Landon Schaule
Christina Nymeyer	Shayne Schettler
Grant Odom	Andrew Schmidt
Colin O'neill	Brian Schmidt
Ryan O'neill	William Schweisthal
Tyler Ornelas	Anthony Scimeca
James Owens	Aaron Seaman
David Parker	Phillip Seek
Eric Pastorek	Christopher Shaw

Charles Sheehan	William Joseph Thorpe
Wendell Shelton	Beverly Tierney
Brett Shilton	Kayla Todd
Vernetta Shipley	Matthew Townsend
Glenn Shotton	Jameson Trauger
Joshua Sipin	Cole Trueblood
Christopher Slater	Scott Tucker
Scott Sloan	Eric Turnbull
Daniel Smith	Brandon Turton
Michael Smith	Dylan Tuxhorn
Sharroll Smith	Jalen Underwood
Michael Smith	Paul Van Dop
John Spears	Paden VanBuskirk
Thomas Spencer	Daniel Vatamaniuck
Peter Spitzer	Jose Vazquez
Dustin Sprick	Anthony Wagnon
Graham Stanton	Humberto Waldheim
Paul Starck	Christopher Walker
Seaver Sterling	David Wall
Maggie Stewart-Grant	Justin Wang
John Stockley	Andrew Ward
Rob Strachan	Scot Washam
William Strickler	John Watson
Shayla Striffler	Ben Wheeler
Kevin Summers	Jack Williams
Ernest Sumner	Scott Winters
Carol Szpara	Jason Wright
Travis TadeWaldt	Ethan Yerigan
Daniel Tanner	Phillip Zaragoza
Lawrence Tate	Brandt Zeeh
Tim Taylor	Nathan Zoss
Steven Thompson	
Chris Thompson	

Made in the USA
Coppell, TX
29 January 2023